# TEN YEARS OF YOU

Julia Oliveira

Copyright © 2025 by Julia Oliveira

All rights reserved.

No portion of this book may be reproduced in any form without written permission from the publisher or author, except as permitted by U.S. copyright law.

# Contents

# 1

◦

## PROLOGUE

June 2018

"Ms. Briggs, you have someone here to see you." Her PA, Cheryl called in through the speaker of the phone on her desk.

Katie was busy writing something down she did not want to forget, and so didn't question who that someone could be. She took a sip of her bitter coffee and turned in her office chair to do some work on her computer. Katie had completely forgotten to answer her PA and had only realised when she spoke through her speaker again.

"Um, Katie? He seemed pretty eager to see you, should I let him through."

"Hmm, yes. Okay." Katie said nonchalantly. She wasn't thinking straight, too caught up in her work as usual. She had no scheduled meetings for that day and therefore this person could not have been that important.

She should have questioned Cheryl. She should have at least been curious enough to wonder who it was. She should have stopped Cheryl from allowing this stranger into her office. She should have done all of these things, but she didn't.

The noise of her door clicking open was what had finally taken her mind away from her work. The thing was, this someone was not a stranger at all. Katie's eyes strayed away from her computer and caught with a pair of deep blue ones. He hadn't seemed to change at all, physically that was. He was dressed in an expensive dark suit, a grey overcoat and designer shoes.

For a moment, he took in her appearance too and noticed how a lot of things had changed. She looked different, but the only question on his mind was were her feelings different too?

Katie sat there with her mouth slightly agape, her palms were beginning to get clammy, her heartbeat was quickening. She was clearly beginning to lose her composure. She was panicking but trying so hard to hide it. She had no plan. As much as Katie had wondered if she would ever meet him again, she highly doubted that. She did not fill her head with hopeful daydreams; she was a busy woman now.

"What the hell are you doing here?" Katie almost spit out. Her tone was harsh but not harsh enough.

Her shock had been replaced with anger and all she could do was question this situation in her head. How could he come here and stroll in like this? How could he just show up now? After what happened, after everything that happened.

"I'm here to see you of course..." he gave her a small, nervous smile. His voice was gentle and slow, almost apologetic if you asked Katie but she would not fall for this again. He wanted to fix things but Katie knew better. She was surprised to find him stepping closer and taking a seat in front of her. The surprise was not a pleasant one.

"Why?" her voice was monotonous and she crossed her arms as she spoke.

"I- I... I wanted to mend things. I wanted to say sorry for everything I put you through-"

"Oh save it Colin. I don't want or need an apology, it's five years late anyway." Katie couldn't stop the bitterness from coming through in her words. But if one was to know the full story, they would not question her clear disgust and stubbornness at the entire situation playing out before her.

"I needed that time, to make myself better. For me and for you."

Katie was beginning to discover she was not the only one who had changed. Colin was not his usual confident self. His eyes had become a person in themselves, they were pleading and his head was not held high like she had always remembered. Suddenly his voice rang in her ears, 'I never beg for anything Katie, you'll be the only one begging.'.

Although the old Colin was someone she had grown to love entirely but hate completely, she wanted him to go back to the way he was. For her own sake, Katie needed him to be a part of her past the way she had left him. It was better for her to hate him the way he was than to see him the way he had shown up right then. She wanted him to be a part of her memories and nothing else yet here he was, right in front of her, almost coming back to haunt her. Katie was unsure about everything and was still trying to process a lot of things in her mind.

"You've really made it big haven't you. I always knew you would do well." His voice was tender and kind. Her subconscious had welcomed it with open arms, wanted it to wrap around her like a warm blanket but she knew better. His words were the truth: she had made it big. She was a someone now, just like him. She was running this magazine, better than anyone had before. She was doing what she loved, finally.

"Talk to me Kate." Colin urged her, his voice going back to how she had remembered it all those years ago.

"I don't want to say another word to you." It was then that he noticed her voice was at its calmest since the beginning of the conversation, although he knew she was not lying. The way she sighed and shook her head after the confession made his chest tighten.

"Katie I'm sorry, I really am. But things are different, I've changed. I'm clean now."

This discovery was something she was not expecting, it was making her want to jump into his arms and tell him how proud she was of him but she didn't. The discovery awakened a small seed of feelings in her again, one she knew would only bloom into something unneeded in her life in that moment. That was why every other part of her wanted him to leave and never return. Her heart might hate her head for it at first but eventually there would be no regrets.

"Get out. Get out of my office now and don't come back." Tears pricked her eyes as she spoke.

He didn't want her to be upset, he just wanted to thank her. Through the four years of absolute hell, she was the one thing his mind had kept itself focused on. He would not have gotten through everything without the thoughts and memories of his dear Kate. He owed her everything and yet she still deserved more.

She had stood up then and came around to the front of her desk to stand facing him. Colin quickly got to his feet too but was only disappointed when she began to usher him to the door hurriedly. He knew not to be confused by her feelings or actions, he had put her through too much to know this reunion would not be a happy one. Colin should have never gotten his hopes up. It did not matter, he would keep trying, regardless of how long it took.

He froze the door and turned to look at her. He placed his hands on both her shoulders and urged her to look right into his sea-blue eyes. But it was all too much for Katie and so she shook herself out of his arms, wiping a tear from her cheek before opening the door.

"I don't want to see you here again, get out!" she said before pushing him out of her office, all the while he kept repeating 'Katie please, I'm sorry'.

Katie slammed the door shut and was met with a quiet stillness in her empty room. Her back was to the door, her hands spread wide. She slowly fell to the floor in a bundle, hugging her knees in her tight pencil skirt.

She sat there for what felt like hours, bawling her eyes out as all the memories of Colin crashed into her thoughts like a deadly tidal wave causing as much destruction as possible. That was all he was to her- complete and utter destruction.

**2**

**CHAPTER 1**

April 2009

The cramped yet slender gardens zoomed past her as she looked out the window of the train, the many memories of her interview only an hour ago, whizzing in and out of her mind also. This would be her commute now, she thought about it for a moment and smiled to herself.

The morning had been a very strange one. She had woken up jobless, penniless and on her way to another interview which would only bring her more grief and misfortune. But this one was different from all the others, this day was different and she was loving it.

Right when everything seemed to be going wrong in her life, she got the call to come in for an interview which surprised her quite a bit. The meeting had gone better than expected, although Katie still felt the need to have her doubts- she had walked out with a job which sounded way too good to be true.

Views from outside the window swooshing before her eyes had become too much. Instead, she turned her head to face the seat in front of her and closed her eyes. She was surprised to find a pair of deep blue eyes that met her instead of darkness. Their stare was too powerful, her imagination playing tricks on her. She could not cope with the intensity of the reminiscence so instead, she opened her eyes again and blinked away the fresh memories.

Katie couldn't get her soon-to-be boss out of her mind and it was irritating. She would not make the same mistakes as she had last time. This job would be a serious one, she needed it badly and so, focusing solely on work was the only thing that should have been occupying her mind. But still, he lingered in her brain.

"I have just one question for you Ms. Briggs," Mr. Anderson paused for a moment, he had yet to look up from her resumé. "Why apply for this job?" His strange and unexpected question took her by surprise, causing her to let out a laugh full of pure anxiety.

"Well, I guess it's always been my lifelong dream to be a PA." he could sense the humour behind her answer, it made a ghost of a smile tug onto his lips. "I reckon I would be good for the job Sir. I'm a very hard worker and once I put my mind to something, I will always do it." This time, she answered a little more seriously but it only made him sigh from across his desk at her, his eyes still glued to the piece of paper containing all her details in front of him.

"No... I mean why are you here? You're clearly over qualified for any job of this kind." This time after Mr. Anderson spoke he looked up and straight at Katie, his oceanic orbs searched hers for some indication of what she would say next. He noticed how she looked anywhere but at him then and sensed her obvious discomfort.

"I need the job." Katie said bluntly but then hesitated to say anything else.

"I-"

"I may be over qualified but I thought I would give it a shot. Every job I've went for that need my credentials have turned me down so I decided I'd try something else. Everyone starts somewhere don't they?" she blinked at him then, managing to keep eye contact. He seemed to be weighing things up, mulling over the interview in his mind for a moment while she sat in silence in the chair across from him.

"I admire your honesty Ms. Briggs." He nodded, clearly pleased with her answer. It made her feel something that she couldn't quite put her finger on, but it felt good. All Katie could do was nod slightly at him before giving him a small, shy smile in return for his friendly one.

They spoke for another while, Katie trying desperately to answer all of his questions correctly but she was weary and unsure of herself. He could sense it yet said nothing at all, only watched her body language and listened carefully to her answers. She was definitely not the best interviewer that day, but there was something about her that he couldn't quite put his finger on. He always liked to take chances and so, he decided she would become his next one.

"I'm sorry, Carrie, the woman you'll be working alongside couldn't make it in today to join me for the interview. But I'm sure she will be happy with my decision. She'll be teaching you all you need to know over the next couple of weeks." It surprised her how casual this man had been about accepting her job offer, it was quite strange.

"I'm sorry?" She didn't know what to say, she was shocked and confused. Did what he was saying mean she had gotten the job? It all sounded too easy.

"Don't be sorry." Mr, Anderson cracked a smile then chuckled. "You have next to no experience but I'm sure you will do just fine in this job.

"For real?" Katie almost winced at her use of casual language around her now-boss but she could not hide her content. "I mean- Are you sure?"

"Of course I'm sure, do you want me to change my mind?"

"No, no of course not."

"Congratulations." He stood up and reached out his hand to shake hers. Katie soon copied his actions and smiled at him. "We will be in contact later this evening about all the details, when can you start?"

"As soon as you need me. I'd be happy to start whenever." She said as he led her to the door.

"Great. Carrie returns to work tomorrow but she may need to settle back in for a day or two so Wednesday seems like it would be a perfect day for you to start. If you have any questions, please don't hesitate to ask me now while I'm here."

"None at all."

"Well if you think of anything, make sure you mention it later."

"Thank you so much Mr. Anderson." Katie stopped and turned to him once they reached the door. Katie could almost see the confidence oozing from his exterior. He stood straight and tall, his shoulders back and his head held high.

"Please, Colin is just fine." He nodded and sent her a wicked grin. Colin.

She could not get his name out of her head, she wanted so badly to let it fall from her lips. Her foolishness shocked her just then, what was she thinking? Katie needed to give her head a shake, was she happy because she had met this amazing man that morning or because she had finally gotten a job? She wondered why exactly he had this pull towards him, it made him unforgettable despite the fact that Katie had only met him once and for such a brief time too.

Katie could not allow her mind to wander off into silly fantasies with this job, the last one had been hell because of it. She chanted to herself, hoping this would be effective, how she would keep her head focused and succeed in her new job as she got off the train and made her way back home again.

"So how did it go?" she heard her flatmate, Emily, call from the living room in their cramped yet homely apartment. Katie shut the door behind her and plopped herself down on the sofa beside Emily before letting out a deep sigh of relief.

"Great actually. A little too good to be true."

"So you got the job?"

"What? No, of course not." Katie replied dryly, her words practically dripping with sarcasm that made Emily roll her eyes before focusing them again on the small TV in front of them.

"Sweet, I'm glad because you don't deserve to have a job. Screw you." Emily replied before hiring up the volume. Her friend made Katie laugh aloud then before she settled in on the sofa.

In no time, the two were chiming along together singing "Jerry, Jerry!" while two women gave it their best shot at ripping each other's hair out.

"I'd like to think that maybe one day that could be us, getting famous from the Jerry Springer show seems like the easiest way to climb up the ladder of fame don't you think?" Katie nudged the girl beside her.

"That's what we'll both look like next month if you don't pay your share of the rent. Whether Jerry is present or not." They both chuckled.

"So who did you meet at the interview? Anyone interesting?" Emily asked, as if reading Katie's mind.

"Only my boss. The woman who I'll be spending most of my time with at work couldn't make it so he interviewed me on his own instead."

"So it's a he huh?" Emily wiggled her eyebrows.

"Yeah, Colin Anderson. He seemed okay, hopefully he's not as bad as my last boss." Katie looked a little anxious although she brought up the situation from her last job casually.

"Trust me, no one could get any worse. Your nightmare of a job is over with now, let's focus on the new one. I'm sure everything will be fine this time 'round."

"I certainly hope so."

"When do you start?"

"Wednesday." Katie sighed as she played with one of the cushions on the sofa, remembering every last horrific detail from her job at a publishing house a few months back. "I'm glad it's sooner rather than later, I really need this job. I can't afford anymore fuck ups this time."

"You'll do great Kate, just don't doubt yourself like you usually do. Hey, what did you say your boss's name was again?"

"Colin, Colin Anderson I think." Katie replied, beginning to doubt herself of her new boss's name.

"That sounds kind of familiar." Emily scratched the back of her head for a moment, trying to recollect her memories of the name. "Let me look him up. See if I can find anything online about him- Wow, he's hot." She spent no time waiting around and had quickly taken out her phone to scroll through her google search of him.

"I suppose he is yes..." Katie didn't want to let her true feelings show, she bit her lip as she tried desperately to think of an easy conversation changer.

"Oh c'mon, you can't deny it. He hasn't got any social media accounts but there's tonnes of pictures of him on all of these gossip sites. Oh my god, he used to date Dahlia Stephens. Look Kate, look." Emily waved her phone in the other girl's face, desperately needing her to be as interested in the subject as she was.

"Yes, I can see. Great." Katie nodded, clearly not as absorbed in the fresh gossip news as her friend.

"Maybe I can quit working at the hospital and just get a new job with you. I bet he's way better looking in person. If that's even possible."

"It would not surprise me if you did that Emily." She laughed softly before smiling.

"You have it so so good right now do you even realise it? You're going to be working for this guy while I wipe sick people's asses at the hospital. I don't know how many more nightshifts I can take before I lose my goddamn mind."

Emily was a nurse at the local hospital which wasn't too far from where they were both living. Although she loved her job, it could be difficult and challenging at the best of times. The hours were tough and the pay wasn't exactly ideal but it would do for now, she thought.

The two women met each other while both attending different colleges that were close to each other. Katie admired Emily's dedication to follow her dreams and found her to be a little crazy. She was not afraid of boundaries at all. Emily ran away from her prestigious lifestyle and family who wanted her to follow their dreams through their daughter. They wanted her to become a lawyer but

Emily was not having it. With help from her very supportive and filthy rich grandparents, she went to medical school instead to be a nurse.

Katie, on the other hand, went to college on a strict scholarship which helped her along the way. Without it, she would still be jumping from cashier and waitress jobs back in her hometown. She was not from a wealthy background, she did not talk as eloquently as her friend and she certainly would not have gotten her degree if it weren't for her grades that were extremely difficult to keep up. But despite coming from completely different backgrounds, the two girls made the best of friends.

Who would have thought the two would cross paths a couple years ago, on a night out in the city? Even after they met and became friends, Katie never thought she would be sharing a dingy apartment with her while they both tried to make a living together. And she most definitely did not expect to be lounging around on a cheap, stained IKEA sofa with Emily watching The Jerry Springer Show every afternoon before she got ready for work. It was crazy how life had worked out for Katie, but she would not change a thing.

"Son, I don't think you really thought this one through. Are you crazy? The girl is clearly educated but not qualified for this job."

"Oh Dad... she'll do fine. Don't worry about it."

"You're wasting this company's money by employing a woman who is obviously incompetent in this particular area."

"Carrie will teach her everything she needs to know. Everything will work out now stop stressing."

Colin rolled his eyes at his father who was noticeably getting more frustrated by the minute. He could not understand the reason behind his hang up. Ms. Briggs wasn't even going to be Colin's PA,

she would be the extra help Carrie needed and definitely nothing to
do with his father.

"I'm giving her a week- if she doesn't perform up to my standard
she can go." Jeffrey Anderson spoke with great finality in his tone as
he looked at his foolish son who stood before him. Colin held back
from saying much else, he knew he was not fully in charge of the
family company yet and although his title was CEO, his father had
all the power when it came to decision making.

"Sure Dad. Whatever you say." Colin spoke nonchalantly before
finding his coat and sliding his arms into it. "Now I'm afraid I have
to run. I have a very important meeting to catch."

"You're going out with David, it's not a meeting if it's in a bar with
your friend." Jeffrey refrained from narrowing his eyes at his son.
Something he had grown accustomed to since the very day his son
could open his mouth to speak. He had always been a pain, but
he loved him just as much as any other father could love their son.
Colin was a difficult child and over the last couple of years, Jeffrey
had learned he was a difficult adult too.

"How do you know that?" He challenged his father.

"Carrie told me."

"Carrie! God damn it I told you not to tell." Colin called in to his PA
next door, not being fully serious. He knew he would feel her wrath
if he actually talked to her that way all the time.

Carrie was a short and frail fifty-something year old who worked
as Colin's personal assistant and secretary for quite some time at
the company. She helped him with everything one could possibly
need help with. Colin was clearly not as organised or brilliant at his
job as his father and so, Carrie practically ended up running the
company for his son.

"I'm sorry! I let it slip by accident this time." She called back.

"If you weren't so goddamn sexy Carrie, I'd fire you right now on the spot." Colin joked with the older woman who rolled her eyes from inside her office. Although Colin could not see this, he knew she was doing it. He grinned at his father who gave him a look of pure disapproval.

"Colin how inappropriate?" Jeffrey spoke with dissatisfaction although he knew his scolding would not work, it never did on Colin. He looked at his watch and felt the need to speak again before Colin headed out of earshot. "And it's only three thirty son! What the hell are you finishing up work almost two hours early for?"

"Sorry Dad, I need a break after that long lunch. I'm really tired." He said from outside in reception area then.

"Get back here now." Jeffrey almost yelled while his son made a beeline for the elevator.

"I can't hear you." He called childishly before entering the elevator and pressing the ground floor button as quickly as he possibly could.

He took a cab to the bar nearby and soon enough he was waiting inside for David. Colin was always bad at time keeping, but it made him feel just a little bit better knowing his friend was far worse. He waited for over ten minutes before David showed up and sat down beside him.

"I ordered for you." Colin said to his friend before nodding to the drink than sat next to his on the table. "What took you so long?" he asked before taking another mouthful of his drink.

"Stacy man, she won't leave me the fuck alone about Puerto Rico." David took a big gulp of his drink, both men knowing he would soon catch up with Colin.

"What did you say to her that night? Did you tell her the truth?"

"I don't even know, I was so out of it I can't remember. But I said something and now she won't stop until she gets answers. She turned up at my apartment right as I was about to leave, I've never seen her that angry."

"You can't really complain David, she has every right to be angry at you. You cheated on her with some random girl when we went away a couple weeks ago. You two have been dating for a while now of course she's going to be mad." Colin rolled his eyes at his friend's foolish whining.

"What are you trying to say?" David was clearly offended then.

"I'm saying it sucks to be you right now, I wouldn't want to trade places but you're better off just telling her everything."

"What she doesn't know won't hurt her right?"

"But she does know, you told her but you just can't remember." Colin said, matter of factly. His friend shot him a look of dissatisfaction which led him to add "I'm just saying." As he held his hands up in surrender.

"Maybe I can still get out of telling her the truth."

"I don't think so man-" Just then, David's phone began ringing.

As soon as he looked at the screen his facial expression changed dramatically. He looked like he was going to throw his phone across the room, his face burning red with fury.

"Stacy?" Colin quirked an eyebrow as he asked although he already knew the answer to the question.

"Of course it's Stacy. Fucking hell." The other man muttered to himself before declining the call only for her to call again.

"You're screwed you know that right?" He laughed at David.

"Whatever." David grumbled. "You know what? I'm just going to turn it off. I'll figure something out later... So? How's that new little PA of yours getting on?"

"She doesn't start until tomorrow. My Dad's been lecturing me already about it." Colin let out a deep sigh then.

"Well I'll be sure to drop by during the week and see if she really is anything special."

"Of course you'd do that." He rolled his eyes at David, he was barely out of a relationship yet but wanted to jump into bed with someone new already.

**3**

**CHAPTER 2**

April 2009

"So we have to keep digital and paper copies of everything. Here's your planners-don't worry you can write everything in that's important later, I'll give you mine to copy from."

"But there's three planners here, don't I just need one?" Katie asked the older woman in confusion.

"Yes dear, I know. Colin is a very busy man, well... when he feels like showing up to half these things."

"Really?" she was puzzled. "Wouldn't clients get annoyed if he doesn't turn up to his meetings?"

"Well his father, Jeffrey is the one who actually owns everything here. He's really in charge. That is, until he hands it all over to his son which won't be happening anytime soon because of simple reasons like this. I tell that boy so many damn times but he will never listen." Carrie shook her head as she mumbled the last part, but her words were still clear enough for Katie to comprehend.

She began to wonder just how incompetent Colin actually was? Sure, he was charming and friendly, but it seemed that wasn't what ran the company. Not turning up to events or meetings whenever he felt like it was not a normal thing a CEO should do.

"Carrie!" Colin called from inside his office, "Would you come here for a minute please?"

"Sure. Come with me Katie." The pair of women left their shared office and walked in to find Colin on his cell phone, lounging lazily at his desk.

"Um, Katie if you wouldn't mind giving us a moment? Thank you." He was very polite whenever he spoke to Katie but she wondered why she wasn't allowed to stay. Carrie was training her in and helping her get settled which meant she was by the older woman's side a lot during work hours.

"No problem sir." She nodded before entering her office and closing the door.

"Carrie." Colin said rather sweetly, giving her a big smile. She knew exactly where this was going, standing there with her arms crossed and a stern look on her face.

"What do you want me to lie about now Colin?" Carrie rolled her eyes.

"What? I never ask you to lie for me... ever."

"Y-"

"Anyways... take a seat for a moment, I just want to get an update on how Katie is doing."

"She's perfect actually, it's really great to have someone helping me with everything. I have to admit over the past couple of months with John being in and out of the hospital  work has been piling up on me and can be a bit of a struggle."

"So you need her here?" Carrie was unsure what the point of this conversation was just then.

"Yes? She catches on quickly, she's done everything up to standard so far and she really does seem dedicated to the job. Is something wrong?"

"No, of course not. It's just that my father will be here in the next day or two to see how she's getting on. If she doesn't perform in the job up to his standards he wants her to go, which I think wouldn't be fair to you or Katie. And so- I might need you to talk her up a bit once he visits."

"Talk her up?" the woman questioned, a curious yet humoured look on her face.

"Yes. Like you know, make her sound amazing, maybe even exaggerate how much she's needed."

"That won't be necessary, she's already doing wonderful. Wouldn't you agree?"

"Oh yes, I definitely would, but my father thinks otherwise. I wouldn't have hired her if I thought different."

"Of course you wouldn't." Carrie said sarcastically. "There's no other reasons you could've hired her."

"None at all." She heard him say as she walked to his door.

"Katie's doing fine Colin, I don't think you have anything to worry about." She stopped and turned to him before she opened the door.

"But you know how Dad is, nothing's ever good enough and I really do think she deserves the job. She needs it and she hasn't had much luck finding other positions around the city."

Colin was clearly allowing his emotions to make decisions within the company for him, but he could not help it with her. Although it was strange to feel the way he did, only knowing her a couple of days, Colin didn't want her to have to look for a new job since she had told him how difficult it had been for her already.

"I understand." Carrie gave him a small smile and a nod before she headed out the door but not before she heard Colin's phone ringing.

"David, hi..." was all she could hear of the conversation.

Soon enough Carrie had given Katie more tasks to do and showed her how to use the photocopier before leaving her to it alone. It was then that Colin came out of his office and walked up beside Katie.

"Hi Sir, is there anything you need me to do?" she asked as she lifted up the lid and switched sheets.

"I'm fine for now but I was thinking maybe you could take an early lunch today? I might need you around during lunch time."

"Sure, when should I leave?"

"Right now is fine."

"Okay, I just need to finish this-"

"Don't be silly, the photocopier won't move during your lunch break." Katie couldn't help but laugh at his words.

"Um sure?" she felt his hand on the small of her back as he directed her toward the coat hanger in the reception. "Should I be back in an hour?"

"Give or take a couple minutes if you like." Colin smiled warmly at her, making her insides melt just a tiny bit.

"Thank you Sir." Katie couldn't help but allow a smile to fall onto her lips also. The two stood there looking at each other for a moment in silence before she snapped out of her daze and began to grab her coat. Once she was all set, she headed for the elevators.

Colin watched carefully as her silhouette swayed from side to side, he could not help himself. Although there were plenty of other distractions from work- she had become his favourite one.

Katie looked at her watch as she exited the elevator, checking the time to ensure she was not late back from her break despite Colin's casual suggestions about time. She was not looking where she was going and before she knew it she had bumped into a man rushing past her.

"I'm sorry." She smiled at him, hoping she had not knocked anything out of his hands. The man's facial expression changed from one of annoyance to content the minute he laid eyes on her.

"No need, it was my mistake. I need to watch where I'm going." His voice was a little too sweet for her liking, but she smiled and turned back to walk out the main entrance of the company building. His face stayed in her mind for a minute or two but had faded by the time she reached the nearby coffee shop.

"So where is she? I came all this way to introduce myself."

"Sorry man, she had to run some errands for Carrie. She won't be back for a while. Maybe next time."

"It's cool." David nodded before he sat down beside across from his friend.

Carrie was near the door to her office and listened carefully to the two men, knowing exactly what Colin had done. She did not usually want to listen in on any of David and Colin's conversations as they were never appropriate for her to hear and so got back to work once they changed the subject.

David spent a long time with Colin, both deciding their plans for the weekend, but all that was on Colin's mind was saying goodbye. There was nothing particularly surprising about his friend's situation with Stacy. She broke up with him the day after they went out for drinks together and he had not seen her since. Despite Stacy being the one cheated on and also the one to end their six-month relationship together- she had not stopped calling and texting him.

Hearing of David's story made Colin feel slightly uneasy although it shouldn't. Colin had been with a couple of women but not as many as David. Most of those women were from long-term relationships and he had never given in to the temptations placed before him whilst in any of those commitments. He was struggling then to have a non-judgemental approach to his friend's stupid decisions even though when they were in Puerto Rico he did not care in any way.

"So..." Carrie raised an eyebrow at Colin once he said his goodbyes to his friend. She was leaning against the frame of his open door, a knowing look on her face.

"So?" He was uncertain where this conversation was going.

"Where's Katie?"

"She went on an early lunch."

"Funny how you sent her for her break early and it happened to be just around the same time David paid you a visit huh?" Carrie almost grinned at the young man.

"That did not register in my mind actually. Is that all Carrie?"

"Sure it didn't Colin." She rolled her eyes at him.

"Hi." Katie appeared at the doorway then and smiled at the two of them.

"Why are you out of breath? Is something wrong?" Carrie seemed concerned.

"No, no. I just didn't think I'd make it back on time. It's fine though, I made it." Katie laughed, which felt like the sweetest music to Colin's ears. "Anyways I better get back to work." She smiled in at Colin then to the woman next to her before hanging her coat up.

The first-time Katie saw Colin actually doing work at his desk was during lunch time that day. Carrie just left along with a couple of the other staff and so Katie decided to knock on his office door.

"Come in." she heard him say.

She stood at the opened door for a moment and waited for him to look up from the paperwork on the desk in front of him. Colin was surprised to find her waiting expectantly a few metres away from him but she had yet to say anything.

"Is there something you need Katie?" He asked, not quite sure what she was doing.

"You said you needed me around lunch time earlier?" Katie replied politely.

"Oh, yes. Take a seat." Colin was trying his best not to come across as sheepish or timid, he was usually very confident around women but it was difficult with her around.

"Okay."

"How are you finding everything?" he almost felt nervous having a conversation with her then, he needed to snap out of it.

"Great."

"I'm sure you love working as my PA." he said in a cocky tone that only made her chuckle.

"What? You mean as a PA to your PA."

"Well yes, that sounds correct actually." Colin laughed after he thought about it. Katie paid more attention to how the skin on either side of his eyes crinkled when he laughed rather than his words.

"Thank you, Sir."

"For what exactly Katie?"

"The job of course." Her little laugh was breathy and light, it fluttered around the room. "It feels weird to actually be working again."

"Again?" He asked, remembering how she had no experience stated on her resume.

"Sorry, I meant just working." She lied. "I have to say, I wasn't sure if this was all real in the beginning- you gave me the job so quickly."

"Well I took a chance, it seems to be paying off. You're a great help to Carrie. How is the commute? Do you have to travel far to get here?"

"Just one train ride away. The station's really near our apartment too so that helps."

"Our?" he had a curious look on his face. Did she share a home with her boyfriend? He wondered, although he knew it was not his business.

"Oh, sorry. My friend and I share an apartment together. She's a nurse so she's at work all the time so it was getting very lonely by myself when I had no job." Friend was the only word that stood out to Colin in her sentence.

"And where are you from originally?"

"Detroit but I moved to Chicago when college started, I've never looked back." Colin noticed the way in which she said the last part. He sensed some feelings of accomplishment behind it but did not want to pry.

"Have you much family back home?"

"Um, no. A lot of friends though."

Katie remembered her days at the girls home she lived at during her teenage years after being passed around in care when she was younger. Katie smiled at the thought of all the friends she had made then and how she really should keep I closer contact with a couple of them.

But then her mind wandered off and thought about what other questions her new boss might ask her. She shifted uncomfortably in her seat a little, the smile melting from her lips. Colin noticed this and felt the need to speak.

"I'm sorry, I didn't mean to be so nosey. I just like to get to know my staff a little better."

"Oh, there's no need to apologise Sir."

"Please, I've told you already- you can call me Colin." He said politely as his lips tugged upward.

"Right." She remembered back to the interview. "Are you originally from Chicago or?"

"Yes, my mother and father met during college here and married. Dad set up the company a couple years after that and now here we are today."

"And did you go to college here too?" Katie asked then, she guessed that they must be very close in age. He looked young but then again, there was a possibility he was older.

"Oh no, I didn't go to college. I started working here as soon as I finished high school."

"Oh right." She nodded before smiling at him.

The two chatted for another while but time seemed to fly. Colin had felt a little more relaxed after talking with Katie for longer and getting to know what she was like. Although they were talking rather casually, she remained polite and professional somehow.

Carrie returned to the office and spotted the two of them laughing about something at his desk. She smiled as she took in the sight of the young pair from the reception.

"Interesting." Patrick, the receptionist said as he too spotted Colin and Katie. He had a look of humour on his face when Carrie looked at him.

"Colin seems to be quite the charmer." She rolled her eyes before she asked how Patrick's children were doing. A few moments later, Colin heard a knock on his door and Carrie entered.

"Apologies if I'm disturbing something but I'm afraid I'm going to have to steal Katie away from you for a while."

"Sure." He said before Katie got up and followed Carrie out of his office.

Katie spent the rest of the afternoon organising her planners and diary. She was copying important dates from Carrie's planner while the older woman was busy with other work when she came across a date at the beginning of June that caught her eye.

"Um Carrie? What's this?" Katie saw that every Friday in the month of June had 'Gala' writing underneath.

"That's the Summer Gala we hold every year dear. It's an amazing night, everyone dresses up and enjoys the dinner and fundraiser afterward."

"Oh, I see. But why is it noted for every Friday in June? I was just wondering should I put them all down in my planner or is there a specific night?"

"Well, the planning committee haven't decided which date to pick yet so you can just copy what I've put down."

"Thanks Carrie. So do we all attend this gala or is there a strict guest list?" Katie enquired, wanting to know more.

"Well the company throws two galas a year. One in the summer and one in the winter. The summer one, a lot of important staff members are invited but only a few workers are invited to the winter gala. It's mostly for big investors and clients but the good news is, I strangely am always invited to both! Which means you will too. You really will enjoy it, it's a nice night to spend out with everyone and not have to worry about work."

"It sounds like a lot of fun." She smiled at Carrie then before getting back to work.

It had taken her quite some time to finally reach the end of Carrie's planners where she discovered the dates for the winter gala. Katie looked up at the clock once she was finished and realised it was time to go home. She said goodbye to the other woman who called her back before she could leave their office.

"Katie." She had called.

"Mhm?" Katie smiled.

"It seems like you and Colin are getting along so far. But I just wanted to give you a few words of advice."

Katie began to get nervous then, maybe she had caught her ogling at their boss when Katie thought nobody was looking. She couldn't help but feel embarrassed but realised Carrie was not concerned about that.

"Colin is still young, he isn't as business savvy as his father and half of the time he doesn't know what he's doing. Just don't be afraid to give his head a shake sometimes, because he definitely needs it. Don't hesitate to tell him when he's wrong and you don't always have to be polite." Katie chuckled then, holding back her needed sigh of relief.

"Thank you, Carrie." She nodded before heading home but not before stealing a quick glance into Colin's empty office.

# 4

## CHAPTER 3

April 2009

There was a fussiness in Katie's stomach that she could not shake as she stepped off her train that morning. She was early, too early, but after a restless night she figured getting up and ready for work a half hour before she usually did would calm her a little.

It was the day Colin's father, Jeffrey, visited the company and inspected Katie's work so far. All she could think about was making a good impression in order to secure her job. She was surprised at how full the office was already when she stepped out of the elevator and onto her floor. What was not surprising at all to Katie, was Colin's absence.

Although he was supposed to be the CEO of this company, he certainly did not act like it. Katie had learned this in just over a week of working alongside him. He turned up to work late by over an hour most days and left early if he felt like it. Colin's lunch breaks, when he took them, were also much longer than anyone could possibly need for lunch but that was none of Katie's business.

Carrie would pester Colin a lot about his lack of time keeping but he would brush it off sweetly whenever she brought it up. Katie decided that having two women nagging at him about being late would be too much so she stayed away but still observed everything from afar.

Colin was expecting his father since the first day Katie started. He knew the exact day he would be coming for a visit, but his plans the night before did not coincide with his commitments the morning after, meaning he would have to prioritise his great night out partying over his meeting.

It was 9.15 when Carrie began to reassure Katie that this meeting was only going to be a casual one and that Jeffrey Anderson was as kind and well-mannered as his son. Her words did little to make Katie feel better but she only smiled at the older woman and thanked her for the advice given.

Once Jeffrey arrived, both women greeted him at reception. It did not take very long for him to ask the whereabouts of his son. Katie noticed how stern his expression was at the mention of Colin. But Carrie tried to make excuses for him, a failed attempt at covering up the real reasons he had for being twenty minutes late.

They decided to give Colin another ten minutes to turn up but then Jeffrey started the meeting with Katie alone.

"So, I'm glad to finally meet you Katie. Carrie seems to be a new woman with you around to help her."

"It's nice to meet you too Mr. Anderson." Katie shook his hand when he reached out for hers from across the table before he gave her a polite smile.

"Look Katie, I want to keep this meeting short and sweet. I'm aware that you're working great so far but I'm still a bit unsure about whether or not you're the best fit for the job. I mean, you have next to no experience, which is something vitally needed for this job. Something my son has forgotten about." Jeffrey said the last part more so to himself than Katie but she could not close her ears or unhear it.

"I understand Sir." She did not know how to react, was she getting fired already? Many things went through her mind then. "But I do think I am capable. I am dedicated and sure enough that I can say I will try my very best at whatever you ask of me in this job."

Katie could not tell them about her other job and all the experience she had there, because they were nothing but bad experiences. Her old boss's reference would have been as good as none, which is why she decided on the latter. Although she wanted to make Mr. Anderson aware of her experience in order to keep this job, Katie knew better.

Jeffrey could see how her hopeful expression gradually fell from her features and turned to that of a concerned one. Then suddenly, he thoughts of a plan.

"Listen, I think this may work out for now. But on one condition."

"Yes?"

"You will have to work between helping Carrie as a PA and also help with the summer Gala we're throwing. It can be very stressful I assure you but if you can get through it, we will extend your contract."

The offer did not seem too bad once Katie began to think about it. It meant that even if she could not stay after the Gala, she would have some experience when she looked for a new job around the city. Either outcome from the deal would have positives to it, although she found staying was probably the more desirable right then.

"Do you think you could do that Katie?"

"Of course." She beamed at the older man. "I would be delighted to accept your offer Sir."

"Good." Jeffrey couldn't help but warm to the young woman already. Maybe it was her optimism and confidence, she was determined and he liked that in a member of staff. "I'm happy to hear-"

Just then, Colin came through the door, almost stumbling in his step. At first, Katie did not take any notice to how much tension filled the room in the short time since Colin made his appearance.

"Sorry I'm late." Colin muttered, not his usual confident self.

"What good is your apology when the meeting's over." Jeffrey replied, rather gruffly before turning to Katie and forcing a smile although he was in no mood once he took one look at his son. "Thank you, Katie. I'll be in touch to organise your role in the planning committee soon. I wish you the best."

"Get outside now." Jeffrey growled in a low tone to his son in an attempt to stop Katie from seeing him this angry.

"Hi." She mouthed out to Colin as Jeffrey walked out the door. Colin only gave her a small smile but it did not reach his eyes.

Katie found herself stuck in Colin's office then, not knowing where to look as she tried her very best to avoid listening to the conversation unfold outside the huge windows. The blinds were only pulled slightly so she still had a good view of the angry father and the irritated son.

"Almost every single time I turn up here you're late. What the hell is wrong with you?"

"I'll try my best to not let it happen again Dad, what else can I say?"

"Why were you late?"

"My alarm never went off." Colin lied easily to his father who stood in front of him, eyeing him up with aversion and clear distaste.

"You're lying. Did you even shower? I can smell the alcohol from here."

"I don't know what you're talking about-"

"This isn't high school anymore Colin, snap out of it and realise that this job is very important and serious or else you'll find yourself working behind a counter at Wendy's in the next few months." Jeffrey was beginning to grow tired of Colin's senseless excuses. When would he learn?

Jeffrey stormed out of the office after another minute or two of lecturing although he knew Colin was not listening. As soon as he re-entered his office, Katie jumped up from her seat to leave, feeling a more than a little awkward then.

"Good morning Colin." She mumbled as she walked by him, noticing then how different he looked from up close. His eyes were blood shot and his hear was dishevelled, like he had not touched it since he got up out of bed that morning. Despite Colin's terrible run in with his father just seconds ago, he couldn't help but smile to feel a little better at the sound of her calling him by his first name.

"Morning." He croaked out before she was out of earshot.

Katie entered her office where Carrie was sitting down at her desk.

"So, how did it go?"

"Better than expected actually. Mr. Anderson made a deal with me that I'll be working until the Summer Gala with both you and the planning committee and if that goes okay, he will extend my contract." Carrie could see the contentment appear on the young woman's face when she spoke.

"That's great to hear Dear."

"I'm really happy with how it worked out."

"Is Jeffrey gone already?" Carrie asked.

"Yes, um, he left just a minute ago."

"That's strange, he usually says goodbye."

"He seemed a bit... angry with Colin so maybe that's why he left so quickly."

"Oh, I see. What's new eh?" Carrie rolled her eyes as she flicked through pages that were on her desk, looking for something between the words.

"Is he usually always like that when he visits?"

"Most of the time yes. He's constantly at Colin to try and step up but he never seems to listen. Jeffrey made this company what it is today, he still works all the time at home and visits almost every week to check up on everything. He's a busy man despite Colin being the CEO."

"I hope Colin is alright-"

"Don't worry about him Dear, he's brought all of this on himself. The only person who can change it is Colin. Remember what I told you the other day Katie, you have to be hard on him sometimes or else he'll never learn."

"I understand." Katie smiled before getting on with her work for the morning.

"Okay I have two mochas here," Katie put the two drinks on the table in the break room for her two co-works, Shannon and Dylan, to take. "A Frappuccino and two lattes. Patrick? Where's Patrick, I have his americano right here too."

"I think he's doing something out at reception." Shannon said before taking a sip of her coffee.

"I'll bring it out to him."

"Thanks Katie." Her co-works almost chorused as she left the room, balancing three cups in her hand.

"No problem guys." Katie said over her shoulder. "Here you go Patrick."

"Who's the extra coffee for? Carrie's cutting down."

"I thought I'd bring Colin some."

"I see. Thank you!" Patrick smiled at her before she headed for Colin's office.

She knocked at the door, not knowing why she was nervous to speak with him. She blamed it on the awkward confrontation between him and his father earlier that she witnessed, trying desperately to brush it off before she entered his office. Katie entered as soon as she heard him say 'Come in.' but was surprised to see him actually working on his computer.

"Hi." Katie said shyly as she sat down on the chair facing him at his desk.

"Hi." He did not look away from his screen until he noticed she took something from her bag and placed it on his desk.

"It was my turn to do the coffee run today and while I was out I thought I'd pick you up something."

"What's this?" he sniggered, looking down at the folded piece of wrapping before him.

"It's a double cheeseburger from McDonalds. I got you an espresso too." Katie gingerly pushed the coffee cup closer to him then, hoping he would take what she had brought him.

"Yes, I can see that but why?"

"Well, I thought you needed them. They help me when I'm hungover." Colin couldn't help but laugh at her honesty.

"How did you know?"

"How could you not know? Would be a better question to ask." Katie said humorously, smirking at him as he began to drink his coffee.

"Okay, okay. So maybe I'm a little hungover."

"A little?" she laughed aloud. "You turned up almost two hours late, looking terrible- sorry to offend- and smelling of drink."

"The one day you're close enough to smell me is the day I come in hungover. Jesus Colin, get it together."

"Me smelling you is the least of your problems right now. It's funny how that's the only reason you think you should be getting it together." The entire conversation was light-hearted and easy, comforting for Colin.

"You're only here a little over a week and you're already beginning to sound like Carrie." He grinned before taking a bite of the burger she brought him.

"I'll take that as a compliment even though I know that was not your intention."

"This is delicious." Colin said, changing the subject. "I haven't had one of these since middle school."

"So, rough morning huh?"

"It has been, until you walked in." he openly flirted with her but she knew better. Colin joked around like this with Carrie also.

"Oh be quiet." She rolled her eyes at him. "Your hangover should start to disappear in no time once you finish that burger and coffee."

"I'm not sure anything will cure this hangover Katie." He massaged his temples then.

"Trust me, it's one of the most important things I learned through college." This made Colin's chest vibrate with warm laughter.

"What did you study exactly in college? I forgot to ask."

"Didn't you read my resume?"

"I may have scanned through it a bit, yes." He lied.

"Is this you wanting to get to know a member of staff like the last day or are you just being nosey now?" He looked at her with a small smile on his face, with his eyebrows raised in surprise.

"The sass! Carrie has taught you well I see."

"I studied business and marketing for four years."

"You probably know more about all of this stuff than me."

"An eighth grader would know more about business than you." Katie said, daringly.

"Don't forget I am still your boss."

"I'm just checking where the line is so I don't cross it again. I'm kidding, seriously. I've learned the hard way a degree isn't really much without experience."

"So how long ago did you finish college?"

"I graduated when I was twenty-two, so nearly two years ago."

"You went a whole two years without getting a job?" Colin was puzzled. His question led to a long pause as she tried to lie her way out of this.

"Yes... well I had the odd job here and there but that was it."

The pair talked for another while until Katie realised the time and said she had to get back to work. It seemed almost every day she would end up in his office, having small chats with him despite them taking up too much of her work time. Carrie noticed how Colin had warmed to the young woman so quickly and every time she saw them together, they seemed to be friendlier and friendlier with one another.

Jeffrey rang Katie a couple days after his meeting with her and told her when and where she would have to meet with the planning committee. As soon as the call was finished, she instantly felt nervous for the day she had ahead of her tomorrow. Although she knew what floor the conference room she needed to go to was on, she did not know anyone who would be there and it made her anxious just thinking about it.

For the time being, she pushed it aside, let out a deep sigh and got back to work until the workday was almost at an end. Carrie had left work early that day to attend a hospital appointment with her husband so Katie could not share her worries with her close co-worker.

Although she joked around with Colin, their conversations together never led to anything with much meaning. She could not vent to her boss about the work she had to do. Katie packed up her things and was putting on her coat when Colin knocked on her door.

"Hey Katie, how's everything?"

"I'm fine thank you Colin, is there something you need?"

"Would you be able to file these reports for me? You don't have to do it now, I left it a little too late in the day."

"Oh, it's okay. I have time." She took them from him, their hands brushed off one another's for a split second, causing Katie to look up at him and pause for a moment."

"So you're actually sticking to doing some work around here since your father's visit huh?" Katie had begun filing the paperwork and only spoke when she noticed Colin remained in his spot at the door.

"I guess so-"

"Hey man, what are you doing in there? Oh- well hello there." Before Katie could have a conversation with Colin, another man who looked familiar had appeared at the door beside him.

"Hey David, I thought you were waiting outside for me?" Colin asked.

"Yeah. I was getting a little bored, just thought I'd come in and see what was taking you. I hope you don't mind."

"David this is Katie, my PA." Colin introduced his friend.

"Your PA's PA actually." Katie smirked at Colin as he laughed at what she had said. David clearly did not get the joke but took her hand once she held it out for him to shake. She was surprised when he pulled her closer and kissed her on the cheek causing her to blush.

"Hi Katie, nice to meet you again."

"Again?"

**5**

**CHAPTER 4**

April 2009

"Again?" Colin couldn't help but feel a tinge of jealousy when he looked at Katie, still blushing. Had they met before? He wondered, he certainly hoped not.

"Yes, we met downstairs in the lobby a while back." David smiled at Colin while Katie was trying to recollect her memories.

"Oh yeah. I remember now, I bumped into you." She laughed a little. "Apologies, again."

"You're a fine thing, I must say. You should come work for me as my PA. I'll pay you double what this chump is paying you." David said playfully.

"Thank you but I'm fine here." Was all Katie said, completely unaffected, before she went back to filing. Colin narrowed his eyes at his friend, the two men still standing at her office door.

"Are you guys heading out somewhere?" She decided to start another conversation with them as to not make it awkward, they seemed to be going nowhere yet.

"Yes, we're heading out for drinks." Colin answered.

"You're welcome to join if you want? We'd be happy to have you in our company." Katie found something charming about her boss's friend, but also something she found uneasy.

"Thank you for the offer but I have some work to do here and I think that would be a little inappropriate don't you think?" She raised an eyebrow at the two men.

"Well maybe it wouldn't be so inappropriate if Colin wasn't there, it can be arranged. I won't tell if you don't-"

"David? Man get out, I'll meet you downstairs in a minute."

"Whatever." The young man rolled his eyes before adding, "I'll be seeing you around Katie." He winked at her, making her blush again. Colin couldn't help but notice her pink cheeks and shy smile appearing on her face again, making him furrow his brows for a moment.

"I'm sorry about him." It was then that Katie looked up at him from the paperwork in the filing cabinet. He seemed a little irritated, she hoped it was not because of her.

"It's fine really."

"I guessed so." He mumbled angrily before turning around to leave, but not before she placed her hand on his arm, stopping him in his tracks.

"I'm sorry Colin, did I do something wrong?" She asked in slight bewilderment.

"No-"

"If I overstepped with your friend, it wasn't my intention."

"Forget it Katie, it doesn't matter." Colin said before turning around and heading for the elevator, angrier at himself than anyone else for being jealous over nothing.

He did not say much to his friend once he got into his car and they drove to a bar nearby. David noticed his irritation and eyed him with curiosity.

"What the hell is wrong with you?" David laughed at the sight sitting next to him in his car.

"What the hell is wrong with you?"

"I can't ask someone out on a date now without you having a problem with it?"

"I wouldn't have a problem with it if you hadn't just met her minutes before and if she wasn't my PA."

"Whatever man, let's just get something to drink and talk about something else."

Katie thought about what just happened all the way home on her train. She hoped Emily was at the apartment when she got back so she could vent to someone about the tiring and confusing day she just had, also the one she was awaiting tomorrow when she met with the planning committee at work.

"Emily? Are you home?" she called once she turned the key in the lock and opened her front door.

"Yeah, I'm just in the kitchen." A wide grin appeared on Katie's face once she saw Emily placing two plates on the countertop. The smell of dinner filled her nose and she couldn't help but wonder what her friend had made.

"Did you make dinner?"

"No, it's breakfast." Emily said sarcastically.

"I'm glad you know how to cook because all I seem to do is burn everything." Emily noticed how Katie seemed a little deflated once she took a good look at her. She wondered if something was wrong.

"You're welcome. Now, let's sit in front of the TV and watch some good old Jerry Springer."

"Thanks for this Emily." Katie finally said once they were settled down on the sofa.

"Oh, don't worry about it. Hey, is everything alright? You seem a bit off." Usually when Katie returned she was lively and chirpy.

"Yeah, the weirdest thing happened when I was finishing work today though. I don't really understand."

"What happened?" Emily lowered down the TV. "Jerry can wait." She said.

"Well, Colin's friend, David, dropped by- the two of them were going out after work- and he was kind of flirting. I'm guessing he's just a flirty guy and he does it all the time but you should've seen Colin's face. He was definitely mad."

"Yes and then what?" Her friend was eating up everything she was saying instead of what was on the plate in front of her.

"Well he just stood there for a minute but then David suggested I join them for drinks and when I said it was inappropriate he said maybe if Colin wasn't there I would agree. But of course- I get it- he's obviously like this with everyone considering how fed up Colin was with him. I know his friend was only joking around but then Colin told him to leave and apologised for his behaviour."

"So who was Colin mad at? You or David? I don't understand."

"I'm not sure, I was hoping it was his friend. But then he left in a huff and I stopped him and asked what was wrong. All he said was 'forget it' and shrugged me off. I mean what's the problem?"

"Sounds strange to me. Maybe he was jealous huh?" Emily nudged her friend as she wiggled her eyes.

"Of course he was." Katie said sarcastically. "Even if he was, I didn't do anything. If I was as brave as Carrie I would march in there tomorrow morning and tell him he shouldn't speak to me in that tone ever again."

"Only Carrie would get away with that." Emily had learned a lot about Carrie over the past few weeks despite never meeting her.

"I know, maybe I should just leave him to it. I don't get paid to deal with his problems, I get paid to help Carrie- oh, that reminds me- and help plan this summer gala for the company." Katie buried her face in her hands for a moment.

"Oh come on Katie, it'll be alright. Once the first meeting is over and done with, you'll do great. It's just because you don't know anyone yet but every meeting will get better as times goes along."

"I wish I believed you. I know I have to do it, since it's now a part of my job but it's just meeting new people that throws me off sometimes. Especially since I'm going to have to work with them until June. I just don't want them to be horrible like my co-workers from my other job. I suppose- everyone I've met so far in the office seems lovely, hopefully the same goes for the planning committee."

If only she had been right.

Katie was always early to work. Since she had started working for Colin, she had never been even a minute late although he was not so good at time keeping himself. She wanted to make a good impression and so that was why she arrived outside the meeting room for the planning committee almost five minutes early.

She was surprised when she looked around outside and found that no one was there. Maybe everyone hadn't arrived yet? She thought to herself. After waiting until ten on the button, Katie decided she should go inside the meeting room and wait there instead.

A dark shade of red crossed her heated cheeks when she discovered the room was already full of people, who were then looking at her in perplexity, as if they had never saw a late person before in their lives.

Katie's realisation that she was in fact late for a meeting she had arrived early to make her scrambled her words when she finally spoke.

"Hi, I'm so sorry I'm late. I've been waiting outside the past five minutes, I didn't think anyone was-"

"We usually all make an effort to ensure we arrive here at least fifteen minutes early, Ms... What is your name?" A tall woman who was standing next to a whiteboard in front of the others spoke with such impatience and displeasure that Katie felt the need to take a step back although they were both on different sides of the room. The woman's stare made her red cheeks only darken another shade or two.

"Katie Briggs. You must be Catherine, it's nice to meet you." Katie tried her best to not let how intimidated she was show in her exterior to the room full of people.

"Oh, Katie! Mr. Anderson has told me you'll be helping us out here in the weeks coming up to the Summer Gala." She was surprised when Catherine's facial expression and voice warmed a little, but once the woman spoke again- Katie found herself wondering why she had thought the woman was going to be nice. "Go get us coffee." Catherine demanded.

"Um, excuse me?" she quirked an eyebrow in bewilderment.

"Coffee? Take everyone's orders and go get them as soon as possible. We've been waiting for you the past fifteen minutes."

"But how am I supposed to carry everybody's coffee back here?"

"Alice, you go with her." The older woman used the very same tone she had used with Katie on Alice. But Alice did no questioning like Katie, instead she submissively mumbled something and nodded before walking towards her.

It took only a minute or two to write down everyone's orders, all fifteen of them.

"Don't be long!" They heard Catherine say as they were leaving.

Alice seemed like a quiet girl, she could only have been a year or two younger than Katie and she said almost nothing on the way to the coffee shop. Katie was too busy running through the events that had just happened.

"So, is Catherine always that mean?" she finally asked Alice once they had ordered and paid for their coffee. The girl tried to stifle a giggle.

"Wow, don't let her hear you say anything like that in front of her. She'll come down on you like a tonne of bricks." Alice blurted out although she felt bad afterwards. What if this girl told Catherine what she had said?

"I'm guessing that's a yes then."

"She can be very- demanding. But you'll get used to her."

"Great." Katie rolled her eyes before the two of them struggled to hold all of their order. "I'll get the first door." Katie mumbled and held the door open for Alice.

"Thanks."

"So is being a part of the planning committee any good? Or am I going to have to go through hell for the next two months?"

"I wouldn't know. All I do is take notes and get the coffee. I'm just glad someone's hear to help me because usually I have to take two trips carrying all this coffee back to work."

"Oh that sounds terrible." Katie replied with sympathy. Alice wasn't sure why she was saying this to Katie but decided that she would whether it was a good or bad decision.

"It is." She nodded at Katie. "So are you new?"

"Yes, since a few weeks ago. I work with Colin and Carrie upstairs." Katie answered as the pair entered the lobby of their building.

"Colin?"

"Yes, you know, Jeffrey's son."

"No one calls him Colin on my floor."

"Oh." Katie furrowed her brows for a moment before Alice asked her another question.

"How are you finding it?"

"It's been great actually. How long have you been working here?"

"Oh, I'm just an intern here. I don't get paid or anything but I've been working on and off since last summer. Usually I'm with the accountants but I've been thrown into the planning committees meetings for the past while to help out with the finance planning even though Catherine reminds me time and time again she does not need an accountant's help. She's been planning these galas for years apparently, and there's never been a mistake made. So I guess that's why I'm told to do these coffee runs and put up with sitting there completely uninvolved in their conversations."

"So you're studying in College?"

"Yes I'm only a sophomore but I'm just about done this year of college which means I'm going to be working here over the summer."

They got to know each other a little more on the elevator ride up to the meeting room and were not surprised to find that Catherine's awful mood had not changed since they had left.

Katie discovered it was not just Catherine who would be nasty throughout the entire meeting, but most of the people in the meeting room too. She was told to sit there and listen, her input was not needed.

The meeting felt never ending but Katie managed to get through it all. She talked a little with Alice until the elevator reached her floor. Alice said her goodbyes but not before reminding the other girl to turn up at least fifteen minutes early to the next meeting. She used a high-pitched voice mimicking Catherine that made Katie laugh when she said it.

Carrie noticed how unenthusiastic she was when the older woman asked how the meeting had went but it did take some time to finally get Katie's truthful opinion.

"And then Alice told me that she usually has to take two trips to the coffee shop because no one else is there to help her."

"Oh dear, that doesn't sound like what you're signed up for."

"I'm sorry, I shouldn't be complaining already about work. I'm so grateful for the job that even if I have to go through those meetings, I know it's worth it."

"No Katie, you don't need to worry. I completely understand. I know Catherine a while now and she seems like quite the... hmm I'm not sure what word to use for her but anyway, don't feel like you can't say anything to me about work unless it's something good."

"Thanks Carrie." Katie beamed at her, delighted that she was back to her office, working alongside someone that she actually liked.

"Hey, would you mind getting Colin to sign these for me?"

"Sure, no problem."

"Thank you sweetie."

"Good afternoon Colin." Katie said, only allowing a certain amount of warmth come out in her voice. She remembered how he had spoken yesterday before he left. Colin was sitting at his desk, texting on his cell phone when he looked up to see the beautiful sight before him that was his assistant. He then reminded himself that Katie was his assistant and he needed to snap out of it.

"You look different today." He furrowed his brows at her.

"Glad to see you're getting a lot of work done, as usual." Katie mumbled as she looked through the papers she had in her hand.

"You know me too well." Colin smirked, his tone was light and playful- clearly he had forgotten about yesterday, but not for long.

"Can you sign these please?"

"Of course, anything for you Katie- that's it." He clicked his fingers as she laid the papers on the table for him, pointing at where to sign. "It's your glasses. Are they new?"

"Oh god no. I have these things years. I just didn't have time to put my contacts in today." He had managed to break her cool exterior in a matter of seconds.

"They suit you." Colin said as he signed his name then handed the papers over.

"Thank you Sir." Katie said politely before turning to go but he stopped her.

"Apologies for David yesterday."

"I don't think David is the only one you need to apologise for?" she said daringly, raising an eyebrow at him. Katie knew she may have been crossing the line but decided to just go for it anyway. Colin had already shown he was not your typical boss, his father was the one in charge and judging from Colin's behaviour, it would stay like that for a very long time. He sighed deeply before knitting his fingers together in front of him on the table.

"Sit down for a moment will you Katie? I promise I won't be long."

"Sure."

"Look... I'm sorry about yesterday. I shouldn't have been so angry with you over nothing. I was just frustrated with David, he never stops."

"I get it." Katie nodded at him, accepting his apology easily.

"Would you have went?"

"What?" she was confused then.

"With David, if I wasn't there of course."

"Like a date?"

"Well yes, he seemed to think that would be a good idea."

"Oh no, I'm not looking for a relationship right now." Her words were probably a little too personal to share with her boss, but she did so anyway. They only made Colin feel a cocktail of relief and disappointment although he knew both were not justified.

"Why not?" Katie looked up then and noticed how big and bright his eyes were. They stood out amongst his dark hair and tanned skin, a sight one must see in person. She was too zoned in on Colin's eyes to realise she had yet to reply. The silence stretched longer then, making him feel the need to talk again. "Forget I asked that please, I shouldn't have."

"Don't worry about it." Katie laughed lightly, pushed up her glasses on her nose and before they both knew it the conversation had stirred in a different direction completely.

It wasn't until a half an hour had passed and Carrie knocked on Collin's door looking for Katie that they realised how long they were sitting there chatting.

"Katie we're about to head out for lunch now, do you want to come with or are you busy?" Carries eyes wandered between the two of them knowingly. She had heard their laughter from her office and wondered what the two were talking about.

"Sure, let me just grab my things Carrie." Katie smiled and got up from her chair.

"Great, we'll meet you outside." The older woman said before leaving Colin's office.

Colin wished she didn't have to go yet despite knowing they had talked for so long already. Katie turned around then before leaving and laughed a little.

"Every time you call me in here I feel like we end up talking for a lifetime. You're such a bad influence Mr. Anderson." She said jokingly, almost flirtatiously if you asked Colin.

"We were actually just about to leave for lunch right now Carrie. I hope you don't mind if I steal her from you for a bit." Katie's head shot back to look at Colin after he spoke. Carrie could not see Katie narrowing her eyes at him.

"What's another hour going to do huh?" Carrie said playfully. She hadn't seen Colin smiling the way he was when she came into his office in months. "Have a good time you two." She grinned before closing the door behind her.

"Lunch?" Katie raised an eyebrow at Colin from across the desk.

"Yes, I thought I mentioned it earlier no?"

"No. You didn't." Katie crossed her arms. "And I think you just said it in front of Carrie right then because you knew I would say no if you had've asked me earlier."

"C'mon Katie. It's just lunch."

"Fine. I guess I'll have to put up with you for an hour straight..." she rolled her eyes and made him chuckle.

"Fine. I guess I'll have to put up with you for an hour straight..." she rolled her eyes and made him chuckle.

# CHAPTER 5

May 2009

"Shit." Katie muttered under her breath as she tried desperately to carry everything she had in her hands. She stopped for a moment in the lobby of the building on the main floor to catch her breath although she knew she did not have much time to get to the planning committee meeting.

"Do you need some help with that Ms?" Someone from the front desk asked.

"If you wouldn't mind, thank you."

"Where are you taking these?" the woman asked as she took one of the boxes of flowers from Katie.

"The meeting room on the twentieth floor." She replied before the tow made their way into the elevator. "They're for the gala in two weeks." Katie felt the need to say as the woman looked quizzically in the box at all the flowers.

Catherine had changed her mind about the flower arrangement she wanted set out on the tables despite knowing that the gala was such a short time away. That meant that Katie had to get up an hour and a had earlier than usual to get the train over to the other side of the city, pick up the new versions of arrangement Catherine might like and bring them back here in time for the planning meeting.

"Oh, I see." The woman who was helping her nodded and smiled at Katie. Soon enough they were on the twentieth floor and walking into the meeting.

"Thank you so much." Katie beamed at the woman before taking the other box of flowers from her.

"No problem Ms." And like that, she disappeared into the elevator.

Katie took a deep breath before opening the door and entering the room that was already full of the committee.

"You're late." Was all Catherine said. Katie refrained from saying anything although it was difficult to do.

She did not get much sleep at all last night or over the past month because of the gala and all of Catherine's little tasks she needed Katie to do. Most of the time, she had to arrive to work early and leave late which was becoming very strenuous. Because it was coming so close to the gala that would be held in the middle of June, there were so many things to do and most of those things had to be done by Alice or Katie while the rest just made decisions and sat around at meetings.

Catherine did not thank Katie as she struggled to set the boxes of flowers down on the table in front of the older woman. But Katie's patience was beginning to grow thin and so she said a quick "You're welcome." Sarcastically before walking to her seat next to Alice.

Catherine surprisingly said nothing as she sat down, just shot her a glare before the meeting commenced. Just like always, Alice and Katie sat there and said nothing. Katie could not stand sitting there as Catherine and the others looked through all the possible arrangements that did not look that much different to the original ones they chose.

It wasn't until the end of the meeting that Catherine addressed Katie again. She was about to leave but the older woman called her back. She rolled her eyes at Alice who looked a little concerned and then waiting patiently for everyone else to leave the room.

"I'm sure you're used to batting your eyes at Colin upstairs to get your own way but that won't work with me Katie." Catherine was still sitting down, her frame stiff and her words harsh.

"I'm not sure what you mean Catherine-"

"You know exactly what I mean. Don't test me, right now or when we're in a meeting. You do what I say and that's final."

"I wouldn't call it testing you Catherine. I'm aware of the fact that both Alice and I have to run around and do everything you don't want to do yourself and that's okay, that's why I'm here but don't expect me to be happy when you are constantly rude to me. I'm here to do what you say, not bow down to you." Catherine seemed taken aback when she spoke first, it took her a minute to register what Katie had said.

"You listen here Katie," Catherine spoke through her teeth, leaning over her table to stare at the younger woman. "I know you need a good report from me back to Jeffrey in order to keep your job so why don't you stop trying to challenge me and be quiet from now on. You seem to have it easy upstairs, all cosy with Colin but down here you work and don't complain."

Her comments about Colin made Katie's heart sink. She had done nothing wrong? But Catherine seemed to suggest otherwise. It made her feel self-conscious, did others feel that way too? Katie wasn't advancing in any way in her job because of how close she had become to Colin since she started working there, but maybe people didn't see that she worked hard and that was the only reason she was kept on. Things were beginning to look the way they did in her old job, and she didn't want history repeating itself but Catherine shook her to the bone.

"Got it?" Judging by the look on Katie's face, Catherine knew she had won. Katie only nodded and left the meeting room, her mind wandering into dangerous territory.

She needed to call Emily, she was worried and getting more upset by the minute. Katie was glad that Carrie wasn't in the office when she reached it, she remembered that the older woman said she would be in later that day because of a hospital visit with her husband again. She thought it was the right time to try Emily on her phone although she may not answer unless she was on a break in work.

Katie walked back and forth as she tried to get hold of Emily three times. On the last try, when it finally rung out again, Katie lout of a short sigh but jumped when she heard a knock on her door.

"Hey." Colin grinned at her at first, but then he noticed how pale and shaken she looked. "What's wrong?" he asked, clearly concerned. He took a step forward only for Katie to take a step back.

"Nothing, I'm fine." She smiled but it didn't reach her eyes.

Colin had noticed over the past while how exhausted and deflated she seemed. A worried expression crossed his features as she sat down at her desk and began working. He sat down in front of her.

"How was your meeting?"

"Good." She blatantly lied. Katie decided that after talking to Catherine that she could not discuss her hatred for the planning committee to anyone, especially not Colin, her boss.

"Oh c'mon, I'm sure it's not going as well as you're letting on to be. I know that Catherine one can be a major bitch."

Katie tried her best not to laugh at the unexpectedness of his truthful admission but only scoffed loudly while trying to contain her laughter. He made her smile and that made him feel a little better about her but her lips set into a line again as quickly as they had grinned at him.

"She's okay I suppose." He gave her a quizzical look, knowing she could not possibly be telling the truth.

"Oh c'mon everything's fine and okay and good with you lately. I know there's something wrong." Katie only continued on with her work, it should not be any of his concern if there was something wrong with her or not. "Look at me." He urged gently. Katie put her pen down and sighed before looking at him from across her desk, resting her chin in her hands.

"I'm just really tired, okay?" her voice was gentle and sweet, like music to his ears. She gave him a grim smile but his eyes were focused on her bright ones. They looked droopy and sore.

"Why don't you leave earlier today? Maybe try catch up on some sleep." His suggestion only made her look down again at her work and continue.

"I have a lot of work to do Colin, is there something else you need that's actually important instead of checking up on my well-being?"

"I-I-" he didn't know what to say then. Why did he care so much? He was not sure.

"I'm a big girl. I can take care of myself. As soon as this gala is over, I'll be able to relax." She said as she wrote something else down.

"Ooo, the gala. Aren't you excited about the gala?"

"Do I look excited about the gala?" she looked at him for a second before getting up to get something out of the filing cabinet next to her desk. He only chuckled a little at her sarcasm.

"Of course you do. Everyone's excited about the gala."

"Maybe everyone who isn't planning it is excited but I certainly am not." She flicked away through the files in one of the drawers.

"Oh c'mon, even the planning committee enjoy their night."

"Well I guess I'll be the first to not enjoy the night then." She knew she was being cynical but she was too tired to care. All she wanted was to feel the relief she would get from the gala being over. It was the thing she thought about the most recently which shouldn't be right.

"You get to dress up." Colin's little burst of excitement was almost laughable, if she had not been in such a bad mood.

"Oh great. Another thing I have to do- find a dress."

"And dance."

"I don't-" before she could continue, Colin grabbed her by the waist and began spinning her around. He took one of her hands and twirled her around, making her giggle a little.

"Colin stop." She tried to say but he continued to turn with her in his arms before finally leaning her backward, holding steadily onto her waist. "Colin!" she squealed, he then stood her back up straight. She could feel his chest erupt with laughter.

"Don't you dare say you can't dance after that." He swayed them back and forth, enjoying the closeness as much as Katie but she would never tell.

Katie couldn't help but take in the scent of his expensive cologne and notice the sprinkle of stubble he had around his jaw and chin. She was looking up at him but his mind was somewhere else. It took him a minute to look back into her eyes and when he did she only let out a quite breath of laughter through her nose before a small smile crept up on her lips, making him involuntarily join in.

The room fell silent but not for long. Surprisingly it wasn't Katie that was the one to pull away first, it was Colin but only after he heard a familiar voice.

"Colin?" the voice called. "Co- of hey man, why aren't you in your office?"

Katie took a step away from her boss once a man entered the office, standing tall in a dark navy suit. His suit looked expensive, just like Colin's and he almost dripped of confidence. His black hair was cut tight and slicked back neatly. Katie didn't know where to look once he grinned widely at her, baring his pearly teeth.

She was puzzled by Colin's behaviour after that. He did not introduce the two of them to each other like he had with David and almost looked flustered upon discovering this man unexpectedly showing up at work. Colin nearly stood in front of Katie, as if protecting her from the man, although she did not pick up on this.

"Vinny, what are you doing here? Come inside to my office." He rushed out the door with the man, looking around the corridor as he left Katie's office as if Colin was doing something he should not be doing.

Vinny wasn't in Colin's office for long, and took off very quickly. After that, Colin seemed a little on edge but Katie knew better than to ask what was wrong. It was not her business, she just continued on with her work- feeling a little better after talking to Colin for a while earlier on. But still, she wondered who this strange friend of Colin's called Vinny was?

Carrie arrived into work soon enough and distracted Katie from her wandering thoughts about Catherine and Colin. Katie noticed how sad and tired Carrie looked when she arrived into the office. Her wrinkles appeared more noticeable on her face and her eyes were glassy and a delicate shade of pink.

"Hi." Katie said, her tone hopeful yet hesitant.

"Hi dear. Is Colin around? I need to talk to him about something."

"Yes, sure. He's in his office. Is something wrong Carrie?" She wasn't sure whether she should ask, but it was strange to see the older woman this way. She was usually chirpy, upbeat and would have said something sarcastic about Colin's lack of work by now if everything was okay.

"We- we've just gotten some bad news back from the hospital this morning. I need to discuss some things with Colin and Jeffrey the next time he's here."

"I hope you're okay. Is there anything I can do for you? Do you want a coffee or anything?" Although Katie knew a coffee wouldn't fix Carrie's broken look on her face, she did not know what else to say.

"No, I'm fine really. I just need a bit of time to process everything. The only reason I came in is because I need to send out those reports for Jeffrey by tomorrow."

"I can do it for you if you like?"

"Oh no, don't worry about it Katie. I'll do it once I've talked to Colin." Although she was becoming visibly more upset by the minute, Carrie still managed to smile at Katie.

She spent some time in with Colin, Katie was quite surprised when Carrie returned to the office, almost fully composed then. She sat down with Katie for a while to explain what happened at the hospital and at the end of it all, there was nothing Katie could think of saying that would make the situation any better.

Carrie's husband had another check up at the hospital that morning when the doctors discovered that things were not going as good as they had initially expected. Her husband would have to undergo an operation as soon as possible, leaving Carrie to look after him. Carrie knew she had nothing to worry about when she told Jeffrey, she had been working there for years and he knew her husband quite well. He was always very understanding when it came to family matters.

Carrie being gone for a few months meant that Katie would have to take over her job, she would have a lot more work to do but she was only concerned about Carrie at that time. Katie could tell how much Carrie was trying to keep it together. She had always been an optimistic woman, and knew that her husband would be fine, especially with her by his side to help him along with his recovery.

Colin was cooped up in his office for the entire morning. Katie didn't speak to him until an hour or two after lunch when he knocked on the door of her office. Carrie looked up at him for a moment but soon realised he was not looking for her.

"Katie." He said aloud.

"Hmm?" she said, still writing. Carrie noticed how nonchalant Katie was with this man then, it only made her stifle a giggle as inspected Colin's expectant face awaiting the younger woman's full attention.

"Um-" he hesitated, not quite sure then why he urgently needed to talk to her. "I need you to review those Jefferson reports for me before next Friday."

"Sure, I'll get right to it." Katie continued on with that she was doing, so engrossed in her work that she still hadn't looked at Colin although that was all he wanted her to do right then. Carrie sensed his wish and was only given solid evidence of it when he clearly looked a little deflated after her sentence.

"O-okay." He nodded before giving a small smile to Carrie before leaving the room.

"Katie..." Carrie let out a small chuckle once Colin was out of ear shot.

"What?" Katie was confused, and took the time then to look up.

"I just find it funny."

"Find what funny?" Katie asked in complete bewilderment.

"You have no clue at all do you dear?" Carrie sighed as she shook her head, a sly smile grew on her lips.

"I guess not." It was the younger woman's turn to laugh then.

"He secretly adores you, or he's on the way to it anyway. And you-you just don't give him the time of day sometimes." The pair burst out into laughter.

For a moment, Carrie had forgotten about the struggles she and her husband were facing and was focused on the fresh romance that would soon enough sprout from these two young people. Although neither knew it yet, Carrie was sure something would end up happening between them- although it may not be ideal, considering they both worked together.

"Sure, whatever." Katie snorted and rolled her eyes before going back to work. She brushed off any trace of Carrie's words that may stick in her mind to make her more concerned about what Catherine had said earlier that morning.

Katie decided to stay late again at work that evening. She had to sort out her appointments and times she needed to be free at for all of the wonderful and completely unnecessary things Catherine would make her do for the upcoming Gala in just two weeks.

Time seemed to fly for Katie when she had so many things to do. She looked at the clock and realised how late it was getting. In her mind, she had thought she only said goodbye to Carrie a couple of minutes ago, but it had actually been almost three hours ago. She grabbed her things and readied herself for the trip home.

She walked into the elevator and pressed the ground floor button only to realised Colin was running to catch the closing doors. Katie pressed the button again to open the doors but it didn't seem to be working for a moment. The doors closed but then after a moment, opened back up to let Colin enter the elevator.

"You know, for a moment there I thought you were trying to avoid me." Colin smirked at her.

"I was, how did you know?" Katie said sarcastically. "Wait, why are you still here, isn't it a little late for you to be working?" She looked at him with a confused expression on her face.

"I needed to look into that Jefferson report. My dad wants me to take care of the investment completely on my own so I had to stay late. Why are you so surprised-"

"You literally can't even ask me that question. You already know the answer." She was trying to keep in her laughter then.

"I don't."

"Maybe it's because you're barely ever on time and you take sometimes over two hours for lunch and- oh wait, you leave earlier than everyone else in the office too. You very rarely stay for a full day in work, never mind staying three hours late." There was a silence in the small space for a moment, Colin was the one to break it.

"Oh yes, you're right." The two began to laugh with each other after he spoke but Katie stopped immediately once the doors opened on a floor that was not the one she had pressed and her eyes met Catherine's beady ones.

"Katie." The older woman nodded at her, keeping her tone very formal yet snooty. Katie nodded back, not saying anything. "Hello sir." Catherine also added.

Colin noticed how Katie seemed to immediately take a step away from him once she caught sight of Catherine. It made him wonder a lot of things. Her presence in the elevator was not wanted at all, for some reason it had made him stop laughing then too- as if the pair would be punished if they continued with their playfulness together.

The ride to the ground floor seemed like it was ten minutes long, although Katie knew it could only have been ten seconds or less. Catherine was the first to exit and they both walked slowly to the front door so that she was gone before them.

Colin stopped outside the door of the building to turn to Katie.

"You want a ride home?"

"No, I'm good. Thank you though." She hesitated, knowing she had to draw the line somewhere.

"Are you sure?"

"Yeah, I don't think that would be- appropriate." Katie didn't want to say it, but she did anyway. Seeing Catherine had brought on those worries again about her closeness with her boss and she did not want to come across a certain way to others in work.

"But it's getting late." Colin tried not to sound worried about her getting home but he knew he was failing miserably.

"I'll be fine Colin. I can take care of myself you know." She scoffed humorously before giving him a shy yet bright smile. "Thanks anyway. Goodnight."

Her soft voice mesmerised him for a moment, he could not even remember her turning to walk away, leaving him standing alone on the street as thoughts of her fluttered around in his mind.

**7**

CHAPTER 6

June 2009

By the time the gala came around, Katie was completely exhausted. A few days ago in work, she remembered actually dozing off into a light sleep a couple of times while sitting at her desk. With Carrie gone and Catherine becoming even more hateful and seething by the day, work was beginning to totally take its toll on Katie.

She was at the point of exhaustion where if she stopped constantly working and took a moment to think about things other than the gala, she would break down in tears. But it was Friday then, the morning before the gala and soon everything would go back to normal. Her workload would still be more than she had at the beginning of the job but she would not have the burden of attending planning committee meetings or Catherine to deal with also.

"I told you to push the meeting with the caterer to review the final menu back by two hours yesterday."

"I did." Katie said, wondering what drama today's meeting would unfold for her.

"You didn't-"

"I would not have answered your question with 'I did', if I did not. I called your cell phone to tell you they could only push it back by an hour but you wouldn't answer. Then I contacted your assistant upstairs who told me you were not around. So after I made two attempts at telling you about the meeting- calling your phone and attempting to tell you in person- I asked him to pass on the message to you immediately."

"You made me miss my meeting."

"I didn't make you do anything." Katie spoke through her teeth then, unable to control herself or the anger that was beginning to bubble inside her. "If you had have picked up my call, you wouldn't have missed the meeting. And if your assistant didn't pass on the message that is not my fault, although I know you wish it was."

The look Catherine gave Katie right then was indescribable, it made every part of the young woman want to shake. She knew she had messed with the wrong woman but she could not stand to be treated the way she had been any longer.

"Go and get our coffees." Katie knew the order off by heart by this time. She looked over to Alice who only gave her a grim look before standing up and walking towards Katie.

"You stay here, she'll just have to manage by herself." Catherine ordered. Katie let out a breath through her nose, trying to contain herself as she began to walk out of the meeting room, everyone's eyes on her as she did so.

Catherine was absolutely livid about missing the meeting yesterday, so much so that everyone's heads seemed to be on the chopping board. She was ordering people around since she had gotten into work and all the people on the committee knew not to cross her at this point. She always got like this coming close to the gala, it was just 'stress' they would say, but not attending the review with the caterer for tomorrow's gala had tipped her completely over the edge.

"Little crossbreed." Katie thought she had imagined it at first, those terrible words being mumbled from Catherine's mouth but, how could she? Katie could tell by the complete silence that fell upon the room after the older woman uttered those words that she had heard correctly.

Katie had a choice then, one she did not want to make. She had never had to deal with people making ignorant comments about her race since many years ago. Katie was mixed race, and she was proud of who she was despite so many times before having trouble with people who wanted to make her race and ethnicity their concern. Deciding whether this time was worth putting her job at risk or not was tough. She could walk out the door, pretend she heard nothing or she could turn around and tell Catherine how she really felt about her. Katie chose the latter over the former, although her decision may have been the wrong one. She turned around, looking at every face in the room before stopping at Catherine's.

"Those words you just used were absolutely repulsive. You're a disgusting woman and I don't care what you tell Mr. Anderson after all this is over, say whatever the hell you want. But I know the truth, that you've had me running around doing every single little thing you could possibly think of to make my job a living hell for me over the past couple of weeks when the workload could have been distributed evenly throughout the committee."

"Well I wouldn't-"

"Screw you Catherine, and get your own god damn coffee." Katie looked around the room then at the many sets of anxious eyes that were on her. She stormed out of the meeting room, leaving behind whatever hell would break loose once she was gone.

She had a troublesome feeling in the pit of her stomach, her breath hitched in her throat and she found it hard to focus on anything as she smashed down on one of the buttons in the elevator. Tears pricked her eyes as she walked out onto her floor and went straight to the bathroom where once she was inside a cubicle, she would allow herself to cry.

Katie was a strong woman, she had been through so much she thought she couldn't, yet she could not help but allow Catherine to make her feel so weak. She was already beginning to regret her outburst although she knew it was somewhat justified. For Catherine to call her what she did because Katie was mixed race was completely unacceptable but she was sure the older woman would have a way of getting out of punishment if something did get out about the awful remark she had said.

It took a couple of minutes for Katie to compose herself again. She had completely untangled in the bathroom alone, all her stress and anger had left her body in the form of tears yet she did not feel any better, if anything she felt worse. The fears of losing her job, of the things Catherine might make up about her strangely close relationship with Colin and the fact that she had to see everyone from that planning committee again tomorrow for the gala made the young woman want to burst into tears again but she had promised herself she was done crying- for now.

She went straight to her office from the bathroom, she had a lot of work to do. The first thing on her list was the Jefferson report that she had put off for over a week. Colin needed it by today, which meant Katie had to finish off the overview as soon as she possibly could. That did not take much time, but it did take quite a while for her to pluck up the courage to face Colin. Katie wondered if and when Catherine might inform both Anderson men of what happened earlier that morning.

It took a deep breath and a fake smile for Katie to finally knock on Colin's door but as soon as she entered, he knew something was different about her.

"And how are you on this fine morning Katie?" Colin gave her a wolfish smile although that did not take the gloomy mood in the room away. Eventually, she broke the silence she had caused.

"I'm okay, thank you Colin." Katie's voice was so quiet and gentle, it crackled out from her throat in a hushed way that he could not describe.

"Is something wrong?" Colin found himself asking her this question almost every day recently. There was an apparent change in her exterior, in her mood and her smile that he could clearly detect and examined very carefully. She had told him so many times that there was nothing wrong or that she was just stressed but he knew there had to be something more than that. No matter how many times he would ask the same question, she would always give the same lie.

"No. Here's the Jefferson report you were looking for, I'm sorry I didn't have it for you sooner." She placed the report down on his desk in front of him and turned to walk away but he grabbed her wrist before her feet could take her anywhere.

"Hey, Katie?" Colin stood up then and walked around from his desk so that he was beside her.

"Yes?"

"Seriously, I can tell there's something bothering you."

Being that close to her then gave him the opportunity to observe her face, her red eyes that looked glassy. If he took another step closer, she did not know what she would do. She began to become upset again, he cared but she did not want him to.

Katie's eyes began to water again, she looked to the ceiling as a solution to stop any from falling down her cheek. She had all of this pent-up anger and frustration she thought she had gotten rid of in the rest room but clearly did not. Katie wasn't sure how to take Colin in that moment. His eyes searched her for some sort of explanation but she refused to open her mouth. He sensed this and did something he possibly should not have done- he extended his arms out to wrap her in a warm hug that lasted a moment too long.

She tried desperately to pull away, but the truth was, that wasn't what she wanted. It wasn't what either of them wanted. It was strange how something so normal felt so much more intense with him- Katie couldn't help but take in his scent and savour his touch. It all felt very natural, for Colin to be comforting her the way he was, running his hand up and down her back as she leaned in closer. A little too natural, Colin thought. It was him who had realised first how inappropriate this looked but did not feel.

Colin pulled away first and noticed the strange look on Katie's face, like she was somehow apologetic yet he didn't want her to be. Her eyes widened a little but the pair remained close to each other, lips lingering, eyes searching one another's as if waiting to see what would happen next.

Katie cleared her throat and stepped away from him, trying to figure out how she felt then. He too was in the same position.

"I should probably get back to work." She mumbled before leaving.

As if Katie was not going through enough that day, her thoughts constantly went back to what had happened in Colin's office. She knew she had so many other things to be concerned about at that point in time, with her outburst earlier in front of Catherine and the entire planning committee. It was just a simple hug, but one she felt was crossing the line too much. But why was she being so sensitive about it? She did not want her mind to divulge into the many questions that awaited her once she had time to think clearly.

Colin was feeling everything at once. Confusion, bewilderment, joy and regret. He felt like there was something there, between him and Katie but then felt foolish for even thinking that in the first place. Nothing could happen, he was just overreacting and needed to stop. He was being irrational. Colin tried to push everything to the side but couldn't help but feel slight embarrassment once he mulled over the situation from earlier. He was the one who initiated the hug, he was the one who was so concerned about her and he felt his interest in her was not only pointless but one-sided.

After heading out for a long lunch Colin returned to find David waiting around in his office. He felt a lot more agitated than he did when first leaving for lunch as he had more time to think about everything.

"Hey, how's it going?" David met him with a smiling face but Colin did not return the expression.

"Fine." Colin grumbled before sitting down at his desk and sighing.

"So is Vinny coming out with us tonight? Maybe he can fix us up with some of that-"

"David." He looked at his friend then, a stern look on his face after cutting him off. "Don't talk about that here, the walls are thin and you never know when my dad's going to randomly appear."

"Sorry bro, I forgot..." David took a minute before he spoke again. "You excited for the gala tomorrow?" he asked, changing the subject.

"Sure, my dad keeps pestering me about bringing a date though." Colin rolled his eyes.

"I think I know the perfect date you could bring."

"Who?" He looked quizzically at David.

"She works right outside your office and you practically drool over her whenever you see her- I don't' blame you though." David's words made Colin a little nervous, could other people see how he was beginning to feel about his assistant? He sure hoped not.

"That's not funny man, I would never bring Katie as my date and I definitely don't drool over her either. But whatever you're into." The harsh words almost burned Colin's tongue as they escaped his mouth but he needed to hide how he felt.

"So you don't think Katie's cute?"

"God no." he scoffed at David who was narrowing his eyes sceptically at the other man. "Besides, I don't want to bring any date, let alone her."

The thin walls Colin had spoken of earlier were what cause the next situation to happen. Katie had heard it all, although she wished she hadn't. She was carrying a pile of documents for Colin to sign when she happened to overhear his conversation with his friend, David. Katie was unsure as to whether she should continue with what she was doing or not. The anger she suddenly felt inside made her carry on, she knocked at his door then entered before he could open his mouth to speak.

"David." She nodded at the young man who stood beside Colin's desk.

"I need you to sign these for me, when you're done you can put them on my desk." Her voice was cold and lacked emotion.

Katie handed Colin the documents but kept her eyes looking down, avoiding his gaze as he tried desperately to catch some hint from her face to figure out if she had heard his previous conversation but it was difficult to do.

"Sure, I'll do it now." He spoke warmly to her but she replied quickly, almost butting across him.

"Thanks." She said before walking out and closing the door behind her. As soon as she did so, the two men looked at each other.

"She definitely heard me, didn't she?" A look of panic crossed Colin's face that made David laugh.

"Why do you care? By the way you were talking just a second ago, you shouldn't be phased."

"I have to go out and ask her, don't I?" He got up quickly from his chair and left his friend standing in his office alone while he went to go find Katie.

She was standing at the copier machine, staring gloomily down at the buttons as she waited for her prints outs.

"Katie." Colin almost sighed with relief when he saw her.

"Yes Mr. Anderson?" she used a more formal voice when she spoke, she didn't use his first name when addressing him which he hated.

It took Colin a moment to inspect the unnecessary situation he had ran into again with her. He did not speak for a minute, and all the way through the silence Katie waited, waited for him to say something she wanted to hear. But what did she want to hear?

It was then that she wondered why she cared as much as she did? Katie wasn't sure then if she wanted him to apologise or tell her that he didn't mean what he said, because both of those things weren't needed. He was her boss and could think of her as repulsive if he pleased. It should not matter to Katie the words he had spoken just moments ago. But still, she couldn't help how she felt.

"Never mind." He mumbled and walked away, leaving her feeling disappointed although it was not justified.

Once Colin returned to his office, he immediately noticed the grin that had appeared on David's face.

"Did she accept your apology?" David laughed again, finding great humour in his friend's reaction to finding out Katie heard everything.

"You have to give an apology before someone accepts it David." His tone was gruff.

"So you're telling me you didn't apologise? You practically ran out there after her."

"No, I didn't apologise. I have nothing to be sorry for."

"Whatever man, are you ready to go yet or what?"

"No, I'm actually going to stick around here for another while. I need to get some things done."

"But you said you were going to leave early today, we're heading out later."

"I know but I have a lot to do."

"So you're deciding to actually work for once?" Colin shot David a glare once he spoke, to which his friend held his hands up in surrender and looked innocently at him. "What? Suit yourself man.

I'm off." He said before leaving Colin to drown in his own thoughts, mostly about Katie.

He hoped by staying a little later he might be able to catch her alone again before she went home. Colin knew he had lots of time to just go into her office and talk to her but he was cowering away from any sort of intent filled meeting. He wanted to just subtly bump into her on her way out, as he knew she would be stuck in her office until the end of the day- she was so busy lately with the gala and all of Colin's paperwork that seemed to be piling up.

Unfortunately for Colin, he never bumped into Katie. She rushed out as soon as it was time to go. Colin, although quickly he got his things together, was not quick enough to catch her before she left.

Confusion fell over Katie on her walk to the train station. It did not leave her that night, not on the train home, not once she got ready for bed, not before she fell asleep. She shouldn't be fantasizing about her boss, she should be glad he said the things he did. At least that way she knew there would not be a repeat with what happened at her last job. But she just couldn't get him out of her head even though there were other matters that needed to be thought about first, Catherine being a perfect example.

**8**

CHAPTER 7

June 2009

Katie woke up with a sore head and a heavy mind. Emily came home from work late the night before when Katie was already in bed so she did not have time to tell her friend about the eventful day she had yesterday. In fact, Katie wasn't even sure she wanted to tell Emily anything, then her run in with Catherine would feel more real. Colin had distracted her from the more serious reasoning Katie needed to do yesterday.

Her worrying thoughts that were beginning to creep up on her the minute she opened her eyes, nevertheless, she dragged herself out of bed and headed to the kitchen for some well needed coffee.

"Hey girl, why are you up so early?" Emily asked before munching down on some toast. She was sitting at the small breakfast bar, looking at the TV as she ate her breakfast alone, until Katie walked in. She immediately noticed her sullen face and the bags under her eyes.

"Couldn't sleep." Katie mumbled as she stuck on her coffee. "You want a cup?"

"I'm good thanks." Emily eyed her friend with curiosity, growing more concerned by the minute. "Is something wrong?" she finally asked.

"Oh god Em, I've made a horrible mistake." Katie covered her face with her hands then, thinking about her outburst in front of the planning committee yesterday morning.

"Katie? Tell me, what happened?"

During Katie's explanation about what happened with Catherine and her remark about Katie being bi-racial, she never once mentioned the other half of her day. Catherine was the main focus of the discussion, like she should be. Katie had already decided that Colin shouldn't be the focus of her attention when she wasn't even sure she would have a job after tonight's gala. She would worry about him later, if it was even necessary.

"I don't even want to go tonight, what if she's kicked me off of the list and I'm not allowed inside? I need this job so bad Em. I don't know what I'm going to do, what if Catherine lies about everything and makes other things up about me?"

"Stop panicking Katie, I'm sure if she does, you can tell the truth."

"But I don't think my side of the story will matter very much to anyone, Catherine's working there a long time before me. I don't think anyone would believe me. I shouldn't have reacted so harshly-"

"Oh stop it. It was bound to happen sometime. Catherine sounds like a major bitch and nothing justifies what she called you, that was completely unnecessary and uncalled for."

"I- I don't know." Katie continued to worry despite talking to her friend.

Anxiety only deepened within Katie throughout the day and the time she spent getting ready. She really did not want to go anymore.

As she did her hair and her makeup, she was thinking about all the excuses she might use in order to get out of going tonight, but she knew if her job was still there, she was needed to help out.

Katie put on her dress, then her shoes and got her things ready. Emily hugged her on her way out the door and told her everything would be okay, whatever happened that night. She took a deep breath and nodded at her friend before leaving to catch her taxi.

In the cab on the way there though, Katie began to become curious. Colin was on her mind again and quickly, she took her phone from her clutch to search something. Being as nosey as she was, Katie wanted to find out what Colin's actual type was. She thought back to when she had her interview with Colin and how Emily mentioned afterward the name of his ex-girlfriend- Dahlia Stephens- the name suddenly came back to her.

Katie was prying, she was sticking her nose where it didn't belong, but it didn't feel as bad because most people knew who she was already, all of the pictures of the two of them were on gossip websites although there were very few of them.

She scanned through a couple of pictures but then decided to stop. Katie put her phone away for the rest of the cab ride but she couldn't forget the image of the glamorous woman who stood alongside Colin in the photos.

Alice greeted Katie with a smile once she arrived at the hotel early to help out before the gala started.

"Hi Alice, you look amazing."

"So do you! How are you after yesterday morning?" Alice asked.

"I don't really know. I feel stupid, I shouldn't have reacted the way I did."

"Yes you should have, you did what the rest of us couldn't. Don't worry about Catherine anyways, I'm sure she won't say anything if you don't."

"If I don't what?"

"You know, say anything about what she called you. She knows how much trouble she would be in and also that the room was full when she said it so she can't really deny it. I bet from now on, she's going to be so much nicer to you because she knows what's at stake."

"Oh, I never thought of it that way." Katie muttered, not being fully convinced.

"She went way too far with you and she knows it- Anyways, I have to get back to work. You have a list waiting for you like the rest of us. It's just inside laying on one of the tables. Everyone's really busy, good luck Katie."

"I'll see you at dinner." Katie smiled at her friend before heading into the dining hall to find her list.

In no time, she was buzzing around the hotel, trying to get things organised for the guests that would be turning up in just a few short minutes. Katie knew she would not be able to rest until after the charity auction when the meal started, she just wished the first half of the night was over already so she could relax and at least enjoy herself a little bit.

She was resetting a couple of tables in the dining hall after she discovered they were different to the rest when Colin spotted her. The hall was almost empty, with only one or two other people flying around organising things and it was mostly quiet.

Colin couldn't help but take in the sight of her in her pale pink dress, the strapless gown exposed more of her bronze skin than he had seen in work before. Once she noticed his presence and looked at him, he could not look away.

"Hi." He spoke first.

"Good evening Colin." He was glad she had used his first name this time. She went back to setting the table, looking away from him then.

"You look beautiful." As soon as the words left his lips, he regretted it. He didn't know what he was thinking before he said them.

"Thanks, I suppose." She continued on with what she was doing, not being phased at all by his words because all she could focus on was the ones he spoke yesterday. I would never bring Katie, god no, I don't want to bring any date, let alone her.

"Listen Katie, I know you overheard my conversation yesterday with David. And I just want to say that-"

"Don't worry about it Colin. I get it."

"No Katie, you don't understand-"

"Look at me. I'm practically the help, and it seems to disgust you."

"It doesn't. God no." he was taken aback by her forwardness. "I just-"

"Yo! Colin, your dad wants you outside for when the guests start arriving." David interrupted their talk before it had even started. Colin took a deep breath, he wanted to say so many things to her right then but didn't.

"You should probably go, we both have a lot to do." The small smile that fell upon Katie's lips as she finally looked at him was full of sorrow, just like her eyes. But there was nothing Colin could do about it, he only nodded and walked off to leave her to her work again.

The rest of the night only seemed to get worse as it went on. After the charity auction, everyone began to find their seats again for dinner. Katie looked over all the names placed around the tables but couldn't seem to find her own. Once she spotted Alice sitting down at a table nearby with a few others from the committee, she immediately went to check if she was supposed to be sitting at their table instead.

"Hey, what's up Katie?" Alice asked quizzically.

"My name." the other woman muttered as she searched the table thoroughly.

"What?" Alice laughed.

"My name, I can't find it anywhere-"

"Katie." Catherina had appeared by the two women's side and looked expectantly at Katie. It was the first time Katie had seen Catherine since yesterday morning, she gulped at the sight of the older woman.

"Yes?"

"You're needed in the kitchen."

"The kitchen? But what would they need me in the kitchen for?"

"No, there must be a mistake Catherine, Katie was just looking for her place for dinner." Alice cut in before Katie had time to say anything else.

"Oh shoot." Catherine pretended as if she had just remembered something. "I may have forgotten to put you down on the list for dinner. I'm so sorry Katie." She said in such an insincere way that made Katie want to crumble into pieces on the ground. She was too exhausted, her entire body aching, to even be angry at Catherine then.

"I'm sure there's a spare space somewhere."

"The numbers exceeded what we expected this year, all the free seats are taken. Katie, we need you to bring out some of the courses for the guests anyways. You should get going to the kitchen."

"But Catherine-" Alice interjected but did not get the chance to finish off her sentence because Katie stopped her.

"Don't worry about it Alice." She said, clearly deflated before she headed off in the direction of the kitchen.

Her heels had begun to hurt her since the beginning of the auction and she wanted desperately to just have a break to sit down- but still, she continued. Katie figured as soon as she was done she could just leave, her night was already mad enough and she did not want to stick around for fear it would get worse.

Colin couldn't keep his eyes off her as she whizzed around the huge dining hall in her flowy dress. Her attire was clearly not suited to the job she was doing and she stuck out among the other waiters in the room. Katie knew this, and couldn't help but feel slight humiliation from this. Jeffrey was quite puzzled by the discovery too, but decided to say nothing, his questions could wait until Monday morning after everything was over.

Finally, the three courses were served to everyone and she could go. Although she wanted to say her goodbyes to Alice, she refrained from doing so. Her stomach was rumbling with hunger and she felt completely wore out. Katie contemplated getting a cab straight home from the hotel but then decided to take her shoes off and walk to the nearest place that served food at this time of night- the first thing that caught her eye was the giant, bright McDonalds sign around the corner. It was relatively empty and despite the strange looks she was getting from everyone around her, she ordered her meal and sat down alone at first.

Little did she know, Colin had walked out once he saw she was leaving. Although he did not know where exactly she had went, it didn't take him long to find her as she was sitting at a window. It took a moment for Katie to realise he was there, she looked up from her food to find him walking towards her.

"If I knew you were following me I would've walked much faster." Katie grumbled before taking another bight of her burger. Colin sat down in the seat across from her and rolled his eyes.

"I wasn't following you, I was just looking for you."

"I suppose I was easy enough to find, I stick out like a sore thumb in here." Colin laughed at her reply although he shouldn't have.

"Not at all Katie." He replied sarcastically before a silence kicked in at their table.

"What do you want? You should probably be getting back to the gala."

"I don't want to go back."

"Why not? You were practically ranting and raving about it a couple of days ago."

"I guess I just can't get my gala on tonight." Katie almost choked on her fries once she heard him speak. She let out a loud, warm laugh that she couldn't help despite the horrible mood she was in.

"Me either." After laughing with her, Colin could notice her mood lighten just a small bit.

"Why not?" he asked. She looked up from her food then to rest her chin in her hand and fix her eyes on his.

"I've had a terrible night Colin. Look at me... I'm a mess." Katie laughed lightly but sadness still shone through in her appearance, her eyes and facial expression.

"You look beautiful to me."

"Despite me sitting here in the middle of a McDonalds, stuffing my face and getting my dress dirty?" She quickly replied.

"Of course." There was no doubt in his words, but it made Katie's smile fall from her lips immediately.

"You shouldn't say that." She wasn't sure what she wanted then. He was taking back the words he had said yesterday that made her annoyed, only to make her want him to take the new ones back instead. Katie confused herself, and if she had have told Colin, he would've agreed that she was confusing too.

"Why not? Why can't I give compliments where they're due?"

"You know why..." she sighed before picking up another fry. "You want one?" she pushed the tray toward him a little in a giving gesture. She wanted the change the subject then.

"Why were you serving food earlier?"

"They needed more people." Katie shrugged her shoulders nonchalantly at him then.

"But that's not your job."

"It's my job to do whatever Catherine wants me to do, that's been my job since the very first day I started working on that committee."

"You didn't get anything to eat?" he asked.

"I wouldn't be here if I did." Katie chuckled then. "Let's go outside, I could do with some air again."

She picked up her tray and carried it to the bin. Colin followed, her clutch and shoes in his hands.

"Thanks." She smiled at him once they were outside and she sat down at the steps of a building a couple of doors up, figuring her dress was already dirty enough. Colin eyed her with curiosity but stood in front of her. "Aren't you doing to sit down?" Katie laughed.

"I don't want to get my tux dirty."

"Oh come on... I'm in a pale pink dress- your tux is black you'll be fine." She patted the ground beside her before he hesitantly sat down. "I'm sure you have a million of them at home anyway." She joked as she nudged him but he seemed to be somewhere else for a moment.

"I feel like I haven't talked to you in forever." Colin said unexpectedly, causing Katie to look up at him with complete curiosity.

"But we talk every day. I'm your assistant." She chuckled. "I'd be doing something wrong if I didn't talk to you, now wouldn't I?" Katie teased him, a smile spreading across her face and lighting up her eyes.

"I know but I mean talk talk."

"Well, we've both been very busy the past while. What with you actually doing work lately, it's very strange actually." She remained light-hearted still, but he held a more serious tone when he talked, as if he was genuinely concerned.

"I don't think I know anybody else who's allowed trash talk their boss all the time Katie." He smirked at her then, deciding to join in on the joking around.

"Maybe it's just me but- it feels like I've always worked for you. Like there's never been a time when I haven't. It's weird." She laughed lightly again at her realisation.

"I thought I was the only one." He admitted as she rested her head on his shoulder then, taking in his scent although he did not know it. She took out her phone and hired an Uber, still leaning into him.

"I'm sorry about yesterday by the way... and today." Katie decided it was the time to bring that up. "I wasn't snooping or anything, it's just that sometimes it's hard not to hear. It was none of my business anyways, it doesn't matter."

"I'm the one who should be sorry-"

"No Colin, honestly, you don't need to apologise. I get it, I'm not your type. I suppose it's a good thing actually, considering I work for you."

"Will you let me speak for a minute, god Katie." Colin said as he laughed aloud. "I didn't mean any of it, it's not true. It's the exact opposite of what I think actually." Katie took her head from his shoulder and sat up for a moment then, taking in his word as she looked at his face that seemed to be very close to hers.

"You shouldn't be saying any of this to me. You're my boss-"

"I wish you didn't have to keep reminding me..." his voice was quiet and low, he was too busy looking at her lips.

"I wish I didn't have to too." Katie trailed off as they moved closer to each other, but she stopped then at a point where it didn't necessarily look like they were going to kiss or not. But were they? Katie was unsure whether it was a good idea, but she still regretted stopping it. "But you are my boss, and you will be for as long as I work for you. I just have to remember that."

There was a mutual understanding that night between the two of them, one that was left unspoken. It did not pass their lips but they certainly would remember it in their minds. He had been so close to feeling her lips on his, something he had to admit he wanted to do for as long as he could remember.

It was strange because he felt as if he knew Katie years, although it had only been months. Colin wanted to know more about her, but that would only happen during their time working together, a relationship outside of the office was clearly not on the cards between them. Both came to a mutual understanding about that although they wished things were different as each felt there was something more- but were too afraid to go for it.

"That's my Uber." Katie said as a car beeped it's horn a couple of feet up from them on the road.

"Do you want me to come with you? Make sure you get home alright?" Katie gave him a pained look then, if only, she thought.

"I think we both know that's not a good idea." Her lips met for a small yet grim smile. "Thanks for cheering me up tonight Colin. I'll see you Monday." Katie leaned down to pick up her things then kissed him lightly on the cheek before walking away. She knew she shouldn't have done it but she couldn't help it. The kiss marked an end to something that had not even begun- they both understood that.

"See you." Was all Colin could say then, as he watched her walk away and get into her cab.

## CHAPTER 8

July 2018

Katie looked in complete frustration at the many bouquets of flowers laid out around Cheryl's desk. A delivery man then passed her on the floor and placed another two bouquets down on the ground beside the desk, there was no more room to put them anywhere else.

"I can't believe this..." she shook her head in disbelief as Cheryl watched close from the corner of her eye for her boss's reaction.

"Did you read any of the cards?" Cheryl asked because of the way Katie was lingering around looking at all the bouquets.

"I don't want to, that asshole's said enough to me to last a lifetime. I don't need another card to read." She crossed her arms.

"Maybe you should talk to him, he seems very- eager to see you again. You know he turns up here almost every day to see if you'll let him in again."

"The only reason I let him in in the first place was because I didn't know it was him." Katie sighed.

She didn't want to think about Colin anymore. She was done with him, or at least that was what she was supposed to say after everything. Her mind was telling her that was the truth but her heart was saying it was a complete lie. For years, Katie had pushed him to the back of her mind, but now, he demanded to be heard and seen and thought about without doing very much at all. One visit and dozens of bouquets were all it took for her mind to be fixed on him again.

The words he spoke in her office kept bouncing around like an echo in her brain, if she had heard that a couple of years ago, they would have changed everything but things were different then- or at least that was what she wanted to believe. Colin had a record of letting her down, she didn't know if her heart could take another heartbreak caused by him but she did have to admit that seeing him again made her think a lot about what possibilities lay ahead if she would just forgive him.

But he completely broke her, left her shattered after so many times of trying to help him. Katie didn't think she possibly had it in herself to forgive him this time. Or maybe that was her head thinking over her heart, deep down, she felt like that statement was false but didn't elaborate on the thought.

"How come I've never seen him before?" a curious Cheryl asked, butting into Katie's thoughts.

"Because he's a part of my past and I wanted to keep it that way."

"Hey what did he do to you that he feels the need to do all of this?" she gestured all around her to the vibrantly coloured flowers. Katie hesitated, still getting flashbacks.

"Things I don't think I can forgive..." she said before she walked into her office and closed the door behind her, clearly not wanting to talk anymore about Colin.

Cheryl felt like she would never find out the story behind all of this. Her boss was certainly a wonder,  before that man turned up but even more so after his arrival. She looked around at all the flowers that surrounded her and read every one of the cards that were in her eyeshot although she had read most of them a couple times before. She did not need to read them a second or third time- they all said the same thing:

I'm sorry x

**10**

**CHAPTER 9**

September 2009

"Hi Katie." Anna beamed at her boyfriend's assistant who was at the photocopier when she walked onto the office floor off the elevator.

"Hey, how's it going?" Katie asked, a friendly smile on her face.

"I'm fine, thanks. Do you know if Colin's in yet?" Katie wished she hadn't asked that question, because she didn't know what to say then. There was an awkward silence for a minute before she spoke.

"Um, no. Not yet. But he should be here soon." She looked at her watch then back at Anna. "He should be here before noon like he usually is. But you can go right in to his office and wait if you want. I'm sure he wouldn't mind."

"Sure. Thanks."

Anna's face dropped once Katie answered her question with a no. That was the third time this week Colin was late for work, and she knew exactly why. Katie didn't want to be the bearer of bad news, but with Colin constantly partying over the past few weeks, meaning she was always the one to inform his girlfriend that.

She had been right, Colin arrived into work before noon, with only a minute or two to spare. He popped his head into Katie's office as soon as he arrived on their floor like he usually did. She noticed how terrible he looked but said nothing about it.

"Good morning." He smiled despite his aching head and tired eyes.

"Anna's waiting for you inside."

She did not need to greet him with anything as polite has his greeting with her. Colin rolled his eyes then and left the room to go to his office, where he knew along with Anna, would be a huge lecture waiting for him once he got inside.

"Hey-"

"Don't." Anna's polite and friendlier exterior that she had when speaking with Katie earlier had been demolished by her rage. She stared at her boyfriend, his bloodshot eyes, and his messed-up hair. He probably hadn't showered, and by the looks of it shaved either. "Don't act like this is a normal Thursday morning and you can just walk in like that as if nothing's wrong."

"Anna...." Colin felt the need to explain then, although he really didn't want to.

"Where have you been huh? Where were you last night?"

"I went out-"

"Like you always do." She had become visibly upset although she promised herself she wouldn't, not this time.

"God damn it Anna, what's the big deal? You knew from the beginning what you were getting yourself into with me."

"I didn't think it was this bad." She shook her head then in disbelief. "Were you with Vinny again?"

"Vinny's my friend, of course I was with him."

"I wouldn't exactly call him a friend Colin." Anna scoffed at him then. "Look at you, you're a mess."

"So what? I like to go out okay? I like to enjoy myself everyone once in a while. What's the problem?"

"Every once in a while? Colin, it's almost every night at this stage. You need to take a break sometimes. It's not just the alcohol it's the-"

"I told you not to talk about that, not in here." His paranoia had kicked in then and he neared her when he spoke.

Within minutes, Katie could hear the two shouting at each other from inside his office. She tried her best to ignore it, like she usually did, but it seemed that their arguments were getting worse and worse each time. She sipped on her coffee and continued to type on her computer although the noise was off putting to say the least.

"Go on then! Storm out of here like you usually do Anna."

Although their voices from next door were muffled, Katie could still make out most of what the couple were saying. First, the voices stopped, then the door to Colin's office opened. She saw Ana walk briskly past her door, on her way to the elevator Katie could only assume, then watched as Colin slowly took a step or two forward, coming into full view for Katie.

She watched as he took a deep sigh then covered his face with one of his hands in frustration but only for a moment. Colin turned then and caught her staring at him. She gave him a sympathetic look that only made him frown a little.

"C'mon, are you almost ready for our lunch meeting?" Colin took a step towards her door and called into her as if nothing had happened.

"Yeah, sure. I'll be right there Colin." Katie went along with his act, she did not mention Anna once on their way to lunch which he was glad of.

She took notes like she usually did, but her mind began to wander at times when Colin's face seemed to be the only thing she could see in the busy restaurant. Katie tried to stay focused throughout their time together with a client, but with each meeting it seemed to be a growing difficulty.

By the time to two were finished, the restaurant had become empty, with only one or two tables full. They said their goodbyes to the client but as Katie was about to grab her coat, Colin insisted on buying them coffee.

"Unlike you, I spent my night sleeping instead of partying. I don't need one."

"Watch your mouth Kate."

His tone was a lot more serious than Katie had expected, but the fact that he had casually called her by her nickname made her feel a little less in trouble than she first thought. He called a waiter to the side then and ordered both a coffee.

"You're unbelievable, I swear." Katie rolled her eyes but then noticed the solemn look on his face as he looked down at the table and decided not to push it. "What's wrong?" her gentle voice felt as if it had melted into his ears. He decided to look up then because of it, both their eyes caught with one another's.

"I'm just tired."

"I wonder why?" she spoke with easy sarcasm, causing him to narrow his eyes at her.

"I already have one woman giving me shit over my partying habits, I don't need another."

"Oh c'mon. Carrie isn't at work enough anymore to whip you back into shape. I think I need to take over now."

Carrie had decided she would only work part time after her husband had made a slow recovery. They only saw her once or twice a week then, which was more strange for Colin because he had been so used to her being around and keeping him on his toes when he needed it.

"You don't, trust me." Colin grumbled before saying, "Thanks" as the waiter brought two coffees to their table.

"I don't think you're just tired." She leaned her cheek on one of her hands as she looked at him, wanting to know more. He looked as if everything was crashing down on top of him and Katie couldn't help but be a little worried then.

"Anna and I aren't working out. And I don't know what to do." He didn't seem that much fazed by the whole situation, his voice was unwavered and his eyes held only a certain amount of sadness.

"I'm sure you'll work things out."

She gave him a small smile, but there was no honesty in her words. She was being his PA in that moment and not his friend because she felt he had a terrible enough morning without Katie telling him the complete truth.

"I'm not so sure anymore."

"Do you want me to be honest, or should I just keep my mouth shut?" Katie couldn't help it then.

"I guess I want you to be honest, yes."

"Do you love her?" he paused for a minute after hearing her question and thought about it.

"Well, we've only known each other a couple of months Katie."

"But do you care about her- a lot?"

"Of course I do." Colin didn't like where this was going, but he continued on with the conversation anyway. He took a minute then to assess his short relationship with Anna and wondered why it felt different to all his other one's- and not in a good way.

"Well then why don't you even try to make a compromise?" Katie didn't understand and had been wanting to ask him this since he and Anna first got together.

Anna was a sweet girl, she was always friendly with everyone around the office if she ever visited. Katie talked to her a lot more than she had expected, they got along good. But if she were Anna, she doubted she would be able to continue in a relationship with someone who didn't seem that bothered about her.

"Because why should I have to? She knew what I was like from the beginning. I shouldn't have to compromise having a good time because she doesn't agree with it."

"This is why you're wondering what's wrong and why you two aren't working out. You can't see it from her side of things, only yours. I can't say whether that's mutual between you two because I don't know much else about your relationship only what I see." He took a minute to take in what she was saying.

"I'm sorry, I've said too much, haven't I?" She worried after he hadn't said anything for a minute or two.

"No. Not at all. Thank you for just being honest with me." He gave her a sweet smile that gently grew on his lips. The two shared a moment then, where Colin's smile was contagious and his eyes were something she couldn't turn away from.

She really didn't have a clue about what was going on with him lately- one of the main reasons Anna argued with him all the time. And that was the way he wanted to keep it. Colin hoped Katie would never see his other side. He would try his best to keep it away from her.

"Katie, the copier's broke again. Can you try and fix it? I really need to send these papers out before the end of the day." Shannon stuck her head into Katie's office.

"Sure, just give me one second and I'll be right out." She finished off the work she was doing quickly and walked out to try and fix the problem.

"What are you two doing?" Colin was strolling past them, a fresh cup of coffee in one hand, a folder in the other when he saw Katie with her head between the wall and the back of the photocopier.

"Katie's fixing the copier for me sir." Shannon replied as if this was what Katie did all the time.

"Can't we just get a new one? I'll say something to my dad about it."

"Sure, thank you. It's been acting up a lot lately."

"It's fine for now, I think I might have gotten it working again- for now." Katie stood up then and went to the other side to tap something in on the small screen.

"Where did you learn to fix photocopiers Ms. Briggs?" there was humour in his tone but she was too busy to notice his teasing.

"Back at my old office." Katie froze completely then, knowing she had said something she was not supposed to. The silence felt deafening, Shannon looked Katie and Colin, who's smile had turned quickly to a frown.

"Your old office?" he asked in confusion.

"No- no I meant, um."

Katie tried desperately to make something up but couldn't think of a way to get herself out of this one. Colin had noticed a lot recently how she would mention another job and then take back what she had said. He never thought much of it but judging by the look on her face then, it seemed like her old job was supposed to be kept a secret. Colin couldn't help but feel curious then as she almost squirmed at his next question.

"I thought you just worked a little here and there during your two years after college. You never mentioned working in an office?" By that time, Shannon had noticed the tension and decided to leave- she could use the copier later.

"Colin I-I..."

"If you worked in an office before you worked here why did you tell me you had no experience Katie?" he knew something was wrong then, her face paled and she look as if she wanted to run as far aware as possible- her eyes wide with shock.

"Can we not talk about this here?"

"No, I want to know now-"

"Please, Colin?" she knew she shouldn't have reacted that way but she needed time to think.

He didn't push it much further but still wanted to know right there and then. She brought him into his office and paced back and forth for a moment or two while he watched eagerly.

"Promise you won't judge me Colin? Promise you tell." A look of complete desperation fell upon her face that made his heart drop a little in his chest. What had happened to her?

"No, of course not." He said quickly, still looking a little mad at her.

"I worked as a marketing assistant for almost a year after I finished college at Pierce. I was an intern there my last summer before school ended so it was easy to get the job with no other work experience."

"Why didn't you say anything? Katie, you could've gotten a job in marketing if you'd put it on your resume."

"I couldn't."

"Why not?"

"For the same reason I don't want to tell you." Tears began to appear in her eyes as she remembered back but she didn't want to seem weak. She looked up in an effort to get rid of them. Colin took a step towards her then to go and comfort her but she put her hand up, needing a minute to just figure out how she was going to tell him what happened at her old job.

"From the minute I started, me and one of the marketing specialists higher up seemed to get along great. I never thought of him as anything other than a colleague and a friend. I was promoted after only a couple of months working there, which caused some rumours to spread. But then they got worse and worse and eventually I had to leave."

"Katie..." his voice trailed off once he focused on her exterior, how clearly distressed she was from telling him what had happened.

"I didn't want future employers to know I worked there in case they started asking questions, got into contact with my old boss and believed the rumours that made me leave."

"But you've been working here for so long now, you know me. You could've told me by now." He seemed to be more annoyed at the fact she hadn't told him specifically- it was almost as if he was wounded by her lie.

"I'm so sorry Colin. I really am." She hung her head in shame, all the names she had been called in her old office came flooding back to her but his voice stopped them all.

"Come here." He said. "Stop it. There's no point in being upset about it now, you're here and you're here to stay. Forget what happened at Pierce Holdings." He held her fore arm as they stood close to one another, his soothing voice calmed her worries. He wasn't talking as her boss then, but as her friend. The lines had begun to blur quite a lot lately, but neither seemed to take much notice of it.

Colin had told her to forget about what happened but for him, that was difficult to do. He was staring at his cell phone that sat on the desk, a couple of minutes had gone by since Katie's confession and she went back to work. Colin was curious, and a seed of doubt had been planted in his mind once he analysed the situation and story carefully. He wanted to believe her, but wasn't entirely sure- and what was why he called David.

"Hey Colin, what's up?"

"Do you still talk to that friend from Pierce Holdings?" Colin inquired.

"Um, yeah. Why?"

"Next time you see him, ask does he know a Katie Briggs."

**11**

— ● —

## CHAPTER 10

September 2009

"She definitely slept with that guy man, there's no doubt about it." David tried to keep up with Colin as he walked quickly through the busy streets.

"How can you be so sure?"

"My friend's an accountant, he works with some of the marketers there and he even knows the guy that she was telling you about. He's got a wife and kids at home."

"No." Colin said with great force, his feet bringing him to a halt. "No that's not true. It can't be true. I know Katie."

"I guess you don't know her that well." David shot back at him before the two continued on walking up the street again. Colin was being so quiet, his friend felt like he needed to say something. "Listen man, you probably just made a wrong judgement. It's cool, I'm sure she wouldn't be that stupid to do it again."

The thought of Katie being with someone did not sit well, and the thought of that someone being married made him feel sick. How could be continue the way they were after he found this out? He was still somewhat in denial.

"It's a good thing you didn't listen to me about tapping that. You dodged a bullet right there. I dodged a bullet too." Colin didn't mention it then, but David was being such a hypocrite. His friend had forgotten too easily about his relationship a couple months ago with Stacy and why it ended.

"David I'm not in the mood right now, can we just stop talking about it." His patience was growing thin.

"But you're the one who brought it up on the way here?"

"And now I wish I hadn't." Colin cursed himself for even calling David up and telling him about Katie. He was snooping in something that as a boss would be okay, but as a friend, was definitely not. "Let's just go get lunch." He grumbled.

It was a busy Saturday afternoon in the city, and the pair were meeting up with Vinny later, after their lunch. Colin had never bumped into Katie outside of the office, so he wasn't expecting to see her sitting at a table across from a guy in the very same restaurant he and David were in.

David didn't notice her at first, but once they sat down and Colin seemed off, he turned around to look at what his friend couldn't keep his eyes off. David laughed before looking at Colin.

"Speak of the devil." He said.

"Let's just stop talking about her, I don't want to think about it anymore for the time being." Colin replied, annoyance clear in his stiff frame and his tone.

But Colin couldn't keep his wandering eyes at bay. Throughout his meal and conversation with David, he would scan Katie's table and take in the little things. She had left her hair down, her dark, wild tendrils fell below her shoulders- a sight Colin had never seen before. She always kept her hair up at work. When she laughed, it was in a shy and quiet way, although seldom, Colin thought she looked as if she was enjoying her lunch.

"So Anna- what's happening with her?"

"Nothing."

"Nothing? Weren't you two breaking up last week?"

"We mended things. For now." Colin mumbled his last two words to himself rather than to the other man.

"And how long will that last huh?"

"You know, David, you really are trying to talk about everything I don't want to talk about today. Good work." He said dryly before taking a mouthful of his drink.

"What?" David questioned, as if innocent. "I just think you're wasting your time man. I mean, she isn't exactly your type. She's not into the same things are we are."

"We're doing okay for the time being."

"Has she come to terms with the fact that you aren't as innocent as you seemed to be."

"She definitely doesn't agree with my habits, but I can stop when I want and I don't want to just yet."

"Anna's a stick in the mud. She's so uptight all the time. You need a fun girl to be around."

"You sound like my Dad, except you're saying the exact opposite of what he thinks." Colin chuckled.

"I'm just being honest." David held his hands up in surrender.

"Why don't you focus on getting your own girlfriend before you look at my options huh?" Colin said, humour evident in his words.

"Whatever."

"Shit." Colin muttered under his breath as he took a quick sip of his drink.

"What?"

"She's coming this way, shit." Colin was clearly panicking then, he was looking everywhere except at her, and was freaking out over nothing. So much so, that David would have laughed- but Katie stopped at their table then and interrupted.

"Oh hey you two, what are the chances of meeting you here?" She said in surprise, a warm smile melting onto her lips that made Colin want to hide under the table.

"Hi Katie." David spoke first, as his friend was unable to do so for a minute or two.

"Hey." Colin said awkwardly.

"Lunch?" she looked at their two plates and asked- being her friendly self.

"Yeah, we're meeting up with some friends later. Just need something to soak up the alcohol filled night we have ahead of us so we don't get too drunk too easily." David spoke again.

"Well, eating is cheating and all that. But I suppose it's worth cheating for in a place like this. The food is amazing."

"You sure got that right." David laughed while Colin tried to find the words to speak. Katie eyed him with great curiosity but spoke nothing of how strange he was acting, choosing to frown instead.

"Anyway, I was just on my way to the restroom when I saw you two and said I had to stop and say hi. I'll see you." She walked past their table then, making a bee line for the toilets again.

"See you Monday." Colin finally plucked up the courage to speak, although it was only after she was out of earshot. David couldn't help but snort with knee-smacking laughter once Katie was gone.

"What the hell is wrong with you?" he asked Colin between laughter.

"Nothing, why?" his friend continued to eat as if everything was completely normal, and their awkward encounter with his assistant had never happened.

"You were acting like a shy school girl with her man. Grow some balls."

"I just don't know what to say her, after what you told me about what she did back at Pierce Holdings. I feel like I've done something wrong." He felt extremely guilty when he saw her just a moment ago. How was he supposed to work alongside her without telling her what he had done?

"Hey Colin, your Dad was here earlier. He wasn't too happy when he found out you were on a long lunch... again." Katie filled her boss in as soon as he had arrived back from his lunch with Anna.

"Oh god." He then began to let out a string of curses under his breath that Katie had so clearly heard- she stifled a giggle but failed terrible at holding in her laughter.

"He told me to give you these." Katie walked up to his desk and handed him a bunch of files before continuing to speak. "And he said once you read through these, he needs you to make a presentation for the meeting in two weeks."

"God damn it!" Things were getting worse by the minute for Colin.

"And your friend, um, Vinny called." Colin sat up straight then, looking at her with great concentration which was a rapid change from just a second ago when he had his face buried in his hands.

"What did he want?" he asked gruffly. "I told him not to call the office anymore." He then mumbled to himself.

"He told me to tell you specifically his exact words: 'Pick up your god damn phone'." Katie put on a funny deep voice that Colin would have laughed at if he weren't so stressed out then- and if he hadn't found it difficult to remember the things David had told him about when Katie used to work for Pierce Holdings.

"How was your lunch with Anna? Did things go okay?"

"Fine." He was looking down at his desk, flicking through some of the things his father had left for him. Too busy to notice how her face dropped and her posture slouched slightly then.

"Oh, okay. I better get back to work." She said, obviously deflated.

Colin had been so short and snappy with her lately. And even when she saw him out with David last Saturday, she knew something was off with him but didn't want to think of why. Because she knew already it his apparent change in mood came after she told him about her old job. Katie didn't say anything, she knew Colin had a right to be angry with her but she just didn't think it would last this long.

"Yes, you definitely need to." He mumbled, past remarkably. His clipped tone made her stop in her tracks on the way to the door and turn around.

"Colin?" once he looked up at the calling of his name, he noticed the hurt evident in her deep brown eyes. "I know I made a mistake, but I was afraid. And I'm sorry-"

"You failed to tell me something so huge that happened to you in a past job. It wasn't just a small mistake Katie, it was something that had been going on for months." His tone was stone cold, she had never seen him this distant. But Katie's mind went from focusing solely on how Colin felt to what he said.

"Months?" she scrunched her brows. "I never told you anything about how long the rumours went on for Colin."

"Well I'm sure it went on for quite some time for your boss to fire you over it." He tried to fix his slip up.

"I also never told you I was fired by my boss. I said I had no other choice but to leave my position- that could mean anything-"

"So you weren't fired by your previous boss at Pierce Holdings?" he gave her a seething look then.

"Yes I was but that's not the point I'm trying to make-"

"It's the point I'm trying to make." Colin cut across her again, he didn't know why he was getting so angry about all of this, but he couldn't help it.

"Who did you talk to there?" Katie sighed quietly, closing her eyes for a moment as she did so. She remained calm and had yet to raise her voice- causing more frustration on Colin's part.

"What?"

"You must have talked to someone. I'm almost sure by the way you've been acting lately, it can't just be because I lied in my interview."

"I'm your boss Katie, I have every right to look into your past jobs." Colin replied, justifying his snooping although it never felt right to do so, not at the time and not right then either.

"I know." She agreed and nodded. "I just wanted to know, to see how biased their story would be-"

"You slept with a married man, I'm not sure there's much of a story to twist in order to make you look worse than you already do." He was frank and straight with her, spitting out his words like venom that could only tip Katie over the edge. The office fell completely silent as she evaluated the situation, but the silence was only for a moment.

"Do you honestly think that?" Colin took a minute to think about the question.

"Of course I do, why else were you fired from the job?"

"I told you they were rumours Colin-"

"Rumours can be true or false. You weren't very specific."

"I didn't sleep with anyone." Katie said, almost through gritted teeth.

"Are you sure?" he insulted her further, making her wonder where this side of Colin had come from.

"You know what? You're like the rest of the people I've come across in work. I thought I was done trying to convince people of the truth but I guess not. I guess I can't just be a hard worker and earn a promotion solely because of that. I need to jump into bed with married men in order to get as far ahead as I can." Colin had never looked at that angle of the story until just then when she brought it up- but it was starting to make some sense in his mind then. She spoke with great sarcasm then, "Because I'm a woman, and women need to use their bodies to achieve anything in the corporate world. They need to use their looks to get them what they want because god forbid they actually have brains and are hard workers like the men in this world!"

"You're really bringing gender into this?" Colin, although he doubted himself greatly, continued with his argument as if her point was not making his opinion sway.

"Why was I fired and not the man who I supposedly had this affair with too? He was higher up in the company yet they kept him on their payroll? He gets rewarded and I get punished, for a rumour he started because he couldn't face the fact that I was not interested in him in that sort of way."

"Katie..." he could see how her anger was beginning to boil over, like water in a sizzling pot.

"Oh all the people in the office loved having some interesting new gossip for their lunch time talks and coffee breaks. They believed it because it was the easiest thing to do for their egos. They didn't get the promotion because I slept with one of our bosses, and not because I worked harder than them to get it. I worked my fucking ass off for months only for the promotion to be a hindrance rather than something positive." Katie was ranting on, but she did not care. She wanted him to understand without having to explain herself, but she guessed he couldn't.

"And who'd believe me when I told the truth? No one. Not even you."

Her voice broke with her last sentence, raw emotion was cracking through in her voice that made him feel nothing but heavy, thick guilt. He looked down at his desk then, unable to keep up eye contact with her.

Katie was almost breathless after she said everything she needed to say. She turned to leave again and this time, Colin did not mumble any smart remarks under his breath. She was disappointed with him, but not as disappointed as he was in himself at that moment.

She didn't stay late after work that day, she left as soon as she possibly could. Katie couldn't concentrate after her outburst in Colin's office and she feared she would have to face him again before the work day was over- fortunately he did not leave his office either. Once he decided to go and apologise, he poked his head into her office only to find she had already left.

Colin sighed and thought to himself about the situation he was in. He should have never listened to David, but he had taken some stranger's word instead of Katie's and knew there was more than an apology needed after the way he'd spoke to her earlier on in the day.

He mulled over the situation, not being able to rid his mind of the thoughts of an upset Katie, while she rushed home to find some comfort on the sofa in front of the TV. She hoped Emily was there when she returned to their apartment but wasn't sure if she was on a shift today.

"Hey Em." Katie was delighted to see her friend's face as soon as she entered the living room of their apartment.

"Hi, how was work?"

"Remember I said I told Colin about my old job?"

"Mhm." Emily lowered down the TV then and sat up with her legs crossed on the couch, understanding that this was going to be an interesting conversation. It took Katie a moment to talk then as the two of them sat there on the sofa. Emily noticed how Katie's happy expression from just a moment ago was fake, as it began to melt from her face and her eyes began to water.

"He talked to someone at Pierce Holdings. He's been real ratty with me the past couple of days and now I know why. We had an argument about it and I flipped out- which I really regret because he's my boss and he has every right to check up on my work history- but at the same time I just think he should've at least asked me about it first before jumping to conclusions, right?"

"What did he do when you flipped out?" Emily inquired curiously.

"I didn't really give him a chance to say much." She sighed then and sunk into the sofa a little more along with her mood. "He didn't believe me Em." Katie shook her head then in defeat, her friend could clearly see how bad this made her feel so reached out to hug her- an attempt to stop Katie from feeling any worse than she did in that moment.

"It's going to be okay Katie. You know the truth and that's all that matters. If Colin doesn't believe that those rumours people believed were just rumours, you don't have to prove anything to him."

"I just wish he didn't believe whatever he heard so easily. I thought I was done with all of this, I didn't think I'd have to focus on what happened at Pierce Holdings again but I guess I was wrong."

"This will all blow over in a few days Katie, trust me." But Emily's words were not reassuring in the slightest. Katie began to panic a little and it was seeping from within her.

"I really shouldn't have gotten so angry at him. It's just- sometimes I forget he's my boss and the more we work together the more I forget."

"Stop wanting to change it Katie. You had every reason to be mad. You aren't the type of person to get mad over silly things. Trust that you made the right decision- you were trying to prove you were innocent and you are. Maybe Colin won't believe that right now but I'm sure if you talk to him tomorrow and try to explain- if you feel like you need to explain yourself- that he'll listen. He seemed like a nice guy from the things you've told me about him."

Emily had to get ready for work after a little while, leaving Katie to watch The Jerry Springer Show alone. She said her goodbyes to her friend before Emily left for work. The apartment fell into this thick silence except for the TV that was playing in the background. Katie had lowered it down for a minute, feeling a headache coming on.

She took a deep breath and rested her head back on the sofa again, but still, nothing could calm her racing mind. This time, her thoughts were not on Colin, but on everything that happened in the past. The evil stares from people at work, the feeling of walking into a room when you know people have just been talking about you in, knowing that no matter how much you try to tell the truth, no one believes you.

Katie decided to busy herself with something a little different to The Jerry Springer Show, and began to make herself some dinner. But as soon as she began chopping some onions and other vegetables, she heard a knock on her door.

**12**

**CHAPTER 11**

September 2009

Katie hesitated for a moment before dropping her knife and heading for the door. She didn't know what to say, or how to react once she saw a deflated looking Colin staring back at her.

"What do you want Colin?" Katie asked in exasperation, looking anywhere but directly at him.

"Can I come in?" His voice was apologetic and almost sweet. He had been fighting with himself the past couple of hours over what had happened in his office earlier on and the guilt was eating him up by the time he returned home. He knew he should not have turned up at Katie's apartment but he couldn't wait any longer to apologise to her. "Please." He urged gently once he saw a look of hesitation fall upon her face.

"Fine." Katie had to stop herself from rolling her eyes as she allowed Colin access to her living room, closing the door after he entered and stood awkwardly a few steps away from the door- feeling like he was intruding.

He followed her then into the kitchen where she continued with her cooking. Not much was said between the pair for another couple of minutes, Colin only stood there and watched what she was doing.

"How did you know where I lived?" Katie asked.

"I finally read your resume." She could have snorted, if she was not in such a terrible mood.

"Oh." She spoke although she did not look up from what she was doing, an attempt of shielding any interest she had in that conversation.

"I'm sorry Kate."

"Great." She raised her eyebrows with sarcasm. "Is that it? Because you can leave if it is." Colin didn't know what to say next, there were too many things floating around in his mind and he could not choose which to say first.

"Please, I over-reacted-"

"You think I'm a homewrecker?" she put down the knife then and looked him straight in the eye. A stare that made Colin almost squirm.

"No. Of course I don't."

"But you did, you told me I slept with a married man."

"I shouldn't have listened to the rumours, I thought they were true."

"But why? Why did you think they were true? What have I done to ever make you think I would do something like that?" The hurt was coming through in her voice. It filled Colin with even more guilt and regret than he already felt.

"I-I don't know." He shook his head.

"I just wish you had have asked me Colin. Before you drew your own conclusions."

"I don't know what to say. I just hope you can forgive me for jumping to conclusions. I should have trusted what you said in the beginning."

Although Katie felt he was genuinely sorry, a part of her still wanted to be angry with him. But how could she? He was her boss and their relationship meant they couldn't take things so personal if a situation in work arose like this one.

"Do you want some?" Katie asked uncertainly as she began cooking again.

"I'm sure you don't want to cook for me after what I did today."

"No, I don't." she stated bluntly. "But I'm cooking for myself already."

Colin hadn't left yet, so she assumed he was staying for some dinner although the mood had not gone back to normal by then. He knew he wasn't going to be welcomed by her with open arms immediately after his apology, but the food was the first step back into her good books for him.

They sat on the sofa and ate dinner, their conversation growing more and more as the time grew later. But Katie was holding back, he could sense it. There was always something more she wanted to say but couldn't because of a previous thought that stuck in the back of her head, one that she needed to say aloud sometime.

"Colin, we can't be friends anymore." She finally allowed the words to come out.

"Why not?" a look of concern crossed his face but Katie knew he would get over it. She took his plate and stacked it on top of hers before placing it on the coffee table.

"Because you're my boss and I'm your assistant. That relationship should come first but it hasn't been and it's becoming a problem."

"Don't be ridiculous-"

"If we weren't friends I wouldn't have been so angry at you for snooping. In fact, I wouldn't even have to think of it as snooping because that's your job as my boss."

"It's not like us two being friends is getting in the way that much Katie." Colin seemed to be in denial.

"So why are you here then?"

"Huh?" he asked, confused.

"If we weren't friends, you would never have felt guilty enough to turn up at my apartment on a Tuesday night- something that would be inappropriate if you were just my boss."

What she was saying was entirely correct, and probably how it should be but sometimes things weren't exactly how they should be and that was fine. But Colin knew better than to object her reasonable statement. It made perfect sense and would be easier if they were not friends anymore, although Colin was left in a state of bewilderment at himself that night.

After saying his goodbyes and thanking her for dinner, he left her small apartment and made his way home- feeling hurt by Katie, a strange feeling. One that should not have felt as bad as it did but he could not help it.

October 2009

"Good morning Sir." Katie nodded at Colin who was early for once.

"Morning Ms. Briggs." He gave her a bright smile and replied but said nothing more although he wanted to. Colin closed his office door behind him and got to work but it didn't take long before she was in his office- giving him orders passed down from his father.

Katie said what she was told to say and nothing more. It had been a couple of weeks since Colin turned up at her apartment and the pair had been working alongside each other instead of with each other ever since. Although she was glad she had said what she did that night, it felt strange to not have an actual conversation with him that didn't involve work matters. Katie tried to tell herself that was what was best but her reassurance meant very little as she sat in her office she used to share with Carrie and sorted out the stacks of paperwork that she had been working on since yesterday.

It wasn't until later in the day, when Katie walked to the photo-copier that she had any other contact with Colin. He stood waiting for his printouts and tried desperately to avoid looking at her for a long period of time, all the while praying that the copier didn't jam again. He really needed to get a new one soon.

"Hey." She said, her voice sweet as always, he thought.

"Hi." He nodded at her and smiled a little, but soon enough he could not ignore the awkward silence that fell once he had finished speaking. It felt so weird to not talk to each other, and it made Katie feel full of regret- she was the one who had caused it.

"Doing anything for Thanksgiving?"

Colin had decided Thanksgiving was an appropriate conversation to talk about with a colleague at work, or was it? He felt unsure then and wanted to take back his question. As October drew to a close, he realised it had already been over a month since their discussion about being only co-workers but still Colin felt very... uncomfortable about it. He couldn't put his finger on it. He always felt unsure about whether he was crossing that line again between boss and friend.

Colin wanted to know so much more about Katie, his mind wan-dered into the countless possibilities of who she was or what she had done but he couldn't ask, not anymore. The only thing that was holding him back from getting to know her more, being around her more, was Katie herself. If she did not want to have any sort of friendship with him outside of work, he didn't want to push things that were only one sided. He could not make her want to be his friend- but there was so much more that he needed to know, and might never know about Katie.

"Oh, I don't really do much for Thanksgiving. I'll probably just have dinner with some friends."

"What about your family?" as soon as he looked up from the copier, he noticed the look on Katie's face but could not entirely detect what it was. She looked as if she was uneasy by the question so Colin decided to pretend he had never asked. "My mom always has this huge dinner on Thanksgiving that I'm forced to go to." He laughed a little and rolled his eyes, trying to break the ice again.

"It can't be that bad." Katie chuckled, her features warming again at his words.

"Trust me it is-"

"Hey Colin, fancy bumping into you here?" David joked, cutting into the pair's conversation before it took off in any other direction. The sight of David made Katie's face drop quicker than her smile had appeared on her lips. "Hiya sweetheart." Colin's friend then turned to his assistant who was trying desperately not to glare at him.

"Don't call me sweetheart." She said monotonously.

"What would you prefer I called you then?" David replied flirtatiously despite Katie's boredom.

"I would prefer you didn't call me anything actually." She scoffed before handing Colin a sheet of paper. "Would you be able to make five copies of this for me please?" she ignored David from then on and once Colin nodded she returned to her office.

"Dude?" David's eyebrows knitted together as he looked at Colin.

"What?" his friend acted oblivious.

"You told her, didn't you?" there was a short pause before Colin decided he wouldn't lie.

"Yes, I did. Why does it matter to you?"

"So uncool man."

"Why do you care? You were disgusted by when you thought she did what your friend told you."

"So were you." He narrowed his eyes at Colin then.

"Whatever. It's not like anything would have happened between you two anyways, she hates you now so I'd stay away from her whenever you come in here." David had a look of annoyance on his face but the other man ignored it.

"Was there a point in your visit or did you just come to flirt with my assistant?" Colin asked.

"There was actually a reason I came here. It's about Vinny-"

"David? Not out here, let's go into my office." He spoke in a hushed tone as he looked around, examining the office to see if anyone had noticed their conversation. "C'mon." he said as he brought David into his office.

They spent only a couple of minutes in the office before David said his goodbyes and Colin went back to the copier to do what Katie had asked of him but was surprised to see her back there again.

"Katie, let me do that."

"Oh no, it's fine. I saw that you left the pages on top of the copier and guessed you didn't make copies yet. Don't worry about it." She smiled politely at him but he wanted there to be more behind her smile.

"I got side tracked, I'm sorry."

"You'd never make it being an assistant, I can tell you that for sure." A playfulness could be detected in Katie's voice that uplifted him instantly.

"I'm afraid we can't all be as perfect as you Ms. Briggs." he teased her then before the two chuckled.

"It's okay. It gets a little frustrating sometimes but I'm trying to come to terms with it." Katie replied sarcastically before rolling her eyes and taking her pages she had just printed out.

Colin wished he could see her smile for another minute or so after she turned away and walked back into her office. Regret filled him up inside, that he did not say just one more thing to keep her in his presence for a moment longer. She was a distraction, but the good kind, although she would never know.

Katie made Colin feel strange, he thought their professional relationship was becoming more excruciating by the minute. But what could he do? He realised more so than ever that really enjoyed her company, but only after the night he turned up at her apartment.

Colin wondered to himself as she walked away what it was that he felt for her? What it was about her that he could not shake? Maybe it was better if he never got an answer to those questions, but she left him in such a state of sweet bewilderment that she was totally oblivious to.

**13**

**CHAPTER 12**

N ovember 2009

"Where the hell is he?" Katie was trying her best to look in any other direction than at Mr. Anderson right then as he muttered under his breath. She pretended she could not hear the older man's quiet mumbles of exasperation that had started as soon as he came into the board room and realised his son had not turned up yet.

Katie could clearly see the anger building behind Mr. Anderson's melting composure, it made her feel nervous- not for herself, but for Colin because she knew what was coming next.

"I apologise Mr. Jefferson, but I need a minute to call my son and find his whereabouts." Jeffrey Anderson forced a friendly smile onto his face although he felt like he was way past boiling point at that time.

"Oh, take your time Jeffrey. I'm sure he's stuck in traffic... Again." Henry Jefferson said the last part more so to himself than anyone else in the room.

Just as Jeffrey stood up from his place at the table surrounded by his and Henry's associates, Colin burst through the door- untidy hair and a heavily breathing mess. He was under the scorching stare of his father, who he would have to deal with as soon as this meeting was over but Colin did not want to think about that right then.

The younger man kept his head down low as he apologised for his tardiness and sat down. Katie noticed how tired and drained Colin appeared to be. She wondered what had happened to make him that late, and cursed herself for even feeling sorry for him. This was what he done- constantly- she needed to try and whip him into shape like Carrie did when she was around all the time.

"Where's your copy of the report Colin?" Jeffrey nudged his son who was then sitting beside him. He knew straight away that Colin did not have a clue what he was talking about and it only irritated him further. He gave his son so many chances to step up and be an adult, but it seemed like it was doing him no good at all. Colin would never be grateful enough for the things his father had handed him so easily in life.

"The report? Um, I-"

"I have it right here Sir." Katie butt in before Colin could finish his sentence. "My apologies, but I was supposed to give it to Colin yesterday before I left work." She lied, smiling at the two men apologetically before she handed Colin the report he was supposed to have looked over so many times before this morning.

Katie held in a giggle once she examined Colin's quirked up eyebrow as he looked through the report, clearly never seeing the contents of the pages before in his life. She knew this meeting was not a joke and Colin's terrible effort at being in anyway dedicated to his job was no laughing matter- at least not in front of all these men and women who clearly cared about their job and took it very seriously.

The meeting was excruciating, Katie kept getting distracted by the clear tension between father and son while taking the minutes of the meeting. She couldn't help but feel sorry for Colin as the meeting drew to a close, because she knew what was coming next and it wasn't going to be pretty.

Katie went straight to her office as soon as everyone left, she did not want to be in the way of the two men once Jeffrey started his lecture with Colin. She only ever half heard the stern speeches Mr. Anderson would give Colin and although they seemed to be every time he turned up at the office, they were usually in private so that no one could hear. Katie wondered how Colin did not just change, even she was tired of hearing Jeffrey's complaints by then and that surely meant Colin was too. But it seemed like he would never learn.

Shannon called in to tell Katie she was going on a coffee run and she decided to tag along and help carry the order back to the office. Shannon was thankful for Katie's presence and decided to be her nosey self and ask what had happened at that morning's meeting that had Mr. Anderson in such a fuss.

"The usual." Katie rolled her eyes, not because of Mr. Anderson, but because Colin was never on time anymore. He was so careless when it came to his job and his excuses were not enough. Mr. Anderson's patience was growing thing.

"I've never seen Jeffrey that angry before. He walked past me back in at the office and it sure looked like Colin was in for an earful." Shannon added

"Tell me about it. My office is right beside Colin's and you can hear everything so clearly from my desk. I can't listen to another lecture, it seems like it's useless anyway. Colin never understands."

Once the two women got back, Katie took her coffee and lingered at Colin's office door for a moment before knocking and entering when he called for her to come in. She noticed how tired and run down he looked although she would never tell him that. He had yet to look up from his phone since she entered. Once she realised he was not doing much work at all except texting and scrolling through his phone, she sighed heavily and sat down in front of him comfortably.

"Colin."

"Hmm?" he mumbled although his attention was still on his cell phone.

"Are you serious right now?" Katie asked in confusion as a little annoyance fell over her.

"What?" It was only then that he looked at her and took in her appearance. "You're wearing your hair down today." He said his observation aloud that caused her serious look to falter a little.

"You're sitting in here doing nothing at all related to your job, and the only thing you can make note of is that my hair is different? You need to work, you need to do your job."

"Chill Kate." He laughed, finding her orders quite humorous but it only made her narrow her eyes at him in disbelief.

"I know you must love hearing your Dad's many complaints and speeches but I'm getting tired of hearing them so please, just do some work for once please."

"And if I do start working, what am I going to get in return?" he looked at her again with a wolfish grin on his face and flirtatious eyes that captured hers. She then heard the message tone on her phone and took it out of her pocket to see who it was.

"I thought I had this on silent." She muttered.

"Who is it?" Colin was curious.

"Just someone." Katie stared down at the message from Sam, one of her friends she grew up with. She would answer her later, she thought.

"Hot date?" He asked playfully.

"Shut up." She rolled her eyes at him.

They were terrible at acting professional she thought to herself, although did not dwell on it. Both she and Colin had slipped so easily back into the friendship that she declared they were not supposed to have weeks ago. Katie couldn't complain though, she preferred it this way but that was only because there had not been another problem like the one previous when Colin discovered the rumours that were going around her old job.

"I hope he's at least half as hot as me, but I know it's probably impossible or whatever." This was the thing that made her laugh aloud then. The room fell into a comfortable silence once she quietened down and she began to look at him again, eyeing him with concern this time.

"Why were you late earlier?" her lips set into a small grim smile as her eyes moved from his eyes to his desk.

"I overslept." He hesitated before adding "I was out late last night." Colin watched her movements carefully from the corner of his eye after his admission.

"Can't you just keep your partying for weekends?"

"Are you my mom now?" She heard him snort, which made her look up and roll her eyes again.

"Whatever. Anyways... The only reason I'm here is because I went on the coffee run and brought you back an espresso, here."

"I was wondering when you were going to stop bickering and give me my coffee."

"Excuse me?" She asked with her eyebrow raised. "I've had enough of your sass today. This mine now, go get your own coffee."

Colin watched as she took a sip out of the cup and smirked at him before standing up from the desk. She waved him goodbye and headed for the door, knowing that her stern talk with Colin was never going to happen anyway.  Although she felt defeated, she was entertained by him for at least five minutes that day. She thought maybe next time she'd get through to him about needing to take his job serious, or not maybe no.

"You owe me a coffee!" he exclaimed.

"I think you're the one who owes me one by now Colin." She did not turn back when she spoke, leaving Colin to watch carefully as her dark tendrils bounced up and down below her shoulders.

"This is amazing Katie, honestly." Sam, Katie's friend smiled between mouthfuls of her food.

"Oh c'mon Sam, I'm a terrible cook you don't have to lie to me." Katie rolled her eyes at the other woman, making the others who were sitting at the table laugh a little.

"I'm honestly shocked, but I have to say- it's better than last year." Anna said playfully, looking over to Leah then grinning.

"Hey, it wasn't that bad." Leah protested although she knew it was not the truth.

Anna was referring back to last year's Thanksgiving meal and how much of a train wreck it had become. Leah was usually a good cook, but the pressure had gotten to her by Thanksgiving day. Katie remembered the smell of burnt food when she walked through

Leah's front door and how Cassie, Leah's daughter looked in awe at the black smoke rising from the oven.

"We had to use a fire extinguisher Leah." Sam snorted.

"Yeah, okay. So maybe dinner in mine didn't work out as good as this but c'mon, usually my dinners are amazing."

"True." The three other women nodded in agreement.

The conversation had stirred towards Cassie and how she was doing. Leah told them she was staying with her Dad for the holidays this year and how much she missed her already, although it had only been a day since she had last seen her. Leah loved Cassie in a way the other women said they understood but really couldn't, not until they had children of their own. She was what made Leah get up in the mornings, and after coming from a broken home and troubled past, Leah would do everything and anything in her power to make sure Cassie never ended up in a girl's home like she had when she was younger.

Leah always had the funniest stories about Cassie to tell whenever they all met up and they gladly listened over the rest of their dinner. Everyone helped to clear the table and after pouring out another four generously measured glasses on wine, Katie began washing up despite the other's trying to convince her to relax while they did it instead.

"I remember how much you used to hate doing the dishes back at Clearview Anna, you can't fool me." Anna laughed then at the memory although she and the other two still felt guilty for not helping out. They knew how particular Katie could be though, so instead kept her company in the kitchen.

"Where's Emily?" Sam asked, forgetting all about Katie's chirpy housemate who usually made an appearance when they visited their old friend.

"She's at her grandparents' house for the weekend. It took her a lot to get the entire long weekend off so I'm sure she's living it up while she can."

"Poor Emily, she always seems to be busy with work."

"I know, her schedule can be all over the place sometimes. I'm glad I work a typical nine to five kind of job because I don't think I'd last if it was any other way."

"That reminds me, how is work? What happened after that horrible woman Katherine treated you the way she did?" One of the women asked.

"Nothing really. I'm just glad I don't have to work with her again, I don't want to cause any unnecessary trouble, I have a job and I'm happy with it so it's best to just leave that trouble behind me. Work's been good though." Katie smiled as she spoke her last sentence, her mind turning to thoughts of Colin although she wished it hadn't.

She wondered how he was then, what he was doing, if he ended up going to his parent's house or if he was out partying instead. Katie was in such deep thought, that she did not even hear her phone ringing from the other side of the small kitchen.

"You want me to get that?" Leah asked as she walked towards her phone that was sitting on the counter.

"Yeah, can you just see who it is for me please? I'll give them a call back later."

"Colin? Who's Colin Katie?" Leah smirked at her friend as she saw how her face turned to an expression of panic although she tried to hind it.

"Don't answer that! Let me get it." Katie said frantically as she took her hands from the soapy water and quickly took the phone from Leah's hand. "Just give me a minute, sorry." She apologised to her friends before walking further into the living room for some privacy.

"You might want to dry your hands first!" Anna called before the three women laughed in the kitchen.

Katie was not listening though; her mind was in a different place as she stared down at the caller ID on her phone. What would Colin want at this time? She wondered. It was beginning to get late in the evening and she was sure he would be busy. Despite thinking he had called the wrong person, she persisted by answering the phone hesitantly.

"Um... Hello?"

"Katie, thank god you answered. I was afraid you might be too busy."

"You meant to call me?" she sounded surprised, which made Colin regret calling her in the first place. She was probably preoccupied with her friends, it was Thanksgiving after all. "Colin?" Her voice broke into his wandering thoughts and made him speak again after the short silence.

"Yes, sorry. I'm still here. I did mean to call you I'm sorry if I'm disturbing something."

"No it's fine." She was a bit concerned then by tone of his voice, he sounded troubled. "Is something wrong?" Katie asked quietly, turning so she had her back to her friends although they were too far away to hear and were in the middle of a full-blown conversation of their own.

"No- well yes. Everything's wrong. This day just keeps getting worse." He groaned.

"What happened?" She sounded genuinely concerned, it made Colin glad he called her instead of someone else.

"I was hoping I could tell you in person rather than over the phone. But I get it if you're busy tonight, I just didn't know who else to call..."

Katie felt sorry for him then and curious to know what it was that was making him act like that. She knew she was more concerned than she probably should be about her boss, which made her hesitate before answering him after a minute or two.

"Well my friends are still here and I'd like to spend some more time with them because I don't get to see them much-"

"Okay, I understand. Sorry for bothering you."

"You didn't let me finish." Katie's laughter was like music to his ears, he could almost feel her chuckles untying the many knots that had built up in his stomach.

"There's more?"

"Yes, there's more. We had dinner kind of late and they're already on their third glass of wine so I'm guessing they'll be too tired to stay the whole night. You could come over later on if you wanted."

"Really?"

"Sure."

And just like that, Katie had asked her boss over to her apartment. The sentence sounded weird when she said it on her head, and after she organised a time and hung up the phone, the weird feeling she had did not fade away. She was trying to justify her growing friendship with her boss in her mind, thinking of reasons she could use although she knew she was clearly overstepping. And if it were anyone else but Colin, it would feel wrong, but it was not anyone else and Colin had become a significant part in life over the past couple of months.

"Booty call?" Sam teased, taking another sip of her wine as Katie returned to the kitchen.

"Of course not Sam, it's way too early for booty calls." Katie joked, to which the women replied with more laughter.

She masked her concern with a joyful smile, not wanting to delve any further into the mystery that was her relationship with Colin. Because she was afraid of what she might realise through the many questions that popped in and out of her head.

Instead, Katie focused on the three women that stood in the kitchen in front of her, the three women that helped her get through her childhood and the girl's home they used to live in. They had many more crazy stories to reminisce about before Colin's arrival. She would try to forget about the feelings that were arising from all the close contact with Colin although that would be a difficult thing to do.

It took a lot of convincing to finally get Anna to call an Uber. She was protesting like a child, despite falling asleep on the sofa several times- the wine had most definitely done its job. The two other women were tired too and felt it was time to go back to their hotel room to rest for the night, it was getting late.

In the middle of all the commotion, there was a knock on the door that made everyone in the room stop. Katie looked at the clock hanging on the living room wall and made a wild guess of who it could be on the other side of the door.

"You try to get her coat on and I'll get that." Katie giggled, the wine had kicked in for her too although she did not drink as much as her friend. She wished the sight of Colin standing in the doorway would sober her up, but it only worked a little.

"Hey." He smiled warmly at her, making her stomach flutter.

"You're early." She stood out of the way so that he could enter the hallway.

"Yeah, sorry about that."

"Well my friends are still here, so you're going to have to introduce yourself."

"Great." He grinned again at her as she led him through to the living room. He was not expecting to see two grown women trying to force a coat and a pair of shoes on another as soon as he entered the room but guessed this was his own fault for turning up earlier than he was expected.

"Woah." He said under his breath in surprise.

"They aren't usually like this, I promise." Katie had heard him and replied. "Everyone this is my friend Colin." She spoke loudly and tried her best not to hesitate on the word 'friend' as she spoke.

"So it was a booty call after all..." Sam muttered under her breath to which Katie nudged her, praying that Colin had not heard.

"Hi, I'm Sam."

"I'm Leah."

"And who is this?" Colin held in laughter at the sight of the other woman sitting on the sofa.

"Whoever you want me to be." Anna tried to sound flirtatious but her words were slightly slurred and her eyes were unable to stay more than halfway open.

"Oh god." Katie covered her face with her hands for a moment, cringing at her friend's choice of words.

"You two look like you need help." He ignored what Anna had said and walked towards the sofa she was sitting on.

"We've been trying to get her ready to go for the past five minutes. I just want to go home already." Leah groaned.

"Let me try." Although none of the women thought he would be of great use to them in their situation, they were surprised at how quickly Anna got ready to go for him.

"What's your name?" he asked her again as he tied one of her laces.

"Anna." She giggled.

"Anna...I used to have a girlfriend called Anna. She wasn't half as pretty as you though." Colin said, being the charmer he always was, despite knowing this girl would probably not even remember this conversation in the morning and the fact that he might never see her again. Katie froze once she hard Colin speak but tried to pretend she had not heard him. Used to... Maybe that was what Colin had been talking about earlier on the phone.

It took another five minutes of trying to keep Anna awake before their Uber turned up. Katie said her goodbyes before her friends left. She noted the wink Sam gave her when Colin was not looking and the nudge from Leah who whispered "He's hot. Goodluck." Before she left. Katie rolled her eyes at her friends' reactions to Colin, if only they knew he was in fact her boss and had only called her to vent about his recent breakup. She did need the good luck Leah had wished her but not in the way her friend was expecting.

"So you broke up with Anna?" Katie sighed, there had been a moment of silence since she closed her front door and stood looking at him in the living room.

"No. She broke up with me."

"What happened?" She was not expecting things to be put to an end by Anna, and initially assumed it was the other way around.

"She came over to my place earlier this morning to get ready to go to my parents and we got into an argument."

"About what- Sit down if you want." Katie added as she herself sat on the sofa near him. He followed her command and began to answer her question, although he would never be able to tell her the full truth about his break up with Anna, or about the true reason behind all their fights and arguments since the relationship began.

"Just pointless crap."

"Colin..." she shook her head, wondering if she should be honest with him or not.

"What?" he asked, just in time as she had made up her mind.

"That's the problem. You think it's 'pointless crap' but it must mean something to her. I guess you didn't follow my advice a couple of weeks ago about compromising."

"I tried- for a while." Colin tried to justify his actions in the relationship he cared very little about, especially towards the end, but he knew he was lying to himself and Katie. He didn't try, he hadn't tried very much at all and that was the reason he and Anna hadn't worked out. Katie could see he was debating with himself then and attempted to see things from his perspective also.

"I get it Colin. You're young, you like to drink and party and have a good time. And Anna- well from what you told me she doesn't like to do those things as much as you. I know you don't want to be held back because of some girl, and if you feel that way about her then maybe it is best that you two go your separate ways."

"But I look like even more of a fuck up to everyone now, I can't even make one relationship work out."

"Sometimes people want different things, you can't change and neither can she." Katie's words of wisdom were soothing for him to hear at that moment in time. They were different to the ones he had been hearing all day from his family, who did not approve of his break up.

"My Dad's been lecturing me all day about it."

"I'm sure he just wanted things to work out for you two."

"No- they all loved Anna, thought she was good for me. Only because they want me to settle down a bit but I'm enjoying life at the minute, because one day I'll be just as boring and bland as them. I don't want to just be with someone because it makes them happy, I want to be with someone because they make me happy."

"Well you seem to have worked it all out then by now." Katie smiled sweetly at him then.

But she could tell he was holding back then, like there was more he wanted to say. After all, he would not have turned up here just to discuss something with Katie he had already figured out the answer to. He wanted to say more and it was only then he realised it was usually that way with Katie. There was always something more he wanted to say, to ask, to do, yet he refrained from doing so.

# 14

CHAPTER 13

November 2009

"He's your boss?!" Sam exclaimed despite being in a busy coffee shop surrounded by many people.

"Keep it down for god's sake. We're having a conversation with each other, not the entire coffee shop." Katie looked around, feeling quite paranoid.

"I can't believe I tried to drunkenly flirt with your boss last night." Anna groaned as she rubbed her head and took another sip of her coffee then.

"What the hell was he doing at your apartment last night if you work for him Katie?" Leah came across as more concerned than judgemental. She was especially protective over her friend and after what happened at her last job, she certainly didn't want people to get the wrong idea if they found out.

"He called me and asked could he come over, he needed to talk to someone and I suppose I was the only one that wasn't busy on Thanksgiving."

"Your boss comes to you looking for relationship advice? That's strange." Katie couldn't help but feel like her friends were beginning to gang up on her and she didn't like it although their reasons were justified- they didn't want something happening to her like in her last job.

"I know, I know. But it's hard to explain, we get along great and-"

"Katie, before you say anything else I want you to think about it carefully. We do have our reasons for questioning you like this."

"It's not a regular occurrence Leah." Katie began to get offended then.

Sure, she had just been friends with the last guy at Pierce Holdings but it was different to how she was with Colin. Neither Colin nor Katie had any sort of attraction towards each other, it was purely a friendship, but with the other guy at her last job, Katie learned quickly that he was beginning to get feelings that were purely one-sided. She tried to get away from the situation quickly because it escalated but she learned he was a very spiteful and angry man when he did not get what he wanted.

"I just don't want anything to happen to you again. That's all." Leah justified her probing.

"He was hot though." Anna said, making the situation worse.

"I get it Leah. It's fine." Katie said, feeling defeated.

But what happened at Pierce Holdings was not entirely her fault and it shouldn't stop her from talking to Colin- well maybe it should but it hadn't, that had already tried the professionalism in the office but things had slipped back to the way they were at the start. She felt she had enough to be thinking about without her friends' questions getting in the way too. She was confused about all of the certain ways she was beginning to feel about Colin and was trying to ignore them, all the while remembering his visit the night before.

She took a mouthful of coffee before her mind wandered back to Colin's admission that things weren't as good as they seemed with Anna or with his life in general. He said he felt like no one understood, and his father was beginning to grate on him more than usual about finally settling down. But the problem was, from what Katie could grasp, was that Colin didn't want to settle down, he wanted to 'enjoy himself' as he put it, for as long as possible.

Although Katie agreed with him in some ways- he was still young and had plenty of time to settle down and find someone like his mother and father wanted- but at the same time the excessive partying was beginning to be too much. It was effected his work for so than usual over the past couple of weeks and Jeffrey's patience seemed to be growing even thinner with every visit.

Colin seemed to be quite rebellious, maybe a bit too rebellious for a twenty-something year old man who had been given a job and all the financial support he could ever want from his family. But that was none of Katie's business, she guessed.

Katie listened for what felt like hours, she remembered every disappointing word he had to say, every deflated look he would give her after he took a breath from speaking. Every day when she went into work and he turned up at whatever time he felt like it, Katie would spend a few minutes of her time talking to him, chatting, catching up and joking around but when he showed up last night, that was the first time she had a proper meaningful conversation like that with him. He was so vulnerable and it scared Katie then, because of how concerned she was for him over nothing but little things that he would eventually get over.

"We should definitely go out tonight. It's our last night in Chicago and our flight isn't until the afternoon tomorrow so we have plenty of time to recover." Sam's voice broke into Katie's thoughts then and she only nodded despite not having a clue what she was getting herself in for that night.

Colin stared at the screen on his phone, he had scrolled through his contacts and before getting to Vinny's name, had paused to look at Katie's instead. His finger lingered over the name before he locked his phone and looked up at the room full of people. It was ironic, how alone and alien he felt with so many people, with so many familiar faces.

He knew it wasn't a good idea to call Katie, she would say it was 'inappropriate'- a word she liked to use a lot around him. But he felt like that night, maybe Vinny wouldn't be able to help him party away what he was feeling, or find him anything strong enough to take the pain away.

In fact, calling Katie was a terrible idea, the thought of it made his stomach flip but there was something in the back of his mind that was silently pushing him to do it. He would be better off, he would probably not regret it as much as he would regret going out with Vinny or David. If she rejected him or was busy, at least he could say he tried the alternative first instead of the norm.

When she spoke, it was what he wanted to hear, although at first, he thought she was shooting him down. Maybe talking to her would help him out that night, because drinking had not been doing him any good so far. Her friends were funny when he first arrived, he knew he was too early but was waiting around for so long that he decided to turn up earlier than expected. Even the sight of Katie left him feeling slightly uplifted, before she even opened her mouth.

She didn't know it, and maybe he would never tell her.

It felt strange to talk to someone the way he did with her then. He felt like he just opened his mouth and let every worry that had been on his mind fall out. Colin never had a conversation with anyone like the one he had then, not with his brothers, not with Anna and not with David, his closest friend. But it was different with Katie, he couldn't describe it or make it sound logical in any way- turning up at your assistant's apartment late one night to open up to her, but the time he had spent with her so far made him feel like she was the right person to go to.

Katie didn't judge him, she tried her best to understand what he was saying and she made him feel like his feelings weren't unreasonable or foolish. It was good to feel understood, he hadn't felt like that in a long time. He knew it was probably wrong to call her after what happened in her old job he didn't want anyone to find out or think their relationship was anything that it wasn't, but he was selfish and he needed someone. Especially after his argument with Anna earlier on that day.

He remembered her shouting, almost screaming at him in frustration. Anna wanted him to care and maybe it would be convenient for him to be a great boyfriend to her, it would definitely get his father off his back, but you couldn't will feelings to life, no matter how hard you tried or how much you wanted it.

Colin understood completely why Anna broke things off between the two of them, he knew it was only a matter of time before she did so it wasn't a huge shock to him although he wished the timing had been better for him. Right before going to his parents' house for Thanksgiving was just the most inconvenient time, he would never hear the end of it that day from his mother and his father. They would complain like they usually did, and it had all gotten too much for him, that was why he had been standing there staring down at his phone for so long before he finally called Katie but he definitely did not regret it then as he looked back on it.

"Let's do another shot!" Leah shouted over the music in the club. Katie looked unsure, which made Leah add "C'mon, I won't get a night out like this for another year or two. I'm enjoying it while I can."

"Oh fine then." She laughed then at her friend before she and the other three women ordered and took their shots.

The night had been going extremely well so far, they danced until their feet were hurting and continued dancing for the rest of the time they spent at the club. Sam had been making the most of her night, she kept telling them she never went out to clubs anymore- she'd become such an adult.

It wasn't until Katie decided to go to the bathroom that she realised someone she knew was at the club too. She had been fixing her hair for a moment or two and then left to head back to the dancefloor to meet her friends when Colin's familiar face came into her eyesight. Although the sight of him was gone before it she even had a chance to analyse it, she knew it was him.

She didn't think much of his short appearance, knowing how much he liked to party, and guessed she would probably not even see him again that night as he disappeared so quickly. Once she was back with her friends, Anna dragged her back onto the dancefloor- 'this is my favourite song' she exclaimed.

Before Katie could protest, a pair of hands grabbed onto her waist and sway with her. Anna wiggled her eyebrows at her friend, knowing who the person was before Katie did and moved away a little to dance by herself. Katie swung her hips to the music and laughed a little, but she had only been dancing for a moment until she realised the hands had a voice.

"Guess who?" He said confidently in a sultry tone, his stubble tickling her skin shyly causing a shiver to crawl down her spine. He flipped her around then so that she was facing him, surprising her.

"Colin." She laughed then, the alcohol was making her senseless. She did not think about how inappropriate this coincidental meet up was, only how handsome he looked standing so close to her.

"Katie." He grinned at her wickedly before they began dancing again, although Katie noticed something strange about him.

His pupils were extremely dilated and he seemed fidgety and more alive than she had ever seen him before. She ignored how alert and hyperactive he was and danced with him for another while. He would sometimes try to take it a little too far than she was comfortable with- him being her boss and all- but went back to less intense dancing with her when he knew she was uncomfortable. His bellowing laughter made her giggle too although she felt dizzy and all she wanted to do was sit down. For a while they only danced and subconsciously pretended that they were not boss and co-worker.

"Who are you here with?" she eventually asked, needing him to bend down so she could shout into his ear over the loud music.

"Vinny and some friends. You wanna join us?"

"No, it's fine-"

"Listen I have to go, I might see you again in here before the night's over." He cut across her then and bounced off dancing in a different direction towards the bar where she saw the friends he was talking about. She did not even have a chance to reply to him before he was gone. So instead of thinking about it she went back to Leah and Sam, deciding to sit down next to them.

"I need a break." She admitted to the two of them before sighing but still swayed along to the music.

"Was that your boss just there?"

"Yeah." Katie said as the three of them watched him from the bar.

Her eyes followed him as he and Vinny seemed to be speaking in secret, separate to the rest before they disappeared in the direction of the bathroom. Katie didn't want to think about him again that night, but her feelings and thoughts of Colin seemed to be piling up inside- she could only bottle it up for so long.

There was something about him that made her want to know more, want to do more and want to say more but she couldn't. Colin wasn't interested in her, she knew it and that was a good thing because she worked for him but something about that made Katie's stomach churn in disappointment. All the 'If onlys' played around in her mind that she would never voice. It was as if all her suppressed feelings had crept up on her and now she could not shake them away anymore especially after his admissions last night to her, although she knew she would just have to deal with it.

Katie savoured her last couple of minutes in the club before it was time to go home, but not without noticing Colin's disappearances and reappearances a couple of times before the end of the night. Her eyes had a mind of their own and no matter how hard she tried to keep them away from him, she could not help it.

She decided to go home to her friends' hotel room and had a good night sleep there although the next morning was when reality hit. Her friends and their questioning about the nature of her relationship with Colin seemed to scare her a little. She didn't want to think about it any longer.

Katie woke up early and made a cup of coffee quietly before heading out to the balcony to enjoy the view. The fresh air was crisp and made her forgetful, but then the appearance of Leah seemed to put her calmer state of mind back into reverse.

"Hey." Leah spoke quietly before sitting down beside her.

"Morning." Katie yawned before turning her head again to look out at the skyline. They shared a quiet moment until Leah broke it again.

"Do you like him Katie?" she knew exactly who her friend was talking about and decided she could not pretend she was clueless.

"I don't know. We're just friends Leah, but I guess we cross some boundaries sometimes. I can't help it and neither can he."

"Has he like... made a pass at you yet?"

"No. Of course not. I think it's just a little crush that's purely on my part. You've all just made me realise it but it'll pass, I know it."

"I'm sorry for being so shitty about it all. I don't mean to judge Katie, honestly. I just don't want anyone else ruining your job like the last one." Her heartfelt apology for her probing yesterday made Katie smile warmly at her friend then.

"I get it. Thanks for looking out for me Leah." Katie really did appreciate each of her friends a lot. It was only then that it sunk it that they were going to be returning home that afternoon. She felt sad but knew they would all organise another trip together soon. Katie would miss them, and until their next visit she hoped her boring life would at least get a little more interesting.

## 15

**CHAPTER 14**

December 2009

"Oh look, it's only nine thirty- you're in early." Katie said sarcastically as she looked at her watch and strolled into Colin's office.

"I know. I can't tell what's gotten into me at all today?" Colin replied, going along with the sarcasm. He took off his coat and hung it up before sitting down at his desk.

"I have these for you." She placed papers down on his desk which made him roll his eyes, already beginning to regret coming in today at all.

"When do you ever have good news for me?"

"Never." Katie said nonchalantly before adding, "Don't forget about the lunch meeting today. It's nice to see you in here almost on time- I was beginning to think you didn't even know a nine thirty even existed." She said in a witty tone as she walked out of his office and into hers, making a huge smile appear on his face before he laughed lightly. Then he let her words settle for a moment and immediately got up from his chair.

"Wait what? We have a lunch meeting? With who? For what?" Colin had already made a way into her office and looked down at her sitting at her desk.

"One question at a time please. Christ."

"Why so sassy?" He raised an eyebrow at her, his words forcing her to snort.

"When am I ever sassy?"

"There you go again, being sassy." Colin crossed his arms then.

"Whatever." She was the one rolling her eyes then. "I know you would be completely oblivious- as always- so I made this up for you." She took out a few pieces of paper stapled together from her drawer and handed it to him.

"What's this?"

"The details and things you need to know before our meeting later. Make sure you actually read them please Colin."

"It's almost like you're the boss here. Crazy." He said sarcastically.

"Someone has to run this place." She retorted as he left again.

"Watch your mouth Kate!" he called in a half-playful tone that made her chuckle.

"No can do sir!"

Katie busied herself for a couple of hours before her meeting although the time seemed to be going very slow. Colin had not made another appearance in her office until it was time for them both to go. She got her coat and the two set off out of the building to the restaurant where they were having their meeting.

Although it was a casual thing, Colin felt slightly nervous. Katie knew this was understandable, considering he never really cared for work and most likely did not know much about what the meeting was going to be about despite Katie giving him the notes earlier. She just wished things would get better and her boss would actually try to be interested in his job sooner rather than later.

Colin always knew how to wing things like this that were work related. Throughout the meeting, Katie took notes and watched as he kept up conversation, he was confident and calm despite the earlier nerves. The pair finished up early and said their goodbyes to the man they had the meeting with. They stayed in the restaurant to finish off their coffee and food.

"Eat up." She said, "We have got work to do when we get back."

"Okay, I get it Katie you don't need to keep telling me." Colin rolled his eyes at Katie's reminder.

"My bad." She raised both her hands up in surrender before taking the last mouthful of her food.

"Let's go for a walk." He said as he finished up his food too.

"I'm not sure, shouldn't we be getting back soon."

"Katie relax, we have over half an hour before lunch is over." Colin checked his watch as he spoke.

"I was lying, I just don't want to go on a walk with you, it's nothing to do with getting back late." She teased as she stood up from the table then.

"You're just going to have to put up with me." He grinned at her before grabbing her arm, placing money down on the table and bringing her with him out the door.

"I guess I really have no choice." Katie laughed lightly, pretending as if being in his company was a chore.

They walked for a couple of minutes until they reached a park and found a bench to sit down on. Colin got comfortable before turning to look at Katie again.

"Aren't we supposed to be walking?"

"You know Katie, I think you're being too sassy today for your own good." He said before looking out at the view of the park and people passing by.

They talked about small things like the weather for a while until the conversation changed to one about Thanksgiving. Although they never mentioned their meeting at the club.

"So how come you didn't go home for Thanksgiving to your family?" Colin asked, the question of family at been brought up- it made Katie feel nervous as she decided whether to tell the truth or not.

"This is my home." She laughed before wrapping her coat tighter around her, the freezing temperature was becoming too much for her.

"You're originally from Detroit no?" he asked, remembering their conversation from months ago, one of the first few days she had started working for him.

"Yeah I am. But Chicago is my home now." She looked down at her fidgety hands for a moment as she thought about what to say next. Initially, she did not think of telling Colin everything about her family life but then something changed her mind- she remembered the night he had turned up at her apartment and completely opened up to her about many things, family being one of the main ones. She thought about it for a second longer before deciding to tell the truth. "I don't really have much of a family Colin."

He noticed then how she had avoided eye contact for the longest time. She looked at her hands sitting in her lap to the people walking past as she sat there, thinking about how she was going to explain to him in the simplest way possible her family situation.

"Those women you met at my apartment are my friends from the girls' home I used to live in since I was a young girl. I suppose they're my family in a way."

"What happened?" he asked, a look of concern on his face.

"My mom wasn't around much as a kid. She never really took care of me properly and my dad- well I don't really know him either. I was taken into care and that's where I met Leah, Anna and Sam."

"I'm sorry to hear that Katie, I really am." He gulped before placing his hand on her shoulder and looking her in the eye, something she had been avoiding until then.

"It's fine really. But it took me a long time to be able to say that. It was tough going but me and my friends, we're some of the lucky ones. I got a scholarship for college and came to Chicago and the rest ended up making it out okay too. I had to learn it wasn't my fault that my mom and dad were never there. I wasn't the problem and I know that know- that's why I'm able to sit here and talk about it." A sad smile crossed her face that Colin returned, it made him feel strange inside to see her the way she was right there.

"What happened to your mom and dad Katie?" he saw how difficult it looked for her to answer so he added "You don't have to tell me if you don't want to. I'm sorry for asking too much-"

"No it's fine. It's good to just get it all out in a way I suppose." She gulped and took a deep breath before continuing to answer his question. "I never knew my dad. My mom never told me who he was. But my mom-um... well my mom was an addict. I would always be left alone when I was younger, she was barely ever around most of the time so." She shrugged her shoulders as she finished her last sentence before looking at him- feeling as if a weight had been lifted off her shoulders. She told him about how drugs had torn away any life she could have had with her mother. It made him feel guilty, for all his secrets he would definitely not be revealing after hearing what she had just said.

"I- I'm sorry about thanksgiving. I feel so stupid complaining, all those things I said about my family. It's probably nothing compared to what you've had to go through. I'm such a dick, god." He felt foolish then but she tried to reassure him.

"No, Colin. You shouldn't feel bad. Everyone has problems and sometimes we just need to let everything out. It doesn't matter if mine are worse or better than yours, your problems are still problems." Katie said in a sweet voice that made him want to reach out and grab her hand, he needed the close contact then although he stopped himself. That was not in the nature of their relationship.

Their conversation led to a less serious topic and Katie shared funny stories about living in the home she spent most of her early life in. They laughed and talked and he made her feel like for a moment she was the only person alive besides him, in this park, in Chicago, in the entire world. She couldn't put her finger on what it was- maybe the way he looked at her, the eye contact, the interest he took in every word she said, maybe it was everything.

After a while, Colin's mind seemed to be somewhere else for a minute. Until he finally spoke of what was on his mind, something he had put to the back of his thoughts for a while.

"Hey who was that guy you were having lunch with a couple of weeks ago when you bumped into David and I?" the question came out as casual as it left his lips despite how nervous he felt awaiting the answer.

"When was that?" she had almost forgotten.

"I'm not sure exactly, a good while back. I think it was September."

"Oh, him." Katie laughed before rolling her eyes, not noticing how nervous he was to hear her answer. "Emily, my roommate set me up with a guy she works with. It didn't work out though. We went on a couple of dates but that was it." It seemed to Colin as though Katie sounded disappointed by this. It almost made him feel jealous but he would never admit it to himself.

"Why?" His curiosity surprised her, made her question whether he was joking or not but when she looked up to see he was awaiting a reply she only laughed a little again.

"Well he works with Emily at the hospital, he's a doctor. I think what he does is amazing, I admire anyone's dedication to their job but- I don't know. It just felt like he was too caught up in work all the time that it made things really difficult. He was always so busy."

"Well I'm in no way dedicated to my job so I'm never busy at all. I could give you all the time you wanted." His reply made her almost raise an eyebrow at him, wondering what he had meant by his comment.

"And?" she chuckled.

"What would you do if I, you know, made a pass at you?" his seriousness made her almost choke. She would be lying if she said she had never thought about it.

"Hey, I'm nobody's rebound Colin." She tried to joke, not taking him seriously.

"Katie." He called her name and she looked directly at him then, his eyes felt as if they were drawing the honesty out of her but she still continued to hesitate for quite some time as they sat on the park bench.

"I-I'm not sure what I'd do Colin." She was the one who seemed to be in deep thought then. She had not given him any sort of straight answer because she really did not know what she would do.

The fact that Katie had answered the way she did gave Colin a small bit of hope that he needed. The conversation turned to something else then before they realised the time and got back to the office. Katie joked about how much of a bad influence he was on her on the way back and Colin had laughed but his mind had been swept away by the thought of her.

She did not leave his mind at all that day. He tried his best to do work and convince Katie that he really was trying to be interested in his job but it was so difficult for him to focus when she made everything blurry for him without doing much at all.

If Colin knew she was thinking about him too that day- he would have been surprised. But that was the truth. After his question, Katie felt confused, as if she was split in two- wanting to be professional and wanting to be with him or at least give it a try. She knew which one she had to choose and felt so deflated once she had realised this.

It was something Katie had been thinking about for a while, but it was and could only ever be something she imagined. Colin was a nice guy, she enjoyed talking to him and being around him. Over the past few months, she had gotten to know more and more about him which only made her feelings grow although she had not faced them until recently.

If Colin had been serious when he asked her the question that was on both their minds, it must have meant there were some mutual feelings. He could be irresponsible and inconsistent at times, but he was sweet too and always had something funny or witty to say. But there was one problem- he was her boss.

They spent the rest of that day and many more thinking about each other and what they were to do with themselves, knowing it would probably never work out anyway. Katie thought about how recent his split from Anna was and figured Colin couldn't have been that serious with his question. She brushed it off, thinking that was what was best.

"Good news Katie, I've completely gotten you off the hook for the gala." Colin said before taking a sip of his coffee and going back to sitting in a relaxed position in the coffee shop.

"Really?" her eyes lit up with joy, it made him smile.

"Yeah. I know they need a lot of extra help this time because it's been postponed until mid January- but I've managed to find someone else to help the committee out. My father even thinks it was a good idea to just have you focus on being my assistant. He says I need you more than the planning committee."

"Thank you so much Colin." Her genuine smile and the look of delight on her face made him feel warm inside.

"No problem, I know how hard it was for you the last time to balance everything. It can be stressful having to look after me."

"It sure is." She replied light-heartedly before the two of them laughed together. "That reminds me, I have to find something to wear for the gala soon."

"I'm sure you'll look beautiful in anything." She scoffed then at his words then placed her coffee down on the table to look at him.

"Nothing like some good old-fashioned bootlicking. What do you want from me now?" she narrowed her eyes at him, being playful again.

"Me? Bootlicking?" he acted surprised and shocked by her words. "Never." He smirked at her. "I'm just speaking my mind."

"Colin."

There was a little warning in her voice that she wished she didn't have to use. It made her think about why they were even here having coffee together. It was outside work hours, they decided to go stop by somewhere after work ended before heading home. She suddenly felt a wave of cautiousness wash over her, was anyone they knew from work around? What would they think if they saw her there with him? Colin could see panic slowly cross over her features and it did not take much to realise why.

"I'm sorry, I think I have to go now." Her voice was quiet as she rushed to stand up and put on her coat.

"Wait, Katie. We haven't finished our coffee?" he too got up from his chair then.

"I just realised I have something to do back at home before work tomorrow." She grabbed her bag and headed for the door, Colin behind her with his coat in hand.

"Katie." He called after her and once they were out on the street she turned around to face him.

"Yes?"

"What's wrong? I'm sorry. I shouldn't have said that. I take it back- well I don't actually, I meant it. But- but just pretend I never said."

"Colin what are we doing?" she asked with a sigh, wishing she did not have to be the one to say it.

"We're going for coffee." He pretended as if that was just it until she gave him a knowing look.

"I don't think we should have. Not after that day in the park. I just don't want people to get the wrong idea if they see us." Colin's stomach dropped, her words made him think that she was not interested and the feeling of rejection crept up on him until she spoke again. "I can't just go for coffee with you, not because of you but because of the way I feel." It pained her to say it but she needed to.

"Katie-"

"I work for you Colin? And as long as I do, we can't do anything."

"You won't work for me forever."

"I suppose I won't no." she paused for a minute, thinking to herself. "But for now, I do." Sorrow filled her words then.

"We could try things out, see how it goes and if it does work out maybe you could look for a job somewhere else?" The idea did sound appealing but that was only after initially hearing it. She needed more time to think about it and he understood that. But he felt it would work, and if it didn't at least they had tried.

Colin decided to walk her to her station and the conversation had turned to something less heavy. It was freezing outside and the sky was already almost black. She walked close beside him, wanting to hold his hand, wanting some sort of contact. He only decided to bring up what they had been talking about only a couple of minutes ago when they reached her station. He turned to her and said a gentle goodbye before leaning in and kissing her softly. It only lasted a moment but left her wanting another.

"Please, just think about what I said earlier."

A small smile crept onto her face that she could not hide, she nodded and they went their separate ways.

**16**

### CHAPTER 15

January 2010

Colin's words played over again and again in her mind, as if they were still fresh but it had been over three weeks and she still could not make up her mind. His lips lingered, the feel of him so close felt as if it was a ghost hanging over her. She felt like everything was right, when she left out the detail of him being her boss. She needed to make a decision but the pair had been busy over the holidays and Colin understood she needed some time.

Over the holidays had been quite lonely for her, she spent Christmas day with Em and her grandparents but decided to come home after that to their apartment alone. Everything had gone back to normal and soon enough it was January and the gala was near.

It was a Thursday night and Katie had come home late after getting the last of her things she needed for the gala. She fell onto the sofa with a sigh before kicking off her shoes and turning on the TV. Emily appeared from her room dressed for work and buzzing around their living room and kitchen.

"Hey Em. Looking for something?"

"I can't find my shoes anywhere." She complained as she began to look in the most unrealistic places she could in the apartment. "What's up?"

"Nothing, I'm just tired." Katie sighed as she stretched her legs then on the sofa.

"From all that shopping, I suppose." Her friend wiggled her eyebrows before she checked in the kitchen again. "Aha! I found them."

"Where were they?" she turned around on the sofa to look at her friend as she put on her shoes.

"On the floor at the sink. Did you find everything you were looking for?" Emily asked, being her chirpy self before she made her way back over to the sofa to look through Katie's bags she had brought home.

"Just about."

"Oh my god, those shoes are amazing."

"You like them?" Katie smiled at her friend.

"Of course, they'll suit your dress well. Maybe this time you'll actually be able to wear them for the whole night because you'll be given a seat." Emily had heard all about what happened at the Summer gala and was definitely not impressed with Katherine.

"Colin keeps trying to reassure me everything's going to be fine this time- I sure hope so."

"Have you been talking to him lately about- you know?" Emily put on her coat as she spoke before wrapping a scarf around her neck and fishing around in her pockets for her gloves.

Katie had told Emily about Colin's proposal, she was glad to have someone to talk to about it without feeling like she was being judged. Em was always a very understanding person, something

Katie appreciated greatly over the years of their friendship, especially when disaster struck at Pierce Holdings.

"Not really. I'm still trying to decide what to do. I'm just so unsure Em. I don't want any rumours to start like back at my old job and the only thing that would make it worse this time round if Colin and I got together would be that they were true."

"Listen Katie, take your time. It's obviously a difficult decision to make. I'm sure you'll make the right one in the end."

"Thanks Em."

"No problem, I'll see you tomorrow okay?"

"Goodnight." Emily heard her say as she closed the apartment door behind her and headed off for work.

It didn't take long for Katie to get ready for bed, she was exhausted. She had a quick snack and then got everything ready for work in the morning. Her bed welcomed her tired and aching body, it didn't take long for her eyes to feel heavy and for her to drift off to sleep.

The noise of her phone on the bedside table ringing loudly woke her up. She looked around the room, not ready to get up yet. Once she picked her phone up she was surprised to find that Colin was calling her and it was three in the morning.

"Colin?" She croaked out, thinking there must be some mistake, until she heard him answering and the state he sounded like he was in.

"Katie, Kate. Thank god you answered." His words were slurred and he began mumbling something else that she could not understand.

"What the hell Colin? Are you drunk?" she didn't want to sound like a scolding mother but it was late- or early depending on how you looked at it and she needed all the sleep she could get for work the next day.

"I'm sorry. S-so sorry. I-I just..." he took a deep breath, one that Katie couldn't tell was to try and stop himself from vomiting on the street. "I don't know where I am. What should I do?" his voice was breathless and she could really tell then by his voice how drunk he must have been. She heard car horns go off loudly in the back-ground that made her wince.

"Are you in the middle of the street?" she didn't want to panic but that was exactly what it had sounded like.

"Maybe." he said as he stumbled around on his own, trying to find something to hold on to.

"Colin for christ's sake." She pinched the bridge of her nose then, already feeling herself wake up.

"I don't know where I am." He repeated again.

"Well first of all get the hell off the street. Go to the sidewalk and try to hail a taxi okay?" Katie spoke slowly as if talking to a child, trying desperately to will it to understand.

"Okay okay." He stuttered. There was silence for a moment or two before he said "I'm here but there's no taxis- Oh wait!" he sounded excited then.

"Do you know your exact address?" she hoped the answer would be yes but sadly she was met by more silence. "Colin-" she sighed.

"I know it, I know it. It's um... um it's-"

"I'll take that as a no then." She said monotonously. He could sense somehow despite his drunken state a hint of annoyance in her voice which led him to apologise again and again. She took a minute to think before giving him more instructions. "Colin I need you to hail down a taxi and put me on loudspeaker okay?"

"Okay. I got it." He said but Katie wasn't entirely convinced until she heard a car door open and close. "I'm in the taxi now Kate."

She spoke over the phone to the taxi driver and told him her address. She felt this was the best solution to the problem. Katie would help Colin inside from the taxi and let him sleep on her couch before work tomorrow.

It took a lot of strength to help him up the stairs of her apartment building and by that time he seemed to have gotten worse. His speech was difficult to understand and he mumbled to himself under his breath.

"God damn it Colin." Katie shook her head at the sight of him once she shut her front door. But Colin did not understand, he was too drunk and the only thing she could make out was his apologies that were of no help to her. She helped him take off his jacket and then to the sofa where he lay down, thanking her every step of the way.

"Here, use these for tonight." She spread out blankets on top of him before he tugged at her hand so that she would come closer to him.

"Thank you Katie. You're the best."

"I know." She rolled her eyes, still annoyed at him but couldn't help caving a bit. "Get some sleep, we both have work tomorrow."

"Goodnight." He said before turning on his side. She switched off the light and went to bed, wondering whether it was even worth her while trying to go back asleep, she would be up for work in an hour or two anyway.

She fell asleep for what only felt like a couple of minutes before her alarm was waking her up for the day. Katie rolled over and let out a sound of exasperation and annoyance. She just wanted two more minutes in bed but knew she would be late if she stayed in bed, she would end up promising herself every five minutes she could get up in another minute. With all the willpower and strength she had left, she forced herself to pull back the covers and get ready for the day.

Once Katie was dressed and almost ready to go, she went to the kitchen to make a cup of coffee before checking on Colin who seemed to be in a deep sleep. She decided it was probably time to wake him up but he was not budging.

"Colin for god's sake, get the hell up." She shook him again and heard him mumble something although he still looked to be asleep. She would give him another minute or two while she drank her coffee.

The sight of Colin's jacket crumpled up on the floor behind the sofa made her roll her eyes. She reached down to pick it up and fold it when something dropped out of the pocket. Her eyes were wide with shock as she stared down at the floor. A small Ziploc bag was lying there, willing her into disbelief. She did not know what to do initially but then this spontaneous anger washed over her.

Katie picked up the bag and looked at the white powder inside then at Colin who was stretching. He had yet to notice her discovery and was in a playful mood.

"Who knew I'd end up in your place after last night huh?" he wiggled his eyebrows but then saw the look of disgust on her face.

"What the hell is this?" she was calm although breaking on the inside.

"Where did you get that?" Colin avoided her question.

"It was in your pocket."

"Why did you go through my pockets Katie?" he was talking as if she was the one who did something wrong.

"I wasn't going through your pockets. It fell out but that's not what this is about Colin." Her stare was unbearable.

"It's not mine-"

"Bullshit." The words came out harsh off her tongue but she could not help it. She remembered seeing him at that club a couple of weeks ago and everything seemed to make sense then, she knew it was definitely his.

"It's only a gram or two Katie what's the big deal?"

"Do you hear yourself right now?"

"Give it back."

"Take it." She threw the bag at him.

"It's not any of your business what I do, I don't know what your problem is-"

"You know exactly what my problem is." Her direct eye contact made him almost squirm, there was no getting away from this easy. "After everything I told you about my mom. After all your crap about trying things out. You knew how I felt about things like this and still you wanted us to be together. How long were you going to hide this from me if we did try?"

"It's not a big deal Katie-"

"It's cocaine Colin." She sounded just as exasperated as he did then. A silence broke out between them, vexation seeped through onto her features but he seemed to be as annoyed as she was. "You obviously don't get it. Just get out Colin. Go."

"Fine then." He said in a huff before grabbing his jacket and marching out of her apartment.

How dare he? She thought. How dare he make her out to be an over reactor, she had a right to be angry at him. Katie had told him about her mother's addiction and how it ruined any chance of a relationship with the only parent she knew. How could he continue to go ahead and voice his feelings for her when a relationship with him would never work out whether he was her boss or not.

She couldn't help but feel somewhat betrayed, Colin could have saved her from her ideas about the pair being together if he had just been straight with her or at least pretended he wasn't interested because she definitely would not want a relationship with him if she had known that all along.

Tears pricked her eyes but she promised herself she would not cry. It was not worth it and she needed to come out thinking positive about the situation- at least she had found out now rather than later when she was more emotionally attached to him. They had not took anything further than the kiss they shared at the train station that night and things could go back to being at least some type of normal.

The situation was confusing for her after her anger had fizzled out. She could not even try to describe what she was feeling. Just then, a confused looking Emily stepped into the apartment.

"Was that Colin I just passed downstairs?" her eyebrows were raised and she looked at Katie for an answer before reading the features of her face like a book. Her expression turned to one of concern then. "Are you okay? You look upset. What happened?"

"Nothing, I'm fine." She lied before gulping back some of her coffee.

"Was Colin here?" she eyed the sheets on the sofa. Emily changed the subject because she could tell her friend did not want to talk about it but she would get the truth out of her some time.

"Yeah, I didn't know what else to do with him. He was drunk and needed a place to stay."

"Hasn't he got his own home to go to?"

"Well yeah, but he was so drunk he couldn't even tell me where he lived last night on the phone."

"You look tired."

"And you look tireder." Katie gave her a small smile then that made Emily chuckle.

"I sure am exhausted. That night shift took a lot out of me. Anyways, have a good day at work."

"Thanks Em." Katie wished she would, but knew a good day was definitely not ahead of her.

She put on a brave face and headed to work, but was unsure whether to be surprised or not by the fact that Colin was not there. She guessed he would turn up later in the day although she was dreading it the entire day. The thought of seeing him made her feel nervous, what way would she act towards him?

Carrie turned up just after lunch time to check up on things. She took off her coat and sat down with a sigh.

"No sign of Colin?"

"Nope." Katie pretended as if she did not know why and Carrie was too busy to even detect any untruthfulness in Katie's response.

The entire day Katie found it difficult to concentrate, her mind kept wandering back onto the topic of Colin. The events of earlier were burned into her brain, the image of the small Ziploc bag wouldn't fade. She could feel her stomach drop again just as it did only a few hours ago, she could sense the disappointment fizzling in and out, reminding her of all the things she had wanted to tell him about her mother's addiction that she was glad then she had not shared.

She sat there that day in her office with Colin on her mind and nothing much else, like many other days recently but it was different this time around. Katie felt some sort of unjustified sadness that he was not everything she expected him to be. The ghost of his words lingered yet she knew whatever daydreams she had over the past while would never come true, not now.

Yes, Colin was on her mind again, but this time for all the wrong reasons.

**17**

**CHAPTER 16**

August 2018

Katie gathered up her things and put on her coat before saying goodbye to Cheryl and heading downstairs to go home. She noticed a fuss at the front door with some of the security guards and kept her eye on them as she began to exit the building. She was surprised when she saw the two men talking to Colin who looked outraged.

"Look, we told you a couple weeks ago, you aren't welcome here-"

"What's going on? Colin, what are you doing?" she noticed how his face lit up instantly once he set eyes on her and felt terrible because of it. If she was going to stand her ground and not forgive him, she didn't deserve to so easily make him feel the way he did when he saw her.

"Trying to see you."

"Is everything okay here?" One of the men asked, about to step in because Katie was frozen in her spot, her indecisiveness glowing on her face. She took a minute to nod at him slowly.

"Yes, it's fine. You can leave him." She said before taking his arm and guiding him down the street before she stopped and turned to him.

"Colin..." her voice was a warning that he would never take full notice of, he was blinded by his love for her, by his hope of reconciliation.

"Katie I just wanted to see you."

"You have to stop showing up at my office, it's not fair on either of us. You need to get over it and go home."

"I haven't been in a couple of weeks but I just thought I'd try again."

"Well you need to stop trying."

"Why? You never stopped trying for us, so why can't I be the one to do that now?"

"Because there's nothing left for you to try for."

"Katie, I just want you to give me one more chance-"

"You had plenty of chances and you fucked all of them up. I can't even describe how happy I am for you that you've pulled yourself together and you're clean now Colin but that won't change a thing anymore. We aren't meant to be together, it took me a long time to understand that, and you need to now too."

"Please, just have coffee with me and then I won't ever turn up at your office again. I just need to know, I need to know what happened to you after you left. I want to know how everything's going, I want to make sure I didn't fuck up your life completely-"

"One coffee, as soon as I'm finished, that's it." She knew she was caving, but she couldn't help it. Ever since his first appearance at her office, Katie couldn't keep her mind off Colin. She wanted to know how he finally got the help he needed, she wanted to know he was okay after all these years.

"Great. Let's go then." His smile squashed all her doubt for a single moment as they stood looking at each other on the street.

For that small second, Katie felt like she had been transported back to the first few months she met him, the first few months when that smile was new to her. It was contagious, and Katie used every piece of self-restraint she had left to keep a straight face. She felt sorry for him, for how her rejection was making him feel, for his desperation, and so, agreed to meeting up with him.

"Oh no, I can't go right now. I'm busy." That wasn't a lie, but Colin felt like it was. The smile fell straight from his face until she spoke again. "Give me your number and we can organise it another day when I'm free."

And just like that, Colin felt so uplifted again by the few words that came out of her mouth.

Hope. That was exactly what he felt. Hope and nothing but it.

**18**

**CHAPTER 17**

January 2010

Katie stared at herself in the mirror for another moment, fixing a piece of her hair that had fallen out of the pretty bun she had put it in before grabbing her clutch and the things she needed. She waved Emily goodbye before going outside for her cab she had ordered.

To say she was a bundle of nerves was an understatement. Her hands shook as she placed them gently on her lap, trying to calm them but it was no use. The thoughts of Colin had not left her and she knew that there was a high possibility of a well-needed talk with him that night although she didn't know if he would even show up-she would not be that surprised if he didn't.

The drive was not long and soon enough she was paying the driver and exiting the cab. As soon as she got inside, she was greeted by co-workers and even saw Alice working in the background just like she had alongside her during the summer gala. She made a note to herself to go say hi once she was finished talking with Shannon and Dylan.

"Guess who's still not here yet?" Shannon said in such a way that suggested she had juicy gossip for both Dylan and Katie.

"Who?" Katie asked.

"The same person who didn't show up for work yesterday." Dylan already knew the answer to Shannon's question and spoke nonchalantly.

"Uh-huh. I can't say I'm surprised, Mr. Anderson seems to be going off the rails a bit lately- well even more so than usual. Do you guys think he'll even turn up tonight?"

"I don't know. I'm sure he will- it's the gala after all and Jeffrey will be so pissed if he didn't make an appearance. Maybe he's just running late." Katie's suggestion made the two others snort.

"Yeah, sure." Dylan rolled his eyes.

They seemed to have a different view of Colin completely but Katie still wanted to give him the benefit of the doubt- even after what happened on Friday morning. She talked with the pair for another few minutes outside in the lobby before promising to find them later on if they were not sitting at the same table for dinner.

"Hey, are you okay?" Shannon asked before she left them. She put her hand on Katie's shoulder and expressed a look of worry shared by her and Dylan.

"Yeah, yeah. I'm fine."

"You seem a little preoccupied. Is something on your mind?"

"Honestly, I'm good. Just a little tired but looking forward to tonight. I'll see you guys later." Katie smiled and left the pair still not looking fully convinced.

They said their goodbyes as Katie walked off not in any direction in particular. She wanted to find Alice and at the same time keep her eyes open to spot Colin if he turned up. She found Alice sorting out name cards at the tables and was glad to see her and not Colin just yet.

"Hey, you need some help?" She asked Alice who was surprised to see her.

"Oh, hey Katie. No it's fine I'm just finishing up here."

"You look amazing." Katie pulled out a chair at the table Alice was working on and sat down to talk.

"Thank! So do you. I'd say you're so relieved you don't have to do this with me like the last gala." Alice laughed a little as she fixed something on the table. Katie sat her chin on top of the chair back she had been sitting sideways on and smiled at the other woman.

"Yeah, for sure. I'm glad I don't have to deal with Katherine this time around." She rolled her eyes and Alice nodded in agreement.

"Did you ever tell Colin or Jeffrey what she said about you?" Alice asked in a quieter voice then as she looked around the almost empty dining room.

"God no. I didn't want any trouble although that's what she deserves. I'm just happy I don't have to work with her anymore."

"Hey, what are you two ladies doing in here by yourselves?" A familiar looking face appeared before them, but Katie couldn't quite put her finger on who it was.

"It's 2010, I think women can handle being by ourselves without needing any help." Katie couldn't help but say, earning a snort from the dark-haired man.

"I'm sorry. That's not what I meant- sad attempt at trying to flirt and find out where your dates were at the same time." He admitted earning a giggle from Alice. "Vinny." He held out his hand for Katie to shake before turning to Alice then.

"Cute but unfortunately I haven't got a date." The other woman said as Katie remembered who he was then.

"Unfortunately." He repeated the word causing Alice to laugh a little again.

"Hey, aren't you Colin's friend?" Katie asked causing him to turn and look at her sitting with her chin resting on top of the chair. She had made no effort to flirt back with him like her friend had- which drew him in further but he would never admit it.

"Yes, don't you work for him?" he pretended as if she did not look familiar but he knew her face.

"Don't we all?" she retorted as she sat up then and moved her hands around to motion to all the people working quietly in the room. "I'm his PA, Katie." She felt the need to add, not wanting to come across as snarky.

"Oh yeah. I think we've met before." He nodded at her. Alice could see his interest in Katie and decided to go find something else to do.

"Well, I have to go find Katherine. I'm sure she has endless boring tasks for me to do." Alice rolled her eyes. "See you later on Katie. Bye Vinny." She smiled at her friend and the man before walking off. Katie gave her a look that seemed to be saying: Don't leave me here alone! Come back please. But she only smiled smugly at her as she waved them off.

"I better get going too. It was nice meeting you again Vinny."

"Going to find your date?" he asked with an eyebrow raised but she had already begun to walk off.

"Ah! There you go again- trying to find out if I have a date or not. Sneaky. Ten out of ten for effort Vinny." Katie laughed nervously then, she had turned around on her way out to speak to him but avoided the question. She earned a wolfish grin from him that made her stomach feel a little fuzzy but she ignored it.

"I'll see you later Katie!" he called.

"If you're lucky." Katie said, feeling like her witty self again- she had forgotten about Colin for only moment. She left the dining room with a big smile on her face that she would not tell anyone the source of.

"Katie? Why aren't you inside?" Alice looked disappointed as soon as she saw her friend.

"I'm coming back out here to find Dylan and Shannon." The other girl rolled her eyes at Katie then. "Oh and thanks for leaving me in there alone." Katie said sarcastically, as she spoke her eyes scanned the lobby and finally latched onto Colin's.

It almost took her breath away, she was not expecting to see him after her talk with Shannon and Dylan a couple of minutes ago. Katie was never usually a coward, but the sight of him then made her want to run and hide. She did not want to talk to him- not yet.

"I was just trying to help." Alice grinned at Katie.

"He was flirting with you too." Katie stated.

"Yeah but he seemed so much more into you."

"How could you tell? We were only talking to him for practically a minute." Katie scoffed, taken away from her worries about Colin again although her eyes still jumped back and forward from Alice's face to his across the room.

"Trust me, I can tell."

"Whatever."

"Katie. Can I talk to you for a moment please?" Colin used his most formal voice she had ever heard once he came up behind the two girls and spoke.

"Sure." Katie tried to make sure her voice sounded calm but it made Alice look at her with curiosity. "I'll see you in a bit." She turned and spoke to Alice before Colin walked off with her to somewhere a little more private.

They walked down a quite hallway and through a room with doors that led out onto a terrace. Katie only followed Colin, she did not pay much attention to where he was bringing her but looked around once outside.

"What do you want Colin?" She finally asked as she crossed her arms and looked up at him. He was standing directly in front of her, lingering, not quite knowing how to say what he wanted to say- that he was sorry, that he should have explained to her, and most importantly that he wanted to be with her. This small thing should not stop them from trying to be together. Instead, panic took over.

"You can't tell anyone Katie." Was all he could say. He shook his head slowly, his eyes wide and pleading with her.

"Colin-"

"Promise me, please." He sounded desperate which made Katie think about it for a moment. It really was none of her business what he did after work hours and it was not her place to spread the word- she understood that entirely. But she wanted to help if this was something he would soon come to have a battle with. She needed to know.

"I promise I won't tell anyone, if you answer my questions." He let out a sigh of relief then and waited to hear what she was going to ask.

"Thank you, thank you so much Katie."

"Is this a reoccurring thing? Do you do it a lot?" she asked and it took him a minute to answer.

"Not as much as I drink, no. It's just a bit of fun K-"

"Don't say that, don't say that to me." She raised her hand up in a gesture for him to stop.

"I'm sorry." He couldn't look at her then and moved his eyes away to the side.

"How long has this been going on?"

"I really can't remember. It's just something I sometimes do Katie. And I'm not going to try and tell you how I feel about it because I know you won't ever agree with me- and that's because you and I have experienced different things. But I know what I'm doing and I can handle myself."

"I wish I believed you Colin." Katie shook her head and looked down with concern. It looked as if an entire series of events flashed in  her eyes, as if a movie was playing in her pupils that Colin would never be able to watch.

"Hey, Katie..." he cupped her cheek and lifted her head lightly so she was looking up at him then. "Please stop worrying about me. I'll be fine."

All Katie could do then was look at him with despair and sorrow filled eyes, misery crept up onto her features. He could not comfort her no matter how hard he tried. She moved her head away from his hand and stood up straight, not wanting to say what was needed to be said, what was making her so nervous and unhappy.

"You do know this means we can't be together."

"I should have told you Kate. I know, but I didn't think you'd understand." He should have told her, but at the time it seemed better to never speak a word of it. He was afraid she would judge him for something he knew he had control over- or at least that is what he thought. She would think the worst when that was not the truth.

"That's not the point Colin." He didn't understand and it made a weak irritation come through in her voice. "The point is I can't be with someone like you."

"Someone like me?" he sounded hurt, but she was stubborn and had strong views about drugs that he would never be able to change.

"Someone who's idea of a bit of fun is cocaine." Her voice was strong and she sounded surer of her words than at the beginning of the conversation. "I can look past some things when it comes to relationships but not this."

"I understand." It killed him to say it, but it was the truth. He did understand and he knew he could not push a relationship on someone who did not want to be with him. It did not matter how much he wanted to try with Katie, it meant nothing at all if she did not feel the same and her words certainly made him feel this was all one-sided.

"We probably wouldn't have worked out anyway." She looked out at the view beyond the terrace and shivered as the cold air she had been ignoring for the entire conversation crept up her spine. Katie was only trying to convince herself she had not missed out on something while the indifference she seemed to possess from Colin's view of her standing there only felt like a stabbing pain in the ches.t

Her words hurt, this entire conversation pained him. The rejection and unrequited feelings left him completely wounded but he would never admit it.

"I'll keep your secret Colin, but I don't agree with it and I want you to know if I think it's beginning to consume you I'll have to step in."

She cared. She should not deny it, but also, she couldn't make it worse by jumping into a secret relationship with him. Feelings would only become more intense, everything would turn into something more complicated than she needed and it would not be good for either of them.

But Colin would never be able to see it the way she did. He felt as if everything that he was feeling had become more indescribable, as if all the words he wanted to say were being shoved back at him by her. They were choking him, making him feel as if his lungs could not work anymore. She made him feel that way without even knowing.

"Thank you." He nodded at her, not quite taking in her words completely. "Maybe we should go back now, I'm sure dinner will be soon." He rubbed the back of his neck with his hand, slouching in on himself as he stared at the ground.

"Sure, good idea... And Colin?" she placed her hand on his arm just as he turned to lead the way back out to the lobby again.

"Yeah?"

"I hope things can just go back to how they were before this all started." The words wrapped around his skull, made him feel deflated and full of hope at the same time- the strangest he had ever felt.

"Me too." But Colin was unsure if he was lying or telling the truth. He ignored it for the time being and they both got back to the gala that was just about to start. The pair went spate ways as Katie was spotted by Carrie and her husband who she would soon be introduced too while Colin disappeared into the crowds of well-dressed people.

"What are you doing?" Alice laughed as she stood beside Vinny, making him jump in surprise. She had spotted him again looking at name cards on the tables.

"Nothing." He tried to hide the name card he was holding in his hand but he was not doing a good job at it.

"Is that yours?" she nodded toward the card he held.

"Maybe..."

"Hmm. Seems like you're looking for someone else's name card too." Alice narrowed her eyes and smiled slyly at Vinny.

"Nope. Definitely not." Vinny tried to convince her but it was no use.

"Katie is sitting over at that table right there," she turned around and pointed directly to a table only a few feet away from them. "Just, you know, if you were wondering,.." Alice said before walking away with a smile on her face.

Vinny looked around as he walked over to her table, he didn't want to look suspicious or to be caught by anyone else. Quickly before someone noticed he switched his name card with the person who was sitting beside Katie and walked briskly away from her table to where he was supposed to be sitting. After placing the random person's card down where his used to lie, he walked out of the dining room and waited a while for everyone to enter and be seated.

He walked slowly back to the area where Katie's table was and pretended to look around for his place at a table. By that time, her table was almost full and she sat there with a gloomy expression he could detect even from the corner of his eye.

Vinny walked around to her table, he could feel her eyes on him but continued to look at the cards until he found his own beside hers. He looked from his name over to her face then, a huge grin appearing on his face then.

"Oh look, what a coincidence seeing you again."

"I guess it is." Katie rolled her eyes at him before shuffling her chair to the right a bit so that Vinny could sit down.

"I told you I'd be seeing you later."

"You must be really lucky I suppose." He could see a sly smile cross her lips before she took a small sip of her freshly poured white wine.

"Of course I am." He was charming and it made her mind be transported to a different, less complicated place than the topic of Colin. She would savour it, even if it was only for the night. "So your date?" the pair's eyes met for a moment and the hopeful look on his face made her giggle a little.

"He couldn't make it." She lied.

"How foolish of him. You won't need to worry about him now that I'm here with you."

"Quite persistent, aren't you?" she stated playfully, being sucked in by his aura and confidence. She did not think twice about it, understanding it was only a bit of fun, an exchange of one witty comment to another.

"So I've been told before."

Vinny went on to make some Dad joke about the amount of cutlery on the table that made her laugh aloud at the ridiculousness of his statement. They talked through each of their courses and in that time she had learned a few things about him. He and his father owned a successful tailoring business in the city- so successful his sister was even called Taylor after the trade- that one made her roll her eyes but laugh none the less. He had been friends with Colin for a couple of years and lived in a house in the Gold Coast Area of the Chicago city. He too, like Colin, was born and raised there.

Katie had not gone into great detail about her life before college, only stated she was from Detroit but moved to Chicago to study and never left. They talked about the city and the places they loved to go and before she knew it, dinner was over. There were fundraising opportunities and auctions for charity after their food and some music. The night seemed to fly and Katie thought it may have had something to do with the man sitting beside her. It made her wonder even more about him, but she would not admit that to him.

When it was time to go Katie tried to find Alice to say goodbye but she couldn't be seen anywhere. Vinny walked her outside to the cab that was waiting on her and wished her well. He was quite the gentleman, charming and charismatic. He had that tall, dark, and handsome look about him too.

"Hey, Katie wait." He grabbed her hand gently before she got into the cab.

"Yeah?"

"I was wondering if you might want to go out sometime?" he decided to just go for it. What was the worst that could happen?

"Oh... Vinny I'm not sure." She looked to be thinking deeply about something then but he still gave it one last try.

"Look, how about I just give you my number and if you ever feel like getting a drink or something to eat we can go? You don't have to say yes or no right now." His suggestion made her face brighten up a bit and she nodded at him.

"Sure, I'll definitely think about it. Thanks." She said after they exchanged numbers quickly and she got into the cab. "I'll see you around Vinny." She had rolled down the window then just as the cab was about to drive away.

"Maybe, if you're lucky." He repeated the words she had used a couple of hours ago, a huge smirk appearing on his face as he spoke. It made Katie chuckle loudly in the back of the taxi.

"Maybe!" she called back between her laughter. Once she settled down her mind began to cloud with the idea of Vinny. It made her smile but she knew it would not last for long. Colin would soon seep back into her thoughts but at least for the rest of the night she had someone else to think about.

Neither Vinny nor Katie had noticed Colin standing at the front entrance to the hotel during their encounter, but he had been watching and saw the whole thing. As soon as Katie had taken off he walked towards his friend and decided to have a talk with him.

"Vinny, man? What the hell are you doing here?" Vinny could tell Colin was angry before he had even turned around and saw the dark look on his face.

"Hey Colin. What's happening? Fancy bumping into you here." He wore a smile on his face despite knowing what this conversation would bring.

"Didn't you hear me? I asked why you're here?" He walked closer to his friend and looked around as he spoke to Vinny, hoping no one would pay much attention to them.

"Relax man. One of my friends got sick and couldn't make it, he switched his name to mine instead. Why let a good dinner go to waste eh?" Vinny was trying to pretend as if it were normal for him to be there and it only added to Colin's frustration.

"You're not supposed to be here or even around me while I'm at work. I don't want people catching on to anything." He spoke his last words in a hushed tone and through his teeth, a furious expression on his face.

"It was fine, I spent the night with that sweet little PA of yours anyway. We haven't even had a conversation tonight until just now." He was brushing everything off as if it were nothing and his comment about Katie only sparked more anger within the other man.

"Katie?"

"No, Carrie." He said dryly but Colin did not find his joke funny.

"Don't go near her-"

"Hey, relax man. She's just your PA? She seems like she can handle herself just fine, I'm sure she doesn't need you to try and protect her." Vinny laughed lightly then as he walked to the edge of the pavement and hailed a taxi.

"Whatever Vinny." Colin felt truly wounded then from the realisation Vinny's words brought with them.

She was just his assistant, and he was just her boss. The way it would stay from then on.

# 19

## CHAPTER 18

May 2010

"Colin your dad's looking for you. He's called like a million times today and wants to know where the hell you've been for the past three days."

Katie had knocked but heard no answer from him so decided to enter his office anyway. She came in with her head down looking at the paperwork in her hand. She almost jumped when she realised Colin was not the only one in his office. Colin's new girlfriend had been sitting on his lap, their mouths locked in a deep kiss.

"Woah Katie, have you ever heard of knocking?" Colin pulled away from the kiss he was sharing and sat up a little straighter.

"Hi Laila." Katie said, not looking at all phased by the interruption she had caused. "And yes, I have actually. I knocked twice and there was no answer." Laila gave the other woman a small smile before kissing Colin on the cheek.

"So you just decided to come in anyway?" he sounded baffled by her actions.

"I figured you had probably fallen asleep again, it's what you usually do when you arrive back after your three or four day benders."

Katie replied dryly. Laila whispered something in Colin's ear and giggled before standing up.

"I was just going anyway."

"I'll see you tonight." Colin said before she leaned down and gave him another kiss, one more than Katie thought she did not need to see.

"Bye Colin." Laila's voice was so sweet it could probably rot right through your teeth. He smacked her on the behind before she left, a wide grin on her face. Katie gave him a look that showed she was unimpressed but said nothing until she heard the door closing behind his new girlfriend. The pair's eyes were locked on one another's but she was the first to break the silence.

"You're a pig you know that?" Katie commented on his last action and it made him laugh loudly.

"Leila doesn't seem to mind."

"Of course she doesn't." She rolled her eyes, falling directly into his trap.

"What's that supposed to mean?" Colin tried to draw more out of her, he wanted her to feel jealous although he knew he was being ridiculous. This was the closest he had ever been to seeing her show the smallest bit of jealousy since he and Leila had gotten together.

"Nothing." She mumbled to herself before looking at him then. "We have more serious things to talk about at the minute other than your girlfriend."

"Oh here we go." He rolled his eyes, knowing exactly what was coming next.

"Where the hell have you been Colin?" Katie asked in exasperation, not moving her eyes even an inch away from his.

"I've just been a little- er... busy." He scratched the back of his neck with his hand then. It wasn't exactly a lie but was definitely an inadequate excuse.

"Too busy to come to work?" she sat down and placed the papers on his desk before crossing one leg over the over.

"Yes."

"Colin." She sighed, saying it like she had said it so many other times before. It made him feel guilty, but he had been too busy having a good time with Leila and his other friends to come to work. "You need to focus Colin. How long is it going to take you to realise that this job isn't going to last if you keep disappearing for days on end without any contact."

"Did you miss me?" an absurd question, of course, and one that was said in a playful manner although he wanted her to answer in a serious way.

"Miss you? It doesn't make much of a difference to me- considering when you're here you never do any work either." Exactly what he did not want to hear.

"I'm sorry."

"Ah, there you go again with the apologies. Nice one." She said dryly.

"C'mon Katie? When exactly was it that you became my mom?" Still, he persisted with the playfulness. He wanted to stir the conversation away from any serious topics. Usually Katie would give in by this time and just laugh it off but she was exhausted that day. She had been up late doing things that Colin should really have been looking after himself and she was growing tired of his slacking off all the time.

"Colin I know you think this is funny and yes maybe it is a little, but that's not the point. You need to start working because I'm just your PA and I can't do my job and try to do as much of yours as possible too." Katie had been too tired to get mad. She sounded completely deflated then and had sunk a little deeper into the chair after her confession. It made his stomach churn at the sight of her.

"I'm sorry." He repeated, not knowing what to say then, guilt beginning to creep up on him.

"Sorry just isn't good enough at the minute I'm afraid." She shook her head and looked up from her lap. "I'm tired Colin. I've been up all night trying to sort out this presentation that I've been convincing your dad is entirely your own ideas and you haven't worked a full day of work in weeks."

"I'll try this time, I promise Kate."

"Whatever you say. Anyway, I need you to review these for me. And call your dad please, he's been looking for you." His conscience had kicked in then as he noticed the bags under her eyes and the way she spoke with no enthusiasm at all. She did not believe him and when he thought about it, why should she? He had made the same promise over and over again not only to her but to his family who were growing tired of him too. Colin tried then to get his mind off that subject, he wanted to think of something else and not allow the guilt to intensify.

Katie got up and walked slowly out of the room, their conversation only making her feel even more drained and made her posture slack as she walked. The high he had been feeling had quickly subsided from witnessing her low- a low that he had played a part in creating. He tried his best then to do the work she had given him and even called his dad that day for a phone call he wished to never endure again.

She was too preoccupied in her office to notice him slip out after lunch that she had skipped. Engrossed in her work, Katie decided on not taking any breaks. She didn't noticed Colin who was walking hesitantly into her office until he sat down on the chair in front of her desk facing her. He was trying to balance two coffees in his hand and a paper bag she did not know the contents off.

"Colin..." she warned him.

"Hold up, I just wanted to bring this as a sort of truce."

"What is it?" her curiosity had overtaken her irritation for just a moment.

"I thought you might need a coffee and I noticed you didn't go for lunch today."

"Go on." He looked as if he had more to say, but he bought some time by handing her the bag so she could look inside. She took out the sandwich and the box of donuts before placing them on her desk, trying her best not to cave.

"I guessed you liked them the most since whenever they're in the breakroom you usually try one of them first." He said as she eyed the box of four deep fried treats.

"Thanks Colin." She nodded, a small smile crept onto her lips that she wished she could hide. But she still did not sound very pleased with him. "I suppose I should really take a break. And I'm guessing by the two coffees you're going to take one too?"

"Yes, but not for long, I promise."

They talked about the presentation he was doing for the board members at the end of May and what he needed to do to be pre-pared for it. Although Colin sounded as if he genuinely did want to start getting back to work, Katie knew his attitude would only last for a while. She had been working with him for around a year by then which made it difficult for her to be convinced.

Katie did not want this to turn out like their quick chats usually would, with both losing track of time and talking about things non-work related. But she also did want to mention something that had been on her mind for a while. She even felt a little nervous to talk to him about it but when the topic of conversation turned to one about Colin's relationship with Laila, she knew it was probably the best time to say what she needed to say.

"She's really great Katie, not like Anna at all."

Katie could see how happy he was with his new girlfriend, it was genuine and new for him but she doubted whether it would last or not. Anna certainly did not make him as happy as Laila seemed to do, but there was something about the pair's relationship that she found somewhat compelling. She could not put her finger on what exactly it was that did not sit well with her about the new woman she had been introduced to but she hoped that it would work out for Colin and that her apprehension was only some small sliver of jealousy that had been left over from the relationship they never had.

"You two seem very happy together." Katie nodded at him, a small smile on her lips that made Colin wonder what was going on inside her head. He had hoped to make her jealous in some way, but at the same time there was truth behind his words- he and Laila were doing better than he had expected.

"Maybe it's just the honeymoon faze, that's what you women like to call it?" his question made her stifle a giggle.

"You women?"

"Yeah, you know. I've heard about it being called something like that anyway." He rolled his eyes and looked at her again, noticing the way she sat forward a little on her chair.

She seemed as if she wanted to say something but was nervous. He hoped she would have something to say about his new relationship, that she would disagree with it in some way. Sure, things with Laila were going amazing but that did not mean he was entirely over his assistant, considering nothing much had happened between the two either. Katie finally spoke up and said what she had been keeping in for a couple of weeks, but it was everything Colin did not want to hear.

"How would you feel if your friend Vinny and I started seeing each other?" the words cascaded with such inelegance, it made Katie want to cringe but she tried her best not to.

"Seeing each other?" he knew what she had meant but needed her to clarify.

"You know, like dating. I met him at the gala and he gave me his number. I just wanted to know what you would think, since he is your friend-"

"I'd think it would be weird if I'm honest." He did not want her to start seeing Vinny, he wasn't right for her.

"Why?" She wondered.

"Because he's my friend. And you two wouldn't go together trust me."

"Well I think I can figure out that on my own, thanks Colin." Katie said, frustration beginning to creep up on her.

"Hey, don't be mad at me. I'm just answering your question." He raised his hands up and let out an obnoxious laugh. "You sound very hurt for a hypothetical situation Kate." He spoke matter-of-factly.

"Well I'm not. But I also don't need your permission I was just asking how you'd feel."

"Sounded like you were asking for permission to me."

"Well I wasn't."

"Then why bring it up in the first place?"

"I-I don't know."

"Katie, Vinny just isn't for you. Sure, he's my friend but he's also an asshole. I'd say this to any girl that asked me about dating him... This is all hypothetical, right?" Colin sounded as if he was almost warning her and it made her feel a little defensive, Vinny was a really great guy.

"Of course it is. He gave me his number at the gala and I wanted to know what you would think while I'm trying to decide what to do." She lied.

"You want the truth? I'd recommend you delete it and find someone else. Just a few words of warning from me." He said before standing up and walking out the door.

"Maybe I will, yeah." She tried to sound like she was taking his words into consideration when really, that was not the case.

Colin left the room with a smug looking smile on his face that Katie couldn't see. He thought he had handled that conversation and gotten through to Katie, if only he had known the truth. While he was feeling like he had won a competition that did not even exist, Katie wondered why Colin was adamant on her and Vinny having a relationship together. Her worry lingered over her like a rain cloud on a day you forgot your umbrella, it stuck in her brain all the way through the rest of her day at work and her train ride home.

It was only when she came through her front door and kicked off her heels that she decided to voice her thoughts to Emily who was happy to listen- not having much excitement in the relationship department in a while.

"And then he starts giving me all this 'just a word of warning' bullshit. I mean, what does that even mean?" Katie had begun doing her makeup on the sofa beside her friend, holding the mirror close to her face so she could do her eyeliner correctly while Emily flicked through the channels on the TV.

"Why don't you ask him next time you're talking about it?"

"Oh god no. I'm never bringing it up again, he really pissed me off earlier. I mean, what has he got against Vinny? They're friends for god's sake."

"So you're just going to not tell Colin that you and one of his close friends have been dating since February? What are you guys going to do when you get a little more serious? Colin's bound to find out."

"I don't know. We'll have to tell him sometime- I just don't know when." She had a worried expression on her face that made Emily turn and look at her.

"Hey, Katie. Don't stress over it. If you like Vinny, then go for it- well I mean you did go for it- but I mean, don't be afraid to fall for him just because Colin might not agree with it."

"Why are you so good at giving advice?" Katie stopped doing her makeup for a moment and smiled at the other woman. "Thanks Em."

She did not tell her friend that she was a little concerned, maybe Colin was actually giving her a warning because it was needed, or maybe it was just him being selfish and not wanting the pair to start dating. From what she had knew of Vinny since they started dating back in February, she had gathered it was sweet, kind and caring.

He treated her well, as she did with him also and Katie couldn't find any major faults since then.

"I better go get dressed, Vinny's picking me up in twenty minutes." Katie said once she was finished her makeup.

"Go girl, hurry." Emily laughed.

Katie appeared from her room a couple of minutes later ready to go. She said her goodbyes and Emily told her to enjoy her night. She jumped into Vinny's car outside her building where he had been waiting for her.

"Hey." He said before leaning in for a quick kiss.

"Hey." A wide small crossed her face then as she drank him in.

"You ready for dinner?" Vinny asked as he started driving off on their way.

"Yeah, I'm starving." Katie admitted before the pair laughed together.

"You aren't the slightest bit dramatic are you Katie?" he joked around.

They enjoyed their dinner and a drink or two together, before Katie knew it the night was over. It seemed time would always fly when he was in her company when all she wanted was for it to stop. His smile and laughter lifted her up and his witty comments just like hers made Katie laugh. She got along great with him and whenever he was around she felt this kind of excited nervousness in her stomach.

Since her conversation with Colin earlier when Vinny was brought up, there had been some small doubt in the back of her mind that maybe Colin was genuinely concerned for her and that his warning was needed and justified. It made her feel cautious when she thought about it, uncertainty had grown on her throughout the day. But from the moment she set eyes on Vinny that night, through the chatter and the laughter, he seemed to make all that doubt fizzle out- Katie felt she had nothing at all to worry about when she was with him.

Colin was moving on from something that had never been, and that was what she needed to do too.

# CHAPTER 19

July 2010

The noise of the curtains violently being drawn made Colin stir under the sheets of his bed although he did not fully wake up, only rolled over onto his side. Then, he heard her voice and that was the strangest thing he could think of hearing early in on a Friday morning.

"Wake the hell up before I go and get water to throw over you." Katie held her coffee and presentation sheets under her arm as she opened the second curtain in Colin's bedroom to expose his delicate eyes to the bright light of the 11am sun.

"Katie." He moaned loudly, still not making any attempt to move from his spot in the bed. It took a moment for everything to process in his mind before he sat up in bed and looked at her in disbelief. "Katie? How the hell did you get in here?"

"You really shouldn't keep a key on top of your door Colin."

"You broke in?"

"It's not breaking in if I use a key." She had not stopped buzzing around the room, taking the occasional sip from her coffee. She managed to locate where exactly it was in his wardrobe that he kept his suits.

"You're coming in without my permission so- same thing."

"Oh c'mon, it's not like I haven't done it before. Now what are you doing still in bed? We have that presentation today."

"Can't I go back asleep for just-"

"Colin it's eleven o' clock, and the meeting with the board members was supposed to be at nine." She spoke matter-of-factly and stood at the end of his bed with her arms crossed. She was definitely furious with him but wasn't letting it fully show... just yet anyway.

"Okay, okay. I'll get up." He groaned.

"Oh take your time. I know it's really hard for you to actually do a full day's work and all. You weren't supposed to wake up three hours ago or anything." Passive aggressive sarcasm oozed from her voice then. A frustrated sigh could be heard coming from her mouth as she walked toward the dresser near his bed and picked up the coffee she had brought for him.

"I would get up, but I sleep naked- or maybe you want to stand there and watch me get dressed?"

"Now is not the time for your incessant flirting. Don't worry, I was just leaving. You better be ready to go in less than five minutes or I swear to god Colin-"

"Sure you were." He grinned at her as he took the coffee from her.

"I'm telling Laila." Katie said dryly as she left the room, clearly joking.

"Telling her what? That you wanted to see me naked in here? That you turned up to get a little action?" Colin said loudly so that she could hear as he began to get changed. His playfulness made Katie roll her eyes to herself, he really was the most ridiculous person she had come across so far.

"A little action? Christ no, I can get my own boyfriend. I don't need to steal anyone else's." She called from the other side of the door making him laugh a little.

"Whatever you say Katie."

Within a couple of minutes Colin had appeared from his room, ready to go. But before they reached the front door he had stopped in his tracks and taken out his phone that he began texting on. Katie tapped her foot impatiently as she waited before questioning him.

"What are you doing?"

"Give me a minute Kate, I need to text Laila."

"Surely you can do that in the taxi on the way to work."

"No can do, it's urgent."

"Sure, we're already..."she checked her watched and announced sardonically "Two months late. What's another five minutes going to do huh?" Katie had brought up the fact that the presentation had been postponed more than twice over the past two months because Colin had not showed up.

"Thanks for understanding." He gave her a smug smile before the pair rushed out of his apartment.

"You're lucky I've sweet talked everyone into pushing the meeting to eleven thirty." Katie nudged him once they had finally hailed a cab and gotten inside.

"All hail Katie for doing her job." He began to use a bowing motion to her in the back of the cramped cab, only making her look the other way.

"If only all I had to do was sweet talk people into believing you aren't the tardy fool you actually are. My job would be a piece of cake." She retorted as she leaned her elbow on the window and rested her chin in her hand.

"Tardy? Is that all you can come up with?"

"It's all I think is suitable enough to say right now. If we weren't in the back of a taxi, trust me Colin I'd have a lot more to say other than the fact that you can't ever not be late for anything."

She refused to look at him and continued to stare out the window at the swooshing streets that flew by. He could tell she was mad but keeping it together until all this was over and knew it wasn't fair that she was running around after him like a headless chicken doing the work he had promised to look after but never actually got around to doing. Because of that he said nothing at all in response and she was glad.

"Take these and just read everything that I've wrote down in red only. I have the slides on my USB key and I'll be changing them every time I know the next one is due." Katie shoved the papers he needed for the presentation at him once they entered the elevator up to their floor.

"Got it."

"And please try not to screw this up Colin."

"I won't, I promise."

"If only your promises could make me feel any less nervous than I am right now." Katie shook her head, clearly not impressed by his whole demeanour. He was so calm, relaxed and seemed to almost be taking this whole thing as a joke.

"Jeez, sorry."

"Just remember-"

"Ignore the writing in red pen." He had the audacity to joke with her then as the pair stepped out of the elevator. Katie gave him a warning look before he chuckled and held his hands up in surrender. "Alright I'm just kidding, I know. Red pen only."

"I could kill you right now." Katie said, only being half serious. The other half wanted her to smile and laugh at his stupidity but she refrained from doing so.

Colin appeared to have a talent that morning in the board room-winging it. She had noticed from previous meetings also that he was very good at pretending to know what he was talking about when in fact, he didn't. He was the most unorganised and lazy person she had ever met yet when looking at his life from the outside, he seemed to be so confident and self-assured.

Katie was almost envious of him then as he stood in front of the board, pretending as if the ideas he was describing were his very own. The men and women in the room seemed to be satisfied with how the presentation, all but one of course: Jeffrey. His father sat there at the end of the meeting, not looking fully convinced. Colin could sense this despite the reassurance from every other member of the board. Many shook his hand and smiled at him, expressing their excitement for the future.

He tried to feel happy inside but that was difficult, he was forced to feel nothing at all except the slightly bit of guilt that full credit wasn't given to the brown-haired beauty that was his PA. She packed up her things, not seeming fazed in any way by the clear attention Colin was getting from her own work.

"Congratulations. You managed to make it through the entire thing without fucking it up." Katie's bad mood had lifted a little and a small smile crept onto her lips that she wished she could get rid of.

"Language." He warned her playfully which made her narrow her eyes at him.

"You're a very lucky man Colin. I'll give you that." She shook her head slowly as she picked up her bag and the rest of her things. "I don't know how but you get away with murder here. Good job, I'll be in my office if you need me." She said her goodbyes before heading to the floor where they usually worked.

Katie sunk into her office chair with a deep sigh escaping her lips. Finally, she could relax- that was, until Colin was handed more work she would be forced to help with because he refused to put much effort into anything at all work related. She heard a knock on her door a few minutes after she had started getting back to work and looked up to spot Colin standing in the doorway.

"Hey." He gave her a smile that would give anyone butterflies in their stomach. She used that as her excuse so that she didn't feel bad for the way he made her feel from such a small gesture.

"Something you need?" she asked, smiling back at him.

"I just wanted to say thanks a lot for earlier and all of the work you've put in over the last couple of weeks. Oh- and for putting up with me."

"Anything else?" Katie sniggered at him before she put her pen down on the desk. Just then, her phone began to ring. Colin watched carefully as she took it from her bag and looked at the caller ID. Hesitantly, she answered but not before looking at Colin.

"Hello."

"Hey babe. Are we still on for tonight?" Vinny asked.

"Um, I'm in work at the minute. But yes, we are. I'll call you when I'm finished, 'kay?" Her voice was sweet and gentle, it made Colin curious about who was on the other end of the line.

"I'll see you then."

"Bye."

"Who was that?" Colin couldn't help but ask which only made her look uncomfortable yet she answered.

"Just my roommate." She lied and used a tone that made Colin feel like there was no room for elaboration even if he wasn't convinced. It took him a minute to realise that it did not matter if she was lying or not, he should not be concerned about who she talks to.

"Colin." He heard his father's voice from behind him. Katie rested her phone on the desk and sat up straighter once she noticed Mr. Anderson. "We need to talk. Hi Katie." He added.

"Hi Sir." She smiled at the older man before her eyes were drawn to Colin again who looked a little nervous.

"Sure dad." He said before the pair left and headed towards Colin's office.

"Great job out there son." Jeffrey said, eyeing his son's every move as he awaited a response.

"Thanks." He said as he sat down at his desk. He noticed his father's poker face as he sat opposite him, cross one leg of the other.

"I didn't think you could do it, but I'm glad you proved me wrong- for once." He said the last part quieter than the rest but Colin was happy that he had earned at least partial approval from his father, something very difficult to achieve. He hesitated for a moment with a reply, knowing he had two choices: to pretend the presentation was his own or to tell the truth. The happiness he felt from his father's words did not outweigh the guilt he felt, and so he told the truth.

"Dad... I have something to tell you." Although Colin looked ashamed, he knew he would feel better afterward.

Vinny woke up to the shrill sound of his phone ringing on the bedside table beside him. Katie was tangled in his arms, making it difficult for him to grab his phone without waking her. She shuffled around in the bed for a moment but went back to sleep once he picked up his phone, stopping the ringing.

"Hello." He spoke quietly, half asleep.

"Vinny man? What the hell's keeping you so long? You haven't been answering any of my calls or texts." He heard Colin say from the other end of the line.

"Why are you even calling me it's late-"

"It's only twelve o'clock Vin." He remembered Katie was exhausted from work and ended up falling asleep on the couch a couple of hours ago. Vinny brought her to bed and the pair drifted off again but he thought it was later in the night.

"I'm in bed Colin. What do you want?" he grumbled as he dragged himself out of bed and outside his bedroom where he would be able to speak louder without worrying about waking Katie up.

"Bed? Did you forget we planned on going out tonight or something?"

"Um, no. That's next Friday not tonight." He was beginning to grow impatient with Colin.

"Dude, it's tonight. Get your ass up out of bed. I'm at your door."

"Fuck." Vinny muttered under his breath before he went back into his room and grabbed some pants. He ran down the stairs and opened the door to find a confused looking Colin staring him up and down.

"You aren't going out in that." Colin chuckled loudly, causing Vinny's annoyance to grow.

"Keep your voice down, Jesus." He demanded as his friend walked into his kitchen, making himself at home.

"When did you become such a grandma? The night is young, c'mon."

"I can't go out tonight."

"Why the hell not? You can't cancel now- have you got the stuff?"

"For god's sake Colin, don't speak so loud-"

"Vinny? Is everything alright?" Colin heard a sweet and sleep-filled voice call from in the hallway although when he turned his head he could not see anyone. He could see a shadow on the stairs but couldn't make out who it was.

"Yeah, everything's fine babe. Go back to bed, I'll be up in a minute."

"Oh... 'Babe'? Has Vinny got a woman upstairs waiting for him?" Colin wiggled his eyebrows at a very uneasy looking Vinny.

If Katie had have known who Vinny was talking to, she would have never gone downstairs that night. Of course, she knew they could only keep their relationship from him for so long until he found out, she just didn't want him to find out the way he did. Vinny heard her footsteps and his eyes went from Colin to her's. She was still hazy from waking up only a minute or two ago and stood there behind Colin who had noticed Vinny's change in direction.

Katie was the first to see Colin's face and his reaction once he set his eyes on her standing there in nothing but Vinny's t-shirt and her crazy hair all over the place. She didn't know what to do, and was as shocked as he was in that moment, her mouth slightly agape as she waited for some sort of reaction from him. It took only a minute, but it felt like an hour for the couple as they waited for Colin to say something, anything at all.

"Wow." He shook his head in disbelief, almost glaring at Katie which made her fill up with guilt. "You two? That's just- wow..." Colin was speechless and a small, choked laugh escaped his mouth as he looked between his friend and his PA.

"Colin-" Vinny walked towards Katie and wrapped an arm around her, he could tell by the look on her face she was very nervous and almost scared to see what was going to happen next. His attempt at comforting her was not very successful as she examined the look of aversion that formed from every part of his demeanour.

"It looks like you two are busy here, I better go." He said before walking briskly past them and out the front door. Katie was almost shaking, worked up over something so small but she didn't want to tell Colin this way, she wanted the couple to ease in gently to the idea of their relationship being something Colin would see and know of.

To say he was furious would have been an understatement yet Colin knew it was unjustified so didn't want to let it show. His stomach sunk once he saw her, a million questions filled his clouded mind that he wished he had have asked instead of storming out like he did but he couldn't allow his emotions to get the better of him. All he needed was time to think and to come to terms with the situation but the only thing that kept popping into his mind was how long had they been seeing each other? He remembered back to that day Katie brought it up in her office and couldn't help but wonder.

"Katie don't be upset, he'll get over it." Vinny tilted her head up to look at him once they heard the door slamming outside in the hall.

"I know, I just wish we could've told him some other way." She was definitely a worrier, Vinny had discovered this and made his best attempt at trying to comfort her before they went back to bed. She was happy that he was there for her and calmed her down a little but she was also tormented by the fact that she cared so much what Colin thought and how he felt after finding out.

Vinny was the first to fall asleep but Katie, she lay awake all night wondering why she could not wipe away Colin's disappointed expression from her mind. She thought she was over him, it certainly had felt that way when she was around Vinny. She really liked him and enjoyed his company, in fact by this stage of their relationship, Katie even thought she might love Vinny but was holding back a little. She did not know the reason behind her hesitation, Katie was afraid of what it might be.

Why? That was the start of the questions running around her mind that night but she would never tell.

**21**

## CHAPTER 20

J uly 2010

"How long?" Colin finally had the chance to ask Katie on the Monday morning after a long weekend of anticipation. He watched as she gulped before taking another mouthful of coffee.

"Since the gala- well it took me a while to get back to him. But that's where I met him."

"Why didn't you guys tell me?"

"Because I knew this was exactly the way you'd react Colin." Katie spoke in exasperation, growing tired of this conversation already.

"Because my two friends have been lying to me and seeing each other behind my back for months." He tried to make her understand but she was in no mood for his explanations.

"You know what Colin, I don't need to explain myself to you, or anyone. Sure, he's your friend but he's also my boyfriend now and we kept things a secret for a while because we needed time to think. That was our decision and you need to respect that. I'm sorry we had to lie to you but we're together now and you need to understand that."

Her sobering words hit Colin like a punch to the face. They were together- and there was nothing he could do about it. He was with

Laila and Katie was with Vinny, all he needed was time to come to terms with it although he knew it was going to be difficult.

"I'm sorry." Colin said genuinely, shaking his head a little. "I'm happy you found someone Katie, I'm sorry for over overreacting." He said, thinking back to that day in the park when she talked about her date and trying to find someone.

Katie willingly accepted his apology but he had one last thing to say before their conversation was stirred somewhere else.

"What I said a while ago about Vinny not being good for you, I meant it."

"Colin-" she began to warn him but he raised his hand up in a gesture for her to stop speaking for a moment.

"But. There is a but Katie if you'll let me finish."

"Fine then." She rolled her eyes at him.

"But it's your decision and I have to respect that. I'll let you figure things out for yourself." He nodded at her.

She found his words to be very cryptic then but shrugged off any doubts she had from them, because every time she thought about Vinny she felt reassured.

"Bora Bora?" Katie asked in complete bewilderment.

"Yeah it's an island in the south Pacific." Vinny replied, looking at her with a hopeful expression on his face.

"I know what Bora Bora is Vinny." She said dryly.

"So..."

"So." She replied, not knowing what else to say.

"What do you think?"

"I think it's too much." Although Katie didn't want to be ungrateful, she had to be honest. His gift really was far too extravagant for her, especially considering they had not been dating very long.

"C'mon Katie." He pleaded with her. Her apprehension puzzled him, any other girl he had been with would've jumped at the idea of going on a vacation with him even if they were not together as long as he and Katie had been.

"What about work?"

"What about it? I'm sure we can twist Colin's arm. You told me before you never take any holidays."

"I know, it's just-" The excitement he could not contain had made her stop speaking for a moment, she tried desperately to find the right words to say without crushing him. "I don't want you to think I need things like this to keep me happy. I really don't deserv-"

"I know exactly what you're about to say and I'm not going to let you say it. You need a vacation, you've been telling me how stressful work has been."

"I don't want to sound like a bitch Vinny, I really am grateful. I just feel like it's too much."

"So what? Live a little." He exclaimed with great enthusiasm, so much so that it made laughter erupt from the pit of her stomach.

"Thank you Vinny." Katie gave him a sweet smile before he hugged her and kissed her on the forehead.

"Anything for you babe." And just like that, she had decided she was going to Bora Bora in a couple of weeks' time.

Colin had the same reaction as Katie when he found out. She didn't expect much else from him.

"Bora Bora?" he asked, as if hearing Katie's conversation the night before and repeating her exact initial response.

"Yes, Bora Bora. I was hoping to get the week off at the end of August." Katie stood in his office waiting nervously for his reply.

"Isn't it a little early to be going on vacations with him?" When she thought about it, Colin almost sounded jealous.

"You and Laila go on weekends away all the time and you aren't together as long as Vinny and I." she spoke matter-of-factly. He knew he could not deny it, but hated being wrong. "Anyway, I didn't ask what you thought about the vacation I asked if I could get the time off." She spoke in a sassy tone, not being bothered by what he thought.

"I'll have to check my schedule."

"When was the last time you checked your schedule, like ever?" she almost snorted at him.

"You're skating on very thin ice Katie."

"I've already checked your schedule, because you never do and it doesn't look like you have much on."

"You really need to stop sounding like a know it all." He rolled his eyes.

"What are you going to do if I don't?" she raised an eyebrow, leaning forward with her hands on his desk.

"Are you threatening me Ms. Briggs?"

"It sounds like you're the one threatening me."

"Sit your ass down so we can go over this week's meetings." He had lost the discussion again so changing the subject was all he could do.

"Um, I think you've forgotten the whole point of this conversation. So can I take the days off or what?"

"Sure, but only if you sit down." It pained him to say yes but he had no other choice. Katie was excellent at her job and put up with him so much without taking many days off, she was due some vacation time but he just wished her time didn't have to be spent with Vinny.

"Of course I will master Colin." Katie said sarcastically before sitting down.

Their walk through of the week ended how it usually did, with the conversation trailing off from being anything important to everything unnecessary. They were sharing funny Jerry Springer stories and laughing about how Katie and her roommate Emily watched the show religiously when Laila stormed into Colin's office, taking the pair by surprise.

"Colin baby, where have you been all weekend? You weren't replying to any of my texts- oh... hi Katie." The way she said the other woman's name sounded as if it burned her tongue to even pronounce it.

"Laila- I'm at work, can we talk about this later? Katie and I are in the middle of something."

"No. Can't she just leave?" Katie avoided eye contact with the other woman but noticed the look on Colin's face and decided it was best she left.

"Um, we can pick this back up when you two are finished?" Although it killed her to be polite, she did so anyway before she picked up her files and left, shutting the door behind her.

It seemed that Laila's true colours were showing more and more since the beginning of her relationship with Colin. At first, she did not seem as rude and arrogant as she was becoming during her recent visits to the office. It was none of Katie's business so she did not intervene, although Colin always had something to say about her relationship he had recently discovered.

After about a half an hour, Laila strutted out of Colin's office and walked straight towards the elevator. Once Katie knew she was in the elevator, she got up and was about to knock on Colin's door when he opened it, looking like he was in a rush. She took a step back, not expecting him to be right there in front of her. The pair stood looking directly at each other, drinking each other in. They hadn't been this close to each other in a while, it made him savour every last second. He had been trying to catch Laila before she left in a huff after their argument but then he looked at Katie and decided he would deal with his girlfriend later.

"I'm sorry, I didn't expect you to be there." Katie laughed lightly before looking up at him again.

"I was just about to come and get you, sorry for the interruption." He lied before moving out of the way of the doorway so she could enter the room.

"Great, now where were we?" she said as she took a seat and he closed the door behind her.

"Will you come to a brunch next Saturday at my parent's house?" he blurted out, taking her by surprise.

"Brunch?"

"Yeah, like breakfast and lunch-"

"God, do I seem that clueless?" she threw her eyes up to the ceiling and muttered under her breath. "I know what the word brunch means, I'm just wondering why you're asking me?"

"I just remembered when Laila came in that we meant to invite you." When she heard we, she assumed he had meant he and his girlfriend so decided to ask was he just inviting her or was this a couples' thing.

"Just me or can Vinny come too? You know, since he's your friend." His heart sunk a little at her words but he didn't let it show. Of course she would assume Vinny was invited, why would she want to come along and sit there with Laila and him?

"Sure, Vinny can come along." He said although he knew Vinny wouldn't agree to go, he knew what the deal was between Colin and himself.

"Cool, I'll ask him after work. Why the brunch?"

"My mom and dad usually host one every month, it's kind of fancy and really unbearable most of the time."

"Why's that?"

"Because it's my family." He said in exasperation, making her chuckle a little.

"I'm sure it won't be that bad." Katie suggested although she knew Colin could be about his family.

"Trust me, it will be. And I'm going to have to find some excuse for Laila not to come."

"Does she not want to be around your family either?" she seemed puzzled.

"God no, it's the other way around. Of course my mom and dad don't like her. They usually have something to say about most of my girlfriends unless they're like Anna." He sounded irritated but Katie was already beginning to take his parent's side with this one, she wasn't sure she liked Laila's company either.

"So... What happened with you and Laila?" Katie was too curious and had to ask although she probably should have kept her mouth shut.

"Nothing, we're fine." He lied and looked at an unconvinced Katie.

"You don't have to tell me if you don't want to, I probably shouldn't have asked in the first place I'm sorry." She let out a small laugh.

Colin had been trying to keep this show of a relationship looking perfect for Katie because every time he saw her he was reminded of the rejection she caused. Things with Laila were good for the most part, but sometimes he needed a break. She was the definition of high maintenance and lived a very fast-paced life that he initially though he could keep up with but in the end, was feeling left behind.

"I just needed some space during the weekend. And she thinks that because I wasn't answering her texts or calls that I was cheating on her or something. I turned off my phone Friday night and didn't switch it back on until this morning before I came to work. I even told the doorman to tell her I was away when she came to my apartment on Saturday night looking for me."

"Would it not be easier to just tell her you needed the weekend to yourself?"

"She'd think I was doing something I wasn't supposed to be doing, hell I even told her this morning and she thinks I was sleeping with someone else. I just need some time off."

"All that partying is catching up on you huh?" Katie tried to be light-hearted about the situation although Colin's exasperation and sullen look in his eyes as he spoke made her want to just give him a hug. "I get it, sometimes you just need time to yourself, away from everything." He looked up after she spoke, glad she understood but wished Laila did too.

"She can be very... hands on sometimes and it's a bit too much. But most of the time, everything's great." He nodded, feeling as if he was explaining himself to her.

"Relationships can't be perfect all the time, they do need work but I'm sure you two will sort things out."

Although Katie was trying to make him feel better, her words were only making him feel worse. He wanted her to be jealous or to hate Laila. He wanted her to say she wasn't the one for him but Katie had Vinny now, there was no chance she would ever say the things he wanted her to. He just needed to get over it and Laila was keeping his mind off her but was she only a distraction or would she make him feel better in the end? He hoped the latter was true.

"How are you and Vinny doing? You two seem to be doing fine."

"Yeah, everything's great actually." She didn't want to elaborate because Colin's relationship clearly wasn't doing well at that moment in time. Colin could see she was holding back and wondered what was wrong.

"Do you love him?" he blurted out, not so much because of his jealousy but because he was curious.

"I-I think I do actually." A smile lit up Katie's face as she thought about it to herself. "Do you love Laila?"

"Of course." He said without hesitation but he wasn't quite so sure of himself on the inside.

He knew he didn't grin to himself like Katie had during her admission, his eyes didn't glaze over with memories of himself and Laila together and it made him feel hollow then when he made the comparison. It also made him feel the sudden urge to tell Katie the truth about Vinny, to spoil the moment because of his envy but he knew that would be cruel and uncalled for. She needed to figure things out for herself, that was what he agreed to do in the beginning and what she seemed happy doing but it was so difficult seeing her so happy because of his friend instead of himself.

"Good." She gave him a small smile as she nodded slowly at him although something about his words didn't sit right. She ignored the feeling and then changed the subject back to what the conversation should have been about- the weekly plan they needed to discuss.

The two went about their day like they usually did except their conversation lingered in their thoughts. Neither could shake this tinge of regret they felt nor the guilt they felt for feeling it in the first place. Katie was almost sure she loved Vinny and because of that she wished her mind would stop going back to that night at the gala when she told Colin they couldn't be together. Colin just wanted to get over that night and felt guilty for trying to convince himself of the love he clearly lacked for Laila.

But Katie knew she could never be with Colin, his bad habits were too much for her to take. She couldn't be with someone like that and although he felt he had a hold on the situation, Katie knew it wasn't that simple.

Colin and Katie felt split in two, conflicted by the feelings they once felt for each other. Colin's were stronger than Katie's for sure, but they had certainly not left her entirely. They wouldn't for a very long time.

# 22

CHAPTER 21

July 2010

"I wish you could come with me." Katie groaned as she stretched out under the covers.

"I know but I'm busy at work." Vinny lied. He felt terrible for having to lie to her but it was for her own good, he needed to keep some parts of his life a secret, at least for the time being.

"I feel so nervous going on my own." She did feel a knot in her stomach although she had agreed with little hesitation at the start to attend the brunch at the Anderson's house.

"Don't worry, you'll be fine. And afterward we can go somewhere nice for a couple drinks, I'll be finished whatever I need to do by then at work." The thought of that calmed her nerves a little.

"Promise?" she asked despite knowing he wouldn't let her down.

"Of course. Now where did I put my shoes?" he mumbled the last sentence to himself as he walked around the room fixing his tie.

"By the sofa in the living room." Katie said, still lying in bed but sitting up slightly so she could take in the sight of her beautiful boyfriend.

"Oh yeah." He nodded to himself.

"Do you want me to make you something to eat before you head off?" she called after him but he soon entered her room again, shoes in hand.

"No, I'm good. I don't want to take away from your time getting ready."

"Are you sure? I'm making breakfast for myself anyway."

"Maybe I could stay for a while longer." He contemplated.

"Great, let me just throw something on." She said before getting up out of bed.

The pair chatted over a small breakfast that Katie prepared for the two of them, it was still early in morning but she didn't want to eat too much before heading to the Anderson's. She had plenty of time to get ready so sat with Vinny for a very long time, in fact maybe a little too long, Vinny was late for his appointment at work. He rushed out the door, kissing her goodbye and promising to see her later that day.

By that time Emily had arrived home from her night shift at the hospital and with a yawn and a stretch, she threw herself down on one of the couches in the living room. Katie was procrastination getting ready and so went to sit with her friend for a while to catch up before she got dressed.

"So have you picked what you're going to wear yet?" Emily asked during their conversation. She could sense her friend's nervousness.

"Yep but my outfit is the least of my concern at the minute. I wish I wasn't going alone. I just don't like not knowing what to expect."

"How crazy can a brunch get?" Emily smirked at her.

"I know, I'm just being silly aren't I?" she laughed lightly.

"I'd love to get dressed up and go to some fancy brunch with you at Colin's mansion, it's too bad I'm a nurse working shitty hours. Otherwise, I would've invited myself." Katie noticed how exhausted Emily looked and felt guilty then.

"I'm sorry, I really shouldn't be complaining."

"Oh don't worry about it Katie. You should probably go get ready. I'll be with you in spirit." Emily joked.

"You're right, maybe I should." She nodded to herself before getting up from the couch. "Do you want me to make you something before I-"

"Go and get ready woman! I'll make myself something in a little bit." Her friend chuckled as she flicked through the channels on the TV.

Katie took her time that morning to get ready. She showered, did her hair and makeup before putting on her dress and slipping into some heels. Colin had warned her how fancy these things were with his parents to avoid any confusion when she turned up. Katie was looking forward to seeing Colin, but dreading Leila's company even though it would surely only be for a couple of hours.

She had never fully expressed her growing dislike for Colin's girlfriend to anyone except when it came up in conversation with Vinny, that was it. She felt it wasn't anything important Colin needed to know although at the beginning Colin had shown clear distaste towards her relationship with his friend. Katie didn't have to get along with Laila, she was Colin's PA and his friend but his relationship should not concern her.

Katie was secretly pleasantly surprised when she discovered Laila couldn't attend the brunch that afternoon. She had turned up in her Uber right outside the gates of the Anderson's huge estate feeling more than a little overwhelmed. She talked over the speaker at the entrance and in no time the gates were opening for her. She walked up the long drive, wishing she had asked the Uber driver to bring her right to the door of the property all the way up.

Colin greeted her in a matter of minutes of walking in the door. He had been there all morning and she had only arrived when he spotted her standing awkwardly alone in the busy reception room. Despite being dressed in a pretty floral off the shoulder dress and spending some time on her hair, Katie felt only barely presentable when she looked around at everyone else. That was another off-putting thing to add to the list. She did not let that stop herself from at least trying to have an enjoyable time.

It was in the first few moments of greeting Colin that Katie found out Laila would not be at the brunch. She had asked where she was when she quickly realised she was not dangling from Colin's arm where she usually would be. Colin didn't let it show, but he was happy his girlfriend couldn't attend and that Vinny was absent too although that was what he was expecting all along. It gave him more time to spend with Katie alone. He knew he should feel guilty for even thinking that but he didn't. Since Colin found out she was seeing Vinny, they didn't seem to talk as much as before.

He showed her around and watched as her face lit up with surprise at every next turn they took in the house he grew up in. Katie was amazed at how big the house was, she couldn't imagine living in anything like this. She was used to cramped spaces or sharing rooms which she preferred to call cosy, she liked cosy but it was still nice to see how the other half lived.

As soon as the tour was finished, he brought her back to the reception room that seemed to be getting even more crowded by the minute. They had a mimosa or two before a man about the same age as Colin made his way over to the pair. He greeted Colin casually but his eyes zeroed in on the drink he had in his hand.

"Don't you think you've had enough already Colin?" Katie was surprised by the man's forwardness and gulped back a small sip of her drink, her eyes going in any other direction than at the stranger.

"Dude, this is only my third one. Chill."

"And your last one." The man said with great tension behind his voice. Katie looked at him through the corner of her eye for a moment, hoping he wouldn't catch her but cursed herself when she realised he was staring straight at her. "I see you've gotten bored of Laila, it took you long enough."

Katie's eyes widened at the harsh words that came out of his mouth and how rude this person was being. Who was he?

"I guess you're jealous because you stopped getting some off that gremlin of a wife of yours a long time ago." Katie was growing more uncomfortable by the minute and tried to take a step away from Colin who wrapped an arm around her waist when she did so, never taking his eye from the man.

"Whatever, you're probably drunk already Colin. Lay off the alcohol, for mom and dad's sake- we don't want you causing a scene again like the last time." He said before beginning to walk off.

"And at least when I do get tired with Laila, I don't have to stay in a marriage I'm bored shitless with. Tell Veronica I said hi by the way." Colin raised a glass to the man but he already had his back to him.

"Colin..." Katie tugged at his sleeve to get his full attention. "Who the hell was-"

"Glad you could finally meet Kevin, my twin."

"Twin?" they shared some small similarities but she only noticed that once he said it.

"Not identical obviously... that bastard wishes he looked as good as me." Katie was left speechless, she never knew Colin even had siblings, never mind a twin. "Don't ask me why I've never mentioned him before Kate, I'm guessing you already know why."

"Okay." She whispered, nodding her head slowly, baffled.

"Let's get another drink." He said after he polished off his third one. He began walking but Katie grabbed his arm to stop him.

"Maybe we should slow down a little," he gave her a look that made her add "I want to enjoy lunch with you." This earned a softer look from Colin.

They took the brunch a lot less serious than the rest of the people there, although Katie did have to stop Colin when his behaviour was getting a little out of hand or when he was bad-mouthing people too loudly. Katie wondered if she was happy that Laila wasn't there because she was rude or because it gave her time to spend with Colin alone? She didn't want to think about it an she certainly had many easy distractions that afternoon. Colin left her alone for a minute or two as he went to the bathroom to pop some pills she would never know about and while he was gone she was approached by another man who looked similar to Colin and his brother.

"Hi there, you must be Katie?" he said her name at the end as if it was a question. She laughed nervously and shook his hand he held out for her to take.

"Yes, it is Katie."

"I'm Andrew, my dad asked me to come over and make sure you're okay for everything." He nodded towards Jeffrey who was standing with a group of people, his wife beside him.

"Don't tell me Colin is actually a triplet instead of a twin?" she tried to joke but would not be surprised, he had kept his family a huge secret up until then. She earned a chuckle from Andrew he smiled at her before he spoke.

"I'm flattered actually, I'm Colin's older brother so I'll take that as a compliment. Where is my brother anyways?"

"He's gone to the bathroom, I'm sure he won't be long." She answered politely. She talked with Andrew for another minute or two and decided she liked him a lot more than Kevin who was just plain rude. Andrew was just about to go check on his brother when he arrived back in the room, a scowl plastered on his face at the sight of him.

"Hey little bro, I'm just getting to know Katie here-"

"Okay, cool. Katie, let's go somewhere else." Katie furrowed her brows in confusion at Colin's rudeness.

"Colin...." Andrew looked at his younger brother who was beginning to lose the run of himself despite it only being the early afternoon. His eyes were bloodshot and he seemed to be in some daze where frustration would break through every now and then.

"Let's go." Colin said as he took Katie's arm and led her off. She turned her head and gave Andrew an apologetic look although she felt there may be more behind the way Colin was acting, she certainly hoped he had a reason.

He took them outside deep into the garden's of the house to get some peace and quiet. Katie noticed how flustered and upset he looked, she couldn't help but feel sorry for him. Clearly, Colin's problems with his family were deeper than he discussed all those months ago. The pills and the alcohol did not seem to be giving him the high he excepted, instead he was facing a terrifying low that he could not even begin to describe to Katie.

"What's wrong?" Katie was so concerned then as she saw his eyes almost crumple with emotion. She had her hands on both his shoulders, silently demanding his eyes to meet hers.

"I'm fine-"

"You aren't fine."

"I should've never asked you to come here in the first place. I hate these damn things!" he raised his voice despite Katie's soothing voice.

"Why can't you just skip them?"

"Because then that's another crappy thing I do to add to the list of things my mom and dad can nag me about." He said in exasperation.

"Come here Colin."

He looked as though he was close to tears. She enveloped him in a tight hug for a moment, something he looked as if he needed desperately. He was glad her gesture eased his anxiety a little and savoured every moment. It seemed that things took a turn for the worst so quickly in the past couple of minutes for him and he needed her to help him calm down.

"You're going to be okay, you just need to take a deep breath. The brunch is nearly over and once it is you have the entire day to do whatever the hell you want." Katie's voice was sweet, he heard it so close to his ear because of the hug she was giving him.

"You're right." He said once they both pulled away and she held him at arm's length.

"I know. Of course I am." She replied with a hint of playfulness in her voice that made a smile crack onto his lips. "And I don't have to come to any more of these things if you don't want me to." He wished he had never said what he did earlier, as he thought she might be someone good to have around during them as a calming force.

"I-I just, god I don't know. I just wish everyone wasn't so god damn perfect around here. Everyone in my family seems to be so great at everything they do except for me." She could sense his insecurities coming out then.

"Perfection is just an illusion Colin. No one's perfect and even if they were you need to stop looking at everyone else and focus on yourself. You'll never do anything good for yourself if you keep comparing what you do to others. Because there's always someone out there that's going to be better than you at something so what's the point in taking tallies of who exactly that is?" Her words caressed his brain like no others, as if they were the first things his ears had ever heard. He understood what they meant although his insecurities stopped him from being able to fully agree with her, they did comfort him at least. "Now let's talk. Why didn't you tell me you had siblings?"

"I guess I just didn't want to talk about them, I hear enough about how great they're doing already without having to tell anyone else about them. And as you can tell, we all don't get along that well..."

"I get it. No one wants to be reminded of people they don't like very much." She nodded at him in agreement, knowing all he needed was for someone to understand.

He began to tell her about a lot more than before although he still held back. Maybe it was the alcohol that was making him blurt out his feelings, he had drunk a lot more before arriving at the brunch that Katie didn't know about. Katie listened, that was all she needed to do and she did it well.

Katie reassured him that if he ever needed to talk, she was there for him. In that moment, she didn't care whether he was her boss or not, she didn't think about whether that was the right thing to do for their work relationship or not. She had stopped caring about that so much quite some time ago. All she wanted was for him to be okay, especially as he looked so full of sorrow standing right there in front of her.

Katie was curled up in a ball in bed under the thin white sheets. She watched with quiet joy, almost mesmerized by Vinny as he walked around the room trying to pack his things. She looked around the room then that they had been staying in for the past week and wished she could stay a week more.

She had such an amazing time and because of this, Vinny did too. Work was getting really stressful for her and he was happy to see her eyes surrounded with smile lines instead of dark circles. But when tomorrow came around, it would be time to go home and back to reality although he wished she could be full of ease like this all the time. He too didn't want the vacation to be over just yet, his holiday blues seemed to be spreading to Katie too.

"I don't want to go home tomorrow." She groaned in bed as he packed another t-shirt in his suitcase.

"Me either." He replied and looked up to find her sitting up in bed.

"Have you much more packing to do?" Katie asked, wanting him to come to bed soon.

"No, I'm just about finished."

"Great, come get in beside me." She patted the mattress beside her, a wide grin on her face.

It didn't take long before they were curled up together, his arms enveloping her in a tight embrace. She turned to look at him, feeling the hair along his jawline creeping up. He kissed her passionately on the lips, sending shivers up her spine. Katie pulled away and looked into his eyes. Unable to hide her content, a smile crept onto her lips as he traced shapes on her bare shoulder.

"I love you." She finally admitted, keeping it in for long had been unbearable but she wanted to make sure she was being completely honest. But she knew then, she was so sure of herself.

"I love you too." As soon as the words passed Vinny's lips, she couldn't help but giggle a little in excitement.

He began kissing her neck, intertwining their fingers as he held her hand.

Katie was glad she told him but realised it was probably the first time she hadn't got Colin in the back of her head throughout the entire trip. She had been worried about him because she left, his partying seemed to be getting even worse than before. Katie just hoped he'd been looking after himself while she was gone or else Jeffrey would be on his case.

The thought of Colin left a bittersweet taste in her mouth. She didn't want to worry about him, but she couldn't help it. Whatever she did, Colin lingered in her thoughts and she was beginning to become tired of it.

**23**

**CHAPTER 22**

September 2010

"So she hasn't told you anything?" David asked, quite shocked by Vinny's confession about his relationship with Katie.

"Well, a few things here and there. But not much at all, it's making me wonder whether I even want to know more or not. If she hasn't told me then maybe it's because it's bad."

"Why should it matter if it's bad or not? She's your girlfriend it's not like it's going to change anything." Colin tried not to glare at Vinny but David could see how hostile his friend was becoming when Vinny talked about his girlfriend.

"I just don't know if I'm ready or not."

"It's her past not her future. It won't affect you whatever it may be."

Colin tried his best not to become enraged by Vinny's constant talk about Katie. He had heard enough about their trip and relationship all together to last him a lifetime. He knew that it was pure jealousy, but he couldn't shake it which only left him full of envy after hearing about how sweet she was or the things she did that made Vinny know she always had his back. If only Katie realised who Vinny really was, she would run a mile and never look back.

"You sound very defensive Colin." Vinny narrowed his eyes at the other man while David merely watched with anticipation, his head knocking back and forth between Vinny and Colin as they challenged each other. "Something I should know about?"

"Nothing at all." He lied but entered into a stare with Vinny, not yet ready to back down.

"You've been working with her for so long, surely you've found out something about her past. She won't even tell me about her mom or dad."

Colin was quite taken aback when he found this out, as Katie had told him a lot about her broken family life and what it was like to live in a girls' home for most of her childhood and teenage years. She had been a little reserved at the start but Colin realised after talking to Vinny that he knew a lot about her life before Chicago. He was confused by this and why she was keeping things from her boyfriend since the pair seemed to think their relationship was perfect.

"Look Vinny, if Katie wants to keep things from you, it's not my problem. They're her secrets to tell, not mine."

"So you do know something?" David still remained quite, absorbing the whole conversation entirely. He could feel the tension building in the booth but couldn't escape it as he would need to get past one of the two men in order to leave.

"I don't know much and I don't have to tell you anything. If she wants you to know, you'll know. It wouldn't be fair on Katie-"

"I'm your friend Colin, why are you so concerned about Katie? It's not like she's going to find out."

"It's not my place." Colin said with finality in his tone yet Vinny persisted.

"You two seem a lot closer than you make out to be..." He sounded suspicious, which made Colin let out a small laugh.

"What's wrong with that?"

"Well, it is his girlfriend." David decided to speak up, earning a glare from Colin.

"What are you going to do? Make her stop hanging around me so much? She's my PA, we work with each other. I'm the only reason you two even met in the first place."

"And you were pissed about that, that I was even talking to her that night."

"You're starting to sound a little jealous Vinny?" Colin almost smirked then, knowing that the tables were turning. Katie had shared more with her boss than with her own boyfriend, it must have made Vinny angry, as he seemed to be reaching boiling point. "Don't you trust her?" He added, savouring the feeling of tormenting Vinny with Katie.

"I don't trust you. Katie's not the problem."

"You two won't last anyway." Colin said nonchalantly, he knew this for a fact but Vinny mistook his confidence as arrogance. His anger got the better of him and he tried to jump up from the table to hit Colin but David stopped him and made him sit down.

"Jesus man, look where we are. Don't do that shit in here." David looked around, seeing if anyone had noticed.

"You aren't worth it anyway Colin. Katie's with me and not you."

"I know that, you think I give a shit? I have Laila." He used Laila as some sort of excuse, as if having her around would stop him from catching feelings for him assistant and avoid the complete jealousy he had toward the couple but she was not just a thing that could make block what he was feeling. Laila was his girlfriend, but maybe not for long. He was unsure if their relationship was going to go far and wondered what had kept her around for so long in the first place.

"Seems like you do."

"Whatever, I'm going home." Colin threw down money on the table and grabbed his things. David and Vinny looked at each other as their friend walked away but neither tried to stop him.

"Hi Laila." Katie noticed the woman standing at the desk talking to Kevin, a desperate look on her face. She couldn't tell what was wrong but had already sensed her visit was not going to bring any joy to anyone.

"Do you know where Colin is?" she turned around to look at her boyfriend's assistant. Katie felt as if she was going to begin interrogating her and still felt asleep, it was very early in the morning to be dealing with Laila and her mystery solving. "Hello?" Laila demanded an answer, causing Katie to become irritated easily by the woman.

"Colin?" Katie scoffed, "Colin doesn't usually turn up here until after lunch some days, so if you're looking for him I'm afraid you're in the wrong place."

"I've checked everywhere and he isn't returning any of my calls or texts. I don't know what to do." She almost rolled her eyes at Laila's panic, how foolish she was to even look in the office for her missing boyfriend.

"I'm sure he'll get back to you soon. He's a grown man, he can take care of himself."

"What makes you so sure of that? Have you been talking to him? Where you the one he was with last night?" Laila tried to grab Katie's arm but she pulled away and tried not to scowl at her.

"I don't know what you're trying to say but-"

"I'm asking if you're the slut he was with last night or not."

"I have my own boyfriend, one I don't feel the need to keep track of twenty-four seven."

Katie furrowed her brows before leaving the woman at the front desk, Kevin's mouth fell open in surprised by Katie's straightness but he said nothing more to Laila before she stormed out of the building. Katie went into her office and hung up her coat. She took a deep breath once she sat down and got her phone out to call Colin. She too, was curious to find out where he was and why Laila was acting so crazy just a moment ago.

Of course, she received no answer from Colin but he surely had read her text. As soon as he arrived into the office right before lunch time, he made a beeline for her door and entered without knocking.

"You wanted me for something?" he asked, looking totally oblivious and innocent yet there seemed to be something on his mind.

"Me? No, but Laila sure did when she turned up here this morning at half eight." Katie put her pen down and looked up at him.

"Oh, I thought it was something important." Colin rolled his eyes before leaving and making his way into his own office.

Katie stood up then and followed him, wanting to know more than what he was giving out. His office door was already shut but she opened it without knocking and stood in front of him, staring right at him.

"Jesus Katie, next time why don't you knock-"

"You never knock at my door." There was a silence for a moment as he took off his coat and hung it up.

"Good point." He nodded, not being able to deny.

"That's it? You're just going to brush it off like that?" she asked.

"Brush what off?"

"Laila's visit this morning. I'm sure she's told you about it already."

"She's fine now, I've dealt with her."

"You've dealt with her? God, you sound like such a dick right now." Katie said in exasperation, earning Colin's full attention then.

"Excuse me?"

"Why don't you maybe communicate with your girlfriend a little more so she doesn't come into the office insinuating ridiculous things about me?"

"What did she say?"

"Why does it matter? You've dealt with her now haven't you?" Katie was angered by his dismissiveness and repeated his words in annoyance.

"What did she say about you?" he asked between gritted teeth, clearly he was in no mood that day but Katie did not care.

"She thought I was with you last night for some reason."

"Oh for christ's sake." He mumbled, pinching the bridge of his nose.

"Why did she think that Colin?" Katie's voice was quieter then than before, she waited for a reply from him but was nervous to hear what his answer might be. "Did- did you tell her about-"

"Oh of course I didn't Katie. That girl would accuse anyone of sleeping with me just to solve the little mysteries in her head."

"Why is she like that?" She asked, curious by Laila's clear para-noia. "Why does she think you cheat on her all the time?"

"Because she's so dramatic." He said casually as he sat down at his desk.

"Have you ever done it before? Is that why she always thinks the worst when you don't pick up the phone or go missing?" Katie was simply asking a question she though may be the very reason for the clear lack of trust between the couple but didn't think her question through when she realised how offended Colin seemed to be.

"You think I cheated on her?" he asked, clear distaste in his expression.

"Well it would make sense why she's so protective and suspicious every time she turns up here at the office-"

"How dare you."

"Hey, you don't need to get so defensive about it. I'm just asking a question, it's not like it's random or anything. You have to admit it would make sense."

"I don't give a crap if it makes sense or not. I didn't cheat on her." He said between gritted teeth, she noticed how irritated he was becoming and even took a step back from his desk.

"Colin," she breathed out, "I just wanted to try and understand why Laila acts the way she does. I didn't think you'd take it the wrong way."

"You didn't think I'd mind being called a cheater? Get the hell out of my office Katie, I'm not in the mood." He raised his voice even louder. Everything felt like it was coming all at once in his stomach, feelings of jealousy and anger brought on from being deprived of Katie and the total exposure to her relationship with Vinny seemed to be boiling up inside him. He couldn't control his anger when he spoke then but didn't care. Vinny didn't deserve her and if she wouldn't be with Colin because of his habits then she certainly shouldn't be with his friend.

It took her a moment to process what he had said and she was shocked that he had clearly lost his temper from her question.

"Gladly." She gave a snide reply before turning around and strutting out of his office. Just as she opened the door he spoke again, making her stop in her tracks.

"You swan around here as if your relationship is perfect. Maybe you need to focus on your own instead of questioning mine."

"Do you see Vinny in here three times a week looking for me because I've completely slipped off the face of the earth?" there was a silence for a moment, she was waiting until she knew Colin was not going to answer her, for fear of proving her point. "I don't care about your relationships Colin, I was just asking a question. Maybe the fact that you're getting so defensive about it proves my point."

"Look at you. So damn smug because you think Vinny's absolutely faultless. You think you're so superior when actually, you only look like a fool and you don't even know it. If you think my relationship has gone to shit yes I'll admit it has okay? That's what you want isn't it?" He was visibly unfolding before her eyes but he wouldn't let any emotion breakthrough in his voice or demeanour other than complete rage. It made Katie take a minute to reassess the reply she had for him in her head. His feelings of inadequacy that she had seen come through at the Gala all those weeks ago and at Thanksgiving last year were beginning to show again, making her soften her voice and her facial expression but he was not backing down any time soon.

"N-no Colin. I don't want that." Her voice was gentle and she took a few steps toward his desk, catching his eyes with her deep stare. "That's not what I wanted, I want you to just be happy-"

"Bullshit Katie. You've been poking holes in my relationship from the very start."

"Colin?" she didn't want him to think of her the same way he thought about his family.

"God, you're such a hypocrite. If you think my relationship is bad, trust me, yours is much worse." She was puzzled by his words and needed to know more.

"What are you talking about?" she asked in bewilderment.

"You're so oblivious. You think Vinny is so perfect and innocent."

"Okay Colin you need to just spit it out already. For months- ever since you found out about us- you've been hinting at something. What is it about Vinny that you don't like huh? Why are you so angry with me for being with him?" she didn't understand but judging by the grim look that appeared on Colin's face, she knew the answers she was waiting for weren't going to be good.

Silence fell in the office for a minute or two as Colin battled with himself, feeling split in two. He was stuck, wanting to tell Katie the truth about Vinny but knowing that it would probably upset her made him hesitate but only for a moment. Any questioning he was doing in his head was forced to stop by this gust of fury he was feeling.

For a moment, he did not think, he did not worry about the consequences, all that mattered was making her feel something other than joy. He felt terrible and wanted her to feel that way too, but this was just temporary. He knew deep within that telling her like this was not the right thing to do, he had promised to leave her with her happiness and allow Katie to find out the truth herself but he just couldn't wait any longer for her to realise.

"You think I have bad habits? One of the reasons we never ended up together was because of what you found in my jacket that morning. But trust me Katie, Vinny is far worse." He stood up then from his desk and came around to stand right in front of her.

She didn't know what to think once he spoke, she was confused because she was sure she would've found something by then. She and Vinny were together a couple of months.

"What do you mean Colin?" He could tell by the tone in her voice that she did not believe him.

"I have to get my coke from somewhere and more specifically, your boyfriend." He sniggered at her, the light in his bright blue eyes turned to burning evil.

"That's not true-"

"You think he's a tailor Katie?" he asked with wicked laughter following his words. "He's laundering money through his business for christ's sake, how oblivious can you be?" he exclaimed in exasperation, bringing her to speechlessness.

"I-I..." She didn't know what to say because she was in complete disbelief.

"Why don't you check his coat pockets next time you see him? I'm sure there'll be a lot more than a gram or two of cocaine."

Katie's eyes didn't well up with tears, she did not slump down in posture or even get angrier and shout at him. The look on his face was smug and confident, she wouldn't give him the reaction he was looking for. Instead, she walked out of the room saying nothing at all, she stopped quickly to get her things from her office next door and left the building straight after.

She didn't know what to do, whether to even believe Colin's story. She was never one to jump to conclusions suddenly, she needed time to think before she confronted Vinny and asked him for herself but how could she do it? She was afraid of what truth might be and didn't want Colin's words to be true. She loved Vinny, but if she found out the accusations were correct, she knew they couldn't be together.

Colin stood in his office for a couple of minutes in shock. He wished satisfaction would engulf him but he did not feel any sort of content from telling Katie about Vinny. In fact, he almost regretted it. The look on her face when she heard, how her features became void of any emotion after his last words made a sinking feeling in the pit of his stomach. Disappointment filled him up, not at anyone else but himself.

**24**

CHAPTER 23

September 2010

Katie felt numb. Her eyes became dull, losing their sparkle after they set their sights on the contents of Vinny's pockets. The air was knocked out of her and it took her a moment to be able to take a breath. Her head had told her to believe Colin but her heart needed proof, and she had certainly gotten it then. She stood there in her bedroom on her own, left speechless as she stared down at the two or three little baggies she had taken from her boyfriend's jacket.

She knew it wouldn't take long for Vinny to be finished his shower, the bathroom was just down the hall so she should be expecting him soon enough. Katie suddenly felt fear wash over her, she wasn't sure she was quite ready for a confrontation. Many thoughts filled her head, different scenarios that she judged for the best choice because she was frozen, she had no idea what to do.

Maybe it would be better to just tell him to leave and not speak to him again, or maybe she did need to talk to him before she broke things off. She could hear the bathroom door opening and footsteps, panic consumed her. Her eyes welled with tears, that was the first thing he noticed when he entered the room. The second was the contents in her hand.

Their eyes latched onto each other and for a moment, nothing was said, nothing needed to be said. But then, the moment passed and Katie finally spoke.

"Why was this in your pocket Vinny?" he had never heard her voice sound so vacant and broken before. It surprised him but then his walls came up, he was more concerned about her fishing through his things than how disappointed she looked right then.

"What the fuck are you doing going through my stuff?" His tone was stone cold and harsh to her ears. She could tell he was angry, but she was too.

"I asked you first."

"Give me those. They aren't for me." He snatched the baggies out of her hand, he was meeting with someone later who needed them.

"Is this what you do? You aren't really a tailor, are you? You've been lying the entire time- god I'm so stupid."

"You weren't supposed to see those." His voice trailed off as he spoke, he stuffed the baggies back into his jacket pocket and went to the other side of the room to find his clothes.

"Well I did. Now answer me." She demanded. He put his pants on and buckled his belt, never once looking at her.

"It's really none of your business Katie-"

"None of my business?" she asked in vexation. "I'm your girlfriend Vinny. I deserve to know who you really are?"

"I'm still the same person Katie." He sighed.

"You've been lying to me this entire time, for months about what you do." She was beginning to visibly become more upset by the minute but she refused to allow any sadness to come through in her voice, only anger.

"Why does it matter what I do?"

"You're some sort of drug dealer, I can't be with someone like that." She exclaimed in irritation.

"Now how did you figure all that out by just looking through my pockets?" he was suspicious and knew that she must have found out from someone else.

"It all makes sense now." She mumbled, but never replied to his question because she didn't want to tell him that the only reason she even began looking through his things in the first place was because of the things Colin said the day before. Emily had thought there was something off about him in the beginning, she had told Katie to be careful but it was only then that she remembered her friend's warnings.

"Katie this doesn't have to be that big of a deal."

"But it is, I can't be with you." She seemed to be in a daze then, she spoke but it seemed like it was more to herself. Her features had become vacant but there was a hint of sadness there too that came with the realisation of her words.

"Everything was fine before you found out, can't we just go back to how we were five minutes ago?"

"I can't ignore it Vinny. You don't understand."

Everyone was free to do as they pleased, but his line of work was something Katie felt was immoral. She had seen what drugs did to her mother. Her addiction completely destroyed her. Katie knew she didn't want to be with anyone who supplied drugs for people, it would completely go against everything she believed in. Vinny couldn't understand, he thought she was just being dramatic, but that was because he did not know about her past.

Memories flashed before her eyes, all of the times as a young child finding her mother passed out in their house, how she would be left alone for days to fend for herself as young as the age of five, the way her mother would lash out at her and her sporadic behaviour. Katie was only young when all of this happened, but there were still memories that couldn't be repressed. Once she remembered her childhood, she could barely look at Vinny.

"Why the hell not?" he moved closer to her, making her back away just a little bit.

"I'm just not into all that stuff."

"All that stuff? You don't have to be. It's how I make my money, usually girls don't care where it comes from. They're just happy I have a lot of it."

"Well that's not me."

"You didn't mind going to Bora Bora with it." With every step she took back, he took another towards her until she stopped backing away, she didn't want to give the impression that she was afraid of him. Vinny's anger was beginning to flare so she tried to deal with the situation as best she could.

"That's before I knew about it, if I found out before then we wouldn't have even gone together. We wouldn't be dating. If you want half the money for the trip, you can have it. I don't need your dirty money, I have my own." She said. She seemed to be somewhat proud of herself, Vinny noticed and laughed wickedly at her.

"Money is money. So what if it's dirty?"

"Vinny, I don't care what you think about it anymore. I want you to leave. I already told you I don't want to be with you anymore. I just can't, and I can't ignore what you do just because-"

"We're going to be fine Katie. You just need some time."

"I've had enough time, I don't need anymore. We're finished." She was beginning to become irritated by his ignorance. And even though he was standing over her, a menacing look in his eye, she wasn't going to back down.

"We aren't over yet."

"Yes, we are." She refused to look away from his stare although she was more than a little nervous then, what would he do next? He was fuming but she didn't care.

"Didn't you hear me?" he grabbed her arm tight, when she tried to pull away he only held on tighter. She tried not to wince in pain as she pushed him away from her.

"Get your fucking hands off me." She said as he stumbled a bit, taken aback. "You think you can try to intimidate me and I'll shut up? I don't want to be with you anymore. We're. Done. Now get the hell out." She needed to raise her voice but hoped Emily wasn't woken up by all the commotion. When Vinny stood frozen in his spot she pushed him again, he was kind of shocked at first but didn't have time for this girl anymore, she was clearly crazy. He would find someone else quick enough.

"Oh don't worry, I'm going." He said as he grabbed his things.

"Why haven't you left already then? Hurry the fuck up." She watched as he quickly got everything together and left her apartment.

As soon as he slammed her front door shut, her rage was replaced with total heartache and anguish. Vinny had shown his true colours and it made her feel so mindless. Over the past few months she had fallen in love with a man who she couldn't be with anymore. Colin had warned her but she didn't listen, he watched as she became smitten with him. He was right, she was a hypocrite, but it was not on purpose. Katie broke things off with Vinny and it was finally sinking in that she couldn't be with him anymore.

The tears she would not allow Vinny to see fell gracefully down her cheeks as she sat in silence in the living room of her apartment. She stayed there like that for a while until Emily came out after hearing her sobs. But it didn't matter how much guidance and reassurance her friend gave, Katie still felt the pain of the relationship she had just ended.

Colin made his way into work that morning earlier than he had been in the past couple of weeks. He just wanted to see her badly, yet she was nowhere to be seen. He looked in her office, hopeful that she would be where she usually was, organising or taking messages at her desk. But when Colin realised she was not there, his stomach dropped.

He put his things in his office and went to the front desk immediately.

"Where's Katie?" he asked Patrick who was opening emails on his computer. Colin tried not to sound frantic but Patrick could sense there was something strange about his demeanour.

"Um, she called in sick today. I thought she would've told you but I guess not. She said she might need another day or two off but things should be back to normal next week.

"Oh... Okay. Thanks Patrick." Colin politely replied before going back to his office where he sat in a quiet that was everything but peaceful. He tapped his fingers on the hard wood of his desk, not quite sure what to do next, if there was anything that could even be done.

She was surely upset about their conversation but which was upsetting her more, the fact that she had finally found out the truth or the way she had found out from Colin. He knew it was the wrong way to let her know, but in his blind rage, he couldn't help himself and now he was regretting it.

Colin felt like nothing could distract him from the feelings that were beginning to creep up on him, not work or Leila or a night out on the town. He wanted to apologise but wasn't sure how she would take it. Katie didn't return to work until the next week and over the excruciating weekend Colin had to endure, he often had the urge to turn up at her apartment unexpectedly. But that would be inappropriate and he was almost sure that she would send him away from the door.

When Monday finally rolled around, Colin made sure he was in work early that day for her arrival. He could see her mope into her office from the windows of his own and until then, he wanted to knock at her door and talk to her but once he saw the dejected look on her face, everything stopped. Colin admitted to himself that he was a coward, and that he couldn't face her just yet so decided to stay in his office until she came to him.

But Colin was left waiting until the early afternoon when he couldn't put it off any longer- they had a lunch meeting to go to. He grabbed his things and hesitantly knocked on her office door. Once he heard her faint voice saying, "come in", he entered and stood in the doorway, as if taking a step closer to her would result in a terrible thing to happen. She hadn't looked up yet from her work, too engrossed in all the catching up she had to do because of her absence.

"Um... Are you ready to go?" he eventually had to speak first but his words came out jumbled and awkward.

"Huh?" she looked up at him then, their eyes catching for a moment as he drank in every inch of her features wrapped in despair. She had dark circles under her tired eyes but looked as if she had tried to cover them up. "To go where?" She asked.

"We have a, uh, a lunch meeting today. If we don't leave soon we might be late."

"Sure. The meeting- let me get my coat." She seemed to be in a daze that was difficult to get out of and all the way to the restaurant, she said very little.

Katie took notes and listened as carefully as she could but she wasn't the only one distracted, Colin was engulfed by her mood. He wanted to just make her feel better again. After the meeting with the client finished, he asked did Katie want to stay for a while for a coffee but she declined.

"Why don't we stay? Just for a little while." There was a silence for a moment after his suggestion. She avoided eye contact but had gotten used to it by then.

"No. I have a lot of work to do, I should probably get back. I need to catch up." When Katie spoke, she was completely deflated.

The rest of the day at work was the exact same. Katie didn't go near his office, she didn't drop in to give messages and she stayed in her office doing the piles of work she had put off, her door closed tight. As the hours passed, Colin couldn't seem to shake the knot in his stomach, the guilt he felt for making Katie feel the way she did, it was partially his fault.

Sometimes, he wondered if it would have been better to just tell Katie from the beginning about who exactly Vinny was but was it really his place? She would be angry that he was intruding on their relationship but at least she would not feel as much heartache as she did right then. He would have been damned if he did, damned if he didn't and he had already made his decision, he had already held off telling the truth to allow Katie to discover things for herself but was unable to hold his tongue for that long.

It was the first time in months that he left work late that day. A million things were running through his head and it had been so difficult to get any work done so he decided to go home and try again the next day. The office was almost empty when he walked to reception where Patrick was packing away his things.

"You're here late Mr. Anderson?"

"You sound surprised- never mind, I'm surprised too..." Colin mumbled to himself as Patrick chuckled.

"I'll see you tomorrow sir." He nodded before he walked towards the elevator but Colin lingered in his spot for a while.

He noticed Katie's light in her office was still on, he hoped she wasn't working too hard. She would be exhausted from all the catching up she was trying to fit into one entire day. Something in him drew him toward her door, he couldn't resist and he had something to say that couldn't be held in any longer. He wasn't quite sure how he was going to say it, but he needed to at least try to talk to her.

He knocked and waited for her answer before walking in and looking directly at her. He didn't sit down, only stood frozen in his spot in front of her desk.

"Wow, I wasn't expecting you to still be here." She tried to find some humour in the surprise of his presence but failed. A thick, musky stillness evaporated into the air between them. In that time, she checked her watch and realised she should be heading home.

Katie was left waiting for Colin to speak again as she had nothing more to say. She wrapped her coat around herself and began walking towards the door when Colin took her wrist, the contact immediately grabbing her attention.

"I-I'm sorry." Was all he could say. A lump formed in her throat that she tried to gulp back. What could she say next? What was there to do in this situation?

"I'm sorry too." Her voice was barely above a whisper, raspy and full of raw emotion.

"I should have handled the whole thing better. I shouldn't have told you the way I did. But I knew if I told you in the beginning you would think I was meddling with something that was none of my business."

"God I'm so stupid." She shook her head and spoke more to herself than to Colin. "I should have listened to you when you warned me about him." Tears pricked her eyes and he could tell how she was visibly unravelling right in front of him.

He reached out then and cupped her cheek, rubbing his thumb over her soft skin as some sort of solution to her sorrow. She welcomed the contact, tilting her head a little into his hand. They shared a moment where Katie felt completely vulnerable, she allowed his touch to transport her back to all those months ago when they shared a kiss, when they planned to give a relationship together a try.

Maybe it was from the heartbreak Vinny left her feeling that forced her to think irrationally for those couple of minutes alone with Colin in her office that night, or maybe that was an excuse. Maybe it was because truly, she believed Colin shouldn't be with Leila, but with her instead- though there were too many complications that a relationship with him would entail. They couldn't be together, but just for that short time, she imagined they could.

# 25

CHAPTER 24

August 2018

Katie looked at her watch for what felt like the millionth time that morning, still deciding if what she was about to do was the best decision possible- for herself of course, not for Colin. She needed to think about herself, she had said that the day she said goodbye to him five years ago and it was still something she found difficult to do at times. Had she only agreed to meet with Colin because she knew it was what was best for him? Or did she genuinely want to see him again too? She was confused because she didn't know which of the two was correct.

She had convinced herself after a couple of quiet moments spent alone in her apartment that she was going for coffee that morning for both herself and Colin. Closure was the reason that seemed to fit best in her mind, although her heart had a problem with that. Closure meant this was all going to come to an end, closure meant saying goodbye for good and Katie didn't know if she wanted that or not.

Letting go of Colin would be the most challenging thing she would ever have to do, it was something she needed to be completely sure about before doing and she was lacking any sort of certainty. Colin being clean could completely change their relationship, it could be the reason their exchanges would be different from the past, but Katie had to forgive and let him in again if she wanted any sort of close contact with him again after today-which was also something she didn't know if she wanted or not.

Colin found her very convincing the other day, judging from her attitude, tone and demeanour, this would be the last time he would ever be talking to her again. And although it was a sad day for him, he still had that glimmer of hope left inside. It wasn't as strong as the other day when Katie agreed to meet up with him, in fact, it was almost non-existent but still, a small bit of optimism lingered in his brain. He hoped he could get her back, but the chances were very slim. Even that realisation, that he may be setting himself up for rejection and failure, didn't seem to faze him.

She was a bundle of nerves as she good ready for the day ahead of her, which she knew would not be a walk in the park and surely would take a toll on her emotions. As Katie looked in the mirror at her appearance, she noticed the wrinkles forming around her eyes, her aging face was as it used to be except for some minor changes that she zoned in on all too often. Her hands were shaky as she put on her makeup, noticing how close to the time of her meeting it was becoming.

Katie had never felt so torn in two before in her life, not even when she was deciding whether to leave Colin and go out into the world on her own five years ago. She felt weak, she felt alone and she felt like she needed someone to just make the decision for her. Could she ever forgive him? Or would she rather live her life keeping him as a distant memory, one she would never forget, one she clung on to many nights she spent alone wondering why every other relationship after Colin had never worked out. One she also tried to push away when she tried to move on from him.

Going to see him that day would either be eye-opening or would be a tragic goodbye- she wanted to wait and see which of the two would come of their discussion but also, Katie felt like not even turning up at all. She needed to make up her mind, she had little time left and the clock was ticking. Would she stay or would she go?

It took every bit of courage left inside Katie to calm herself, take a deep and grab her bag. She needed answers from him, she needed to hear about how his life was going since she left, she needed to see him again. There could be no denying this and so, she followed her heart and ignored her head.

## 26

## CHAPTER 25

March 2011

"Katie, it's so nice to see you again." Katie jumped in surprise when she heard the familiar voice of Colin's older brother, Andrew, who had just walked up to her and stood beside her.

She was outside the huge house on the veranda that overlooked the huge grounds of the house when he spotted her and noticed she was alone.

"Hi Andrew, I didn't see you there for a minute." She laughed a little.

"Where's Colin?" He was surprised he had left her on her own.

"He's inside with um, Olivia." The woman's name burned her tongue, but she really wished it hadn't. "I just needed some air so I came out here."

"She's a real handful huh?" Andrew nudged Katie who clearly felt some kind of apprehensive talking about the subject. His light-heartedness calmed her down a little and she let out a small chuckle after he spoke.

"I don't think I should say." Katie raised her eyebrows then laughed again. Not only did she not think it was appropriate, she genuinely didn't know what to say about Colin's new girlfriend. Well, she wasn't that new anymore, they had been together since December. He seemed to be completely smitten with Olivia and everything about their relationship made Katie green with jealousy in the beginning, but right then she just felt deflated. Also, Olivia didn't seem to like Katie very much which also made it difficult for her to be around the couple.

"Oh come on, we're all thinking it. Colin hasn't figured it out yet but Olivia is really one to watch." Katie furrowed her brows at Andrew's forwardness.

"What's that supposed to mean?" Katie seemed a lot more offended than he had expected.

"Well... She's different to Laila, she's smart and she knows exactly how to make Colin do what she wants. She has him wrapped around her little finger. It's quite strange seeing my brother like that with a girl."

"I don't think we should be critiquing Colin's relationship. He's old enough to work things out himself." Katie didn't believe a word of what she was saying, but she felt the need to lie and pretend Colin had everything worked out- she didn't like how Andrew was already analysing his brother's girlfriend when he probably didn't know much about her. Maybe she was being over sensitive because of all the things Colin had told her about his over-bearing and criticising family but Andrew needed to reassure her he didn't mean to offend.

"My apologies Katie if you think I'm over stepping, but with Colin, sometimes you have to."

"I can't say I agree." She was still being polite while trying to express her opinion, influenced clearly by Colin because she had seen first-hand how affected he was by his family's constant criticism.

"Look, you don't know Colin like I do. I'm not like Kevin, I know Colin might have already tried to distort your view of me because he hates us all but I'm really just trying to look out for him. We all are, minus Kevin maybe..." he said the last sentence more so to himself than to Katie but she still heard it. "I don't think Olivia's good for him. Sure, she's not as bad as Laila but there's still something about her that just doesn't sit well with me. I'm trying to figure it out."

Katie understood although she refrained from voicing her agreement for Colin's sake. She felt like it would be betraying him to be talking behind his back about Olivia with Andrew. She did however, think Andrew was not like Kevin despite Colin tarring his whole family with the one brush. Kevin was mean and condescending, he always had something snide to say to Colin when he saw him but Andrew, he was different. Colin just hadn't figured that out yet.

"Well she hasn't done anything for me to question their relationship yet so until then I don't think I should be talking about it with you. I understand your concern though, Colin doesn't seem to have any luck with his er... previous girlfriends."

"How did my brother ever find such a level-headed person like you to be in his life?" Andrew asked in some sort of astonishment that forced her to look at him directly for a moment to detect any sarcasm but found none.

"It's not like we're married or anything, I'm just his PA." Katie snorted.

"But you get along with him." Andrew's surprised caused her to question him.

"Why wouldn't we?" she asked before taking a sip of her mimosa, humoured by Andrew.

"You're so sensible and he's- crazy." Katie erupted in laughter then.

"Sensible? I don't know whether I want to take that as a compliment or an insult."

"Why's that?"

"Because Grandma's are sensible, I'm not sure I want to be viewed as a grandma just yet."

"It wasn't meant as an insult, I assure you." He laughed then too because grinning at her.

"I suppose anyone would seem sensible when compared to Colin..."

"Very true."

"He's calmed down a bit since his high school days, but trust me, he's still crazy."

"Really? I can't imagine Colin being worse than he already is." She wanted to know more.

"He was certainly the wild child of the family... God he was such a nuisance for my mom and dad a couple of years ago."

"How?" she noticed how Andrew seemed to be humoured

"If someone told Colin to do one thing, he would do the opposite. Even if he wanted to do the thing someone told him to do, he just wouldn't because he hated being told what to do." Andrew shook his head and the pair chuckled together. "He was a nightmare when we were younger. I remember growing up how bad the arguments would get between him and my parents- it was serious at the time of course but looking back now it's quite funny. You just couldn't tell him what to do at all."

"He sounds like he was a bit of a handful."

"He sure was..."

"Andrew, Katie." Just then, Jeffrey walked outside and nodded at the two of them. "Your mom's looking for you."

"I better go find her then. Bye Katie, nice catching up again."

"See you." She was left standing beside Jeffrey then and felt like it might be time to look around for Colin and Olivia.

"Are you enjoying your morning?" he decided to ease into conversation with her before he brought up what he needed to say to her.

"Yes, thanks Mr. Anderson for the wonderful food."

"It's the least I could do for you Katie." She looked confused then so he continued. "You've really been trying your best to whip Colin into shape. I know it can't be easy working with him but I never thanked you fully for helping him out and trying to get him to work harder- although I'm not sure anyone's help could actually make him a changed man."

"He goes through phases a lot." Katie nodded, talking about how Colin's performance in work varies depending on his moods, she had picked up on this over the past two years of working for him. "He really does try though."

"Even Carrie has noticed the difference. When he works, he definitely works well. But when he doesn't, he's back to his old self and goes missing for days..."

Jeffrey felt torn in two as he stood there with one of the only people in his son's life that genuinely cared for his well-being. He knew Katie was over-qualified and was a great worker, he had a job opening up at the company that was better paying and more suited to Katie's qualifications but he wasn't sure if he wanted to take her away from Colin since she had such a huge effect on him. But he knew Colin was holding Katie back, she could do so many other great things for the company other than trying to boss his son around for his own good.

"How would you feel about a promotion?" he decided he would only ask and not promise anything to Katie first.

"Promotion?" she was a little shocked.

"Yes."

"What would the promotion be? I take over what Colin's doing and run the company?" she asked with humour in her voice before they both laughed. She wasn't taking him seriously; what promotion could she get from her position she was working in already?

"I know you made the presentation last year Katie."

"What?"

"Colin told me, it's alright, I was mad at him- not you." She relaxed a little then but was still confused. Colin never told her and Jeffrey was only confronting her then, months later.

"I was just trying to help him out Mr. Anderson. I'm sorry."

"I understand Katie. But what you did was great work and ever since I've been wondering if you were hired for the wrong job at my company..." Katie was surprised to hear this and was left unsure how to reply to Jeffrey.

"I-"

"Don't worry, I don't want you to make any decisions right now. But I do want you to be aware that I've noticed all your hard work and if you ever did want to look into a different position at work, I'd be willing to tell you more about it."

"Thank you Sir." Katie gave him a polite smile and nodded There was no time to continue their conversation because before she knew it, Colin was walking towards her, a quizzical look in his eye.

"Katie? I've been looking everywhere for you. What are you doing out here?" Trying to get away from you and your girlfriend... She thought to herself but knew she would never admit the truth.

"I was just getting some air."

"Let's go back inside." Colin didn't speak to his father, only eyed him with curiosity before taking Katie's hand and leading her inside.

"Bye Mr. Anderson." Katie managed to say before she was taken inside. Colin's father nodded at her and gave her a warm smile.

Katie didn't want Colin to let go of her hand but as soon as they were deeper into the house, he dropped his hand back down to be by his side.

"Where were you?" he seemed annoyed.

"I was outside? You literally just came out and found me there?" she tried to add humour to the conversation but the sly smile on her face didn't seem to make the concerned look on his disappear.

"Yes, but why? Why were you talking to my dad?"

"He just spotted me outside and struck up a conversation Colin. Why are you being so paranoid about everything?"

"Nothing... it doesn't matter. I thought you'd left without saying goodbye." The way he said it sounded as if it was the worst thing she could ever do.

"No, but I actually should get going soon. I haven't even started packing for my trip yet." The trip, Colin had almost forgot about Katie's trip to see her friends from Detroit. He knew it was only for a couple of days but he would miss her.

"Please, stay for just a little while. I won't see you until Thursday."

"I'm sure you'll survive." She scoffed.

She didn't know how to take his words. They annoyed her but at the same time she though he was being sweet. Even though he had been dating Oliva, Colin continued to flirt and suggest that he cared about Katie more than a friend should. What was he playing at? She wondered, which made her decide maybe it was best that she did call a cab and head home. She pulled out her phone and began to order a taxi.

"I'm going tonight and I haven't got anything ready. I better head home."

"Katie..." he sounded disappointed.

"C'mon, walk me out?" he said nothing but nodded at her before they stood out at the entrance to wait for the car to turn up. This was the first time that day she had got to see Colin alone but she wasn't happy about that anymore.

"I wish you didn't have to go yet."

"You have Olivia for company anyway. I don't know why I even still go to these things." Katie mumbled the last sentence but she knew Colin would still hear her.

"Don't you want to anymore?"

"Sure, but the only reason I started was because you didn't want to face your family on your own. Now you don't so I don't think there's any point in me still being here. I talk to someone else here and you quiz me about it as if your family are plotting against you or something."

"I thought you liked coming here. I'm sorry, you know how I get about my dad and stuff. You were with Olivia and I, then the next you were just gone."

"I do like coming here, but I'm third-wheeling now and it's not like you really need to invite me anymore."

"So you want me to stop bringing Olivia here?" he sounded her but it only angered her more although on the outside, she seemed calm and ready to further their discussion.

"Of course not. God that would just make things even worse..."

"What's that supposed to mean?"

"She doesn't like me Colin. God, how can you even ask me that?" Katie said in exasperation.

"She does like you-"

"Listen I don't need you to try and convince me, I'm not offended. She doesn't need to like me, I'm just your assistant. But I guess I'd rather just avoid having to be around you two together all the time."

"You're my friend too."

"I know." She rolled her eyes but on the inside, she wished she didn't act so jealous and mean in this conversation. "I just know we don't get along, and that's fine. I think it's probably better that I don't come here anymore."

Katie was surprised by how hurt he looked from her statement but even Colin was not worth putting up with Olivia's snide comments and strange looks. In the beginning, Katie came as some sort of support system for Colin because of how sensitive he was to his family, but he had Olivia for support if ever he needed any then and Katie was happy leaving the duties to her for as long as their relationship lasted- which she assumed wouldn't be long.

Despite Andrew's thoughts about his brother being wrapped around Olivia's little finger, she knew that cracks were already beginning to appear but only small things. Sure, Colin was smitten with Olivia but he was a guy who was easily impressed by women. Once, he was smitten with Anna and Leila, but that didn't mean they would stay together forever. This time, she knew there were some differences and the intensity of Colin's feelings towards Olivia were stronger than she had seen in any of his other relationships but Katie just felt like Colin would always be a bad boyfriend after a while. He lost interest quickly and was careless, that's without even considering his reckless behaviour towards himself that would come out for everyone to see in great bouts.

Colin may have been a bad boyfriend and Katie could see this clearly, but that didn't mean she didn't want him. Katie couldn't shake the feelings that had begun to appear again for her boss. And the cliché line that you always wanted what you couldn't have was playing over and over in her head. She couldn't have him, she couldn't want him and that was final.

"But I want you to. I really do-"

"What are you two doing out here?" Olivia asked with great curiosity. She looked at Katie first before turning her gaze to Colin, the look on her face saying everything.

"We were just talking."

"What do you want her to do?" Olivia crossed her arms, acting as if she was almost hurt by Colin's meaningless words from the conversation she had just walked in on.

"Nothing Olivia, we can talk about this later okay? I'm just saying bye to Katie before she leaves for her trip tonight."

"I'll be inside waiting." Olivia gave Katie one last suspicious look before she entered the house again.

"Bye Olivia." Katie waved awkwardly at the other woman who had already turned her back to them.

"I'll see you Thursday." Katie put both hands on either side of his shoulders in an attempt to soothe the frown lines forming on his face.

"I'll see you then." Colin hugged her then, holding on tight and forgetting their discussion only moments ago. He felt disappointed once she finally pulled away and began to make her way down the steps of the entrance to the house.

"Colin?"

"Yes?"

"Try to be good, okay?" her voice had a hint of humour to it but also concern, she was afraid of what might happen if she wasn't there.

"I'm always good." A wide grin formed on his face that made her roll her eyes.

"Behave...." She warned him before his grin was too much and she had to join in too. "Goodbye."

**27**

—•—

## CHAPTER 26

April 2011

"Colin, wake up. For god's sake."

"Hmmm." His incoherent mumbles only added to her irritation.

Katie couldn't take it anymore, the past few minutes she had been trying to wake Colin up for work. It was lunch time already and it amazed her how difficult he was finding it to get up. She wanted to shake him then, left with no other option. Or maybe it would have been better to throw water over him, she couldn't decide if that suggestion was too far or not.

"You know what, I don't even care anymore." She said to herself before going into his bathroom and grabbing a glass full of water to pour over him.

"Ah! What the fuck Katie?"

"Great- you're up." She stood beside his bed and crossed her arms.

"Thanks to you." He said sarcastically.

"It's half one Colin, work will be over in a couple of hours and you're still in bed."

"That was the point. I was going to skip today."

"Skip? What are you in high school again?"

"I wish."

"Colin."

The way she said his name instantly drew his attention towards her. Katie's voice as full of worry and doubt and the expression on her face was no different. She was concerned for him, especially when she saw the state he was in once he sat up to look at her. Katie was tired of standing and so perched down on the side of his bed and turned to him. He said nothing, only looked at her, waiting. Because he knew what was coming next.

"You can't keep doing this Colin." Her lips were pursed into a thin line then, a grim look on her face.

"I'm fine-"

"You don't look fine."

"Well, I'm doing great."

"What happened?"

"What do you mean?" Katie sighed at his attempt to obliviousness.

"Well you haven't been in work all week. You didn't even go to your family brunch last Saturday and no one has seen you that I've been talking to."

"I'm never going to one of those stupid brunches again and you can tell my father that."

Katie realised it all came back to what she thought was the root of the problem- his family, it always was his family.

"What happened?" her brows knitted together with great concern, her voice a little softer than before.

"My dad and Kevin talking shit about Olivia, and of course how much bad taste I have in women when it's none of their business."

Olivia. This was the first time in two weeks that she had heard Colin utter her name. Since her last brunch at the Anderson's home, Katie had realised how the woman's lustre was beginning to dull for Colin. He was no longer wrapped around her little finger as his brother had suggested but there was something that always pulled him back toward her. Even though they clearly weren't right for each other.

"You know nothing I ever do is good enough for any of them, so I don't give a crap anymore."

Katie had heard this so many times before, she almost knew what he was going to say word for word but listened anyway. Colin pretended as if he didn't care, but deep down, there must have been something inside that craved approval or else he wouldn't be the way he was. Katie refrained from saying any of this, she knew how defensive he could get so just listened because for then, that was all he needed.

"Colin, you know I can help you if you want. You don't have to keep doing this-"

"I'm fine Katie. Jeez, I like to have a good time- that's all."

"I'm worried about you." She finally admitted. The glimmer of sorrow in her eye made Colin's chest hurt but he didn't need her help and she couldn't guilt him into going to any sort of therapy or rehab- there was nothing wrong with him.

"Well I can take care of myself, trust me Kate. Now unless you want to see me naked- I'd get out if I were you. I need to get dressed for work. I'm running late in case you haven't noticed." He had returned to his playful self, swiftly changing the topic before Katie could say another word.

"Let's stop off for a quick coffee before we head back-"

"Back? Colin you haven't even entered to go back..."

"C'mon... You know you can't resist."

"Resist what exactly?" she scoffed.

"Spending more one to one time with me."

"Colin, that's all I do with my life nowadays. Look after you, go home, sleep, get up and look after you again."

"You make it sound as if you're my carer not my assistant."

"That's because I am."

"Of course no-"

"How many assistants do you know that own a key to their boss's house and go to wake them up three mornings out of the working week?"

"You're my assistant and my alarm clock then- Let's settle for that." He retorted. Katie tried to hold back her laughter but his care free mood always seemed to loosen her up even when she was stressing over work.

"Fine, whatever. But we're getting coffee to go and then heading straight for work. I have things to do."

"Yeah, yeah, sure."

As soon as they got their coffee Colin followed Katie's instructions. They went straight to work and as soon as the elevator doors pinged open, Olivia greeted them at the main desk. Colin inhaled sharply once he caught sight of her, Katie took note of this but said nothing as the pair walked toward her.

"Hi Olivia."

"Hi." Olivia forced a fake smile as she looked at her boyfriend's PA. A smile Katie knew was false.

"That's a pretty purse. I love the colour." She didn't know why she tried, but every time she saw Olivia she felt the need to try- for Colin's sake.

"Thanks. Colin bought it for me, didn't you honey?" The famous line that Olivia always came out with. Katie had noticed how often the other woman said that in their brief and detached conversations. It was almost as if Olivia was using him in some way- but that was none of her business.

"Yes, now let's go inside."

"Why are you being like that? I haven't seen you in ages and you're acting like you don't care!" Olivia's outburst astounded Katie. There was clearly a reason Olivia's name hadn't been brought up in two weeks- but she decided maybe then was not the time to ask. She would find out later, she always did.

"Olivia, not right now." Colin said with exasperation. "We can talk about this in my office. This is a private conversation that doesn't need to be heard by anyone else but the two of us." He spoke in a hushed tone.

"Fine then." Her eyes burned like rings of fire, glaring at her boyfriend as he took her hand and brought her inside his office.

Katie buried herself in the mountains of work she had in her office for the rest of the work day. It wasn't until she was getting into the elevator to make her way downstairs that she saw Colin again.

"Hey wait for me!" he exclaimed, walking briskly toward the closing doors.

Katie put her hand out to stop them and within no time, the pair were standing awkwardly together in the small space. She wanted to ask about Olivia, but knew it was probably too much of an intrusive question to ask- especially then because things felt different for her.

Katie took a long time to realise her feelings for Colin had crept back up on her again and because of her fresh realisation, she knew it would be over stepping boundaries if she delved too deep into Colin's relationship this time.

"You made it through a half a day's work without imploding, well done Colin." She decided a joke was better than inquisition.

"Thank the lord Kate." He seemed to be a lot perkier than he was a couple of hours ago during Olivia's arrival. "I deserve a drink. Want to come with?" This was nothing new to Katie, Colin had invited her out before for casual drinks now and then, to which she usually declines but that night she decided one wouldn't kill her.

"I think I deserve one too. But just so you remember, we do actually have to do this whole work thing again tomorrow morning- preferably at nine of clock instead of noon like today."

"Sure, you know me Katie, would I ever stay out all night and not show up to work the next day?"

"You'd do it in a heartbeat." She retorted.

"Not tonight, I promise. You'll be with me so I can guarantee I'll be sent home at a reasonable hour to get ready for work tomorrow. Or maybe you'll let loose tonight and we'll both wake up in my apartment with a massive hangover like I did this morning." He noticed how Katie's smile faltered a little at his words and realised what he just said.

"No, I'm sorry. I didn't mean it like that... I meant- Oh nothing."

"It's fine Colin." Katie chuckled at his response. "I know what you meant, don't worry."

"I just didn't want you to think that I meant the two of us would- well you know what I mean anyway..." Katie rolled her eyes, she tried not to feel hurt by his reaction, as if being with her would be awful in some way. But she had to remember- she shouldn't care if he felt like that or not and he was in a relationship so it didn't matter what he thought.

"So, what are you having to drink?" he asked once they set foot in one of the bars nearby.

"Gin and tonic but it's fine, I can get it myself." Katie smiled at Colin before reaching into her purse but instantly stopped what she was doing when Colin put his hand on her arm.

"No, let me. Please... I owe you a lot more than one for the amount of shit you have to put up with." She hesitated for a moment but then decided to let it go.

"Thank you Colin."

"There's no need. Hey why don't you go find somewhere to sit while I order the drinks."

"Sure, if you can't find me, give me a call."

And although Katie promised to only have one, it seemed like the night drifted away on her without giving any signs. She was not completely drunk, but she knew she probably would be soon if she continued drinking at Colin's pace which was reasonably slow on that particular night. She promised the drink she had just gotten would be her last, it was getting sort of late anyway.

"Maybe we should get going after this last one." Katie suggested. "You don't want a repeat of this morning huh?" she nudged him and he nodded with a wide grin on his face.

"You know, you should come out with me some time. It would be fun."

"Aren't we out right now?" Katie asked, her eyebrows raised in a certain way that made Colin chuckle.

"I mean a real night out."

"Colin I know you still think you're in high school but my real nights out are very rare and I'll have you know I wasn't always as sensible as I am now."

"Oh really?"

"Yes, a long time ago- before I became your PA slash carer slash alarm clock." She said sarcastically before taking a sip of her drink.

"When was that exactly? I can't imagine a time when you weren't giving me daily wake up calls."

"College." Her reply made Colin smirk.

"Oh I bet you were a wild one Kate."

"Work hard, party harder." She said dryly causing him to howl with laughter, adding to the already loud background noise. "I'm just kidding, that's kind of a douchey thing to say isn't it? But I'm not kidding about the partying."

"I wish I had've known you then..."

"Why? Am I too boring for you the way I am right now?" Katie raised an eyebrow, a small smirk on her face.

"No... But sometimes you can be very-" he tried searching for the right word as to not hurt her feelings. "Uptight." This made her let out a loud cackle, he was glad she wasn't offended.

"I have to be uptight for the both of us. But trust me, I'm not like that at home."

"I don't believe you but I get it, we work as a great team when you're uptight so I probably should be thanking you."

"You've never really known me besides when I've been working for you, I guess that's why. When I think about it, there's a lot you don't know about me and I've known you like- two years now?"

"Yes, longer than most of my relationships last." This made Katie laugh.

"I know Colin..."

"God I'm such a crappy boyfriend, aren't I?" he sighed before drinking some of his drink and laying it back down on the table, a look on his face that showed some kind of sorrow mixed with regret.

"Hey, I'm sure you're not that bad." She didn't know what to say, because she had worked for Colin through three relationships and his statement seemed to be very true but she couldn't admit that.

"Oh I am. You don't have to tiptoe around it. I never pick the right girls and I get bored so easily because of that. Ever since before you dated Vinny, I've always wondered what it would be like if we were together."

"Col-"

"No hear me out Katie. I know it sounds creepy but I honestly don't mean to be. I just- I don't know, I feel like I might have fucked up with you. It's always been in the back of my head, you know, and maybe that's why I couldn't bear to see you and Vinny together. I should've just told you from the beginning instead of acting like a jealous child about your whole relationship."

Katie had waited months for this and now that Colin was finally admitting his true feelings about everything, she was left speech-less.

"Well it doesn't matter now anyway, you're with Olivia." She felt like she needed to reassure him  that he wasn't missing out on anything, he had Olivia. "You two are-"

"We broke up last week Katie."

"But she was in the office today when we got in?"

"I know, she doesn't seem to really get it. I broke up with her but she keeps trying to get in contact with me. Today I just told her straight, she understands now." Why hadn't he told her? He usually tells her all about his relationships. "I think I was just with her because I knew my family wouldn't like it."

Where was all this honesty coming from? Katie had a million questions running around her head, she didn't know which to ask next.

"Sorry to hear." This made Colin choke a little with laughter.

"Oh don't worry, you don't need to pretend you care. I know you two didn't really get along at all."

"She doesn't have to like me, I understand."

"She does, because you're my friend. She really didn't try at all."

"I'm going to head home, I'm done my drink and I'm up early in the morning. We both are."

"I should get going too then, be the responsible adult I know you want me to be. I'll walk you to your station, c'mon."

They grabbed their things and headed home but the fresh air didn't clear Katie's head like she wished it had. Instead, her head was filled with so many dilemmas, so many what-ifs and she didn't know it but Colin was feeling the same too.

"I feel like I'm always going to wonder what would've happened between us." He decided to be honest, maybe it was a bit of Dutch courage,  but Colin just had to get it off his chest.

"Well you know there was a reason we didn't end up together Colin-"

"What if I quit? I'd stop for you."

"But you need to stop for yourself not me Colin. You don't think you even have an addiction. I'm almost positive you have a little ziplock baggie in your jacket pocket like the one I found months ago. I can't be with someone who does that sort of stuff Colin, I'm sorry."

"But I could do it, I could stop if it meant we could be together, or at least try." The thought sounded nice to Katie but maybe it was a little impractical. "Or else I'm going to be left wondering forever, what would have happened if we ended up together. And I don't want that."

"Neither do I." by then, the two had stopped walking down the quiet street and turned to look directly at each other.

Their honesty had sparked something inside one another, they couldn't believe either one was finally admitting how they really felt. Katie wanted to believe Colin, she wanted to think she was going to be the one thing that made him turn his life around and finally realise his addiction but somewhere in the back of her head, she knew she would be left disappointed. But for then, for just that one night, that one exact moment as they stood filled with quiet excitement at what was going to happen next, she believed him.

He took her in his arms and locked his lips onto hers, something she never thought she missed but she certainly knew it was what she had been craving for months. She wrapped her hands around his neck and kissed him like it was the last time she'd ever see him again.

Before they knew it, they were hailing a cab and heading to Colin's apartment. The night they spent together was worth the wait. Katie felt everything at once, she was infatuated with him for that one night, as he completely unravelled her. Afterwards, she clung onto him like he was her lifeline, for fear that it had all been some sort of dream. He would wake up next to her in the morning and that would make him the happiest person alive, after months of waiting, wanting and yearning, they could finally be together.

**28**

CHAPTER 27

May 2011

Katie attended the Anderson's brunch again, this time she was not tagging along with Olivia and Colin. After their first night spent together, neither could contain their excitement from finally trying to be together. They had both agreed to take things slow, nothing was going to be official for a while as they were still testing the waters. They didn't want anyone to know at work or any of Colin's family to know either, it was only early days and both agreed to keep it to themselves and close friends for the time being.

"Katie! We missed you, glad to see you're back."

"We?" Colin asked with a scoff, his face void of emotion as he spoke to his older brother.

"You know, all of us." Andrew's smile didn't dull despite his brother's clear lack of enthusiasm. He waited for Colin to say something else but instead he only stared at him and took another gulp of his drink. Katie decided to speak to help the awkward encounter.

"Hey maybe we should go find our seats. See you in a bit Andrew." She spoke with a smile on her face but it only made Colin look at the pair of them in disgust, and then of course take another drink.

"When did you two become so close huh?" he asked as Katie practically dragged him away from his brother and towards the dining room.

"Colin, we've always talked a little when I come here. What's wrong with that?"

Katie knew exactly what he would find wrong with that, he wanted her to share the same hatred he had for his family but she couldn't do it. Sure, she wasn't Kevin's biggest fan, but she genuinely did believe Andrew had his brother's best interest at heart, just like his father although he was a bit more forceful with his feelings towards Colin's bad decisions.

"What's wrong with all my family kissing your ass this whole time we've been here? Hmm, I don't know..."

His snarky remark made her quieten down a bit, she didn't want to have an argument with him over something as ridiculous as this. Just then Colin stopped a waiter and placed his empty glass down on his tray before swiftly picking up another full mimosa.

"Hey maybe you should slow down a little."

"All that ass kissing's starting to make you sound like them."

Katie couldn't keep quiet about that comment and stopped completely in her tracks to stand there and look at him. She remained calm, because she knew he was probably hurting and going through a difficult enough time already, he'd been trying to stop completely with the drink and the drugs but it was extremely hard for him. This was the first time in two weeks that he'd taken a drink and she didn't want him to just throw all his progress down the drain because he was hurting. Instead, she wanted him to talk to her.

"Colin, please don't be mad because I like talking to Andrew."

"Next you and that bitch Veronica will be best friends." Katie noticed the burning anger in his voice as he mentioned his brother's wife.

"Don't you think you might be overreacting just a little here?"

"No. Of course not."

"Jeffrey's my boss, do you expect me to be horrible to him too? All he has been is nice to me-"

"But you're here for me, not to bootlick."

"You're being so childish right now Colin. When have I ever come here to bootlick?"

"Maybe when you start getting overly friendly with members of my family. They're trying to hook you in, they seem like they give a shit Katie but really Andrew's only trying to get at me by showing interest in how you're doing or whatever kind of shit you two talk about."

This conversation was making Katie feel even more nervous to mention the promotion his father told her about months ago. She had everything figured out in her head, she just hadn't voiced any of it to Colin. The plan was that if they became more serious, she could stop working directly for Colin and take the promotion Jeffrey offered.

Katie would be more suited to the job, people on their floor wouldn't start talking as much about their relationship and they would be able to be together with ease. Taking the promotion would be beneficial, Colin had always said from the start that she was overqualified to work as his assistant but after hearing his comments, Katie thought he might not like the idea and see her as only attending these brunches specifically to get ahead in the company like he suggested a moment ago with his bootlicking comment.

"Can we talk about this later once we get home? Let's try to enjoy the afternoon."

"Sure." He said between his teeth.

All the way through eating together, there was a clear tension that neither mentioned. Katie tried her best to get along with him but he didn't seem to have any filter. His gloomy mood was steady and unchanging, he had a permanent scowl on his face and was sulking. Katie noticed how many more drinks he had over their food and how he was beginning to lose his composure.

Colin had a lot on his mind that afternoon, he was mulling over his situation with Katie and wondering how he had never noticed how much his family seemed to like her. It seemed like if this relationship ever became serous enough to tell his parents, it was going to be the way it was with Anna and he was going to hate everything about it. He didn't want a repeat of Anna, he didn't want Katie to turn out the way she did. Toward the end of his previous relationship with the other woman, Colin had grown to hate the great relationship Anna had formed with close members of his family. She seemed like the perfect girl to settle him down, would Katie become that girlfriend too?

As that thought came to mind, he noticed his mom wave over at himself and Katie, which only added fuel to the fire burning deep within Colin. When had Katie even spoke to his mom before? It was only once briefly a few months ago but Katie knew Colin wasn't aware of that and would overthink the small, friendly gesture that meant almost nothing. Susan Anderson watched as her son glowered at the young woman beside him and then as Katie waved back with huge apprehension.

"Oh come on..." Colin said in exasperation.

"I'm going out to get some air, why don't you come find me when you decide to calm down?" Katie had had enough and threw her napkin down on the table before she got up and walked out of the dining room.

Susan decided to go find out what had just happened and so headed toward her son who only shook his head and sighed to himself, clearly unmoved by how upset the young woman looked as she exited the room.

"Hey son, is everything okay between you and Katie?"

"Why do you care mom? Everything's fine."

"It's just that she looked kind of upset a minute ago-"

"It's good to know your only concern is my assistant."

"Well I came over here to see if you're alright too." Susan said, placing a hand on her son's shoulder before sitting down in Katie's seat next to him. "Are you?" She searched his face, waiting for an answer.

"Yeah, I'm good..." Colin couldn't keep eye contact with her for long, he could see her features dull once she smelled the scent of alcohol off his breath. He noticed that familiar look of pained disappointment on her face that he could never get used to.

"Are you drunk Colin?" Susan asked, her voice remaining gentle and calm. It didn't matter how non-judgemental she sounded, Colin always viewed her as being over-critical and disapproving.

"No, of course not." He stood up then and decided to go look for Katie, leaving his mother behind- her heart breaking just a little bit more at the sight of her son.

Meanwhile, Jeffrey had bumped into Katie and began a conversation with her that Colin would soon walk in on unexpectedly. At first, Jeffrey asked now she was doing but then he asked about the promotion after a minute or two.

"So have you put any more thought into the promotion I offered you a while ago?"

"What promotion?" Katie almost jumped as Colin's scrutinising voice filled her ears. She was left speechless for a moment as he narrowed his eyes at her then his father.

"Colin-"

"Can we talk alone for a minute?" Katie asked.

"I guess so, maybe then you can tell me what the hell he's talking about."

"Excuse us please."

And for a second time that afternoon, Katie was whisking Colin away to avoid conflict with his family. They headed down the halls to one of the bathrooms situated far away from where everyone was in the house. As soon as they got inside, they locked the door and stood staring at each other in silence for a moment.

"So my dad offered you a promotion..."

"Yes."

"When? Why didn't you tell me?" he asked, clearly wounded by the news.

"The last time I came for brunch here. But before you think I came here just to suck up to your family I want you to know that from the beginning, the only reason I ever decided to go was because I knew you needed me."

"I don't know why you expect me to believe that considering you've been keeping this promotion from me for so long."

"Because I didn't think much of it at the time. I work for you and I enjoy it, most of the time. But then when we decided to get together, I thought that maybe it would be a good idea after all. I just didn't want to tell you about it until I figured everything out and if we were serious enough to the point where it would work out better for the two of us to not work so close to each other anymore." Her explanation seemed to make a lot of sense, but Colin was still paranoid.

"You should have told me as soon as my father offered you it-"

"I should have told you? I'm not obligated to tell you anything about that until I hand in my notice actually Colin."

"God, you sound like you're seriously considering it."

"And what would be so wrong with that? You've said from the start that I'm over qualified to be working in the position I'm working in at the minute. At least then I'd be making my own presentations and doing my own work that I don't need to try and pass off as yours."

"Oh whatever, you were stupid enough to do that for me."

"So, I'm stupid now? You didn't seem to have a problem when you took credit for it."

"I didn't take the credit, I told my father afterward that every single thing came from you."

"That's one person out of the room full of people Colin."

"Are you really holding a grudge over that? Is that why you wanted to take the promotion?"

"I just told you I wanted to take the promotion now because I want us to work out and it would be better if you weren't that guy who's dating their assistant."

"Well I don't think that's going to be a problem anymore." He noticed how his words made her face drop, the blood draining from her face as she tried to compose herself again.

"W-what's that supposed to mean?" she still had hope that Colin didn't mean what she thought he had meant.

"I don't want to be with you anymore Katie." The look on her face made his chest ache, but he had decided that day which he cared more about- his family's disapproval or Katie and the former was something he thrived off while the latter would only bring him praise from everyone.

"I know what you're doing Colin. I know. And I think you're insane."

"What is it exactly that you think I'm doing?" he was ignorant to how well Katie knew him. She had delved into the mystery that was his mind and with that, began to realise there were so many underlying reasons behind Colin's actions that even he did not understand. She had never voiced her opinion the way she was about to right then and it made her nervous but there was no time to be nervous, she yearned for him to understand before he made the mistake of breaking things off with her.

"You can't stand being with me if it means that your parents are going to like me the way they liked Anna."

"Don't be ridiculous." He scoffed, crossing his arms then, showing her how confident he was in his reply but it seemed Katie knew him more than he knew himself with this one.

"I'm not being ridiculous Colin. Maybe if you thought things through a bit more, you would understand. You hate that they like me, it makes you hate me too. We haven't had an argument since we got together until we turned up here this morning and you discovered how warm and friendly everyone has been towards me. And now you want to break up? What about everything you told me? What about how much it would kill you to go on and wonder what it could have been like if we tried to be together?"

"I've changed my mind." He said with finality seeping from his voice yet doubt filling him on the inside.

"Why? Because I'm not a gold digger like Olivia? Or because I'm not annoying enough like Laila?" She waited for a reply but he had nothing to say, he could barely even look at her.

"If you want to be a drunken mess your entire life who craves that dissatisfaction he gets from everyone that's fine. But I know deep down all you want is approval and if you can't get that, you at least want some sort of attention. You need to grow up Colin."

"I'm not drunk!" he exclaimed, clearly feeling defeated by her words. He couldn't stand her in that moment, because she was so right. He hated how her words were making him feel, how they brought enlightenment he did not need nor want in that moment.

"Whatever you say. I'm leaving." Katie wished she wasn't so petty and scornful about the whole thing, but she couldn't help the fury she felt from Colin's decision. But as soon as she walked out of the room and slammed the door shut, her eyes welled up with excruciating tears.

He wanted to run after her, he wanted to apologise for everything and admit she was right but instead he let his anger consume him.

"God damn it!" he said as he punched the wall next to him. Once, then twice, then for a third time. He didn't know what to do with himself once he realised that any hope of a relationship with Katie, the amazing woman he'd been wondering about for the past two years, had completely disappeared as soon as their conversation had ended.

# 29

## CHAPTER 28

June 2011

"Here I go again..."

"You look amazing as usual Katie."

"Thanks, but I know this isn't my best outfit. I don't think I can pull off the sleeves. I couldn't find anything else on time for the gala so this will just have to do."

"What? Of course you can, you look great."

Emily's words were no comfort to Katie, no matter how much she truly wanted them to be. She needed something to calm her down, she wasn't feeling the best and the fact that she had to be in such close proximity to Colin outside work for a couple of hours was beginning to make her feel like not turning up at all. She knew what to expect when she arrived at this gala but certainly could never prepare herself for what her eyes were about to set sight of: Olivia and Colin as a couple again for the first time since their breakup a few months ago.

"What's wrong?" Emily was worried about her friend and even took a few steps closer to give her a hug as she noticed how close Katie was to losing her composure.

"I-I don't think I can do it Em. I really don't." She could tell by the other woman's voice that she was crying in her arms just then.

"Oh Katie..." she held her friend at arm's length then and looked at her red eyes. "I know it's going to be tough for you, but you'll get through it. You're stronger than you think."

Emily had noticed over the past week how her friend's mood had taken a turn for the worst after that night she came home and told her of the news she'd heard about Colin getting back together with Olivia. As far as Emily knew, Katie and Colin had never addressed their break up fully, it had been over before it even began. Katie could barely even look at her boss before finding out about Olivia, and since her new discovery, she filled up with anger and jealousy mixed into one.

Katie was confused, she didn't know whether to be upset or furious. Work was certainly very complicated when you and your boss hated each other, but they really did try to be civil with each other despite Katie finding it the most difficult. Colin found work agonizing, every time he saw her face it never looked the way it used to be. Her smile and bright eyes had changed to an indifferent frown. She wasn't interested in work, she never turned up at his apartment to wake him up- although he had started again with all the partying so was usually late for work- and avoided talking to him unless essential.

Katie hadn't informed Colin yet that she was looking for a new job, she wanted to be sure about another job before she quit the one she had then. But moving from the company she was in was a must, especially since finding out about Colin's rekindled relationship, she felt so betrayed and couldn't work in such a tense and strained environment for much longer. She was stressed enough, trying to work for a man who barely showed up to work and this time around, Katie wasn't going to help him turn things around. She was sick of trying to make Colin understand that he needed to take work a little more serious, it wasn't up to her to make him get up out of bed every morning, she was just his assistant. This had taken her a long time to realise but she understood then.

Even after she took all these things into account, including the pain he had inflicted on her that she was still feeling, Katie still cared about him. This was why she was crying, this was why she was still so upset. The feelings still felt fresh, they hadn't dulled yet because she still liked him, she still cared and this tore her apart also. She knew she needed to get over him but it wasn't going to be easy.

"I really don't know why I still go to these things... Besides, I'll probably be leaving in the next couple of weeks or so." She said as she tried to meticulously wipe away her tears as to not ruin her makeup.

"Well then why not try to enjoy your last gala? Fuck Colin, don't let him ruin your night or your make up. He isn't worth it and you don't want to let this gorgeous dress go to waste do you?" Emily tried to hype her up and it seemed to be making some kind of small change to Katie's demeanour.

"You're right. If it's going to be my last I should try to have a good time."

"Exactly. When are you supposed to leave?"

"I'm going to call a cab now in a minute, I just need to make sure I didn't ruin my make up too much."

"That's the spirit." Emily smiled at her friend who returned the gesture expect hers was not as bright and big as it usually was. The makeup hid the dark circles Katie had under her eyes from lack of sleep well but Em still knew they were there, she still knew that her friend was hurting badly on the inside. "I'll call the cab for you if you want?"

"Thanks Em."

Katie arrived a couple of minutes late but people were still getting settled for dinner. As soon as she walked into the banquet hall, her eyes were cast on Colin who was clearly drunk already despite it being so early in the evening. She tried to put him out of her mind and immediately looked away, turning her attention to finding her seat. As usual, she was sitting with her friends from the office and dinner was more enjoyable than she had predicted. Just as Colin had completely erased himself from her head for the evening, she noticed a concerned looking Olivia making a beeline for her table.

"Oh god what does she want..." Katie mumbled to herself which made Patrick who was sitting to her right, look directly at the other woman. He noticed how Katie looked anywhere but at Olivia although that certainly was not going to stop her from coming right up to the two of them.

"Katie." Olivia let out a deep sigh as she said the woman's name.

"Yes?"

"I need your help."

"What?" she was confused. Why would Olivia of all people need her help with something?

"Quickly, you need to come with me." She yanked Katie up from her chair and almost dragged her outside and down the hall to the bathrooms.

"Olivia, stop. Just tell me what's happened?" Katie stopped in their tracks as she was led down another hallway.

"It's Colin." The way she said his name sent shivers up Katie's spine. She wondered what could be wrong besides the obvious and why Olivia thought it was even a good idea to get Katie involved in whatever dumb thing Colin had done.

"What about Colin?"

"You need to see him, he keeps asking for you and won't talk to me or let me in."

Katie was shocked, why was he asking for her? She didn't want to see him, especially since he was clearly drunk earlier. She was never fond of Olivia, but the look of desperation in her eyes made Katie feel like she had no choice but to go talk to him. Soon enough she was knocking on a bathroom door and calling his name. She heard his drunken slurs from the other side of the door and then a shuffle before he opened the door and let her in. Katie turned to the other woman.

"Aren't you coming in?"

"He asked for you... He won't come outside until you go in there he said and I need him to hurry up, he has to say his speech soon." To say Olivia felt inadequate at that moment admitting Colin wanted to talk to his PA instead of his own girlfriend would be an understatement but this was serious and she wanted Colin to get his act together for the rest of the night. If that meant allowing Katie to be alone with him to sort things out, she would have to suck it up.

"O-okay."

She closed the door behind her and watched as Colin tried to stand up straight. He was failing miserably and this was clear to her. Neither said a word for a moment as they eyed each other in an eerie silence.

"What's the matter Colin?" she finally asked but she was still wearing that same face she sported in work, indifferent and un-moved- he hated it.

"I-I don't know." She rolled her eyes.

"Why won't you come outside for Olivia? You have to say your speech soon-"

"Screw the speech. I can't go back out there Katie..." She noticed the deep sadness in his admission and it made her chest hurt.

"Why not?"

"I'm not ready."

"Are you ever going to be ready?"

"I know my Dad, he's going to flip." His words were slurred and almost inaudible, his red and bloodshot eyes looked sore and ab-solutely shattered. He was a mess, a drunken state Katie had never witnessed as bad before.

"Maybe you should have thought about that before it was too late."

"Please Katie..." he sat on the closed down toilet seat and covered his face with his hands. "Don't be like that."

"I don't know what you want me to do Colin. I can't magically sober you up in the next ten minutes so you can go out there and face a hall full of people."

Her words were cacophonic and severe as they tumbled out of her mouth but it was only the truth. He took a cigarette out of his pocket then and lit it up which surprised her, she never knew he smoked?

"You shouldn't do that in here. Colin you're a mess, you need to go home-"

"What? And prove to everyone how much of a failure I am?"

"I don't think you're a failure." Her voice was a lot gentler than before, her eyes softened as they caught his. She wasn't lying, she didn't think he was a failure and judging by the look on Colin's face, that was all he needed to hear from her right then. "You're just not in a good state at the minute and you need to go home to sleep this off."

"My dad won't understand." He looked close to tears and it shocked Katie to see him in such a state. The thought of his father's disapproval almost crippling him was evident in the way he sat, spoke, and looked at her. She felt like she needed to protect him, wrap him in her arms for a moment and tell him this would all pass, he would feel better in the morning but that was not necessary.

After all, he wanted this, this was the reason they weren't together. Colin seemed to be falling apart right in front of her eyes, he looked like a different person. Gone was the cocky and confident young man who made her laugh so many times, instead, he was replaced with a timid, doubtful and self-conscious person she had only ever caught glimpses of in the middle of their heart to hearts. It made her forget all the pain he had inflicted upon her for a moment, shattered this façade she had been keeping up for a while. She would help him tonight, but after that, she was done with it all.

"Don't worry about him okay? Let me speak with him. Go home with Olivia and let me sort this out."

Colin was drunk, but he still noticed her change in tone and attitude. He felt like he had gotten to normal Katie back but there was no time to savour the moment. Within seconds she was helping him up and leading him outside to Olivia who was waiting eagerly for them to reappear from the bathroom.

"Bring him home Olivia, I'll deal with Jeffrey."

"But the speech-"

"Do you think he's in any state to say a speech right now?" she narrowed her eyes at Olivia, wondering why she was being so dense.

"No..."

"Colin needs help Olivia. And I think you know what kind of help I'm talking about. He's a mess but it's not up to me to fix him. You're someone who I'm assuming is very close to him, I know you know what he gets up to. This is only going to get worse if you don't talk him into some sort of rehabilitation or therapy." Katie's voice was quiet, not that Colin would be conscious enough to understand the conversation between the two women anyway.

"My boyfriend's fine Katie." Olivia spoke the exact same way Colin had all those times before when Katie brought up this topic. "He's just drunk."

"If you think he's just drunk then you're a moron. I know you know what the problem is, and maybe it was just alcohol tonight, but it's not every other night. He needs professional help but he's in denial about it."

"He'll be fine Katie. Trust me." Olivia put a hand on her shoulder, a condescending gesture that made Katie burn up with anger.

"You're just going to ignore it? It's right in front of you Olivia. Take a fucking look." She pointed at Colin, surprised he was even still standing. "You know what, I'm done. I don't care. Just take him home before anyone else sees him like this. I need to go find Jeffrey."

Katie walked off, leaving the couple alone. Jeffrey wasn't very happy when he heard the news Colin had went home but Katie calmed him down a little. After she was finished what she had to do, she decided it was time to go home too. She was exhausted and more emotionally drained than before she turned up at the gala.

There was no talk of Katie alleviating the problem that night once they were back to work after the weekend. In fact, Colin never mentioned it at all even a week after the gala. Things only went back to how they had been before, both avoiding contact unless absolutely necessary.

It was like any other day at work to Katie until she stepped out of the elevator and spotted Andrew talking to Patrick at reception. She wondered if something was wrong, if she had missed something during her lunch break.

"Andrew? What are you doing here?" Katie laughed a little and smiled at him but then noticed the unwavering dismal shadow that was cast over his features. This conversation wasn't going to be good, she could already tell.

"Hey, have you seen Colin?"

"He didn't turn up this morning but that's normal to be honest. Is something wrong?" Andrew scratched the back of his head, not sure if she knew yet. He didn't want to be the bearer of bad news but the heart wrenching look she gave him made him feel like he had no other choice. Katie was bound to find out anyway.

"I-I don't know if I should tell you yet.." Andrew always felt like there was something more between Colin and his assistant, something more than just a work relationship or friendship. This made him unsure of how she would take the news.

"Did something happen to Colin?" She looked concerned then, he couldn't keep it a secret then, he had already said too much so why not just tell her to whole story.

"He proposed to Olivia."

Katie's stomach dropped once she heard Andrew's confession. All of her senses seemed to fizzle out for just a couple of seconds as she tried to fully comprehend his sentence. It was too difficult, she didn't believe him.

"W-what?"

"He asked Olivia to marry him and they plan on getting married like, really soon. My dad's freaking out because Colin doesn't want to draw up a pre-nup and now he's threatening to cut Colin out completely if he doesn't."

"So, why are you here then?" The blood drained from Katie's face. She wasn't over Colin yet but he certainly was over her.

"To try and talk some sense into him. You know I really try not to get too involved in things between him and my dad but this time I have to step in. This is very serious and dad's not going to lose any part of this company to that gold digger Olivia."

She was trying to come to terms with the news and at the same time not show any signs that it affected her deeply in front of Andrew but that was proving very challenging. She felt so powerless and stupid for ever falling for a man like Colin. She couldn't control her feelings and he kept making her feel worse.

"Katie?" Andrew asked after a moment or two of silence. She seemed to be in a daze.

"Oh yes, sorry. Um... I'm sure he'll turn up in the next couple of minutes, he usually does after lunch. Do you want to go wait in his office?"

"That would be great, thanks."

"No problem, go right in."

She put on a front, but as soon as she got into her office and closed the door, she completely unravelled into a shattered mess. She felt so empty, so used but still, she couldn't find the anger to despise Colin. In fact, it only made her realise how strong her feelings were towards him, once she knew she definitely couldn't have him, there was no chance. She shed a couple of tears and tried to go about her day as if nothing was wrong when on the inside, there was a storm approaching.

## 30

### CHAPTER 29

June 2011

It took everything left in Katie to make it through that day in work after she heard the news from Andrew. She tried so many times to focus but it was impossible. Especially since she knew he was in the room right next to her. She saw him come into the office a couple of minutes after she sent Andrew in there and noticed when Andrew left, not looking very happy at all. She guessed how their conversation had went by the look on his face and didn't expect much else from Colin.

She understood him, she had come to know how his mind worked and what made him feel and do the things he did, but the marriage without a prenup was too far. He was clearly only doing it to get a reaction from his father and losing everything just to anger the people who cared about him was too much. She had never met anyone as self-destructive as Colin, and didn't believe she ever would either.

Katie couldn't take it any longer, she was still in a state of disbelief and decided to knock into Colin's office for the first time in days. Usually, she would communicate through call or text, neither minded that much and it was easier to talk to him when she didn't have to see his face. But this conversation was not one she could shy away from and needed to be in person. She wanted to see the look on his face, his bright blue eyes as he admitted he was getting married to a woman he only knew a couple of months. A woman that he had stated before, was not the right one for him.

She picked up the nearest thing on her desk that needed signing and with a deep breath, began to make her way to Colin's door. It felt like the longest walk of her life, she wanted it to just be over and done with already. There was only a few minutes left in work so then was good time to confront him, she could leave as soon as she got the clarification she was looking to get out of this conversation no matter how awkward or heart breaking it was.

"Come in." he called from the other side of the door, knowing exactly who it was knocking. As soon as he saw her face, it made his heart jump. It felt like the first time she walked into his office just over two years ago, it felt like he had never laid eyes on her before. Colin drunk in her features, every part of her he could see as she walked towards his desk and placed some papers down in front of him. She had yet to make eye contact and he could already guess why. She must have already heard the news, he thought.

Katie felt his eyes on her as she lingered in front of his desk. She had so much more to say but in the moment, she couldn't speak. Her mouth was dry, her palms were sweaty and she wanted to just leave but something rooted her to her spot. Katie couldn't back down then, she needed to know the truth, she needed Colin to admit to her what was going on or else it wouldn't feel real.

"Are you getting married?" she blurted out casually as if it was a normal topic to speak to Colin about.

He hesitated for a minute, he knew the answer was yes but he didn't want to say it for reasons unknown. Maybe it was the way she looked at him when she asked the question or how every time he saw her over the past couple of weeks made every part of his being regret what he said that day at brunch in his family home. The truth was, Colin missed her but it wasn't like the way he would miss her before they were together for those couple of weeks. This feeling of yearning was much deeper than it had ever been before because he knew what it felt like to have her- to be with her, to wake up beside her, to hear her voice at home or outside work.

And how could he do it? How could he admit that he was marrying someone else when the woman that flooded his thoughts was her? Colin felt split in two, one part wanting to tell her everything, to apologise and tell her how he really felt while the other part wanted to lie and tell her how happy he was about his plans to marry Olivia. The latter of the two, was the easiest, and for that reason he chose to lie instead of telling the truth. What was the point in admitting his feelings for Katie? He had messed up too many times already and knew it would be no use to tell her how sorry he was.

"Yes. Yes I am." He nodded but didn't smile, only frowned as the words left his mouth.

He didn't look like the typical person informing you of their plans to marry their other half. Katie could see that and knew this was the very harsh reality that she had to face with Colin. He was digging himself an even bigger hole, making worse decisions than ever before and his only goal was to hurt himself, to push everyone else away.

If anyone else stood in the room and knew what both parties were thinking, they would surely step in and tell them both to speak the truth. Things would be so easily resolved. The person would be able to see how crushed Colin was from seeing the look on Katie's face. They would notice how when their eyes met for a second and both seemed more alive than this entire conversation for that moment. But it was only Katie and Colin in the room and neither was brave enough to make any confessions.

"Is that all?" Colin asked, not being able to bear seeing her for another minute.

"I just wanted to say congratulations. I hope you two are very happy together." She was being passive aggressive then as she turned around and headed for the door. "You can leave those on my desk once they're signed." She called over her shoulder before closing the door behind her, leaving Colin in silence mulling over his thoughts. He picked up the nearest thing sitting on his desk and threw it at the wall in a fit of rage. Katie heard this from inside her office but didn't question it, just grabbed her coat, and got ready to leave.

Katie stared in the mirror at herself, a stranger looked back at her and she tried to figure out why that was for a couple of minutes. She asked herself so many times why she was ever there? Why she even wanted to go to the engagement party when she knew it would only cause her upset and distress. Katie couldn't figure that out, even after locking herself into the bathroom for half an hour. She decided it was time to go, she had been at the party for over two hours and felt like she had made enough of an appearance.

After much frustration and quite a few discussions between himself and his father, Colin finally agreed to writing up a prenup and so he was not cut out of the family. In fact, most of his family members were there that night for the engagement party, although some looked a lot less happy than others to be in attendance. Because no one knew of Coli and Katie's short relationship, no one would understand her heartbreak from being in the same room as him for too long. She wanted to keep it that way so knew it was time to call a cab before she fell apart in front of anyone.

She picked up what little she brought with her off the marble countertop and headed straight out the door without saying good-bye to anyone. She ordered an Uber that was going to take over twenty minutes to get to where she was in the city. Twenty minutes felt like twenty hours for Katie in that moment. She stood outside the venue, letting the warm summer air wrap itself around her bare shoulders and arms.

Katie looked around and sat down on the steps outside, waiting rather impatiently for her car to turn up. She rested her head in her hands and looked out at the passing traffic in front of her. Tears filled her eyes and she felt drained, something that was becoming very familiar to her over the last couple of weeks. Just then, she heard someone come outside too but didn't turn around to see who it was. Whoever it was, she could hear them light up a cigarette and linger at the door for a minute or two.

"Want one?" she heard a familiar voice say from beside her. She turned her head a little to see Colin standing up and holding a cigarette out for her to take. Katie looked back at the traffic and tried to quickly wipe her tears away without him noticing before answering him.

"You know I don't smoke." She said in a low and gruff voice. He surprised her even more when he sat on the steps beside her. He didn't speak so she decided to break the silence. "Aren't you worried about getting your tux dirty?"

Colin remembered the repetition of her words from a long time ago when they sat and waited for her cab after the gala. Except when she asked this time, she used a monotonous tone, like she could care less but still enough to ask.

"I have a million of them at home anyways." He knew she would remember, but didn't expect her to tell him she did.

"Going home?"

"What do you think?" she refused to look at him when she spoke.

"You could be just getting some air like me..."

"Definitely not. I'm not going back in there, I'm going home."

"You're breaking my heart Katie." Colin admitted with a sigh. He needed to talk to her. He craved her attention, the way she smiled and how her laugh would make him feel warm inside, but he would get none of that out of this encounter.

"Really? I'm breaking your heart, that's rich." She scoffed. She wanted him to talk again, because the silence was too deafening, it made her feel nervous. But she never expected him to say what he did next.

"If you tell me not to do it Katie, I won't. Just say the words and I'll call all of this off in a heartbeat." His voice was so calm and gentle, yet there was a great indescribable desperation behind it that Katie couldn't get her head around. It made her look at him, his expectant face thirsty for an answer, for her to say anything at all.

"I can't believe you just said that." She shook her head in disbelief.

"Katie-"

"That's probably the most hurtful thing you've ever said to me. You've stooped to a whole new low, wow."

"I didn't think you'd take it like that."

"What way did you expect me to take it? As some sort of compliment. Is this your idea of being romantic Colin? Telling me you'll call off a wedding for me you don't even want to have in the first place. The only reason you're doing this is to get some sort of reaction out of someone. And if that someone is just me then you can go fuck yourself because if you think I'm going to want to have any say in whether you marry that woman inside that two months ago you told me you weren't in love with then you can think again." She stood up and looked down at him, so much fury whirling around in her stomach that she needed to get out in the form of words.

"I'm not in love with her. I never lied to you about that."

"Great, that makes me feel better. That some guy I was fucking wasn't in love with another girl while I was with him..."

"That's all I am to you?"

"Well I guess so, if that's all I was to you."

"You weren't, you aren't." he stood up then and placed his palm on her cheek only to have her push it away.

"Don't even try to say you cared about me Colin, because I know it's bullshit."

"I do, I just- I..."

"Look around you, look where we are. Now try to tell me you even gave an ounce of a fuck about us. If you even cared about me just a little bit, you wouldn't be doing this. You wouldn't be torturing me every day with all of this." Her pain had not subsided yet and tears fell down her cheeks as she tried to take a breath before speaking again. What she said next was something Colin never thought he would hear, and definitely not in the context she was about to admit it in.

"I love you Colin. You have no idea how hard it is to go through every single day loving someone who just keeps letting you down and absolutely crushing your heart at every opportunity." She turned and began to walk away but he kept following her. He grabbed her arm to stop her from going any further and turned her around to look at him although there were no words that could right his wrong. Especially not after seeing the extent of pain he had inflicted on her.

"I love you too. I really fucking love you Katie-"

"Don't." She held her hand up as she spoke, her eyes were closed, she was unable to look at him. "You don't get to say that to me, it's a complete lie, don't say it again."

"I'm so sorry Katie. I really am..." he was shocked. Colin never thought he would be having this conversation with her.

"You're sorry?" she scoffed, her tears finally beginning to stop but probably not for long. "That doesn't change a thing. Stop acting like a child and learn how to make your own decisions instead of trying to constantly hurt the people around you that care about you. You really didn't want a prenup Colin? Are you fucking crazy? You and I both know this marriage wasn't only to try and hurt me."

"Why are you bringing my family into this?"

"Because I know you wanted a reaction out of them, you always do. You keep fucking up because you crave bad attention, and you know everyone expects this sort of shit from you now."

"If you think they care about me, you haven't learned a damn thing from being around me these past couple of years."

"But of course they do Colin, are you actually that blind? Yes, you have a dickhead of a twin brother, it's not the end of the world. Andrew cares about you, your mom and dad care about you-"

"You think that them constantly being on my back about the stupidest things is caring? They're so cynical sometimes, it feels like they're smothering me."

"Because they want you to do well. They want you to succeed. And sure, I don't agree with the way they show how they care about your wellbeing but I can see there is some good behind their actions. I know how much it affects you Colin but sometimes, when I see both sides of situations I witness, I feel like you're the infiltrator."

"You think they actually give a fuck? They don't. You wouldn't understand-"

"You're right. I wouldn't understand. You know why? Because the only thing I know about my dad is the colour of his skin, I took a wild guess one day when I looked in the mirror and saw myself. And my mom? I can't say I know that much about her either. The only memories I have of her are horrible ones, she used to leave me alone and not come home for days. I'd be left there, starving, wondering if anyone would come find me and take me away. So yeah, I wouldn't understand because I never had anyone to kiss me goodnight or bring me to school every day or support me by giving me a job I really don't deserve. I barely knew my parents so you should be happy that you have ones that actually give a crap about you."

Katie had never been this confrontational in her entire life. She watched as Colin shrunk into himself, his face had paled and he was left speechless from her outburst.

"You think your life sucks because you don't get along with your parents and you have a shitty brother? Well guess what Colin, everyone's life fucking sucks but we all don't have time to sit around moping about it. I've tried so many times to help you and you just throw it all back in my face like this. Well done. You've disappointed another person who cares about you, are you happy?"

"Katie please, I-"

"I don't want to know. You've really hurt me but I guess you got what you wanted now didn't you? Goodbye Colin." She said before walking up the street, she didn't care about her drive home, she just needed to get away from him as quick as possible.

Colin was shaking when she left him alone, his body was in shock from the things his ears heard. His mind couldn't handle it all and it broke down in the middle of the street, alone. He messed everything up, including his last hope at figuring everything out and turning things around- Katie. The realisation of how hard he hurt her hit him, he felt paralysed.

This had all gone too far.

**31**

——— ◆ ———

## CHAPTER 30

J uly 2011

Katie couldn't take it anymore, Monday afternoon, two days after her confrontation with Colin, she decided it was best to just quit work that day. She only went in to get her things and say her goodbyes. She knew she should have handed in her notice weeks ago and she might get in trouble for leaving so abruptly but Katie couldn't face Colin anymore, especially not after their conversation the other night.

She didn't have that much in the office to take with her, most of her things fit in her bag. Katie stood in her office for a moment, taking everything in one last time. She was glad to see Colin was already in his office when she arrived on their floor. There was no way he would have been in early this morning that's why she didn't turn up, she didn't want to be left waiting around hours for an unpunctual Colin who strolled in to work whenever he felt like it.

Colin knew there was something wrong that day when he got into work and there was no sign of Katie. At almost half ten, he knew she couldn't just be running late but he refrained from trying to make any contact with her. When he heard her knocking on his door a couple of hours later, he was surprised why her appearance at work that day.

"Come in." She stood at his door for a moment after closing it, deep reluctance and anxiety etched on her face. He saw that she had her coat on and was carrying her handbag awkwardly as if it was too heavy and wondered what she was going to say next.

"I can't do this anymore Colin, I have to leave."

"Leave? Katie, if this is about Saturday night then I want you to know that-"

"It's about everything. I can't work for you anymore and I'm very sorry that I didn't hand in any notice but I think it's better if I just leave now instead of waiting two weeks."

"Did you take the promotion?" he was curious, this abrupt decision would be less severe to his feelings if he knew she would still be working at the company. There would still be a chance he would see her, there would still be time for him to make everything up to her.

"No." His heart dropped. What would he do without her? Where was she going? He had so many questions and so much to say, that day and the other night but it was like his mind would go blank every time he opened his mouth to speak. "I feel like I need a fresh start, without you still being in the background and I can't get that if I take the promotion your dad offered me."

"W-why? Why does it matter if I'm still in the background?"

"I meant everything I said the other night. It wasn't just because I was angry or upset. And I can't work here at the company anymore because it will remind me of you in a way I suppose."

"Katie, I can't describe how sorry I am about all of this, I really can't. But I need you to know something and-"

"I'm tired of trying to help you Colin. I'm tired of constantly trying to pick you back up and put you together again. You're so self-loathing and self-destructive that no matter how much I care about you, I know we won't ever work out." He rushed out of his seat and towards her, a storm of hurt and distress whirling around in his mind.

"But Katie, I can turn this all around, I swear."

"How Colin? You're getting married in two months and I realised that being your PA is just not good enough. I wanted every part of you, not just to work for you but Olivia changes everything I've ever thought about you so far."

"No you don't understand." He took her face in between both his hands, urging her to look at him as he tried to explain himself.

"I don't want to understand anymore."

"Katie just let me explain, Olivia and I-" his voice was strained and urgent, his desperation did make her curious to find out more but she was also sick of hearing excuses.

"Colin? Oh god, I'm interrupting something. I'm so sorry." Both their heads shot in Andrew's direction, he was standing at the door awkwardly and began to close the door but Katie's words made him stop.

"No, it's fine Andrew. I was just about to leave anyway." She turned her head to look Colin straight in the eye when she said the last sentence before removing his hands from her face. "Goodbye." She said sadly, low enough that only Colin could hear her.

As soon as she walked out of the office and into the elevator, her stomach churned with uneasiness. It would take a while for her actions from today to sink in but she knew it was all only for the best. This way, it would be a little easier to get over Colin because she knew there was no way she could have him. Sure, marriages didn't have to be for life and she definitely didn't think his and Olivia's were going to last a lifetime but it was in Colin's actions, his decision to propose to her and ask Katie to make the decision for him that made Katie understand that she needed to be done with him.

She knew her heart would not be able to take the pain that would be caused by turning up to work every day and having to look at him.

Jeffrey called her a couple of days after her run in with Colin in his office, he offered her the promotion again and seemed eager to get her on board but she told him several times she could not accept the position. She thanked him again before declining again and hanging up the phone after a quick goodbye. Jeffrey told her that if she was ever in need of a job somewhere down the line, that he would gladly take her into consideration and it would be an honour to have her work as part of the company again. He regretted her answer but understood the reasons she had told him- she wanted to look for work somewhere else, have a change of scenery and pace in her next job.

It did take her some time to find a new job, but not as long as it had before she started working for Colin. The job was as a marketing assistant at another firm in the city, it took a while for her to get the hang of things as she had been doing a different kind of work with Colin. Katie knew exactly what date the wedding would take place, although she would never turn up. At first, she felt like she would, it felt like it would help her come to terms with the harsh reality, as if it would be like watching a coffin getting lowered down into the ground but she then decided against it. The engagement party had been too much, the wedding would be much worse.

She decided to take a trip back home for that weekend, her old friends would help to take her mind off everything. But it was no good. As she boarded the plane, all she could think about was how Colin would be getting ready for the ceremony, he would be putting on his suit and Olivia, her dress. They would have said 'I do' before Katie even reached her friend Leah's house.

Leah was the first to see her when she arrived in Detroit, and so, was the first to see how absolutely torn about she looked. She hugged her tightly for a moment before her daughter, Cassie held out her arms too.

"Are you okay?" Leah asked.

"Yeah, I'll be okay." Katie put on a brave face despite how bad she felt on the inside.

"We can talk about it later when all the girls get here. I know you must be feeling really exhausted, do you want to take a nap before they come over tonight? The spare room's ready for you."

"That would be great actually, I'm up since really early."

Kate brought her things upstairs and lay on the bed, trying not to let tears fall from her eyes. But it felt like the hardest thing to do right then, all of these feelings demanded to be felt all at once. Since she left her job working with Colin, it felt like it was getting easier each day, like she was on the way to forgetting about him but then that day everything went back to the way it used to be. She felt completely heartbroken and didn't know if it was even justified, the pain was irrepressible.

Little did Katie know that as she fell apart alone in Leah's spare room, Colin was back in Chicago, also completely unravelling. He was paralysed by pure regret and sadness from the realisation that he would never get Katie back. The only person to blame for all of this was himself, and that made him furious.

She couldn't sleep at all, but she stayed in her room for an hour or two pretending that she didn't pass the time bawling her eyes out. As soon as the tears started, it felt like they would never stop but she did pull herself together after a while. She had been talking to Emily a lot and that seemed to help so she hoped that talking to everyone back here would also make her feel better. Everyone knew what was going on but didn't know every single detail, they were all dying to find out the full story and hoped that their friend was okay.

Soon enough, Katie got up and ready for dinner later that day with the girls. Cassie was staying in her dad's and so Katie spent some time with her before she left. She hugged her mother goodbye and went on her way as soon as Leah's ex-boyfriend, Travis, knocked on their front door. Leah was civil with Travis but there was still some sorrow behind their interaction that Katie noticed.

"How are you and Travis?" Katie finally asked once they had left and the house was empty. They were waiting for Sam and Anna to turn up.

"Fine. We're trying to get along for Cassie but if it weren't for her, I don't think I could possibly be in the same room as that bastard." Travis cheated on Leah, it had been going on for months and she found out, if she didn't, Leah wondered how long it would have lasted before he finally had the courage to tell her. She was heartbroken from the entire thing but never let it show in front of him or their daughter Cassie. "He really is a bastard, but he's a great dad. I have to just separate what he did to me from how well he treats our daughter for Cassie's sake."

"I'm sorry Leah." Katie stood up and reached out to hug her friend. "I'd say it's so difficult for you."

"It is but I've learned to cope. It doesn't hurt anymore and I can say I'm definitely over him now. It just sucks you know? I wish we could've worked out for Cassie but we really can't be together after how bad he hurt me."

"And Cassie will see that when she's older. She'll see how strong you were for making the decision you did."

Just then, the doorbell rang and in no time, the four women were sitting around drinking wine and eating dinner that Leah managed not to burn to flames that time. It didn't take long before the conversation steered from catching up to Colin.

"So the wedding's today?" Anna asked in complete shock.

"Yeah, that soon..."

"That sucks, when we met him he seemed so sweet. Screw him, you don't need someone like that in your life."

"I guess."

"You guess?" Sam wondered why her friend's reply sounded very nonchalant. "Katie the guy's an asshole for what he did to you."

"I know he is but- I think I still love him and it's so hard to even admit that right now because of everything's he's done. With Colin, it was strange. Like, we avoided being with each other for so long, then those couple of weeks we both tried- it was amazing. It was so great and I fell so in love with him, even more so than before we were together and then it felt like it was all just pulled out from under me so quickly without a good enough reason. I didn't have any time to process anything and it felt so unfair, it still feels so unfair. I'm in love with someone who doesn't love me back."

"I still think he's a spoilt brat that doesn't understand there are consequences behind everything that you do. I mean, I can't believe he told you he'd call off the wedding if you told him to?" Leah told it straight to her friend although her words didn't comfort Katie in any way.

"He just needs to learn to help himself. But he won't, he started trying when we got together but after that everything just went to shit again. He hates himself and it's so hard to watch someone be so self-loathing and destructive when you know they deserve more-"

"Katie stop feeling sorry for him. After everything he's done to you, you still can't help but think about his feelings over your own. That's not how it works when two people love each other."

"I get it though," Sam finally spoke up for the first time during the conversation, she had been very quiet during their discussion over dinner but finally felt strongly enough to have an opinion. "Katie loves him, and maybe they would've worked out if he learned how to love himself and her. That's got to be hard trying to come to terms with it all, there's so many what ifs involved." Katie was glad someone was on her side, at least, she thought Sam sounded like she was on her side, right?

"I know, I get that but she has to think about herself right now. Not some guy who keeps wasting her time. She won't be able to get over him if she keeps thinking like that."

"Sometimes it takes a while to get over someone, she will eventually." Katie wasn't as convinced as her friends were but she refrained from saying anything until Leah asked her a very serious question Katie wished she hadn't.

"Would you get back with him if he left Olivia for you?"

"Well, he doesn't love Olivia-"

"That's what he's told you. Judging from your answer, you would consider it, you'd be willing to forget his random proposal to a woman he swore he didn't love when he was with you. Even if he didn't love her and was just marrying her to get at his parents, since he seems to do things a lot purely for that reason, he's still choosing to do that over being with you. He doesn't deserve you Katie-"

"It's just hard okay? Yes, I know I sound like a fool, I sound like a complete maniac but I still love him despite everything he's done. It's so confusing and I don't know why I still feel like this because of him, it's been months for christ's sake." Katie cut across Leah with a short outburst, before tears began falling from her eyes.

They all tried to comfort her, but it took time, as would learning to live without Colin, to live without wondering what could have happened if things were different. But Katie would move on, they were all sure of it.

# 32

CHAPTER 31

September 2011

Katie looked at her phone again as soon as she got out of work and sighed when she saw the many missed calls from Colin. It seemed as if no amount of ignoring she did was going to stop him from trying to reach out to her. She was surprised he hadn't turned up at her apartment yet, but maybe he had gotten some sense and realised that would be crossing the line and Katie would be even more furious with him if he did so. She was trying to get on with her life, it had taken months, and she was still learning but things were getting better for her. She still thought about Colin from time to time, especially when he left texts and tried to call her numerous times every day, but she was strong and independent, she had lived her life without him before, and she would get on fine after him.

Although she had not gotten back out on the dating scene yet, she had been preoccupied with work. Once she kept busy, she would be fine. Her mind would not linger on the continuous scenarios which used to play around in her head a month or two ago. It felt like there was still no amount of work that she could bury herself with in order to get rid of Colin. He still seemed to linger in the background, usually creeping up on nights when she began to wonder what it would be like if things were different a couple of months ago.

Katie had to learn that she couldn't change anything. It was not possible to go back in time and make Colin do everything differently, make herself stay that day at the Anderson's home and calm him down, reason with him that he was making a bad decision giving up on the two of them. When looking at the situation from the outside, it definitely seemed desperate, but Katie felt so much all at once, indescribable sadness, nostalgia and anger all mixed into one. She didn't know whether to hate him or love him for it, because Katie could only remember the bad times with the good, neither could be looked back on without the other.

Colin, although she did not want to think of him, was trying desperately to find a way to make it up to Katie. He knew by then, words would surely mean nothing at all. He was falling apart, of course he turned to his vices, his addictions at times when he felt helpless and alone- which was a lot when he wasn't with her. Knowing that he was the one that ruined everything between them was killing him slowly, and understanding that he might never get her back tipped him over the edge.

But that night, things took a turn for the worst.

Colin tried to call her, like he usually did around the time she was finished work. Her finger lingered on the screen, she didn't know whether to decline or pick up. And for once, the only time she decided she ever would, she accepted the call. Her hands shook as she held the phone to her ear, wanting to hear him speak.

"Katie... Katie. Hello?" He questioned her desperately on the phone, needing to hear her reply, to just say something. He hadn't heard her voice in so long.

But Katie couldn't do it. Tears began to form in her eyes that she forced back, she wouldn't cry, just hang up and try to forget. She was only tempting herself. What good would have come from a phone call? Colin was a married man, nothing he could say could right his wrong. She could never be his friend again.

Colin was left heartbroken as he stood in his apartment, staring down at his screen in complete shock. Why had she answered for once and then hung up? He didn't want to think it was a mistake, that she might have accidentally accepted the call and soon realised what she'd done. The small action tormented him, she had no idea though. Instead of thinking about what had happened, she pushed it to the back of her mind, even if it was only for her trip home.

An hour or so later, she made it home. She was greeted by flashing red and blue lights as she turned her corner. There seemed to have been a road accident, she walked past the many medics and officers rushing around the terrible scene that had unfolded just a block away from her building. She tried to keep her eyes off whatever was happening, she didn't want to be nosey although other people who had gathered around the scene did not seem to care. Katie walked on and went straight to her apartment where she was greeted by Emily who was lying down watching tv in the living room.

Katie had a sinking feeling in her stomach that wouldn't go away, she wasn't quite sure what the cause of the feeling was as nothing had really happened out of the ordinary- apart from Colin's phone call.

"Hey Em, did you see what happened down the end of the street?"

"What? No, it's my day off. You know I don't move from the couch on days off."

"I think there was some sort of crash. You didn't hear anything?"

"Yes, actually. I heard sirens a couple of minutes ago. I wonder what happened."

"Me too. I'm sure someone will find out." Katie fell onto the sofa then and took a deep breath. "God, it's been a long day."

"How was work?" Emily asked between a handful of chips.

"Okay, I suppose." A silence fell then for a moment between the two women before Katie added, "Colin called again."

"Did you answer?"

"Yes." She sighed before looking down at her hands in her lap. "But I hung up straight away."

"Didn't you speak to him?"

"No, I don't want to." Emily had a different opinion to Katie's other friends about the whole situation. She found it weird that he was so persistent in getting in contact with Katie, as if he needed to tell her something important, more than an apology. She felt like her friend needed to face Colin one last time in order to get over him and move on. "I instantly regretted picking up, because now I just want to hear him speak again."

"Oh Katie..." Emily put the bag of chips down and moved closer to her friend. She could see how upset she was becoming. All the progress she had made over the past few weeks seemed to go down the drain from one phone call. "It's alright." She hugged Katie for a moment then looked at her. She was surely putting on a brave face but breaking on the inside.

"I'm sorry, I know it's been so long and I should be over him by now. I really don't know why I haven't gotten over him yet. I've been through breakups before and it never takes this long?"

"Don't worry, just give it time Katie." She wished Emily's words would ease her thoughts that night, but they couldn't. She went to bed with a heavy heart but couldn't sleep. She heard her phone ring from her bedside table and immediately answered. The number was not familiar but the voice on the other end of the line was. It was Andrew and he sounded awful.

"Um.. Is this Katie?" he asked hesitantly, his voice filled with worry.

"Yes, it's me. Andrew?"

"Oh, thank god I got through to you."

"Andrew what's wrong? Why are you calling me?" A knot instantly formed in her stomach as soon as she picked up the phone.

"It's Colin. He's in the hospital. You need to come quick."

"W-what? What happened?"

"I'll explain when you get here."

Katie didn't think she could wait, but of course she listened to Andrew and quickly rang a taxi to the address he told her he was at. Her heart was racing as she stepped out of the cab and walked inside to the reception area of the hospital where an exhausted looking Andrew, waiting patiently for her. The anticipation was killing her, she couldn't take it any longer.

"Andrew, what's happened? Is Colin going to be okay?"

"He was in a car crash earlier this evening Katie. He's suffered from a lot of serious injuries but they're hoping that after surgery, he'll be okay. Have you been talking to him recently?"

"He's been ringing me the past couple of weeks but I never had the guts to talk to him, it's too much for me and I need to get over everything."

"Did he mention anything to you? Are you sure you haven't been talking to him?" Andrew's scepticism made Katie furrow her brows in confusion at his questions.

"I haven't spoken to him Andrew, trust me. Why?" she saw him gulp, hesitation eating him up as they stood there in the reception, people came and went but Katie was paying no attention to anything else but Colin's brother and his confusing questions. She saw the look on his face and how his eyes avoided her at all costs, as if he did not want to tell her the answer to the question. But after a moment or two, he finally replied.

"W-we think he was going to see you when he crashed." Katie's stomach dropped when she processed Andrew's words, was that Colin in the car that she passed earlier on her way home from work? "I'd been talking to him before he left, begging him not to drive. He'd been drinking and doing whatever else it is that he's into... I knew by his voice and when I rushed over after he hung up, he'd already left." Tears filled Katie's eyes at the thought of how bad of a state Colin must have been in. No amount of time apart could stop the overwhelming despair she felt right then from hearing about Colin.

"What's going to happen now? Is he still in surgery?"

"He should be finished up in a couple of minute, my mom and dad are here too but that's it." A question dawned on Katie, where was Olivia? Surely she had been informed and had already turned up to see how her husband was doing? She needed to ask.

"I don't understand why you called me even though I'm glad you did. Like I said Andrew, I haven't spoken to Colin in weeks. We haven't seen each other since before the wedding. Where's Olivia while all of this is going on? Couldn't she have stopped him, couldn't she have made sure he didn't go overboard like he usually does-"

"Colin didn't tell you?"

"Tell me what?"

"Katie, they never went through with the wedding. He called it off after the engagement party. You were still working for him back then, surely he told you?"

A heavy weight fell on her shoulders then, she felt sick to her stomach from hearing the news. Then, she remembered back to the last time she had ever seen Colin, that day in his office he was adamant on telling her something but she refused to listen. Could he had tried to be telling her about cancelling the wedding? Guilt and frustration, that was all she felt in that moment.

"He's been so bad since then." Andrew was not helping her at all but she needed to know the truth about how Colin had been doing. "Just drinking constantly, I'm surprised it took this long for him to do something like this. But he's been talking to me a lot more than before- I can tell he's trying Katie but he just won't listen to any of us, not even me." She covered her mouth with her hands and shook her head in disbelief. All this time, months, she had thought he went through with the wedding when in fact he had called it off.

"Can I see him?" Katie wanted this, she needed this although she thought she was not ready.

"When he's out of surgery, you can come in and see him but I have to warn you he doesn't look like Colin at the minute."

Andrew was right, Colin looked like a stranger when Katie finally got to see him. He was sleeping in a hospital bed, his face covered in cuts, his body covered in bruises. He had a cast on his right arm too, but the most sever looking thing was his swollen and battered face. His eyes were closed but he wasn't in a peaceful sleep. She knew what that looked like from some mornings when she woke up beside him and he was still sleeping. Tears welled in her eyes, some even fell and rolled down her cheek, but she tried to contain herself in front of Andrew and his parents.

She waited at the hospital all night despite Andrew assuring her he would call when Colin woke up. Katie wanted to be there with him, although she was not much help. She needed time to think about everything and that long night gave her a lot of time. In the end though, she still had so many questions that she wanted to ask. The answers were not important right then, the only thing that mattered was Colin being okay.

That night was one of the longest she'd ever went through, all her mind did was race rapidly through the past two and a half years of her life, from when she first met him until right then as she sat in the hospital room beside his bed, waiting for him to wake up.

Colin, in his sleep, was surrounded by a deep darkness. But that would fade and the pain would disappear instantly as soon as he opened his eyes and saw her face.

# 33

## CHAPTER 32

August 2018

Colin's face instantly lit up at the sight of her, as if he was seeing her for the first time again. He had his doubts, in fact, in order to avoid getting his hopes up he tried to imagine Katie not showing up at all that day. But she did, and he was overjoyed. She could see it and it only made her feel confused guilt.

He stood up as she got closer to the table he was sitting at but didn't know what to do with himself once he was standing. He surely couldn't hug her, and shaking her hand would only make it feel like some sort of business meeting, so he lingered for a moment, a wavering smile on his face. She stood too, irresolute, not wanting to sit down and not wanting to remain standing either.

"Have you ordered yet?"

"Yes, mines on the way. You can leave your stuff here while you order if you want."

"Sure." She tried to force a smile before putting her things on a chair and going up to the coffee shop counter. Within a minute or so she was back and sat across from him, a comfortable amount of distance for Katie.

"I'm so happy you came." He couldn't lie and needed to voice how grateful he was for her appearance.

"I'm glad I came too. I think we need to have one last talk so that we can put things to bed and get on with our lives." Her words sank in to his heart, engulfing it, ripping it apart. He tried not to let it show but it was proving to be tough. "So you're clean now?" she had been wondering the story behind this ever since his admission the first time she saw him a couple weeks ago in her office and surely she would get one now that they had time and she wasn't pushing him out the door.

"Yes, I have been for a whole two and a half years now. I kind of went off the rails when you left but after a while I tried my best to get back on track again- with some slip ups of course." Slip ups- she remembered so many of them during the time they were together.

"That's really great Colin. I can't express how happy I am for you." Her genuine smile was dimmed down a little, she didn't want to seem too eager but he could see it in her eyes, her true feelings beaming through despite how professional she was being about all of this.

"I know I did a lot of bad shit four years ago Katie. I know how much I hurt you and I know sorry isn't enough right now for you but I hope one day it can be."

"You hurt me Colin but I'll survive. I've gotten over it, I've gotten over you." Her words held finality that was actually non-existent. What she was saying were lies, she hadn't gotten over him at all.

"I'm glad to hear that." He didn't know what else to say. What could he say? There was a short silence before he thought aloud. "So why are you here then?" she looked directly at him for the first time during their short conversation and took a minute to answer.

"I guess I need closure."

Closure.

He had hoped for a resurrection but what she wanted was to finally end everything.

"Andrew told me to say hello. Hazel too." He saw how a smile tugged on her lips at the mention of the young girls name.

"How are they both doing?"

"He still hasn't grasped fatherhood quite like he guessed he would but he's been doing fine. Hazel's certainly a handful but the good kind."

"I'm sure she is." Katie chuckled then, she was instantly brought back to a couple of years ago when things were going great between she and Colin. It made her think differently, it made her realise again that although Colin had brought her a lot of grief, he had also made her feel so many highs too. Nostalgia took over, wrapping itself around her worries and thoughts about saying goodbye to Colin that day forever, it changed her outlook and before she knew it, she suggested something she never thought she would.

"Hey do you want to just take these to go? Maybe a walk would be better than sitting here." Colin was confused, but went along with it. If she had have suggested bungee jumping over their coffee he would have agreed. He could sense some sort of forgiveness in her voice, as if some walls she had built up were beginning to fall only an instant ago. He had not realised her discovery of truth in this short encounter.

The truth was, Katie didn't want to say goodbye to him forever that day. She wanted to know about everything that had happened in the four years of her absence, the good and the bad. She wanted to forgive him, she wanted to forget and start fresh. But she needed time to think it through, prolonging their goodbye would allow her to make a decision on whether it would be a final goodbye or just a goodbye for now.

The truth was she had been lying to herself ever since he walked through the door of her office again after four years of being gone. He had stuck to her heart, stuck to her brain, and she didn't want to ever forget him.

"Sure."

**34**

**CHAPTER 33**

September 2011

Colin thought he was still dreaming when he woke up the next morning and saw Katie curled up on a chair opposite his bed. She was sleeping soundly and for a moment, he savoured the sight of her. He hadn't laid eyes on her for so long. It was as if he had been walking through the scorching hot desert for weeks and she was a mirage appearing right before his eyes.

It took her only a moment to wake up from her light sleep. She had been dozing in and out of consciousness all night long. Once she saw he was awake, she almost leapt up from her chair, dread and surprise written all over her face.

"Katie?" he was confused.

"Colin? Oh thank god you're awake. Are you okay? Are you hurting- I need to call the nurse." It was as if those two months apart had never happened. She had turned back into the concerned and worried Katie she'd always been when he was around.

"You're here." His entire face lit up, a smile creeping onto his lips. It was an unusual yet funny sight to see- his body was in complete ruins, his face battered and bruised yet he still lay there grinning like an idiot.

"Of course I'm here, Andrew called me last night after the crash."

"Katie, I have so much to say to you-"

"We can talk later okay? Now's not the time. You're badly hurt and you need to get better before we talk about anything."

She had made her mind up last night, for the time being she would pretend as if nothing had happened between them. All that mattered was Colin getting better. Seeing him lying there in that hospital, seeing all his injuries made her realise that she still cared, she still loved Colin and wanted, if not needed him to be okay. No amount of trying to forget could rid her of him.

Colin wanted to address everything there and then, he had so much to say to her- that was why he was going to turn up at her doorstep last night and as she stood there in front of him he had the perfect opportunity but it was not the time anymore. She wanted to wait for his apology, so he decided it was better to do it at her preferred time although he didn't know how much longer he could take holding it all in. He felt even worse after the delight from seeing her again had resided, knowing she was probably really concerned, everyone was and it was all his fault.

It took weeks for Colin's injuries to finally heal. Even as he left the hospital, he still had a cast on his left arm and a slight limp. But Katie was by his side, she visited the hospital almost every day after work to see him and even brought him home the day he signed himself out of treatment and care. She helped him to her car and soon enough they were on their way. She was nervous enough driving her car, as it was something she didn't do often but then to top that off, Colin sitting in the passenger seat next to her made her feel worse.There was a mutual feeling in the air that day in the car, a kind of tension that neither could describe, because both of them knew what was to come.

"I can take them Katie."

"Oh please," she sniggered as she looked at him. "I think I can carry two bags for you. It's not a big deal."

"It's just that they're heavy and I feel bad." He said as she shut her trunk and began walking with him into his apartment building.

"Sorry macho man, but I can handle this. You only have one functioning arm at the minute anyways, it's not like you can carry them." Katie slung one bag over her shoulder as they walked into the elevator.

"Thank you." Colin replied in defeat with a heavy sigh she was sure to hear.

She placed the bags down as soon as they got inside his door and walked through to the familiar living room. Katie lingered as he followed suit and then sat down on a sofa. He noticed she was still standing and patted the empty space beside him for her to join him.

"Aren't you going to sit?" their eyes latched onto each other but Katie didn't move.

Her mind raced, her heart pumped furiously because she knew they had to have the conversation she had been putting off for weeks as soon as she sat down. Strangely enough, and much to Katie's surprise, she had found it a lot easier pretending as if nothing had happened between she and Colin although it was not the right thing to do. Katie deserved an apology, and she needed to talk to Colin about the seriousness of his actions the night of the crash. She had so many questions she wanted answers to and he had so much more to say, which made it difficult for her to understand why she was shying away from the long-awaited confrontation.

"Sure." She sat beside him but kept a small distance. Her palms began to get sweaty but she took one last long breath, an attempt to calm herself. "So..."

"Katie I can't apologise enough for everything I've put you through. And I'll understand if sorry isn't enough anymore but I realised a lot of things after you left- one being that I love you so much and I don't want us to be apart again like we have been." His honesty tugged at her heart, his words made her feel warm inside but she was not forgetting anything.

"Why did you do it Colin? Why did you propose to Olivia after everything you told me about her and how you knew she wasn't right for you?"

"I guess after our argument at my parent's house, I realised how right you were about everything. Olivia never made me feel the way you did, the way you make me feel but I wanted to go against what people thought was better for me. I was hurt and I tried to hurt you too because of it."

"Tried? You definitely succeeded." Her words were brutal to his already guilty conscience but he understood the reasons behind her honesty. He hurt her badly by doing foolish things instead of facing the problem that was at hand.

"I never planned on actually marrying Olivia. I'm sure she knew my heart wasn't in it. But then I kept using it as a distraction from how I felt. I thought we'd never be together again, so what was the point in trying? I was digging myself a bigger hole by proposing to Olivia but it was easier than being honest with you and apologising for the way I'd acted that day at my parents' house. It got to a point that day at the brunch when I saw you with Andrew and my dad that I understood then I wasn't the only one who enjoyed your company.

They liked you too, I realised that you'd stuck by me and helped me so much. You were good for me- it made me feel so crappy because then I thought about how I'd never be able to make it up to you, you'd done so much for me and I wouldn't ever be able to do that in return for you. I'll admit I was drunk but my thoughts were not, I felt like throwing everything away, our progress and time together because being with you would make me feel so much better and I just- I..." Katie noticed how glassy his eyes looked, how raw his words were as he completely unravelled in front of her. She urged him silently to continue and after a moment, he did.

"I don't deserve that. I don't deserve you and how good you make me feel." He shook his head which made her move closer to him on the sofa and wrap her arms around him.

"Don't say that. Of course you do." Colin heard her say close to his ear but her words did not ease his guilt.

"I've caused you so much pain, I've been a nuisance ever since you met me Katie."

"So stop trying to hurt me then? Stop trying to hurt yourself. You deserve to feel good, you deserve to have someone in your life that loves you. Take control, do things that are good for you and others around you. You can't keep beating yourself up over everything." It hurt her to see him this way but she was also glad that he had finally begun to understand the hidden reasons behind his self-destruction after so long.

"You have to learn to forgive yourself, and take care of yourself too." She added, to which Colin replied with a slow nod and an apprehensive, dulled smile.

"But will you?" the smile had fallen from his lips by then, he looked so nervous as he waited patiently for her reply. "Will you learn to forgive me?"

To forgive him would be a very difficult thing for her to do. But she loved him, so although forgiving would be hard, she had no doubt about her decision at all.

"Of course I will Colin." He took her in his arms again for another tight hug.

When he released her, Katie had the time to take another look at his grief-stricken face, how all his heart-wrenching emotions were scattered over his features. His stomach had been tied in a knot from all the guilt, from all the pain he had caused her. Despite her agreement to forgive him, none of the torturous guilt would subside for quite some time. It was going to be tough for him, he loved her and from that love and the hatred he had for himself, he had tried to hurt her too many times. He thought about it every single day since she had said goodbye two months ago- it was the most regret and shame he had ever felt in his entire life. Colin didn't want to feel that again, he didn't want to lose her again purely because of his own pride and selfish actions.

"But I need you to promise me you're going to take care of yourself from now on." Regardless of whether he felt worthy, Colin only agreed for her. She was the only reason, and maybe that was the problem but neither would figure that out for quite some time. "You really scared me last night. You could've killed someone, you could've killed yourself." She spoke sternly then after their emotional heart-to-heart because there were still things that needed to be said.

"I-I know." He avoided her gaze then, her eyes were unbearable to even glance at for those few seconds that she spoke. Her wavering voice only tugged at his heart when she spoke again.

"Don't ever do that again."

"I won't. I know it was stupid of me but I really wanted to see you, I wanted to make things right again for us."

"Well they are now, right?" Their eyes locked onto each other's then, the fire that had been extinguished two months ago had relit. He gave her a small smile and a nod.

"Right." She thought this was going to be the end of the conversation but he had much more to say. Something needed to be addressed, and she was surprised that he was the one to even mention it. She could see his smile falter and his eyes glazing over in sadness. A type of sorrow fell upon his face like no other, it scared Katie but she had to ask what he was thinking about that had changed his demeanour so quickly.

"What's wrong?" she was worried then when he didn't reply, only hesitated.

It took a while for him to finally speak, he had opened and closed his mouth a couple of times by then, attempting to let the words spill out but they were stuck to his throat. With all his strength, he finally spoke of a truth that had been following him around for quite a while.

"I think I have a problem Katie." He looked torn apart after his confession.

There was a minute of silence that felt like an hour, both felt their feelings were being intertwined. His eyes began to water and after she realised this, hers did too. Katie nodded slowly then before engulfing him tightly in her arms for another moment, cradling him as she realised this was what she had wanted for so long, she wanted him to realise how bad things were going because of his addictions and once he had finally come to terms with this, like she felt he had, things could only get better.

"I know, I know." She said softly, still holding onto him tight. "But it's only going to get better from here on out, we can get you the help you need, and everything will good again."

"I can't believe I put you through all this. I want to make it all up to you Katie, I'll go to rehab. I want to prove once I get better, how much I love you. I'd do anything for you." He spoke with great certainty, and loosened himself form her arms so that he was facing her with clear eye contact when he spoke.

"I'd do anything for you too." They both smiled, one that was not too big or too small. For a second, everything in Colin's apartment dimmed, everything that surrounded them had disappeared and the only thing that mattered was the blue and brown in each other's eyes as they were incapsulated in one another's presence. It was brilliantly beautiful, something neither would ever be able to describe, but would always play back in their minds- remembering the day he made a promise to her, how the only way was up from then on.

## CHAPTER 34

September 2011

"Morning." Colin whispered in Katie's ear, his voice was graceful, like a symphony filling her ears as she gently awoke from the long sleep she had.

"Good morning." She groaned and turned from having her back to this stomach, rolling closer into his arms for the first time since he had gotten his cast off the day before. He kissed her on the forehead and smiled as she remained lying there with her eyes closed. He moved his lips from her forehead then, down to her lips and around her jawline, but she still would not budge. A small smile crept up onto her face and once he noticed this, he burst into laughter.

"Are you going to pretend like you're still asleep even though you just said good morning to me?" he asked, humoured by her lack of reaction.

"Of course not." She cracked her eyes open then, a mischievous look written all over her face.

"Good, because I'm making breakfast and if I'm not enough to get you out of bed in the mornings, surely my food will be." He needed something to do, he felt exhausted yet full of energy at the same time.

After the day he came back from the hospital, Katie had spent many nights with him in his apartment. She would come over after work and leave the next morning for work, two weeks had passed already and it was a Saturday, which meant she could spend the entire day with him. While spending most of his time with her was exactly what he wanted and needed, in the back of his mind, he was counting down the days until rehab, dreading when the day would finally come.

Katie was the perfect distraction, but as he stood in his kitchen whisking eggs together for their breakfast, the words "two more days" repeated over and over in his head. He only had until Monday before he would have to leave for three months, only seeing her weekly was going to kill him. Colin doubted himself a lot, he doubted whether rehab was even going to work out for him, and he doubted his strength that would allow him to get through everything, but then he thought of her and remembered why he was doing all of this.

He was haunted most nights by nightmares, always very strange, the kind that made you wake up in a cold sweat. And once his breathing had calmed he would turn and find her lying there beside him in bed, fast asleep. Her presence made him feel so much better, she was his safe haven that he never wanted to let go of.

"Want some help?" Katie padded out from the bedroom to the kitchen.

"No, you can just keep me company." He smiled at her before he began cooking again. Katie sat on one of the stools at the breakfast bar and began tapping her fingers on the countertop along with the music he had just turned on.

"It smells amazing already."

"Of course it does, it's my cooking." Katie rolled her eyes at his statement.

"No need to rub it in even more than you have already Colin. I can't cook, there, I said it." She raised her hands up in mock defeat, to which he grinned. There was a short silence, the pair looked at each other and no words were needed for that small minute until Colin asked a question.

"Are we meeting Andrew at one or two again? I forgot."

"Two." She said dreamily, taken away by everything about him in that moment. She had her head propped up with her hand while she stared at him a little longer. "I need to go pick up some stuff at my apartment on our way too though, so we should probably leave a bit earlier." She said it as if it was a chore, and it definitely was beginning to feel like it was exactly that although she didn't want to admit it. The look on Colin's face made her realise she should have used a different tone, because she know what was coming next.

"Maybe if you moved in here you wouldn't have to keep going back and forth all the time?" he smiled, his features lit up with a kind of hope Katie couldn't agree to, not yet anyway. The undetermined look on her face did not stop his thoughts from clouding with pictures of her being permanently there with him. His apartment could not only be his home anymore, but theirs. The thought made him want to smile even more, but he suppressed it then once she spoke.

"Colin..." she warned him. She didn't want to have this painful conversation again.

"What? C'mon Katie. Think about how great it would be if you lived here with me, if we lived together."

"I practically already do."

"See? You just agreed with me, so why not move in?"

"I didn't agree with you, I just don't think it's the right time yet." She hesitated, not wanting to give her reasons. For today, she just wanted to pretend he wasn't going away in a few days, she wanted to pretend that everything was perfect and that Colin had no vices, only virtues. But he had some things to do before she would agree to take such a plunge as moving in fully with him- one specifically being- finishing rehab and getting clean.

"Why not?" she let out a deep sigh once he asked the question he already knew the answer to, the question that had been answered so many times in the past few weeks they had spent together. Yet he asked again anyway.

"Maybe after you're finished in rehab we can talk about it then."

"But it's closer to your job, more convenient for you."

"You're going to be gone on Monday anyways Colin. I'd be here on my own for months?"

Months- The word scared both of them but they refrained from admitting so.

"It's better if I just stay with Em until you're back. Besides, I can't leave her paying the entire rent on her own until the lease is up, that wouldn't be fair."

"I feel like you're going to keep saying maybe even after I get back." He was truly deflated from the whole conversation, like he usually was once it got this far.

"Of course not. You- you just need to sort a couple things out before we think about taking the next step of moving in together." By then, she had walked around to stand behind him as he cooked. Katie wrapped her arms around him and stood on her tiptoes to plant a soft kiss on his cheek. "As soon as you get back, I promise I'll move in, okay?" he nodded and allowed his lips to curl into a small smile.

"Andrew? Yeah sure, we're just on the way to Katie's apartment before we head to the restaurant." Colin puffed on a cigarette as he spoke to his brother on the phone. Katie pressed the button on her side of the door to roll down his window.

"Katie, it's freezing."

"I don't want the whole damn car smelling of smoke, thank you very much." It had been a couple of hours since breakfast and Colin's cheery mood had taken a turn for the worst. His cravings caused a sharpness in his demeanour, he lacked any patience and was easily annoyed but no matter how irritated he became, Katie would outdo him in sassiness any time.

"Yes, the restaurant. That's why I'm calling, I should have asked you sooner but I've been a little... tied up here. I can't make it to lunch."

"I guess we could try and do it another day- oh wait, I'm going away on Monday- does tomorrow suit instead-"

"No, you guys need to come here, like, now."

"What? Why?" he asked quizzically, surprised by Andrew's some-what panicked tone.

"I'll tell you when you get here."

"Andrew- Hello? He just hung up on me the bastard." Colin scrunched his eyebrows in annoyance.

"What did he say? Can he not make it today?"

"He wants us to go to his place instead. It seemed like something was wrong..."

"Sure, but you'll have to give me directions, I've never been to his place before."

They both went up to Katie's apartment and said hi to Emily before Katie put some things in her laundry pile and packed fresh clothes for work on Monday. They chatted with Emily for a couple of minutes but realised the time and had to leave. It took some time to get to Andrew's house and Colin was terrible at giving directions. He was still in a very ratty mood even after they arrived. Colin knocked on the door to have no response.

"C'mon for christ's sake." He said, a cigarette between his lips. He knocked harder this time.

"Calm down Colin. He's probably in the middle of doing something." Katie rolled her eyes. It took until Colin finished his cigarette with a few violent puffs for Andrew to finally answer the door.

"It's about damn time." He said as he threw the butt on the ground and stood on it.

"Shh. Come in." they both noticed how serious he was and quietened down as they stood into his home, closing the door behind them. Katie looked around at the lavishly decorated house. Although it was not modern like Colin's apartment, it too was filled with expensive furniture and must have been thought deeply about by an interior decorator.

"What the hell's going on Andrew? First you tell me you have to show us something and now we get here and we have to whisper and tiptoe around the place. Spit it out already, what is it that you want to tell us?" Katie nudged Colin in side when Andrew wasn't looking, which earned her an irritated look from Colin.

"Promise you won't tell Mom and Dad yet, I haven't figured out how."

"Alright, what the hell do I care if they find out or not?"

"You'll have to come inside and see what I'm talking about, let's go." Andrew headed for the front living room, the couple close behind him. Katie was puzzled when she saw a white crib in the middle of the room, it looked so out of place. Andrew didn't have a girlfriend or wife, nor did he have any children so what was it doing there?

"Andrew what the hell is that?" Colin asked in bewilderment.

"I have someone I want you two to meet..." Andrew reached into the crib and picked up a small baby, cradling her with great care in his arms. Katie and Colin didn't know what to say, they shard a look of equal surprise but Colin was the first to speak.

"What the hell Andrew? Is that yours? Where did you get it?"

"It's a she, she's a girl. I haven't figured out what to name her yet." Andrew replied, as if it was perfectly normal for him to have a child in his arms, his child.

"You can't be serious?"

"Why didn't you tell anyone?" Katie asked, her eyes fixed on the tiny baby that lay in his arms.

"I only found out yesterday. I've been so busy trying to organise everything since then, I needed to get furniture and food and every-thing else so my head's been up my ass."

"So she hasn't got a name yet?" Katie was filled with curiosity.

"Forget about her name, how did she get here? Where's her moth-er? I don't understand." Colin couldn't wrap his head around the concept of his brother having a child.

"A girl I dated last year for a couple of months totally ghosted me for no reason- well, I guess this was the reason right here. She turned up at my place yesterday with the baby, said she couldn't handle it and that she was just as much my responsibility as she was hers-which is true, but I didn't know anything about it? She never told me, if she did, I would've liked to be there, you know, throughout the pregnancy. She handed me the baby, blurted out this huge speech then left."

"What if she changes her mind in a couple days and you've already grown attached?"

"Well she's my baby too, I'm going to want to see her a lot even if she changes her mind." Andrew narrowed his eyes at his brother. "Aren't you happy, you're an uncle now?"

"I never thought of it like that." Colin's features softened, his whole demeanour turned from irritable to eager. "Can I hold her?"

"Sure- but make sure you hold her properly. Look, like this." Andrew delicately handed her to the other man, both brothers' eyes being stuck to the cute little thing wrapped in a cosy blanket. Colin sat down and Katie soon followed, unable to keep her eyes off the little girl either.

"She's beautiful Andrew." Katie said, a smile crossing her lips then.

"She sure is." Colin agreed.

Andrew was still in shock from the entire situation, he couldn't believe that he was a father- but the time periods added up and there could be no denying it. He wished he had have found out sooner, Andrew had always planned to have children, maybe not yet but sometimes unexpected things happened. He could certainly support a child financially, he had a house that was also too big for him alone and being so high up in the company, work hours could be organised around the baby. Although having a child was not planned for him, he found it so strange how it seemed to fit in perfectly to everything happening in his life, as if fatherhood was meant to come about at this exact time.

He knew he may have been getting a little too ahead of himself, his ex-girlfriend could turn up at his door again tomorrow and demand the baby back, but she was part his then too and he was so happy about it. Since she turned up yesterday, he already felt like there was a bond. Andrew knew it was going to be very hard work, as she was only just over a week old at that stage, but he wanted to keep her. He would need to sort out custody with his legal team once she was settled in well and he had the time.

Katie requested that she could hold the baby then too, breaking into Andrew's thoughts. Colin handed her over and she stirred for a moment or two in her arms.

"I'm surprised she's not awake yet, she's due a feed in a little while."

"So... a name? I'm sure everything's been completely turned upside since she arrived yesterday." Katie asked. He paused, a name was the first thing that entered his mind once he saw her but he had been trying to decide and deal with everything else so wasn't completely sure yet.

"I was thinking Hazel." The way he spoke, it sounded as if he was kind of shy to admit the name he liked the most.

"That's really nice."

They all sat there for another while, talking quietly until the baby woke up and needed to be fed. Colin and Katie stayed for another hour or so before heading home. The car ride was quiet at first, but as they neared Colin's apartment, a sadness washed over him as he realised how little time he had left with his girlfriend before he went away. Katie pulled into the car park of his building and as they both made their way up to the top floor in the elevator, she began to sense something was up. Her hand curled around his and they walked up the long hallway.

"Everything okay?" she squeezed his hand.

"Yeah, sure." He nodded and gave her a small smile but it was in no way reassuring. She was not convinced, and rightly so. "I'm just tired." Colin added as he opened the door and moved out of the way so she could enter first.

"You look tired." They stood in the hallway of his apartment after he shut the door, staring back at each other. Katie took a step toward him and reached up to run her thumb over his cheek. She noticed how dark the circles were under his bright eyes, how deflated and exhausted he looked. Katie was worried about him, but she knew everything would only get better once he took the first step for rehab.

"Yeah, I haven't been sleeping great the past while." He mumbled his words slightly, avoiding eye contact as he was brought back to the many restless nights he had with her by his side.

If he hadn't been sleeping great before, he definitely would not be sleeping at all for the last two nights he had to spend with her he would be kept awake worrying about what was in store for him in rehab. Colin didn't want to admit that he was terrified of what was to come, not even to her. It was like stepping into the complete unknown, he didn't know what to expect, he had no idea how difficult it was going to be to go completely cold turkey and the thought of therapy scared him.

Colin was afraid of failing, and afraid of what therapy might un-cover. He was afraid of relapsing and the disappointment that might cause Katie to feel. He was afraid that rehab just wouldn't work, but he would give it a try anyway. Although he should want to get clean for himself, the only thing pushing him through was Katie. He was struggling already, and he hadn't even left yet.

"Maybe I could change from inpatient to outpatient instead-"

"Colin." Katie warned before giving him a knowing look. She held both hands on each side of his face then, urging him silently to look her in the eye. She knew he was getting doubts about the whole thing and if he wanted to change his mind she could not stop him, he was a grown adult, but she felt like inpatient care would be what was best for him at that moment in time. Katie had said it before and she was going to have to say it again. "Look... at the end of the day, it is your decision. But I really think it would be better to begin with inpatient care. We both agreed on this when we planned it. I know it's scary and the next couple months are going to be even scarier, but I know you can get through it." He knew she was right, but he was getting cold feet- that was- until he looked into her eyes, saw how they pleaded with him. Katie knew what was best for him, and so, despite changing his mind over and over again, Colin would finally attend rehab in two days.

**36**

**CHAPTER 35**

December 2011

"Hop in." Katie said through the opened car window, to which Colin walked around to the opposite side of the car and got in the car.

"Do you like the suit?" he asked about the suit she had gotten dry cleaned and dropped into his rehabilitation centre a couple days ago.

"The suit is the least of your worries right now." She replied with an eye roll and began driving off. He always looked good in a suit, but she wasn't going to admit that to him right then while they were on the way to court to decide his DUI charges.

"It's fine, I don't need you to tell me how good I look right now. I already know it." He looked from the corner of his eye to see if he had gotten some sort of reaction out of her rom his words. Colin noticed how she was trying to hold in laughter and smiled then despite his nervousness.

"How are you feeling?"

"Okay I suppose, considering the circumstances." He held back his honesty for a moment, which led to a short silence until he voiced his worries aloud to her. "D-do you think I'm going to have to go to jail?"

Katie took a moment to look at him and then fixed her gaze back to driving, unsure how to answer his question.

"I don't know Colin. But I've been speaking to your attorney and he thinks he'll be able to get you out of a jail sentence."

"I won't last in prison." He could barely cope being in rehab for this long, and that was nothing compared to prison.

"Listen, let's just take everything as it comes. We'll be there soon, and if you do get a prison sentence, we can worry about it after the hearing."

Her words didn't calm him down at all and his nerves only got worse the closer they got. The hearing didn't take long and much to Colin's surprise, he was not given a jail sentence, only a hefty fine and two year license suspension. The relief he felt once they walked out of the court room was immense. Katie turned to him and gave him a huge hug. They stayed in the same spot for a while sharing a moment of relief.

The car ride back was much louder than the one to the courthouse. They joked and laughed, the mood much more uplifting. Katie's phone cut across their talking when a message came through.

"Hey can you read that message out to me? I'm driving."

"It's from Emily, she asked if you're still on for dinner tonight at seven?"

"Can you text her back saying sure, I can't wait."

"Sure, why are you two going to dinner?" he asked, curious.

"She said she has something to tell me but needs to do it in person, I'm not sure why though because we live in the same apartment. Surely she could just tell me there. Then again, I barely see her when I'm at home. Our schedules are always crossing, I feel like I haven't seen her in forever."

"How come?"

"Oh she's just been really busy with work lately. She's been working a lot of nightshifts and stuff."

"Nightshifts... that must be crappy."

"I know, you can't even handle simple nine to five shifts." Katie scoffed, cracking a smile in the corner of her mouth after she spoke.

"As soon as I get out I'm going straight back to working, and working hard at that."

"How are you going to survive without having me doing all the work for you?" she asked, humour filling her tone.

"Who knows?" he chuckled before adding, "I'm going to have to find someone else to be my PA, Carrie's not going to be able to work full time again like she used to. I was just putting it off after you left since I barely ever turned up to work for a while..." she noticed how his smile faltered then as he mentioned the time after Katie quit working for him.

A short time later, they pulled into the car park of the rehab centre. Katie wanted to talk him to the door and give him a proper goodbye. Once they reached the door, she got closer and gave him a huge kiss. She took his face in both her hands and smiled at him, the most genuine he had seen in a long time.

"I miss you already." He laughed once he spoke, his words came out as a half-hearted expression but truly, he was already feeling apprehensive- it was in his eyes.

"I'm coming up on Friday to see you and then a few days after that you'll be home for a while for Christmas. I'm not going anywhere."

Katie smiled again, an attempt to will one onto his lips also but he just couldn't do it. He decided then, to take her into his arms and held onto her tight for a moment, kissing her cheek and speaking again.

"I love you."

"I love you too and I'll see you in a couple days, okay?"

"Alright." He didn't want to let her go, but he knew he had to.

"Sorry I'm late, my Uber was stuck in traffic- oh, hello." Katie was too busy taking off her jacket and setting her purse down to notice the man that was sitting beside Emily at the table. Once she looked up to see him smiling at her, she felt surprised. Who was he? And what was he doing there?

"Katie, this is Jeremy. Jeremy, this is my lovely friend Katie." Emily beamed from across the table but her friend was still confused.

"So glad to finally meet you Katie." Jeremy held his hand out across the table for her to shake, which she reluctantly accepted.

"Jeremy's my boyfriend Katie, I've wanted you to meet him for a while now." Katie was shocked, but was extremely happy for her friend that she had finally met someone. It seemed like Emily was always too focused on work to ever find a companion, but Katie guessed she had been wrong this entire time.

"Oh my god, it's so nice to meet you too. I'm just so... surprised, I had no clue. How long have you two been dating?"

"What would you say Jeremy, like- six months now?"

"Yeah, around that. I was asking you out for weeks before that though." He rolled his eyes teasingly before shooting Emily a grin.

"He works at the hospital too, if you've noticed I've been working a lot more lately, now you know why." Emily joked as they were all handed their menus from a waiter who had just stood at their table.

Katie wanted to know all about Jeremy and how they began dating. She was so curious, having too many questions to ask all at once. Throughout the dinner Katie learned more about the man her best friend had been dating over the last couple of months, she smiled, laughed, and joked but on the inside, she felt saddened by her discovery. Of course, she was delighted that her friend was dating someone who seemed to suit her well, but suddenly a wave of guilt and sadness washed over her. She had been so caught up with what was going on with herself and Colin to even ask Emily had she met someone over the past few months. She knew she needed to apologise and she decided to do it once she and Emily were alone.

As if reading her thoughts, Emily mentioned Colin, asking how he was.

"He's- he's doing fine at the moment. He has his good days and bad days."

"Colin?"

"Yes, sorry Jeremy, Colin is Katie's boyfriend."

"He would've loved to be here, but he's away at the moment." Katie didn't want to get too into a conversation about her boyfriend, for fear she may share more than Colin wanted her to share. Emily noticed the anguish appear on her friend's face and gave Jeremy a look while Katie wasn't looking that told Jeremy there was no room for any more conversation on that topic.

"I was just thinking that maybe we could go on a double date sometime soon when he gets back." Emily gave the other woman an encouraging smile that she returned but it didn't reach her eyes.

"Sounds good, I think you two might get along." Katie looked at Jeremy then who nodded.

"Sounds like a plan alright." He replied.

Katie was surprised when Emily said she was going to stay at home that night after dinner instead of going back to Jeremy's. He was in work early the next morning and Emily said she wanted to spend more time with her friend, she felt like they hadn't seen each other in ages. They said their goodbyes to Jeremy and got a cab home. Once they were alone, she decided to ask Katie about how Colin was doing, knowing she would get a real reply this time.

"Well I've never used my car as much in life. I used to hate driving so much I would always just get ubers everywhere but now I feel like I'm his personal taxi driver." Katie said light-heartedly which made Emily laugh aloud. "Court went okay today though, he's got a license suspension for the next two years so I should probably get used to being the one driving and a fine too. I know driving under the influence is a terrible thing to do but I'm so happy he didn't get a jail sentence."

"How's the rehab going for him?" Emily was genuinely interested, she knew how difficult it had been on him and Katie although her friend put on a brave face through all the heartache and only seeing him for such short visits at a time.

"He has his good days and his bad days, but I think he's going to be okay. He's home for the holidays in a couple days, I can't wait."

"I'm sure you can't. I hope everything works out good and I'm glad to hear he's doing okay."

Katie felt like everything had been building up inside her, she had to put on a brave face in front of Colin and around his family when they asked how he was doing. She had to stay strong for both of them and keep a positive outlook on things even when she felt like the weakest person in the world. It was all taking an emotional toll on her and she hadn't properly opened up about everything to anyone, not even Emily or her friends back home over long phone conversations. Then suddenly, on top of everything else, the guilt she originally felt in the restaurant came back again- it forced her to speak again but not before letting out a long sigh first.

"Em I'm so sorry about the past while, I've been so tied up with Colin that I haven't even had a long enough conversation with you to find out about Jeremy sooner. I need to try harder, I feel like I've been so caught up in Colin to even realise you've found someone yourself." The look on Katie's face as she explained her feelings to her friend only made Emily furrow her brows in confusion.

"Oh Katie, you don't need to apologise to me, honestly. I understand, Colin has been a handful and we're both in work a lot, plus I've been spending a lot of time with Jeremy, so I haven't been home a lot. It's not your fault I was waiting until the right time to tell you about him. Don't punish yourself for something that isn't anyone's fault." She could see the tears forming in Katie's eyes and felt the need to reach out and give her a huge hug. "Shh, it's alright. Tell me what's bothering you Kate."

"I-I'm sorry. I feel like I'm making this all about me. Everything's fine. We should be talking about you."

"Oh stop, we have all the time in the world to talk about Jeremy. Nonsense Katie. Tell me what's the matter." Emily held her friend at arm's length then to take a look at her tear stained face. She gave her an encouraging smile that Katie gave back, although her face was red, and her eyes swollen.

"I-I just feel so overwhelmed that's all. I feel relieved for Colin but anxious too, I don't want him to slip up once he comes home for the holidays or when he comes home for good. It's all been hard to handle, and I thought I was managing just fine up until just now to be honest."

"You just need to vent, that's all." Emily didn't take the smile off her face the entire time she talked through things with Katie, it uplifted her and comforted her in ways her friend would never understand. After a while, Katie felt like she had cleared all her doubts up and before they both knew it, they were rooting through the freezer to find ice cream and trying to find a TV channel that was doing old re-runs of the Jerry Springer Show.

**37**

CHAPTER 36

April 2012

"You're getting married? Oh my god Em that's great!" Katie exclaimed before she stood up to give both her friend and her boyfriend a hug. Emily had been beaming since she, Jeremy, Katie and Colin had reached the restaurant a while ago for brunch that afternoon, Katie knew exactly why then.

"Congratulations." Colin said warmly to the couple before shaking Jeremy's hand and smiling at Emily.

"Have you picked a date yet? How did he propose? I want to know everything." Katie's words shot out of her mouth at a thousand miles an hour. She was unable to contain her excitement and it made everyone at the table laugh.

"We're looking to have the wedding around November or December, but we just need to try sort everything else out first and see if it suits everyone." She smiled at Jeremy as she spoke.

It seemed quite soon to Katie, but she didn't voice her opinion out loud, instead, she listened intently as Emily explained where she wanted the wedding to be and how Jeremy proposed to her. She was completely surprised by the engagement but at the same time, truly thrilled for her friend. Emily broke the news to her that she would be one of the bridesmaids, which only added to Katie's excitement. They branched off into their own conversation about dresses, themes and decor while Jeremy and Colin continued with their conversation before Emily had told them the big news.

The waiter gathered their empty plates just as message came through on Colin's cell phone.

"Shit." He breathed in sharply as he read the message before turning to Katie. "It's almost two thirty, Andrew just texted me asking were we still coming over."

"Oh yes, I almost forgot about that. We might be a couple of minutes late but we'll still make it."

"Okay, I'll tell him now."

"Sorry guys, I guess we'll have to cut this brunch short."

"Are you two visiting the gorgeous Hazel?" Emily asked, looking between the couple. She had only met the baby a handful of times but she certainly left a lasting impression on her. She was beautiful and even though she was only a couple of months old, already was bursting with personality.

"We sure are." Colin replied from across the table as Katie put her jacket on.

"This was lovely but I'm afraid we have to go now. Congratulations you two, I'm so happy for you.  And don't worry Em, I'll be catching up with you tomorrow, so we can continue our conversation about the wedding plans." Katie winked at Emily which caused her and Jeremy to chuckle.

"Bye." They both said in unison, to which Colin and Katie said also before leaving.

There was a short yet comfortable silence in the car on the way to Andrew's house. Katie was content, she feel so happy and overjoyed for her friend who had found someone she thought she would spend the rest of her life with. And Katie was going to be able to help Em every step of the way with wedding plans, it was all so exciting for her. Colin watched intently as she smiled to herself, then said something that made Katie's content to curiosity.

"Look at you, smiling like a fool to yourself and you aren't even the one getting married." Colin teased her before adding, "I can't imagine what you're going to be like when I pop the question if you're like this because Em's got engaged." Katie's eyes widened a little at the mention of Colin proposing to her. When she turned to look at him in the passenger seat, a boyish grin was plastered onto his face.

"Well... it's different. Em's my best friend, of course I'm going to be excited." Colin scoffed and let out a quiet chuckle before replying.

"What? So you won't be excited when we get married?" He was in too much of a daze with the idea of he and Katie getting married to notice how perplexed and caught off guard Katie felt.

"When? You haven't even asked me yet. You might want to do that first before you start planning anything." She tried to joke away the scary feelings creeping up on her and put an end to the conversation. The car fell silent for a moment while Colin tried to think of what to say next.

"Well- will you?"

"Will I what?" Katie acted as if she had forgotten all about the conversation they were having only a minute ago.

"Isn't it obvious? Will you marry me?" the seriousness of his voice forced Katie to react in a fit of laughter that filled the car but it was matched with Colin's. Once she stopped, the car filled up with a thick silence for a third time that car ride.

"How romantic of you Colin?" Again, she tried to dodge a serious answer with a joking and light-hearted tone.

"You're avoiding the question."

"You can't be serious?"

"Of course I am."

"So Jeremy proposed and now you want to too?"

"I was planning on asking you soon anyways-"

"We've only been dating a couple months Colin, don't get too ahead of yourself."

"But we've known each other for much longer."

"Yes, but the majority of that time we were both with other people or not together."

"We've been dating longer than Emily and Jeremy have been, you didn't bring up how little time they've been dating when Em told you they got engaged." He had a point; one Katie did not want to think about.

"Yes but... Colin are you really going to propose to me in a car ride over to your brother's house?"

"No time like the present."

"You aren't thinking straight."

"Of course I am."

"No you're not."

"You're acting like it's such a bad thing for us to get married."

"Well- now's not the right time to get engaged Colin and what's the rush anyways huh?" she shrugged her shoulders, clearly feeling extremely uncomfortable by the entire conversation.

"Like I said, no time like the present." He was using that tone again, the teasing kind. Colin received a questionable look from Katie then, to which he chuckled again. "What? I'm just testing the waters, no need to worry about me proposing anytime soon. You can relax... for now." She was surprised that he wasn't in anyway wounded by her rejection but was happy either way that he had not taken her hesitation the wrong way.

"Good, because you better not think of proposing to me for another at least ten years." She joked.

"Commitment issues much?" he quirked an eyebrow.

"Over-commitment issues much?" she retorted.

"Touché."

"Can we talk about something else now? All this serious commitment talk is making me feel sick." Katie said half-heartedly.

Colin guffawed loudly in response and they changed the topic of conversation until they reached Andrew's house. He was at the door to greet them, Hazel snuggled up in his arms. Katie immediately asked to hold her as soon as they aid their hellos and began rocking the sleepy-eyed baby in her arms.

"She's due a nap around this time so don't worry if she falls asleep. I'll put her in her crib when your arms get tired."

"I don't think her arms will ever get tired, it's going to take a lot for Katie to let you take that baby out of her arms now." Colin joked as he nudged his brother.

"Oh don't act like you aren't the same when you get your hands on this little princess." She scoffed, rolling her eyes at the two men.

"Very true." Colin replied.

Andrew made them coffee and they all sat together in his kitchen, catching up. Soon enough, Hazel fell asleep and her father took her from Katie to put her in her crib. While he was gone, Katie caught Colin smiling uncontrollably at her and her curiosity kicked in.

"What are you staring at, creep?"

"Just how much of a doting aunt you are." His words made her scoff.

"Aunt?" she quirked an eyebrow at him, crossing her arms.

"Yes- well, you will be her aunt when I get the chance to marry you." He replied wickedly.

"Oh, dream on Colin." She slapped his arm playfully and then took another sip of her coffee.

"What's going on here? I leave you two alone for a minute, are you beating up my brother?" Andrew walked in and expressed mock surprise and disgust as he sat down at the table in front of them again.

"Of course I am."

"Good, you should've hit him harder."

"Maybe I will next time." The three laughed together before Colin decided to ask the question he always asked once he saw his brother after a couple of days. The same question that was always given the same answer.

"So... Have you heard anything from her mom yet?"

"Yet? I doubt I will ever hear from her, or she'll at least wait until all the raising is done. I could tell by the way she was acting that day when she turned up here she probably wasn't going to change he mind any time soon. She seemed terrified of having to look after Hazel. I get it thought, parenthood is scary, especially when you think you might have to do it alone and it's completely unplanned."

"Do you think she will ever turn back up here then?"

"I-I'm not sure." Andrew thought about it for a moment before answering. Judging by the look on his face, he wasn't sure if he wanted that to happen or not either.

"What would you do?" Katie was sparked with interest.

"What could I do? If she wanted to see Hazel, I'd have to let her. She is her mother after all." A frown met his lips after the words left his mouth. A silence filled the kitchen for a moment or two before a thought entered Andrew's mind, reminding him. "Hey, by the way, would you two be able to watch Hazel for a night next weekend?"

"Next weekend huh? We'll have to check our schedule." Colin pretended to think about it although he would say year eventually. Andrew rolled his eyes at his younger brother.

"Don't mind him, of course we'll look after her." Katie laughed.

"Thanks Katie."

The pair stayed with Andrew until the late evening before deciding to head home. Once they got in, they booked a meal and sat down in front of the TV together to eat and binge watch "The Office". By the fourth episode, Katie was curled up in a ball, her head on his lap as they both watched the screen intently. She yawned and stretched her arms before speaking.

"I'm tired, I think I'm going to head to bed."

"Don't you want to wait until this episode is finished."

"I can't keep my eyes open."

"Fine then." Colin rolled his eyes, but a cheeky smile fell onto his lips a moment after and then he decided to scoot out from under her and pick her up and throw her over his shoulders.

"Are you serious right now?" she tried her best not to squeal, her legs dangled in the air as blood rushed to her head from being held upside down.

"Of course I am, you said you wanted to go bed, so I'm bringing you to bed."

She screamed with laughter as he threw her on the bed playfully and crawled on top of her.

"I could have made it to bed myself you know." She replied dryly, holding back a smile at the sight of his smiling face full of complete contempt.

"I just thought you might need some help."

"Get off of me you pig!" she laughed again as she tried to push him away from her.

"What did you just call me?" he raised an eyebrow in mock disgust before tickling her until she cried out for him to stop. They lay there for a moment in silence once both their laughter died down, just smiling at each other like two love sick teenagers.

"Now I'm wide awake." Katie sighed.

"That's a good thing." He explained wickedly as his face inched closer to hers. "We don't have to go asleep just yet." Colin kissed her passionately on the lips before the pair rolled over, so Katie was on top. She used the opportunity to take off her jumper and throw it on the ground somewhere. He helped to undo her bra before they began to undress him too, both giggling uncontrollably.

It was the early hours of the morning once they were finished and they sat in the afterglow of their passions. Colin caressed her cheek as she lay facing him, examining all his beautiful features. She would never get used to how perfect she thought he was. His hand moved from her cheek to her left hand, he held it up and examined it carefully. She almost shivered at his touch, at the feel of his fingers falling over her skin and snaking around her fingers.

"What are you doing?" a breathy laugh escaped her lips, by then she was exhausted.

"What's your ring size?"

"Oh god not this again." She groaned and took her hand from his to cover her face. Katie's reaction made his chest erupt with loud laughter.

"I'm going to have to know someday-"

"Some day, not today." She turned around in bed so that her back was to him. He continued to find the entire thing humorous and only moved closer to her instead of away like she had hoped.

"I'm kidding, I'm kidding." he reassured her before turning her around in bed so she could see his half-hearted expression. He kissed both cheeks and then locked eyes with her. "But I do want to spend the rest of my life with you." He leaned in again and kissed her lips this time. "And I am going to have to propose to you some day." Colin said in between kisses.

Katie couldn't control the huge smile that appeared on her lips then. Her hands went to hold either side of his face and she leaned her forehead on his, her eyes were closed but she was still awake and still smiling.

"And I'm looking forward to that day- just please, don't rush into it. I'm always going to be here regardless of when or how you ask me." He was the one smiling then, and she saw this once she opened her eyes and looked into his deep blue ones. Colin tried to stifle laughter, his body taken over by complete happiness, all he could do was chuckle like a giddy child.

"What?" Katie was quite quizzical but his laughter was contagious, so she had to join in too for a moment.

"I'm just happy, that's all." He said once he got control of himself. "Every day I wake up and you're here I don't believe it's true. I can't believe that we're together, I can't believe we're working out."

"Wow, you're getting very deep tonight aren't you?" Katie teased him then. "How have you been feeling lately?" the conversation turned from being about them to being about him.

Every couple of days she always made sure to ask how he was doing, how therapy was going and if he'd had any urges again. Since Colin signed himself out of the in-patient care, he had been attending a therapy session every week where he tried to tackle his problems from the very roots of their existence. Sometimes Colin thought it was best to lie to Katie and tell her things had been going great, and sometimes he couldn't help but tell the truth about how difficult it was to actually talk to someone about everything.

"Everything's perfect." He lied. He still felt guilt, from putting her through what he had put her through. He still felt inadequate, ready for her to leave at the drop of a hat once she realised all his flaws. At times he even felt unworthy, not just of her but of his family, parents that were trying their best to understand him and Andrew who said he would always have his little brother's back. Colin was truly finding it difficult not to slip into old habits again because of all these things he was feeling. He didn't deserve any of it, he didn't deserve her but she was here and she had told him time and time again that she wasn't going anywhere.

He had been strong enough all this time to not give in to any temptations he faced along the way, but that was only because she had been there to help him. She was one of the only reasons he had gotten this far. Just then, his mind rushed into a state of panic- what would happen when she wasn't around?

"Good." She whispered, breaking into his thoughts with her sweet voice but it was not nearly calming enough for his wandering mind that night.

"I miss you." She admitted from the other end of the phone.

She had finally gotten to the spare room in Sam's house to be alone and speak to Colin after calling him a couple of times that morning and getting no answer. Katie had been visiting her friends for the past few days, and would be there until the end of week. She was quite concerned when Colin wasn't picking up his phone a few hours earlier but it certainly felt like a weight had been lifted off her shoulders after she finally saw his name pop up on the screen of her phone.

Her voice hurt him, it broke his heart to hear her so concerned and he knew she had reason to be.

"I miss you too." He tried to laugh as he spoke before adding, "I've almost forgotten what you look like." To try and lift her up a little.

"How come you weren't picking up earlier?" she asked after chuckling.

"I was still asleep, sorry. I've been finding it hard to sleep without you here so it's taken until all hours before I finally drift off."

"Aw really Colin? I hope you're okay. Don't worry, I'll be home in a few days to kiss you goodnight again." She wiggled her eyebrows, despite knowing he couldn't see her. He laughed, but not with as much force as usual.

"Listen I have to go now, I'm in the middle of cooking dinner. I just wanted to call you to let you know I'm still alive and haven't burned the apartment down- yet." The joke made her lighten up again and stop being so concerned for him. Colin was fine, he could survive a couple of days on his own without her. She had nothing to worry about, she thought.

"Okay well enjoy, I'll call you again soon. Love you." He closed his eyes as she said the last words, unable to speak for a moment. He pinched the bridge of his nose, trying to get the words out of his mouth without breaking down on the phone.

"I love you too. I'll see you in a few days." Were his last words before he hung up the phone and threw it on the floor next to him.

Colin buried his face in his hands and shook his head slowly. He felt like a completely failure, he was a failure. It had only taken two days, two days of her absence for him to fall off the wagon and take up David's offer of going out for the night. He'd been on a two-day binge since then, the drink and drugs had finally wore off completely and he felt the worst he had ever felt. Why was he so weak? That's all he kept asking himself, over and over again.

## 38

CHAPTER 37

December 2012

Katie snuggled closer into Colin as they sat on one of benches outside in the courtyard of the hotel. They were waiting for Emily and Jeremy to arrive, along with all the other guests but decided to come outside for some air. He felt her shiver next to him and put his arm around her shoulder to bring her closer. There was a light sprinkle of snow on the ground, the trees were bare but the day was calm and cool.

"C'mon, maybe we should go back inside now." She said, but he was distracted by the plushness of her fur coat.

She shrugged gently out of his grip and stood up, taking his hand and pulling him up to stand next to her. She linked his arm and they both walked back inside. She noticed he had been distracted all morning, distracted the past couple of weeks again and she was too afraid to ask why. There had been a pattern with Colin that she had picked up on by then from all the time she had shared with him over the last few years, especially since their relationship had started. There were many obstacles he needed to get through, and she had been there every step of the way. She was afraid to ask what had been bothering him because she already knew the answer, because with those many obstacles faced, there were more slip ups.

They sat at their seats arranged for them for dinner a while later but Katie still had worry and doubt weighing her down. She smiled as she watched a charismatic Colin chat with everyone around the table but when they all shared laughter she did not laugh, and when they all became deeply engrossed in conversation she did not open her mouth. Katie played with her cutlery, half listening to everyone around the table while thoughts and memories crept back up on her.

Katie remembered returning home after her trip back to Detroit, she remembered finding Colin and his apartment in a state. He was crying and so was she, the feeling of wrapping her arms tightly around him as if to protect him from any harm that he had or would inflict on himself from slipping back into old patterns was a feeling Katie could never escape. Not that time he slipped up or the time after that a couple weeks later or even the time after that when he promised he would never do it again. Promises were always full of hope and determination, full of love and appreciation for Katie and everything he had done for her but promises were always broken and all the optimism and hope deteriorated as time passed.

As dinner was laid out in front of them, each course only brought back more memories and heighted Colin's obliviousness to what his girlfriend was experiencing right next to him. Katie had begun to wonder if it was her or if it was him. She wanted to blame Colin but she knew so much about him, he told her so much and opened up his chest so many times to rip his heart out and show her what was the problem. The problems that only Katie could see, that only Katie could understand. She had gotten to a stage where she felt she knew Colin more than he knew himself- she had never been that closely connected with someone before in her life. And as much as the feeling was uplifting and joyful on the good days when it heightened her love even more for Colin, it did nothing but destroy her on the bad days, because it was that connection that made her stay every time and it was that connection that she was clinging on to every time he broke their trust and went back to the addictions he promised he would never go back to.

Maybe she was too lenient with him? Maybe she loved him too much? Maybe she needed to remove herself in order for him to get better? Maybe if she did she would lose him and never get him back? A million more maybes flooded her thoughts that she could not shake away. She wondered if leaving him would push him to get better on his own or if it would only tear him apart even more? Katie thought deeply about what it would be like to not have him around and it only made her grip onto him tighter as they danced slowly on the dancefloor after their dinner. She rested her head on his should as he swung from side to side gently. She felt like his slip ups and let downs could equate to infinity and even then she would still love him more than that, she would still be there every time he got the help he needed or went back to rehab or tired again starting fresh. That thought was scary- loving someone unconditionally that had a huge habit of letting you down.

"Are you alright? You seem quiet." Colin had finally noticed. Katie took her head from his shoulder and looked him straight in the eye before replying.

"I'm fine." She smiled at him.

"Yeah, I'm just mulling over everything that's happened today." To say she was completely overjoyed for Em would be an understatement and although the wedding preparation was not long, Katie never thought the day would finally come. Colin let out a soft chuckle before nodding towards the newly married couple who were dancing across the way from them.

"He looks so smitten." He said before grinning widely.

"And rightly so." Katie added before joining in on the laughter.

"Funny to think that'll be us soon." Katie immediately gave him a look of warning once the words left his mouth.

"Colin..." her tone was as cautionary as her facial expression.

"What?" he smirked at her.

"We've talked about this."

"I know, I'm just reminding you what's to come."

"I need no reminder, you've already told me a hundred times already. They're starting to become daily." That was another thing to add to her list of worries that she had forgotten despite Colin's persistence. He laughed light heartedly before planting a kiss on her lips and moving closer to her ear.

"I love you."

"I love you too." She said before resting her head on his shoulder again.

His actions nor his words could stop her mind again as it raced through everything that had happened since his first slip up after her return from Detroit leading up to this moment. Katie knew what she needed to do- but she was having a good day and she didn't want to ruin it despite being able to clearly smell the alcohol off his breath and the giddiness he had throughout the ceremony and the reception that seemed to top everyone else's. She could see he had been trying to contain himself all day, trying to make himself look like he had not passed their two-drink limit although she knew he had crossed that line before they had even sat down to eat whenever Katie would be whisked away with the wedding party or to help Em out. She noticed how he seemed to forget things and run back up to their room several times also, Katie had forced herself into silence, pretend she didn't see anything.

It wasn't until further into the night when everyone was distracted with dancing and having a good time that she had made her decision. This could not be avoided anymore that day, she was going to do something- something she may regret. Katie saw Colin was distracted with Jeremy, Emily and a few others to notice her slip out of the function room and upstairs to their hotel room. She rooted vigorously through the over night bags they had brought with him for a couple of minutes until finally she found Colin's stash. She picked up the small baggie and held it close to her face, examining the white power as it settled to the bottom of the bag. Within giving it a second thought she went to the bathroom and dropped the back into the toilet bowl before flushing it. Katie tidied up the room and then returned downstairs as if nothing had happened.

The weight that had lifted off her shoulders made her feel content with her decision, but it would not last forever. The night went quickly after that, Katie didn't once think of her actions upstairs in the hotel room until she was saying goodnight to an exhausted looking Emily. Jeremy had his arm wrapped around her, as if she would fall to the floor if he let her go.

"Where are you two going?" she asked once they approached her.

"I think we need to call it a night Katie. I'm exhausted."

"Well I'll see you two in the morning. Goodnight and thanks for an amazing day."

She hugged both before they said their final goodbyes. It was then that Katie had realised she was on her own, Colin was no where to be seen for the past while and this automatically made her heart drop. She began to rush upstairs to her room but the closer she got the slower her feet were. She was terrified of what she might walk in on in their room. Had he realised what she did earlier? Was he mad? What would he do when he saw her?

Katie hesitantly put her key card in the door and opened it as soon as the light flashed green.

"Colin..." Her voice held so much caution, she had not realised she was standing at the threshold with the door only opened slightly. She was shaking, and it was completely justifiable- she realised this only when she eventually stepped inside and shut the door behind her. Her eyes widened as they wandered around the room then finally met his tarnished blue ones.

She couldn't look away once their eyes had caught each other's. She wanted to burst into tears, she wanted to scream and shout, but she didn't. Colin's facial expression tore her apart, for a moment she could rip her eyes away from him to look at the room he had just destroyed, the clothes he had ripped out of the suitcase that were strewn all over the floor, and the furniture that lay pulled out from their original places. Katie's lungs couldn't work for a moment, her eyes could not see anything but his rage and desperateness- the urgency that tore him apart yet promised composure, even just for a little while.

"Where is it Katie?"

"Where's wha-"

"Don't pretend you don't know what I'm talking about. Where the fuck is it?" he growled at her, unable to hold back his anger. She had never seen him this way before, it was the first time she had actually felt afraid of him and that upset her even more.

"Colin..." Katie warned as he took a step toward her only for her to take a step back. His eyes were glazed over in a mixture of anguish and torment. Colin was absolutely furious- every part of his body and every word he spit at her showed that clearly.

"Katie?" he waited for her reply still, despite knowing she was holding back. "Katie for fuck's sake tell me where you put my god damn stash!" Colin's booming voice echoed around the room, making her feel tiny as she stood in front of him but that did not mean she felt weak. Katie stood up straight and looked him dead in the eye before replying.

"Why does it matter now? It's gone." Her voice held great force to it also, she could not show him how afraid she was or else he would notice this and use it against her.

Katie's eyes widened as he erupted in front of her, letting out grunts as he punched the wall then pushed the desk over that had been pulled out from the wall already.

"Colin!" she shouted at him, she was furious then too. "What the hell are you doing for Christ's sake?" her yelling only made his anger stronger, he ruined another piece of furniture in the room then stalked towards her until she had her back against the wall and their noses were almost touching.

"You better be fucking joking." His words and expression were void of any emotion, he then paced around in front of her for a moment- fidgeting and mumbling to himself. "This is a joke. This is a joke. Let this be a fucking joke!" The last sentence was spoken with his body facing her.

"You told me you were done with all of this. You said that to me, a couple weeks ago."

"Does it look like I'm done?" his eyes were opened wide, his expression frightened her beyond anything she had seen before. He looked as if he was going insane.

"So you lied to me? You lied to me again."

"I tried Katie, I really did."

"Well why don't you try harder." Her stern voice interrupted his racing thoughts for a moment, but he had nothing to say. What could he say? He was in too much of a state to worry about her feelings in that moment, but knew that once all of this passed, nothing but guilt would cripple him. "Calm down, we can work this out together tonight, and make this be the last time this has to happen-"

"Don't you get it? I can't! Not right now. God fucking damn it."

"If not right now then when Colin? When are you going to stop this for good? It's only hurting you and I."

"I can't I told you already." His voice raised again but she only raised hers louder.

"You keep saying you can't but sometimes I wonder if you're even trying?" Katie was done trying to talk sense into him. "I wonder if you'll ever start trying, if you're just stringing me along." The last part was said more so to herself than to him, she walked to the edge of the bed and sat at it for a moment as she tried to process her thoughts. She saw him walk slowly towards her from the corner of her eye but her gaze never moved from the carpet below her as she hung her head low.

"Babe- please..." his voice was as soft as could be, as if the last five minutes had never happened. He knelt down in front of her and took both her hands in his gently. He was pleading with her, completely and entirely desperate. "Just tell me where it is. I know you didn't throw it away. If you just tell me, I promise tonight will be the last time." He urged her to look at him but instead of catching his eyes, she diverted her stare from the ground to the left of her despite Colin's face being so near and in front of her. Katie took a deep breath and tired not to allow tears to fall from her eyes.

"I flushed the bag Colin. I got rid of it and there's nothing you can do about it now." Katie sounded completely deflated. Her eyes were dead once they finally caught his. She felt nothing but defeat and the last piece of her heart that was still intact broke once Colin's fury arose again and he began to take his anger out on the hotel room.

"Colin stop it! You're really scaring me now. Stop it!"

She stood behind him, barely able to breath as she choked on her tears. She had been so strong throughout all of this, but this time, she could not put up a front. She could not hide her grief or distress at the situation unfolding in front of her caused entirely by the man who was supposed to keep her from feeling such ways. Colin turned to look at her for a moment.

"This wouldn't be happening if you had've just kept your nose out of it."

Colin had the audacity to blame this on her, as if she was not already completely tormented by his actions that night, his words hit harder.

"You have no one to blame here but yourself." Katie shook her head before grabbing her bag and leaving him in the room alone. She headed down to reception but tears brimming her eyes. She organised a cab, not caring how much it would cost and headed back to the apartment she shared with Emily. Once silence greeted her, she took a deep breath and closed the front door. The lease would be up in a few weeks, almost perfect timing as Emily would be moving in with Jeremy after their honeymoon.

Katie didn't sleep at all that night, tossing and turning until the early hours of the mornings. She was completely alone with her thoughts for those few hours in the early morning as she lay in bed. She had turned off her phone so was completely unaware of the countless messages left from Colin once he had calmed down and assessed the situation. It could wait until she had sorted her head out a little and fully processed the events that took place the night before.

Katie, he spoke to the dead line on the other end of the phone, I know what happened tonight- it was terrible. I really don't ever want it to happen again and I truly mean that. I know you're scared, and I am too. But I need to go back, I know I do. Not just out-patient like the last time, I really need to go back. Maybe you don't want to speak to me right now, hell I'd understand if you never wanted to speak to me again after tonight, but if you do I'll be waiting. I love you and I don't want to ever hurt you like I have so many times before in the past.

**39**

— • —

## CHAPTER 38

August 2013

"Yes, that would be great actually. I can meet any time next Tuesday." Katie smiled to herself as she spoke on the phone at her desk in the small cubicle she had become familiar with over the last year.

"Does noon suit then?" The women from HR asked.

"Noon sounds perfect."

"Great, I'll meet you at the front desk of the building then and don't forget to bring a form of identification and your resume. I look forward to seeing you."

"You too, thanks again."

"Goodbye." As soon as she hung up the phone, her smile beamed even brighter than before.

Katie couldn't believe it, she had just heard back from a job she went for last week at LOVE Magazine- she hadn't even excepted to get a reply from them yet there she was, organising a meeting for next week. She didn't want to think too fa ahead or get her hopes up, but she was really excited. She heard her phone ringing once again and answered immediately, afraid that it would be from the magazine again saying there had been some mistake. Instead, she was pleasantly surprised that it was Colin.

"Hi babe, I have bad news."

"Oh really? What's up?" she was immediately concerned. At this stage, Katie never knew what to expect next with Colin so every time he spoke she was waiting for bad news. Luckily this time, it was not the bad news she always dreaded.

"I might be a little late to lunch." She tried to hold back her sign of relief from the other end of the phone before replying.

"That's fine. I'm actually a little busy right now so I might be a couple of minutes late too. Call me when you're on the way there?"

"Sure. I'll see you in a little while."

"Bye." She called before hanging up. They had arranged to have a long lunch together earlier in the week, something they did often despite not working close to each other.

Katie was happy that Colin had finally went back to working for his dad, after months of taking the time he needed to get better. Of course, there had still been some slip-ups since his first time in rehab all that time ago after the crash, but there had not been one as big in a couple of months. This had enabled Colin to return to working for his father but not with the same amount of responsibilities as he had previously. He did not work a full week in work either, but was really trying his best to actually do his job this time around compared to when Katie had worked for him. She wanted to be happy for him, in fact, she was happy for him but at the time she always felt so on edge that he may slip back into old habits like he had done so many times before. Katie had become hypersensitive to his behaviour and over the past couple of days, she had noticed a change in him again like the one only a couple of months ago.

She thought about this all the way to the restaurant that day, wondering why she had not brought it up with him yet before anything could possibly escalate. The truth was that Katie wanted to believe he would never break the good cycle he had kept up for this long, so she had blatantly been ignoring all the signs. Her mind forced her look back on the early days, when she first started working for Colin and she was getting to know the type of person he was- before she knew... He had been letting people down back then too. This thought had crept up on her from what felt like nowhere, she didn't want to think about it anymore. She engrossed herself in another few tasks in work before grabbing her coat and bag and heading downstairs to exit the building.

Colin was only around five minutes late, which surprised her. He apologised once he met her at the table and she stood up to hug him.

"Sorry I'm late." He said again before planting a light kiss on her cheek.

"Oh don't worry about it, c'mon let's eat."

"Do you know what you're going to have?" he asked once he was seated and scanning through the menu.

"Hmm, I'm not sure."

It took a couple of minutes before a waiter approached them and took their orders.

"And would you like anything to drink?"

"I'll just have a water, thank you." Katie smiled politely before turning to Colin.

"I'll have a gin and tonic please." He spoke so nonchalantly, that made Katie furrow her brows at him.

"Colin-"

"Thank you." Colin cut cross her before she could disagree and handed the waiter their menus.

"What the hell Colin?" Katie gave him a look of disbelief as she spoke as soon as the waiter was out of earshot.

"It's just one."

"You have to go back to work after this."

"One gin won't do me any harm."

"I think you and I both know it could." He narrowed his eyes at her statement.

"What's that supposed to mean?"

"It means that for now it's one, then maybe you slip to the toilet and decide you want another so throw it back before you come back to me and then you can't help yourself." He truly looked wounded by her words but there was something irking her more so than usual that day. She couldn't hold back how she really felt.

"I'm glad you feel like I can't handle a drink."

"It's when you have more than one and can't help yourself that I feel you can't handle it. I just don't want you to make another mistake- for your own sake." She remained calm as she spoke, her words softer toward the end of her sentence. It made him pause for a moment to compose himself.

"You're right, I'm sorry." He shook his head. "I promise this is the only one Kate."

They both agreed to change the subject and enjoy their lunch together instead of bickering. Colin had been true to his word, he only had the one drink then drank water after that. They spent their time talking about anything and everything, the time flew. Katie decided to tell him about the interview for the new job she was hoping to get, he was delighted by the good news and was positive she would get the job despite even going to the interview yet- Katie on the other hand, was not so sure. It was just when their plates were being cleared and they both thanked the waiter that the mood changed from being upbeat again. Colin had begun to mention the future again and Katie was not in the mood to talk about what may lie ahead, she never was. In the beginning, it would only be marriage that was casually brought up in these discussions, although after a while children began to be mentioned and this made Katie even more uneasy because she knew that the stress of this would probably take a toll on Colin despite his obliviousness.

"Colin..." Katie used the same tone of warning she had so many times before, as if the subject was strictly taboo.

"What?"

"I don't want to talk about this now."

"You never do. Are we seriously going to be that couple at our wedding talking about how it took the hundredth time for me to propose before you said yes?"

"You haven't asked me once."

"Because I know you'd flip out if I did."

He was right, she would be annoyed but it was not because she didn't love him. Katie loved Colin very much, she wanted to spend the rest of her life with him, but she wanted him to be in a more stable state before they agreed to tying the knot. Colin never seemed to understand this and always thought the only reason she would say no was because there was something wrong with him.

"I just think that you need to be sober for a while longer before we plan anything-" Katie wanted to bring up the drink he had ordered at the beginning of lunch but refrained from doing so. She knew that Colin's idea of sober was just including drugs and nothing else- his drinking habits were being kept at a low but he still drank and it didn't help. But he would never agree to refraining from drinking alcohol although Katie thought it would really benefit him, at least then he wouldn't be tempted to go father than having a drink or two.

"Why is it always me that's the problem? It's never you." He gave her a seething look then that made her straighten up in her chair, trying to calm herself down.

"I don't know what you mean Colin..."

"Maybe it's not me. The only thing holding us back is you. You aren't ready, you don't want to talk about it, you are the one who dictates everything in this conversation."

"Well getting married is a big decision Colin, I don't think it's something to be taken lightly."

"Who said I was taking it lightly? I've been sober for months, you know that, I know that."

"Why are you in such a rush to get married all of a sudden huh? Ever since Em and Jeremy-"

"Because I love you? I love you and marriage makes it more real."

"If you need me to marry you to justify how much I love you then I don't think you want to get married for the right reasons. Just because we both don't have rings on our fingers doesn't mean that we aren't together, or that I don't love you more than anything. I think we just need another while-"

"There you go again, with the vague milestones. I feel like I'm walking around in the dark here Katie. It's like you're too afraid to give me a definite amount of time in case I actually reach that deadline and you have to agree to take things further."

"No, Colin that's not the truth. I want to be able to say yes and to give you a definite time that I'll be ready but- but..."

"But you're doubting me." He finished her sentence, feeling like he had hit the nail on the head. "You're doubting that even if I do stay sober for long enough that you're going to marry me, I'll go off the rails again and you'll be stuck with me." The upset and anger that was clear in his tone made her panic a little, she didn't want him to think those things but he did and she was almost sure she couldn't change the way he saw the situation, no matter how much talking she did.

"Of course not Colin, I believe in you. I really do. And I know that even if things got bad again we would work them out like we always have- I just need more time okay?"

"This conversation's going around in circles. We're getting nowhere here." There was a great tension in the air as they paid for their food and left the restaurant for work again that day. Katie felt terrible, she couldn't stop herself from feeling guilty for the way he felt while Colin remained quiet in his thick and silent anger. All he seemed to be focused on was a wedding, but Katie knew there was more to marriage than just a big day of celebrations and she wasn't sure if she was ready yet. Marriage was something she felt they could both work towards, not right then, but somewhere in the future.

She stopped outside the station that he walked her to before he headed back to work and took the time to exam his hard expression. He was avoiding looking at her despite her eyes begging him to do so. Guilt crippled her for the second time, a conversation needed to be had but not then- it could wait until later when they both got home.

"Colin..." her voice was sugary, delicate and pleading. He remained stoic although she took a step towards him and kissed him on the cheek. "I'll see you later when you get home okay?" The hurt look on her face that she was trying to cover up make up soften up a little- enough for him to answer her before he left her there.

"Yeah, sure babe." That was all of their goodbyes, before they turned opposite ways and went on with their day.

Katie could not stop thinking about her conversation earlier throughout the rest of her time in work, or even when she arrived back at his home. She remembered once she stepped into the empty apartment that he had told her the day before he would be late home. She took off her coat, kicked off her shoes and tied her hair up, ready to start cooking something to eat for the two of them and silently hoping that she would not mess up their meal this time. Colin was far better at cooking than her but she wanted to cook one of his favourite dishes as a sort of apology. Once preparing the food, she had time to think- of what to say, of how to explain herself to Colin. But it was going to be difficult. Katie was unsure how to put into words how she felt about the entire thing.

Just then images flooded her mind of herself and Colin on their wedding day she was reluctant to organise, of children running around through their legs as they tried to do school runs and of happy holidays away on sandy beaches with loud and hyperactive little munchkins she would call their children. Katie's smile brightened up the dim and lonely kitchen for a moment- the moment that lasted long enough for her to realise she wanted that in all the joy of her imagination. There could be no denying that the things she had dreamed about were wanted, only wanted with Colin and no one else. So why was she still extremely reluctant? Colin had been doing great for the past while. Maybe she needed to just go for it, say yes, completely put all her faith in him- but it was not that easy. He had caused her so much heartache, all of which she could forgive and forget about but only partially- and maybe that was the true reason behind her hesitation.

The noise of the landline ringing cut into her thoughts like the sharpest of knives. She immediately stopped what she was doing and walked toward the phone to pick up the call.

"Hello is Ms. Briggs there?" Katie was surprised by the formal tone of the unfamiliar voice.

"Yes, speaking. Who is this?"

"Hi this is Adam Statham from the Whitestone rehab centre." Katie was surprised by the man's call but tried not to show it.

"Oh hi Adam, what can I help you with?"

"I'm just calling to confirm you are Colin's next of kin, correct?" She didn't know where this was going but answered as quick as she could.

"Yes I am. Is there a problem?" Her voice had instantly gotten shaky, she wished she hadn't made her nervousness so obvious.

"Well, I was just wondering when Colin will be available for an-other therapy session as he's missed the last four weeks and it is a huge part of out-patient care." In a short second, Katie's stomach dropped, her knees felt weak, and she struggled to find the words to say next. There was a long pause on her end of the phone until she decided she needed to push through what little of the conversation she had left before allowing her emotions to come through.

"Oh, I'm so sorry. We forgot to inform you, he's been very sick but I'm sure he'll be able to attend next week's session as he's been recovering well."

"Oh that's great. Thank you. Sorry if I was interrupting anything, I've been constantly calling Colin but he hasn't been picking up, has his contact number changed or anything?"

"No it hasn't but I'll be sure to tell Colin to contact you to confirm the therapy session as soon as I see him."

"Thank you Ms.Briggs." As soon as she hung up she immediately walked to the couch on the other side of the room and sat down, her face in her hands. She was in complete disbelief that Colin had been hiding this from her for the past month and then, a wave of worry fell over her like a tsunami.

What else had he been hiding from her? Did she need to go around the apartment and look in his usual hiding places? How was she going to confront him about this? She took her face from her hands and checked the time. Colin wouldn't be home for another while, which meant she had some time to compose herself. Despite this planning in her head, Katie's mind turned to mush, a deep sorrow took over as she sat by herself in their living room trying to stifle the sobs that uncontrollably left her mouth as she tried to make sense of her unconditional love for a man who could not even love himself.

**40**

— ❖ —

## CHAPTER 39

August 2013

By the time Colin reached the apartment that evening, Katie had calmed herself down, although there were still hints of tears left on her face. Colin noticed this immediately once he saw her face and limp body sitting on the couch as soon as he opened the front door. Her eyes were puffed out and red, they had a look in them that seemed to show that she had given up and her lips were set in a feint line.

"Katie? What's wrong?" he rushed towards her, but no part of her body moved except her eyes. They made him shrink down, their deadliness almost made him stop in his tracks, and he squirmed at the sight of them- afraid to look away, afraid to continue looking.

"Your therapist called." As if things could not get any worse, her voice was void of any emotion, yet it still had an edge of iciness to it. "Adam Statham... in case you can't remember his name. It's been so long you may have forgotten."

"Katie-"

"Don't say anything. I don't want to hear any more excuses, any more bullshit or lies come out of your mouth." Her words certainly shut him up, they even made him straighten up. "I felt terrible after leaving you at the station today, I couldn't shake away the guilt I felt because of our conversation and the things you said. I felt guilty because of your lies, and because you don't feel secure enough by the love I have towards you. You need marriage and for a long time today, I even contemplated agreeing to get married as soon as you walked in the door after work." Just as quick as her words had made him stand up straight only a moment ago, they then made him slouch and hang his head in a deep shame.

"I even wondered what it would be like if we just said 'Hey, fuck it. Why not just have children right now?'."

"Why can't we just take the next step Katie? It would make things better, I'd have something more to work hard enough to stay clean for." He instantly kneeled down so that he was at her eye level and tried to take her hands in his, but it was no use. She looked away from him and shook out of his grip.

"You could have everything in the world to stay clean for and even then, I'm not sure you could actually do it Colin." She had crossed her arms before she spoke in a bitter tone that made Colin's heart feel as if it was being torn to pieces. Unlike any other time before, Katie was unphased by the harshness of her words or their impact on Colin. She too was heartbroken. In fact, she wasn't sure she even cared about destroying his confidence, his hope or ambitions and it was entirely because of the truth behind what she said next.

"You would rather push me, make me feel guilty enough to agree to marrying you when I know we aren't ready. You would rather tell me bare faced lies and trick me into marriage with your empty promises and your fake hurt that I don't believe in you enough to think you'll stay clean for long enough. You lied to me earlier, you pretended like you were clean and on track but you aren't."

"There you go again- speaking for both of us. I am ready to get married." She had sparked anger within him, forcing him to address only half of what she had said.

"You are not. You have no idea how hard it is to keep a marriage intact for normal people, never mind you and I." Katie matched his anger and stood up abruptly from the couch, causing him to stand up too and back away a little.

"We aren't normal?" he questioned her.

"No. We aren't. You're a weak, manipulative, self-destructive bastard and me... I'm a fool. I'm weak. I'm too easy on you. I live in a different place up in my own head, thinking that I can fix you and I can save you when I can't. I don't think anyone can save you at this stage Colin. When did you ever think we were normal people? That this relationship was normal? It's not. It never has been. It's been me sticking by you when really, I'm not quite sure if you were worth any of it, and you destroying any progress you ever make."

"Don't say that... You don't mean it."

"I do. I don't want to admit any of it but it's just the truth. And I'm not sure yet who is worse in this situation? You for constantly hurting me, breaking my heart and making promises you can never keep or me for being stupid enough to take you back, to believe your lies, to still continue to love you even though you don't love me."

"I do love you. Of course I love you Katie." Desperation was evident in his voice, in his eyes, in everything that could show emotion- it filled up the room, but it didn't matter, it would never be enough for Katie to take her words back. Regardless of this, she did not believe him.

"You don't love me. And you don't want my love either." She shrugged off his objection, clearly angered by what she viewed as lies.

"I do. I don't just want it, I need it. I need you."

"You want marriage. You seem to be so fixated on it that you disregard all the things that mean I love you because you think marriage proves it instead. I've spent so many sleepless nights worrying about you, I've always tried to encourage you to be your best self and be there for you if you ever need me. Even after everything that happened a couple of years ago with Olivia, I still took you back and even after every god damn slip up, every high and low, I've been with you, and I've continued to stay with you through it all. But Colin I've realised something tonight before you came home- all of these things mean little or nothing to you unless I agree to have a ring on my finger and that's not how I want to start any marriage."

"I don't know why you will never just admit that you're afraid you're going to make the wrong decision and be trapped in a marriage with me because I'm such a fuck up?" Vexation was thick in his words, they were both reaching boiling point, and the water had already begun to throw itself over the edges of Katie's mind after he spoke.

"Because that would give you another reason to fuck up. Another reason to go missing for a few days on a huge bender. Another reason to hate yourself. You're the most self-loathing person I've ever met, and maybe you be trying to fix that problem if you ever went to therapy and tried to help yourself."

"I can't do it." He said in defeat.

"Oh for god's sake Colin of course you can. You can get better, you can address the problems you have with yourself, you can be so much more than what you are right now, but the problem is, you just don't want to get better. You can't go to therapy to talk to someone once or twice a week but you expect to be mentally stable enough to have children while you try to face your own demons?"

"Children could make this better. Imagine starting our own family Katie."

She realised how oblivious Colin was then and it was soul destroying- to see how his eyes lit up at the thought of children, to see hopes and dreams flash before his eyes that would never happen because of what would happen next. It was one of the hardest things Katie had ever done, but she knew it was completely necessary. Colin needed to face the truth and he was going to have to do it on his own because it was clear to her that she was little help to him anymore- no matter how hard she tried to support him. Before he knew it, she was turned her glaring face away from him and stomped into their en suite, Colin hot on her tail.

"What are you doing?" He had an idea of what the answer would be, and was very nervous, but needed confirmation from Katie.

Every part of her hoped that her quest would leave her high and dry, that she wouldn't find anything in her sweep of the apartment. If only she had known better by then, but it was her heart coming through between the hurricane that was happening in her head. She lifted the cistern of the toilet and unhooked the plastic baggie from the lid. Without batting an eyelid, she then made her way into Colin's section of the wardrobe, where she rooted in the second last drawer where he kept his socks. Her search only lasted a couple of seconds before she found another baggie. This searched continued for another couple of minutes as an unphased Katie walked around and retrieved more baggies of white powder from Colin's hiding spots. Each time she found another, Colin's chest would constrict, and his palms became sweaty.

"K-Katie what are you doing?" he felt so defeated as she walked out into the kitchen and reached up into the back of a cupboard and found exactly what she was looking for again. She threw all the bags onto the counter top before cutting into his with her sharp knives as eyes. Everything was silent, it felt like nothing else existed in the entire universe except for Katie, Colin and the grams of cocaine sitting there, staring at them both.

"You want to raise kids up around this?" there it was again, the emotionless voice, the disappointed demeanour. "You want one of them to be running around here and accidentally come across one of these? What will I say every time you go missing for a couple days and they keep asking where daddy is? Will I show them this and tell them their father loves them- and me- but not as much as this?" Every time, she threw her hands in front of her towards the plastic bags, disgust growing more and more with every word she spoke.

"I had an addict as a mother growing up Colin, it was more terrible than I make it out to be. There's one thing I know for sure, and that is that when I eventually decided to have children neither of their parents will be addicts. Children can't save you Colin, they won't fix you, and for you to think anything other than that is disgusting. You need to fix yourself and you need to do it for you- not for me."

"A-are you leaving?" she had that look on her face again, as if her soul had left her body, as if her body was just an empty vessel. Her face was void of emotion as she nodded slowly, realising this was what needed to be done. There had been signs for months, so many times she should have left but she chose to ignore them and stay the entire time- until that evening when the heartbreak had become too much and she could feel nothing but numbness.

"Yes. I am." Her cords clarified her actions only moments previous before a thick silence filled up the kitchen.

"Please Katie, don't go. I need you, you're good for me." He begged desperately for her to stay. She was the glue that had been keeping him together for so long, if she left he could fall apart completely and be left a hopeless pile of dust that could never be fixed again.

"I might be good for you Colin, but you aren't good for me. I have to think about myself this time, my life's consisted of trying to keep you together for so long that I forget how it feels to be Katie anymore."

"I can change, I promise you I can. Things will be different this time."

The distraught look on Colin's face made Katie want to believe him again, but it would only lead to more heartache on her part if she continued to believe the vicious cycle of empty promises.

Katie had to say no this time, she could not go on like this any longer.

She needed to think for herself for once, something she had not done in a long time.

**41**

EPILOGUE

August 2018

Katie took a deep breath as soon as she sat down on the park bench beside him and stared out at the view of the greenery before their eyes. There had been many things eating her up ever since the day she said goodbye to him five years ago. She had promised herself to pack her things that night and never see Colin again despite him wanting her to sleep on her decision. Katie did not take his advice, she had too much and needed to be strong enough to say what she thought would be her last goodbye.

But ever since that night years previous, she had been stuck on the thought of him, although it did fade in and out every so often. Katie was haunted by the way she had ended things, she had always wondered if it was the right decision to make.

"I've been wanting to say a few things to you for years." Katie finally admitted after another few moments of silence. He could tell by the way she spoke, by the uncomfortable look on her face and the way she fidgeted with her hands that her admission was not an easy one to make.

"Really?" he was confused. She hadn't made contact, and when he had finally plucked up the courage to go see her in June she gave him the impression she never wanted to see him again.

"Yes... I-I just wanted to say sorry." She gulped before adding, "For the way I left. I should've handled it better and the things I said were too harsh."

"Honestly, I don't blame you Katie. What I put you through for years, I'm surprised you didn't crack sooner. You shouldn't be apologising to me, I'm the only one who needs to be saying sorry in this conversation."

"I shouldn't have called you weak, or manipulative." She stated matter-of-factly, ignoring his previous words. "And I needed to jut get that off my chest. I think weak is too harsh of a word to have used. And I think you were just happy to have me stay every time you slipped up, I don't think you took advantage of it in a manipulative way." These words that she had been holding in for years were finally allowed to leave her mouth and it only took a weight off her shoulders she never thought would feel so good.

"I needed to hear those words, to make me realise the extent of destruction I was causing to myself and most importantly, you."

"Why did you lie to me that day? Why did you make me feel guilty for not wanting to get married or have children yet when you knew you weren't clean?" there was a long pause as Colin took a few breaths, trying to figure out what to say.

"I guess I was just desperate. I wanted everything there and then. I felt like if you said yes and we got married, it would be more real and I'd have more to get clean for. I know I was wrong and I should never have lied to you, that time or any of the other times but I can assure you right now that no matter how many promises I broke before, I am clean and plan on being clean now for the rest of my life. I followed your advice and I did it for myself- but the whole way through you were always in the back of my mind too. I thought maybe I'd stop loving you after what you told me before you left, or even when I never heard from you for months then years. But I didn't, and that's why I'm here. And I'm not trying to force you or guilt trip you into being with me again because I never expected you to feel the same love I still feel for you after such a long but I thought it was worth a shot."

His words made her feel so much, much more than she had felt through the entirety of his absence from her life. They struck her heart, made tears form in her eyes and a mixture of swirling emotions flutter around in her stomach. She had never found anyone quite as captivating as Colin in the five years after she had said goodbye to him for the last time, and this had been playing on her mind for quite some time recently. Everything she had said in her office to him in June had come back to her, and she wished she still felt the same way because that would make this situation easier- but she didn't.

It was clear to her when she looked into his deep blue eyes, took in his now unfamiliar appearance, felt every bit of pain and hope in his words that she still cared about him. She would go as far as to say she probably still loved him. Did she want to give it one last try with Colin? Yes. Was she afraid of admitting this? Of course. She felt like she had nothing to lose. Maybe Colin did deserve another chance. She knew this time if it did not work out, she would not stay like she had so many times before. But if she didn't agree to giving their relationship another try, she would always be left wondering if it could've worked out or not.

Just then, she leaned her heavy head full of thoughts on his shoulder and looked ahead again. She took in his scent, he smelled like home.

"I forgive you." She said gently, her long-awaited acceptance of his apology was so soft, so uplifting and entirely overjoying for Colin. His mouth widened into a huge smile, he hadn't smiled such a smile in a very long time.

She felt lighter, and so did he. Nothing but bliss and ecstasy filled up the little bench that day as they both sat in each other's calming yet electrifying presence.

And just like that, she had forgiven him.

But this time, it would be different. There would be no more slip-ups, no more empty promises, no more sleepless nights worrying, no more disappointment- only love.

www.ingramcontent.com/pod-product-compliance
Lightning Source LLC
Chambersburg PA
CBHW070735190726
48292CB00002B/274